LONG DARK DUSK

JP Smythe is an award-winning author. The Australia Trilogy is his first series for Young Adult readers. He lives in London, where he teaches Creative Writing.

Long Dark Dusk

Book Two of the Australia Trilogy

J.P. Smythe

HODDER &
STOUGHTON

First published in Great Britain in 2016
by
Hodder & Stoughton
An Hachette UK company

1

A CIP catalogue record for this title is available from the British Library

Trade Paperback ISBN 978 1 444 79637 7
Ebook ISBN 978 1 444 79635 3

Printed and bound by Clays Ltd, St Ives plc

Hodder & Stoughton policy is to use papers that are natural, renewable
and recyclable products and made from wood grown in sustainable
forests. The logging and manufacturing processes are expected to
conform to the environmental regulations of the country of origin.

Hodder & Stoughton Ltd
Carmelite House
50 Victoria Embankment
London EC4Y 0DZ

www.hodder.co.uk

It is in vain to say human beings ought to be satisfied with tranquillity:
they must have action; and they will make it if they cannot find it.

– Charlotte Bronte, *Jane Eyre*

PART
ONE

ONE

She says that her name is Alala, but I'm not sure if I believe her. She says that it has a meaning, that in the language her ancestors spoke it would carry some weight, but she doesn't know what it is now. Nobody remembers. It's a word that has been lost, from a language that went under the sea. She wears a wrap around her head, that comes down to cover the bottom half of her face, a scarf of swirled patterns trimmed with fur, a kind of golden colour that looks like dirt or sick when you're up close, but you know it's worth something from the way she handles it. Along the edge of the scarf, silvery tufts and tassels hang down over her neck. You can't tell how old she is. She tries to hide that from everybody.

Alala buys what I steal; that's our arrangement. That's the joy of her, what makes her so different from everybody else. She'll take anything if she trusts you – doesn't matter what it is. She'll give absolutely anything a price. It's always a struggle to see her, because she has queues: either others with stuff to trade; or junkies who want whatever she sells that they need; or her own people – she calls them her fingers, *fingers in pies*, she says, then twitches her fingers while she says it, even the stump of the half-missing one.

I hold today's merchandise out for her to examine. It's a knife, of sorts: a filthy black blade, threaded with these red knots, like veins. But not blood or gemstones or anything like that, but glowing metallic, running with electrics. When I picked it up it sparked me so violently that I almost passed out. It's serious technology, probably from somebody working on the wall. It's protected, which means it's got to be worth something. I pass it to her, blade first.

'Don't touch the handle,' I say.

'Little girl. Give me credit. You think I was born yesterday?' She doesn't know much about me. Just my name, where I live, where I came from, and what I'm after. That's it. Some people here give her sob stories when they try to sell to her: they tell her about who they used to be, or what they've lost. Who they've lost. I keep all of that to myself. I'm a criminal, escaped and running. Nothing too personal.

'Will they be coming back for this?' she asks. 'They know where you are.'

'They won't be coming.'

'But you did steal it?'

'In a way,' I say.

She nods. She understands. Technically, it was stolen. I found it next to the unconscious body of a policeman who had been chasing me. Finders keepers. He chased me nearly the length of the slums, persistent as any police I've known. Climbed as well, which is rare. Usually they stop when there's a danger of their suits getting torn, but he didn't. I led him the trickiest route I could find, and still he kept it up. He only gave up when he had to; when I jumped a gap I knew he would never make. He fell, and I backtracked slowly, down to his body. Checked he was alive, set off his rescue alarm, took his weapon. Easy.

'I need the imprint. Otherwise . . .'

She reaches down to the pockets that she's sewn into her clothes: lots of them, most secret, so that she can turn any of the obvious ones out, show you how poor she is, without giving away what's in the others. She's got tricks, and they're obvious to anybody who's lived where I have, haggling with the salesmen as I did. Not what I'm after. 'I only have a cheap card, ten units. If I have imprint, it is maybe worth more, but . . .' She shrugs, this exaggerated gesture where she puts her hands up in front of her, empty apart from the cheap money card. 'Take it, go on. You rob me.' She covers her face with her empty hand, makes out that she's not looking at me.

I take out the other package from my pack: the guard's thumb, wrapped in a scarf that looks not unlike the one she's wearing around her neck. She smiles, through her fake blindness, pulls a card from her sash and hands it over, snatching up the thumb so fast, pocketing it even faster. She's got her imprint now.

'Don't be spending this all at once,' she says, handing over the cash.

I walk towards my home – it *is* home, even if it feels transitory – past the junkies, past the families huddled around home-made water distillers and trash-can fires, through the rows and rows of shanty houses with their makeshift walls and corrugated metal roofs. On the ground, outlines of yellow lines still exist, faded nearly to nothing; and then, in some places, you can see insignias printed onto walls: a printed shape of a bird here, a flag there. I go past the warehouses, the sheds, their walls opened up, their insides gutted, replaced with a maze of tents and makeshift shelters. I keep going towards the wall, as far as you can get, before the shanties drop away almost completely, and there's just a few of us, propped up against the back wall of the last warehouse. This is where I like to live. Nobody asks you anything, and everybody keeps to themselves. There's a peace and quiet like I've never known before.

I'm nearly to my own home when I hear the sound of a baby crying. That's the worst sort of alarm. It could be a visitor, but who would bring a baby here? Everybody hunkers down when they hear it, because no good can come of this. This means police and services both, flooding in here like they own the place. Only a matter of time.

I watch the people here pull shut whatever they have that passes for a door, yanking across plates of sheet metal if they have them, cardboard if they don't. Fires are extinguished, because they'll only draw attention. You want the darkness. If you're in the dark and quiet, chances are the police won't bother to check you out.

I miss the warmth I used to take for granted, but I have adjusted. I didn't know how warm it actually was on Australia until I got here. Now I only know months of prickled skin on my arms. Months of it.

The crying's coming from inside one of the warehouses. It won't stay there – you're trapped inside those things, nowhere to run if you're cornered. I climb up onto the top of the closest building, burned out and slightly more fragile than some of the others. Still, it takes my weight. I look over to see if I can spy them, spot any movement. The baby's mother – seems like it's never the father, trying to hide them – will either find somewhere to hide, or she'll be immediately on the move. Either way, this isn't going to end well. I don't know why she didn't have the baby muted; that's the easiest way of keeping them quiet, as cruel a thing as it is to do. Now, instead, the baby will be taken, prised from her hands, because babies here are always taken away from the people that live here. The services swoop in, take them somewhere they'll be better cared for. That's what happens every time. It's what'll happen now.

Unless.

I stay on the rooftops and listen. She's moving. The sound stops echoing, it's no longer coming from the warehouse. Now, she's winding her way through the shanty village. I hear them shouting at her to move on. They won't help her if she needs it.

So I run with her. Maybe I can help her. Could be we get her somewhere to get the operation done. I know that Alala's done some, so her, maybe; though she probably won't touch one that's this hot. I can't hear any sirens from cars yet, so she's still got a few minutes. She could still hide, maybe set the baby unconscious, just for the time being, hide it somewhere. But that's risky. I've seen it where the baby wakes at the worst possible moment, hidden in some compartment in the ground or something; where they open their eyes and don't have a clue where they are, then just start screaming again. They don't even know what happened. Babies always seem to cry when they wake up. When do we learn that it's safer to be awake?

I get from the warehouses to the shanties and I don't stop. Uneven roofs make it hard to sprint, but at least they're stable enough to take my weight.

I spot her, a few rows over. The people who live in those sheds are putting out their fires, hissing as she runs past; but I can make her out just enough to keep a track on her. She's barely my age – younger, I would guess – and I can't see the baby, not at first. Then movement from the pack on her back, and *that's* where it is. Easier to bundle it away than carry it, I suppose. I wonder what exactly set it off crying this time: food; sleep; the desire to be anywhere but here. The mother is panicking. She's looking around, gasping as she runs. She's making this panting noise, the air puffing from her mouth like smoke. It's hard to run in the cold, I've learned. There's still no sign of the police. If I were her, I'd be less worried about running. I would be trying to keep the baby quiet.

But she's not me. She's lived here a lot longer. Maybe she knows something that I don't. I have to change direction, feet slamming onto patchwork rooftops, to keep up, and I'm leaping to another row when I hear the sirens, in the distance.

Damn it. Out of time.

The girl runs towards where Alala lives, over by the entrance, by the fence. Maybe she's going to try and get out of here, get past the wire fences, past the grey-brown of our concrete and into the poorer parts of the suburbs. Maybe it'll be easier to hide there. But it's not like they'll stop chasing her. They'll catch her, and she'll barter. They always barter.

I follow her, silhouetted by the glow from embers of extinguished fires; and then, as she turns to hush the baby, to soothe it, I see her face in the light of the moon. She's younger than I first thought. Thirteen or fourteen. She shouldn't be in here, shouldn't be running. She shouldn't be in this situation.

I have to get her attention. The police are coming closer. I can hear their sirens; their tyres on the gravelled tarmac near the entrance to this part of the city.

'Hey,' I shout, but not too loud. I don't want to get made, not if I can help it. There's every chance that the police want me just as much as they want her. Maybe even more. 'Hey!' She turns and looks at me while she's running, and she stumbles. My fault. She's on her knees, scrabbling, the baby really howling now. The jolt kicked it into a whole new level of panic.

'Go away,' she says. She doesn't want my help. They never do.

Then I hear the engines, unnaturally loud. They're here on bikes, on trucks. The lights of them coming bob wildly, chucking shadows up all around me.

'I can get you help,' I say, but I'm not even really sure that's true at this point. Still, it's worth a shot, better than giving up before you've even had a chance. But she doesn't stop. She hesitates. Maybe. I can see it, in her shoulders, her spine. *Maybe.*

But she's too late. We both are. The vehicles – two bikes and a truck, both armoured, far more serious than you need to deal with a teenage girl and her illegal baby – screech to a stop in front of her. The remains of somebody's shanty hang from the front of the truck, ploughed through and destroyed. Fabric and fragments of metal piping. Technically, nobody's allowed to live here. The police don't care what damage they might cause. The vehicles rumble, which is intentional. They can be silent, but the police use the sound when they want to intimidate whoever they're chasing; when they want you to know that they're unbeatable, inescapable. It's a growl of intent.

The back doors of the truck open, and the officers scramble out. The two on the bikes step down, leaving their engines on, leaving the lights pointed right at the girl. She shields her eyes with her forearm. I duck down, lower the chance of them seeing me. I don't want them to force me to make my move. That has to be my choice.

Miraculously, the baby's being quiet. The mother could still talk her way out of this – as long as they don't search her backpack. I stay back and down, and I watch. The police are all dressed the same, men and women, doesn't matter. Thin black fabric costumes, those little plates across their mouths for the air. Only bit you can see is their eyes; the police are fitted with augments to help them track others, to see in the dark, to react faster. Silly, though: augmented body parts make for an easy target. Take them out, and whoever they belong to is temporarily out of action.

The police spit orders at her. I don't hear what they say, only the fizzing static of their mouthpieces, the high-pitched residue of whatever it is they're actually telling her. When they direct their orders at you, it comes out as a targeted sound, like they're talking inside your head. They're telling her to put the baby down, I'm sure. They'll take that first, and then her, won't want the kid caught up in any sort of crossfire, if there is one. They won't want to damage it.

I can see the police's hands: all twitching fingers, wavering near their sides. No weapons, to reduce the chance of an accident. They'll try to persuade her to go with them of her own accord; they might even tell her that they'll allow her to keep the baby, just somewhere cleaner and nicer. She might even bite, even though she'll know it's a lie.

It's *always* a lie.

I see one of the cops put his hand on the hilt of his weapon. The thin blue light that says it's activated blinks once, twice. The mother won't have seen that from where she's standing. She begins to kneel, swings the pack to her front and opens it, so that she can put the baby down.

It's a show of trust. She raises her hands.

I surrender.

How can she be so stupid? How can anybody be so stupid?

I weigh my options. I've escaped from nine at one time before – easily. A month or so back, I made it away from twelve of them. Barely escaped, but I made it. Amazing what you can do when you have to. I must get their attention, get them away from her. There's no sneaking here in this city, no stealthy hiding. If I can get their attention they'll scan me, tag me. If I'm lucky, I'll be higher up their list of priorities than the baby is.

I shout to get their attention. They look up at me, all but one of them. I see the little lights in their eyes flicker. 'Get out of here!' I yell at the girl, but she doesn't listen. She doesn't take the baby and run. She cowers, pulling the infant tight to her. 'Move!' I scream, but the girl stays still.

Stupid, stupid, stupid. Somebody gives you a chance, you take it. At least, you should. That's how Australia worked.

If I run, they'll take her anyway. They'll chase me, and I'll either lose them or injure them, and then I won't find her when I'm done, because there's no way she isn't already locked up, barred and tagged, and everything will have been for nothing.

And I am so, so sick of running.

Different tack. I jump from the roof, close the gap between me and the police. I watch them scanning the area, their eyes darting around the place faster than real eyes would, the little blue-hued reflective glint of their pupils trying to find escape routes, alleys, hiding places, prepping for pursuit.

That's not my plan, not this time.

I know how to fight the police. Hit one hard enough on the bone between their eyes, right at the top of the nose, and it does more than hurt their skull. Something in their augments scrambles. It's a flaw in their design; they've been outfitted with cheap tech, the government too skinflint to bother getting them anything up to date. Smash one, another, boot yet another in the crotch. Doesn't matter what gender you are, that'll crumple you. I slam my fist into throats, push their faces down onto the gravel.

12

It starts to rain, which is typical. Just a sprinkle, not setting in. I tear weapons from their hands, throw them into the darkness, smash more maskplates, poke eyes. Whatever works. The rain is hot, like the showers I used to love. Haven't had one of those in a while. Too long. The warm water is nice, satisfying, even though it makes it harder for me to see. The augments give them an advantage in the rain, but disadvantaged is when I've always worked best, with my back against the wall; gives me a reason to take risks.

They all fight well, because they've been trained. They've spent their whole lives working at getting better at fighting, building their skills, their aggression.

But then, so have I.

I leave one of them awake, head still lolling, mouth more than a bit drooly. He tried to hit me with his striker, went for the back of my head, but I snatched it, jabbed him in his own neck with it so hard that it crunched something in his throat before the electrics even sparked through his system – but he's conscious, just about.

'Where were you going to take the baby?' I ask him. He makes a noise, but it's unintelligible, tries to pretend that he doesn't know, that he's about to pass out. This is how it always is: you always have to fight for information, no matter how little you actually get. They're audio-linked to their control, who's probably listening to everything they say. They have to make it seem like I'm torturing them. And even when they do give up information to me, there's rarely anything that useful. It's all the same stuff,

13

over and over. I press my hand to his throat, where I injured him before, and suddenly he can speak, his eye – his one good eye, at least, the light gone out from the other – staring right at me. Suddenly, the power of speech returns to him, and he tells me what I already know, croaking out the words.

He tells me that there's no way of finding out where the kids have gone, because that information is all special requisition stuff. It's the same as they always say. He tells me his name, because that's what they're taught. Tell them your name, because it makes you more human. You're less likely to get killed if they know your name. Not that I'd ever kill him, but he doesn't know that. I don't kill, no matter what they might think about me.

I hear the sound of backup: a whirring in the wind and the scream of sirens.

Now there's no choice but to run.

The girl is gone and her baby with her. She must have run while I fought the police. She didn't wait to thank me, but I don't blame her. I run back towards my home and I shout as I go, telling the people hiding behind their walls that the fight isn't over. Most people here are scared. I knew somebody once who would have called them cowards, but the truth of it is that these people are surviving. You do what you have to do. As my mother once said to me: *be selfish*. That's the path of least resistance.

The only time I ever tried to not be selfish, I ended up down here. So now I'm doing exactly as my mother asked. And it was selfish of me, helping this girl. The police have information I need. Not the girl's fault I didn't get it.

I pick up the pace, heading towards the wall. At least it's a target you can see from wherever you are in the city, like a point on a compass. Faster, feet slamming onto the concrete so hard they hurt. Don't go near the rooftops. If they're in the air, that'll get you spotted faster than anything. It's easier to stay down, bolt forward, back past the warehouses, even as the lights of their vehicles start flooding the streets behind me.

Up in the sky, framed against the slight red tint of the dawn, I can see birds flying in formation; a sharp V, an arrowhead, soaring on the gusts coming from the wall.

I stop when I reach the water in front of the city wall. There's nowhere to run to now; the police are too close behind me. The water here is frozen where it touches the wall itself. Patches of ice spread out across its breadth forming precarious bridges into the water that you don't dare walk upon. The only thing this water is good for is drinking. It's too cold to swim in; after a few minutes, hypothermia will set in. But a few minutes are all I need, if I'm lucky, if I get this right.

We call this the docks, because once that's what it was. Before the wall was built, ships came here; and before that it was an army base, and before that probably fields, farmland, forest. Now, the bits that made it a dock are mostly gone. There's no pier, no walkways, just concrete, collapsing at the edge, and the remains of an old crane that's mostly been torn apart for scrap. I sit on the ground where the water meets the land, and I lower myself in, quiet as possible. It's horrible. My whole body arches away from the cold, and I struggle not to squeal as I go in. I push myself to a drifting floe of ice and sink down until only my mouth and eyes are above the water. I can see lights approaching the water's edge. I wait until they're close, until I have to actually hide from them.

When they're close enough, when they've jumped down from their vehicles and are scanning the area, I force myself to go totally under. The cold is murder on my eyes, but I daren't close them, not even for a second. So I look down, through the water, and I can see so far down. Not to the bottom, because it's too dark; but I can see a part of the city from where it collapsed, a fault line that tore the land into pieces; and the remains of people, of possessions, of lives.

Those people didn't know what was happening to them when they died. Not a single part of it was their choice.

I hold my breath; and I pray that my body doesn't let me down; not now, not when I need it the most.

The gasp when I break the water, after they're gone, is wonderful. It hurts, because it's so very cold, but I try and stay down, in case they're still milling around. I wait, bobbing about in the water, attempting to stay motionless, even as my limbs start to ache. It's only when I absolutely have to that I pull myself out. I kneel on the solid ground for a moment. I can't stop shivering. I need to.

I find a fire that's still lit, just outside one of the warehouses and sit next to it as everybody else starts to poke their heads out, to check the police have gone. I warm my hands, my arms; lean in over the coals, just for a few moments, just to feel the heat on my face and listen to the sizzle from my hair as the water slips off.

Then I'm off, before anybody can ask me why I'm so wet; or, if they saw me before, why I was being chased.

My home here isn't unlike my last: three walls, a roof, a floor; a bed, although I had to work pretty hard to make that what I needed it to be. I got a mattress from the waters at the edge of the docks – somebody threw it there; I don't know why and I don't really care – and I let it dry out. But it was too soft, made my back ache, so I had to put wood inside it. My back hurt less, after I made it harder. I also traded for a sheet of filthy torn fabric, but once I'd scrubbed it clean it revealed this pattern that's really quite beautiful. It took me a while to adjust to the colours. They're everywhere. There's nothing dark about being here, not during the daytime. There's a lot of sunlight, so much brightness coming down from the city, between the city walls. It's almost blinding.

I found the docks quickly when I first got here, mainly because I had to. The docks are the parts of the city that nobody else wants. The ground is too unstable to build on, and they're too close to the wall, to the air conditioners that keep the rest of the city cool. They're useful for the homeless, though, for shanties and shelters: big, unbroken concrete slabs on the ground, then a load of old buildings that have been repurposed. There's a lot of metal around, a lot of shards of glass on the ground. This is where you live if you've managed to stay inside the city itself after you should have been kicked out, if you've managed to avoid being chased out. If you make it out of here, you get a place in the suburbs. But that costs.

It looks like Australia, at a glance – people living in cramped conditions, no sense of there being anything

17

permanent about where they live, everybody suffering. But it's different. There's something missing here. At least on the Australia we had the arboretum; and we had a sense of unity, I suppose. We might have been terrified, but we were *all* terrified. Every floor, every section, whatever gang or cult you had allegiance to, everybody was scared. Here, there's no fear. Instead they're resigned. They live hand to mouth, day by day, remembering when things were better; struggling to eat, to stay warm, praying that the fans in the wall won't set too much of a chill in over the night time, that the police won't come and raid and put out the fires, that there might be a job for them in the morning – a lot of good people, just so beaten down it's like they're barely here.

They remember when things were better, and they pray that things will change.

So maybe that's something I share with them, at least.

TWO

I know a man who lives much further into the city, well away from the docks. His apartment is almost central, in a part where you wouldn't think ordinary people can actually afford to live. His building isn't as tall as some, though, and that's something I've discovered: height costs here. His name is Ziegler, and that's all he calls himself. Always that, nothing more. We're on a single-name basis.

Ziegler.

Chan.

He used to be a reporter, he says, which was a good job. He wrote stories, telling people what was going on. And then that was lost, pretty much, because there are direct feeds for everything; eye in the sky stuff, he calls it. *Pie in the sky.* He said that like a joke when he first told me about himself, and he laughed, but I didn't. I didn't get it. Even after he explained it.

He writes articles, and books about the city – he's shown them to me, but I haven't read one yet – so he finds people to talk to from the outskirts, women, men, whoever, and he buys them dinner, and he records their stories. He lets them sleep in his apartment for the night. He has a spare bedroom, painted in this soft pink colour. The bed is small, but it's better than being outside. And he gives his informants clothes: if not new ones, then certainly they're clean, better than what they were wearing when they went there. I got a new outfit, once; he let me pick from the wardrobe. Only the wrapped-in-plastic ones were off-limits.

Ziegler and I have a system. I go to one of the contact points outside the docks, and I drop-e him, ping him a blank message that's totally innocuous. He said to never use names, never give too much information away. They're watching everything, he said. He's pretty nervous about this stuff. He set me up with an ID, a name that isn't mine and that I don't recognise – *Peggy Wolfe*, somebody who I'm sure once existed but now no longer does, except for when I walk into shops as her, or order a coffee on a credit chip Ziegler's given me – but it logs me in okay. As long as I don't have to use gene testing to get in anywhere or use anything, I'm fine; and the docks' contact points are run-down and beaten up, so they don't register any issue with my ID. They haven't been in good repair for years, I'm told, probably never will be. As long as they work, there's no sense in changing them. No benefit. So I type in my details. Username: *Peggy Wolfe*; Password: *AgathaJonahMae*. He told me to pick something that I would remember. If I forgot it, I'd be screwed. I told him I'd never forget those names.

Usually, he turns up at the docks a few hours later and then we'll go to his apartment, and we talk. We have to be careful, he tells me. There's a lot of violence in this part of the city, and we need to be wary of getting caught up in it. We trade. I keep him up to date about what I've seen. He takes notes, records my stories while we eat food that he pays for.

He's always trying to find out details about the crime, the terrorism. Anything I hear, I report back. And when that's done, he asks about me, about Australia. He wants to know about living on one of the prison ships. He's writing a book, he says, about the penal system, how it got to the point we chose to send people to space. And, more than that, what we do with prisoners now. It's a different world, now. Now, everybody's useful, nobody's expendable. They just have to be taught to be better.

There's something he told me, about freedom of the press, the ability to protect a source. Nobody can ask him who I am. He can claim that I'm actually a fiction, an amal-gamation of voices, an approximation. I'm not a single person. But the book? It'll be the truth. He says that too many people don't hear the truth.

He had a wife and a daughter. The daughter died; I know that because the room that his visitors are allowed to stay in was hers, and there's a holo of her on the side, of her laughing and giggling, and when you touch it you can hear the sound of her voice, and how young she was. Younger than me. The wife isn't here any more, and he won't talk about her. But I can see that there's something in all of this; in his story, and in mine. Some truth about her, and what happened. Alala told me that all men are obsessed with the women they've loved.

'Obsessed men do drastic things,' she told me, and then she told me stories from when she was a younger woman, about her ex-lovers. She laughed at her own stories far too much.

So I can get hold of him whenever I want, but if Ziegler wants to find me, there's no way of letting me know. He offered to get me a chip, but I don't want one. I like being off the grid, as he calls it; I like the freedom of being able to cut myself clean away, if I need to. I like the idea that if somebody wants to talk to me they have to find me first.

Today, I spot him before I even hear whispers that he's looking for me. He's dressed in a suit that's far too rich for these parts, and far too flimsy. If you're a native of the docks, you know that you need a heavy coat. You can tell he's out of place here because he's shivering. But more than that, he looks like money. There are no ragged edges to him. His hair is slicked back, aged to an almost perfectly white colour, and he's got a mouthpiece on, a thin beige mask strapped to his jaw. He doesn't want to breathe our air, and who can blame him? It's colder here by the vents, much harsher on the throat, leads to sickness.

Ziegler nods at me as I head towards him. He's got cups in his hand and a bag with something in it, and he holds them out to me like an offering. An apology for something that hasn't happened yet, it feels like. No smile. That's not how he does it.

'Been looking for you. I thought we could have a catch-up,' he says. His accent is thick and sharp. Alala says that it's money that does that; makes him sound rich, different from the people in the docks, even more different from the people who lived on Australia. 'I've gone and stumbled onto something you'll want to hear, I reckon.'

'Mae?' I ask. I'm aware that I say her name too quickly. I trust him, but if I'm too eager, he could use that. All I have to barter with him is information and favours of my own. I don't want to have to give all my good stuff up at once.

'No,' he says. 'No, not Mae.' He looks sad. Maybe it's because he knows what she means to me. Or maybe he doesn't look anything and I'm just projecting. 'Not yet. I am getting there, let me assure you; but nothing quite yet.' He sees the dismay in my face. He's said before how bad I am at hiding it. I've got to get better at that; at lying. Everybody lies here and all the time. On Australia, I think we were worse at it. It was a lost art we'd forgotten about, for the most part. We were used to baring our teeth, our fangs, our tongues. Here? Seems like the truth is held back for as long as it can be, as long as it needs to be.

'My car's around the corner. This is going to take a while.' He puts a cup into my hand, pulls the lid off for me. I smell the bitterness of the coffee. 'But trust me, Chan. It's worth it.' Every time we meet he uses my name again, like that's going to persuade me. In print, I'm anonymous, a *contact*. In person? He can't get enough of saying my name.

We walk to the fences that mark out the edge of the docks. This part of the city used to be an army base. It was flooded and so they abandoned it, and now it's as big a flat piece of tarmac as you can hope to find for the city's homeless. Leaving here is such a brutal change. It's like there's a line drawn across the shanty towns and tented warehouses, and then there's absolute order and structure. No warehouses, no slabs of concrete, no people scurrying about like rats. Suddenly the city is structured and ordered, grids of streets full of houses or lost-cost tower blocks that creep higher and higher into the sky, the closer you get to the middle of the city.

Ziegler's car is parked up on a side road, a clean silver cylinder, an egg clinging to the edge of the road. As he walks close to it, it recognises him. On the curb side, a door folds away from the side, the vehicle opening itself to let us get inside.

'Welcome back, Mr Ziegler,' the car says. 'Did you have a nice time?'

'Fine,' he says, as he climbs in. His seatbelt automatically snakes across his lap. As I sit next to him, the car scans me as well.

'Hello Guest,' it says.

'Hello,' I reply. I hate the voice of his car. Everything here is run by the same computer, Ziegler tells me. I don't quite understand it, but it's everywhere. It's called Gaia. The only reason it talks, Ziegler tells me, is to make people feel comfortable with the idea that they're no longer in absolute control. Ziegler's hacked his AI to keep his car off the grid, though. It's no longer on the same network. She doesn't remember who you are, doesn't ID anybody. Ziegler says that's how he protects his sources. Everything with him is built on suspicion. And, truth be told, that only makes me all the more curious.

'Take us home,' he says, 'doors unlocked. Okay?' He does that for me, because he knows I hate the thought of being trapped. He asked me why, once. I told him that I wanted to know that there was always an exit in case I needed one. He told me that he liked them locked, because he preferred the security. Still, he does it my way.

The car moves off and down the road. Not that you can tell, if you aren't looking out of the windows. It's so quiet. One of the hardest things about being here has been getting used to the sound, or rather the lack of it. The first few days, I couldn't sleep because I missed the engine noise. Even when I was in the guards' section of Australia I could at least feel it: the rumble of the engine through everything; a vibration that was so constant you almost forgot that it was there. In comparison, everything in the city is so quiet and still. They've made it peaceful; Ziegler's told me that was the point, when they started to rebuild. People don't shout. If there's noise – like from the police vehicles, or from alarm sirens – it has a purpose. There's no noise just for the sake of noise.

Ziegler unfastens his breathing mask. It's delicate, a new model, with little purifying tanks on the side. Mine is paper, cheap, throwaway – given to us in the outskirts as the scantest protection from the harsh air, in pity packets sent from the rich to take care of the people they don't otherwise seem to give a damn about. He takes mine from me.

'I should get you a better one of these,' he says. He turns it over in his hands, prods it hard enough to find small tears in the fabric. 'I don't imagine this one does a thing to save your lungs.'

'If you give me a better one, somebody'll only try and steal it,' I reply.

'Oh, and I'm sure you couldn't protect yourself.' That's the first smile of the day. Same pattern as always. He's stoic and stony-faced until he gets more comfortable, and then the smiles come. By the time I leave him, he'll be beaming. He passes me the bag he's been carrying and I tear it open. It's full of pastries. The buns aren't cheap ones, and Ziegler acts like it isn't a big deal that he brings these when I meet him, but he doesn't know what it means to me. Always be grateful, I tell myself. A sensible rule for life.

'You've been well?' he asks. I nod, my mouth full of pastry. 'I saw something about an incursion last night. *Pockets of violent dissent*, the report said. Injured cops, stuff like that, bundling it in with the Amber alert . . .' I don't make eye-contact with him. He's got good instincts – he's called me out before – and he knows that my not looking at him is as good as a confession. 'I don't care if you were involved, you know.'

'I know,' I mumble.

'I care that you're not hurt.'

'Just some bruises. They hit pretty hard.'

'I've got good painkillers. Remind me to give them to you before you leave.' I won't need to remind him, though. He always remembers what he promises. He never writes anything down, because he says that's how people get caught. He doesn't leave even a fragment of an evidence trail; he just puts it all into his brain and out it spools, as and when he needs it.

We don't talk for the rest of the journey. The car's safe, but only just. You can't be sure who's listening in, I suppose; though why they would bother with us is beyond me. There are proper criminals out there. Every day there are more stories about violence on the news. Some days it's worse than others. A month after I got here, there was a bomb at the north edge of the wall, in the train system that people use to get to the other cities. It took out a station and two trains, sucked the ground in like there were no supports, leaving this giant hole.

Terrorists. I'd never heard the word until then. The news kept updating the body count and I thought about the Lows: how they were responsible for more deaths than that in the last month of our time on the Australia. Terrorists. Maybe that's what they were the whole time. They hurt others to cause terror. After that, the police upped patrols along the wall, and all the other places that felt like they could be more dangerous. The poorer high-rises, the ones that nearly reach up to scrape as high as the wall does, they've been hit just as hard.

I stare out of the window. Ziegler has left the glass transparent for me, because I like to see the city shining the way that it does. As you get past the outer suburbs where the people have much less money, where the buildings are lower quality, the city becomes brighter. There's more light here, as the sun breaks out of the shadow made by the wall, as it creeps over the top of us. Then we move to more expensive parts of the city and the buildings change; older brick buildings give way to glass, every side reflecting everything else, mirrors upon mirrors. When two mirrored buildings

27

face each other, you can see them repeated in their own reflections, going on and on forever. It's beautiful.

When they had to pick up and start again, after the quakes and the floods and the fault lines, the people who lived here wanted to make life better for those who survived. In most of the city, they've managed it. The only concession to what happened is the wall that surrounds us. Depending on who you are, you think of the wall in different ways. Ziegler calls it *the bastion*. In the docks, we just call it *the wall*. Different words for exactly the same thing. It's an eyesore, a twenty-foot-tall lump of mole-grey stone that holds us all in. They didn't even try to make it look pretty.

We move fast enough through the streets that they blur. We pull up to a junction and I get just a second or so to focus my eyes before we're off again and everything smudges back together. I see the people walking around, masks on their faces for extra protection – going to work, eating food as they go, carrying bags, wearing clothes that I'm getting used to now, but that were almost alarming when I first saw them – neat as anything, cut in ways that I didn't know you could do and still have them actually hanging off your body. And shoes that look so painful I can't understand why anybody would wear them, and that I can't fathom how people walk in them.

And then I think about my own shoes, about how they were lost, after they took us all when we landed; how they took my clothes, my weapons. Everything. All the things that I had to go through to earn those belongings, those belongings that were mine and that I loved, and they were taken from me. Just like Mae.

Somewhere, in this city, they're all still here. Somewhere.

'You look like you're keeping well,' Ziegler says, snapping me out of my thoughts. 'Healthy, I mean. You've been eating well.'

'There's a kitchen near the border with Morningside,' I reply. 'They're good, do a serving in the evenings. For people who can't afford other places.'

'I know them,' he says, 'They're good people. They do what they can. I've contributed to them.' I don't know if I'm meant to thank him for that or not. Like I should be grateful. He pats his legs, both hands onto his knees. He's still got a ring on his finger that you use to show you're married. But he's not married anymore. She's not here, at least. He very clearly lives alone. But I don't like to ask what happened. Not my business. His hands are older than his face, wrinkled skin all over, bunched up by his wristwatch. There's blemished skin on the knuckles, all the way up to his arms, going under his shirt. He looks old. Old here and old for Australia. But I can't pin it down more than that. 'I even worked at that kitchen, a few years back. Over one Christmas.' He looks at me, scrunches his mouth up. 'You know about, uh . . .'

'I know what Christmas is,' I say.

'Of course you do. Of course.' We had it on the ship. The fat man in the red suit: just another story that we told ourselves. Same story down here as we had up there; only here it's presents, jolly old men. On Australia it was protection. Protection from reality, even for a single night. 'Anyway, I worked there. Did what I could.' And then he's silent again, and I don't push the conversation.

Outside the car, everything is clean and everybody looks happy.

His apartment block – *The Royal,* it says on the sign above the entrance – is taller than Australia by what must be a couple of times. Rows and rows of balconies, all with the same frosted green glass in the front of every single window. We drive underground, through gates and past the security terminals, and the automatic scanners scan Ziegler's eyes while I lie down on the seat so they don't try and scan me as well.

'Hello Mr Ziegler,' the security terminal says, in Gaia's strange, strained mechanical voice, a few pinches away from actually sounding human. Then we park and rush through the car park to the internal elevator, which is so fast to rise that it makes my stomach churn, as if I'm hungry even though I've just eaten. And then we get out on his floor, the 40th, and walk right the way down the corridor, which has a carpet, patterned and soft and slightly too worn at the edges. He sometimes says the same thing as we walk down it: 'I bought this apartment years ago, when it was cheaper, and I can't even afford to think about moving away from here now,' or a slight variation on those words. And then he opens his door and stands back and lets me go in first.

His apartment is different from the rest of the city. Everything elsewhere is clean and white and glass and plastic. But here, the units are made from dark wood and the shelves and surfaces are dusty. Most of the apartment is just one big room. You couldn't be surprised in here. There's no corner you can't see into. Comfortable seats, a table, a kitchen. Around the walls on one side there are book-shelves, running as high as the ceiling. I reach into my pack and pull out one of his books, and I find the space on the shelf where it came from – this perfectly indented space – and I slide it back in. Everything has its place in Ziegler's apartment. It's always obvious where something goes.

'Did you enjoy it?' he asks. He's been giving me books to read. I'm getting better at it, but there are so many words I don't know that he's given me another book to look them up in. That one was a gift; mine to keep forever, he said.

'It was good,' I say. So he reaches in over my shoulder and pulls another out, the next in the series.

'This one is better,' he says. There's a lion on the front, and a little kid – a young kid, blonde – clutching a sword. Behind her, there's a snow-covered forest. 'This is where it all kicks off, where it gets really . . . I don't know. I loved it when I was your age.' He means when he was younger than I am. He acts like I'm not seventeen. I don't look my age, I know. I'm smaller, sharper. When I see people my age here in the city, I barely recognise them. We're like a different species.

He goes to his kitchen and opens the refrigerator, and he pulls out two bottles. He throws me one as I sit on his couch. Raspberry soda. I have discovered that I hate rasp-berry, but I don't say anything. 'Listen,' he says, 'I won't beat around the bush. I told you I've found something. The other survivors, from your ship? I think I know where they were taken.'

*   *   *

I read his articles first, the stuff that he wrote about the day that Australia crashed into this city. They're anonymous, published under the name *The Truth*, and there's a little shadowy outline of a figure next to that name, which turns and looks at the reader and tips its hat when you look at it. Ziegler tells me that's a thing from way back. The reporter, in the shadows, telling the truth to the people. Reporters are all about uncovering the struggles that the people in the city face, the real things that go on below the surface. He says, over and over, that the city isn't perfect, but so many people are trying to make it so, in their own ways. And he's trying to get the word out about them, and about the people that are stopping it. That's the important thing, he tells me. I have read all his articles, all his books. It was a crash course in this world, through Ziegler's eyes. He seemed like a good person; somebody who sees the injustices and wants to do something about them.

And then, when I trusted him – or trusted that he was trying to do good, at least – I found him and I told him the truth about the crash; about who we were, that there were people on board; where we came from. He guessed a lot of it, or he'd worked it out, but he sat and listened for the hours and hours my story seemed to take. Every word, he just listened to it all. I told him about Australia. I told him what it was like to live there, how dangerous. About the gangs, the Lows, the Bells, the Pale Women. About my mother, and Agatha; and about how they died. I told him about Jonah, who I cared for, and who actually – insanely, in that place, when it happened – seemed to care for me. About Mae, who I wanted to save, who I wanted to give a life that I never managed to have, who wasn't yet broken when I found her.

I told him about Rex. The worst of the worst. How she fought me, tried to kill me, over and over. How she died, falling down in the ship, her body a wreck of her own making. And I told him the end of the story: how we survivors landed here, lost and confused and praying for a home to accept us in a way that we had never had before. How we were betrayed.

After I finished talking he didn't say a word. He hadn't made notes or anything. He'd just listened. And then he sat there, silent and still, fingers to his mouth, folded up like a point. I thought about running. I thought he might be thinking about calling the authorities, the police and the services. Worst case, I'd be fighting my way out of his apartment, out of the tower, and back to my new home in the docks. And that would have been another lesson learned about who to trust.

'That's all real?' he asked. 'True, I mean?'

'Why would I make it up?' I replied. 'You can put it in the newspaper if you want.' He smiled and shook his head.

'This is a book, Chan. It's longer. It's a book, and everybody's going to want to read it.' He went to his desk and pulled out a folder and wrote a word on it: *Australia*. And then he told me to start over, and this time he took his notes.

He brings up a screen and stretches it as far as he can with his fingers until the image is so large that it looks almost blurry. His desktop is full of video clips and documents, and he rearranges them, trying to find the ones that he's looking for. They're bad quality, but you can just about make out what's going on.

'Don't ask me where this came from,' he says, but I wasn't even going to. He's got sources, and he protects them. Partly that's why I feel safe with him, telling him my story. Everything comes from one of his sources, and that's all he'll ever say about them. It suggests that he's keeping me as anonymous as he's keeping them. 'This was the day that you escaped. This is you, right here.' He jabs a finger at the screen and it highlights one of the figures, a little ring of yellow around them like a full-body halo. It's me. I remember this. I'm lying on a table. There are straps holding me down, guards all around. 'This is what happened. It's what you told me, you know.' I wonder why he got this; if, maybe, he was checking out my story. Makes sense: trust doesn't come easily. Not like I haven't asked around about him as well. 'This was taken from the other side of the city. There's an old space centre; my guess is, that's where the autopilot in your ship found a homing signal.'

He presses play, and I – the me on the screen – start twitching, stirring. The guards come around, and I fool them, play dead, then break out of my bonds and take them down. I'm fast, I realise. I've never been able to watch myself fight before, but I'm so much quicker than them. I look like I'm in control. That's not how it is inside my head while it's going on. Maybe I don't realise how dangerous I can be, as well. The only thing I don't recognise is the look on my face. I've never seen it from this angle before. I'm kicking the guards, hitting them, using their weapons against them. My teeth are bared the whole time, and it reminds me of Rex; the way that she fought, and challenged the Lows to fight. A nightmare, lashing out.

No wonder the guards in the video look scared of me. Not that I experienced them being scared at the time. At the time, they were threats.

I did what I had to do.

'Now,' Ziegler says, and he exhales loudly, like he's been holding his breath the whole time we were watching me fight. He points somewhere else, but I'm still watching as I take down the backup, the guards who have arrived to halt my escape. I take them down and I'm gone, over the exit ramp just in time and out of the compound. The cameras don't follow me. They watch me stagger-run into the distance, not knowing where I'm going, confused about where I am. Ziegler pauses the video. 'Chan. Eyes here,' he says, and he points to another section of the picture, showing the inside of the place that they were loading us survivors into. 'You couldn't remember where you were, right?' He presses play, and the video continues.

'No,' I say. And I still can't. I left that part of the city and I ran, and I didn't stop until my feet were bleeding and some old woman found me crying in a dark corner. She didn't ask me anything, just gave me something to eat, and she rubbed my shoulders until I'd pulled myself together, and she told me that everything would be alright.

'I still don't. But I heard them saying that it was a transport.' From here, on the video, that's now clear. It's enormous. A truck of some sort. I can see the conveyor, the loading in of the people that maybe I once knew; that I used to say hello to, or stay away from; that, one time, I tried to give something better to.

'Right, and it was,' says Ziegler, 'but we didn't know where it was going.' He swipes through the video, fast forwarding it – hours of it, because in fragments of frames I see the guards that I took out get picked up, dusted off, their wounds seen to, and then a new shift start work, and then it's like I was never even there – until we see the conveyors get taken away. I can see flashes of the people, packed inside the vehicle. The doors shut. A guard walks forward, brings up something in a holo from his wrist; some sort of document. Ziegler freezes the picture and pulls his hands around it, zooming in. 'And then I noticed this.'

Manifest, the top of the document says. *PC1.*

'What is that?' I ask, and he grins.

'PC1. I looked it up, and it's listed as a revision facility. That's just a way of saying it's a prison. It's the sort of place that does some psych testing, but that's all that makes it different. In the old days they just sent prisoners up into space in ships like Australia. Now there are lots of types of prisons, different ways of rehabilitating prisoners, to get them ready to be put back into society. There are different names for them all, but the meaning's the same . . . Getting this feed took some serious favours.' He says this in a way that lets me know how much work he's gone to here. He's going to want something in return and I'll have to play ball. It's a barter system. At least I'm used to that. 'But, so. PC1 is Pine City.'

'Where is that?'

He smiles. He sometimes forgets that I don't know these things, and when he's reminded, it's like there's something quaint about me, something amusing. 'It's in the north, a little town in New York state. Or, used to be a town. They evacuated the whole place when they rebuilt the infrastructure, but kept the prison.' He shrugs. 'I don't know exactly what goes on there. There'll be more information in the archives, but I don't have access to those, and I've used up all of my favours,' he says, but his words fade into the background. 'We'll have to think of something else.'

'But Mae won't be there?' I ask.

He shakes his head. 'No. But, again, the archives could be how we find her.' He sounds sceptical, even as he says the words. 'Everything that the services keep about where they take prisoners will be there.' He smiles. 'But, those files are locked down tight. No press access, no requests for information. I don't even have any contacts who can get to them. Not any more.'

'So we get access ourselves,' I say, and he almost laughs.

'You can't just waltz in there. That stuff is very carefully protected.' I wonder how obvious my disappointment must be. 'We'll find something. We just need a little time.'

'I know,' I say, but that doesn't make it easier. Everything is out of my hands. That's the worst thing about my situation here in this city. I'm powerless. He keeps saying that I should focus on what will happen when the book is written;

that I should be thinking about my life here when it's done and my story is told: back with Mae, starting a life properly, trying to make everything better than it is; than it has been. 'I have to find her.'

'And you will, I'm sure.' He looks down at my drink, which is empty now. The taste of the fake berries is so harsh on the back of my throat. We had real ones on Australia. The soil there was good. Here, it's ruined. Everything's lab-grown and nothing tastes quite right. It's all worse; or, maybe, it's better and I just can't tell. 'You want another?' he asks. I shake my head. 'Food, then?'

'Have you got any bacon?' I ask.

He smiles. 'Absolutely.'

While he fries the bacon, I walk around his apartment. He's got more picture mementos than just the holos. I've looked at these photographs so many times. They're real prints, not miniature screens, fastened behind glass inside wooden or golden or silver frames, propped up on the shelves and on the sideboards. They're of the same little girl. It must be his daughter. Whatever happened to her, I think that's why he is who he is now; why he does what he does.

Now, he's alone, just like me.

Bacon sandwiches. The first thing he ever cooked for me, and the thing I will keep coming back to. He says that the bacon doesn't taste as good as it did when he was a child, when they still had pigs in the city farms. I don't know different from this, though.

'So who has access?' I ask. Apparently it's rude to speak with your mouth full. I couldn't care less about that. It takes Ziegler a second to realise what I'm talking about, and then it clicks. I want to know about the archive.

'Outside the Services and the Police? Only the people who work there, I reckon. The executives. Probably some of the techs. There's no way of seeing who's on file for getting into that place.'

'Where is it?'

'The Smithsonian Archive, near the museums.' That's where we met. 'But you can't get in there.' He knows me too well. 'I told you. You'll get caught, and you'll end up . . . Well, who knows. They won't be kind. They're already looking for you.'

'Maybe they'd take me to Pine City, with everyone else from Australia,' I say. 'It could be like a reunion.'

'You're joking?' he asks, and I smile. He laughs then, like I've given him permission. 'That's nearly two hands I need to count the number of times you've made a joke.'

'Don't worry; you won't need more,' I say.

'Maybe ask your contacts,' he says, sighing, as if he already knows how pointless this is. 'Ask Alala. She might know some way in. But if she doesn't, I think it's a dead end.' The bacon is gone, the smell still hanging around. But he's itching to get to work, to ask me more about the docks, about anything that I've heard; and about Australia.

'So what do you want to know?' I ask. He waves his finger in the air, drawing a line, and he scrawls his short-hand signals.

'Tell me about the Pale Women,' he says. 'You mentioned an emissary, a boy.' He scrolls through notes on his paper. 'Jonah,' he says.

'Yes,' I say. Jonah.

'What was he like?' Ziegler asks.

'He was nice,' I tell him. 'He was really nice.'

THREE

Ziegler's car drops me off after every session, taking me right back to where he met me, but not today. Today I ask the car to take me to the Smithsonian.

'I am contracted for one single ride,' Gaia informs me. 'Further trips will have to be approved by Mr. Ziegler.'

'Just drop me off there,' I say, 'then you can go back to him.' Ziegler mentioned Alala, and she's definitely an option; but there was a time I used to do these things for myself, by myself. Maybe I should start doing that again.

'Thank you,' Gaia says. It took some adjusting, talking to the voices of people that aren't actually real, in cars and stores and pretty much everywhere else. It's easier in so many ways, because Gaia – disembodied and run by software, not even close to human – isn't going to judge me the way that people sometimes do.

I lean back and shut my eyes for a second, rub my eyelids. I don't know what I'm hoping to get out of going to the Smithsonian. I can't get into the archives, and I won't try. Ziegler's right about that part. There will be guards, because everything is guarded. There's every chance they'll identify me as it is, as soon as I set foot in there, into the eyes of their security cameras. I would risk everything on an impulse, and I'd lose.

It's so tiring, being here.

It's not how I dreamt it would be.

Every other car on the road is just like this one. I can see into their seats, if their windows aren't dimmed: the smiling families; the business-suited people on their way to conferences or lunches; the kids, being ferried around, taken where they need to go. There's nobody like me. Nobody is looking around with the same awe at this place, feeling uncomfortable even as their world is so totally comfortable. They're used to it. I'm not sure that I'll ever get used to being here.

As we drive, the buildings get taller and taller. I crane my neck to look at them, to try and see where they peak, where they touch the sky. Soon the streets are too dense, and I shade my eyes against the glare of the glass. And then we're in the part where the towers give way to the very centre of the city.

When they rebuilt Washington, they concentrated on the infrastructure. That's how they describe everything: the layout, the areas, the people who live here. The city is structured like a wheel, with the oldest part – the bit that's meant to be protected, with all the buildings full of important people, important information – in the middle. And there's grass and parks there as well, green and luscious and nurtured. You'll be driving along the road, hemmed in by buildings, and then suddenly everything drops away, and you're surrounded by white stone and polished marble and iron statues; and the streets are three times as wide as anywhere else in the city, and there are gardens and fountains and a general sense of luxury.

Now, the car pulls up in a lay-by outside one of the buildings. 'This is as close as I can get,' it tells me. It's such a nice, calm voice. I've never been able to tell if it's meant to be male or female. Probably that's the point.

The buildings here are hundreds of years old. My favourites are the oldest-looking ones: big, whitewashed walls, spired roofs, windows that stretch almost from the roof to the ground, the stone chipped away at the edges. They're even older than Australia was. There are weapon scanners when you go inside the buildings – the city officials are worried about terror attacks, just like everybody is – but they're still welcoming. Everybody is allowed to learn the history of where we came from, and what we went through.

No. Not *we*. They. I went through something very different.

When I was first finding my feet in the city, I came here a lot. Some of the museums here have art, some have furniture, some deal exclusively with war. But I like the one that's a tribute to what the world was like before anyone who's now alive saw it: a history of everything that went before.

I go through the enormous, old polished wooden doors and let it hit me, as it always does: a realisation that I'm looking at something that doesn't exist anymore. This is a dinosaur. *Tyrannosaurus Rex*, the holo in front of it says; and it's all jaws and teeth sticking from exposed bone, a snarl on its skull. *The world's most fearsome predator. Its name is from the ancient Greek words for Tyrant and Lizard; and then Rex, which means King.* Around it, other smaller skeletons rear up and prowl, animals throughout history, posed as if they're encircling the biggest dinosaur, as if they worship it; or, maybe, as if they're getting ready to attack. It's hard to tell. The smallest, a *Velociraptor* according to the holo, is the scariest. Its teeth are sharpened to terrifying points, its claws like thick curved knives. And velociraptors are fast, the holo says. Fast is sometimes much scarier than big.

I stop now and look at it, and I picture my head in its mouth, the vision coming from nowhere. The big one might share Rex's name, but this little one is what most reminds me of her: smaller, vicious, more dangerous.

Corridors lead off from the central lobby, and people mill through them. Words hang in the air, directing you to the various sections of the museum: *A World Before Us; The Ground Beneath Our Feet; Life Under a Microscope; The Beasts and The Burden; When We Fell*. It's this last one that I walk towards. The passageway is the quietest by some measure. Most people don't want to be reminded of their mistakes, or the mistakes of their parents, their grand-parents. They want to go further back, to a time when stories weren't even written down, when they were passed along, mouth to mouth, generation to generation. And that's how it was for me, and how the lies of what happened to us – why we were on that ship, where we came from – were set. But now? The closest history I can learn is more interesting than the furthest.

The corridor opens into a hall, a diorama at the far end showing the city as it once was, before they set the infrastructure. It was smaller, more squat. There was more green. Most importantly, there was no wall to cordon it off from the rest of the world, keeping the temperatures down and those in the wilderness out. It used to be so much messier than it is now, more organic. You can see the freeway as it roared into the city; the aquarium, a towering building that swelled to bursting in the heat, one of the first major casualties – the brief plaque in front of it says – the metal that held it together splitting and spilling its innards across the road it sat upon. There's the palatial house where the President used to live, one of the oldest buildings in the city, with tunnels and secret places below it. When the heat kicked in, when the riots started as the evacuations left people here to die, the building was torn apart; and when they rebuilt the city and let the people back in, they put up a statue in tribute.

I walk around the diorama and on the other side there's a model of the city as it is now, surrounded by the sweltering wasteland where once there were suburbs, the borders between city and wasteland extreme and enforced. The wall – The Bastion – so large and encompassing. An explanation of how it works: chilled air generated in turbines along its length, then pumped into the city. And finally, the semi-permeable roof ('A scientific marvel!' the tag says) mounted atop the wall, which blocks UV rays to stop burned skin and cancers, things I never worried about on Australia. Things I never even knew about.

Around me, holos of people walk and interact with the exhibits, leaning in and speaking, giving me more information. They're so close that I could touch them, but they're silent until I'm in front of them, until I'm in their eyeline – then they speak. That's scary; like ghosts that only I can hear. I listen as they talk.

'We were selfish,' a woman says, leaning in to peer at the city as it was, 'and we didn't think about what was really important. We didn't protect ourselves. That's a hard lesson to have to learn.'

'We were complacent and we assumed we were safe,' a man says, pointing at the outside of the city, sweeping his hand to show what he's talking about; indicating the countryside and greenery and the water. 'We built and built, and we never worried about the future. It was easier to ignore it. Then the land started falling into the sea.' The holo sweeps his hand across the diorama, and a projection of water spills out from the aquarium, re-enacting the history – water pouring across the green, flooding it, swallowing it. The waves overwhelm the city and when they're gone Washington is left bordering a new coastline of cliffs and scree, a beach of land that never used to line the sea, that used to be towns and farms.

It isn't what I imagined this world would be like. But then, I don't remember what exactly it was I thought we would find down here, beyond a fantasy about grass, about the sky. All I really remember is that we found the button that brought us home, discovered that we had been lied to, and then landed. Somewhere in the middle of that I killed

Rex. Somewhere in the middle of that, Jonah died. Agatha died. Mae was taken.

And at the end of it all, I was alone.

I move to the next exhibit. It was here that I first met Ziegler, when we were both watching this holo-diorama play out: him for the hundredth time, me — slack-jawed with awe – for the very first. I stand in front of it now: *The Prison Ships Australia and South Africa* – the first two countries who volunteered to build ships and send people into orbit around the planet, because the heat was over-whelming, and the portion of their landmass that was actually habitable was growing smaller and smaller. When the program began, every country had plans for ships. They were built in shipyards and the first that went up – the only ones that went up – took prisoners initially, as a test. The irony: they needed the prisons, places that had been used for the people who weren't deemed fit for living with the rest of the population. They were sheltered, often cold. Many were underground, by that point.

If the ships were successful, maybe others could live off-planet. Maybe that could be our real future. But only those two ever launched. After that, the program was aborted. So many people died, overpopulation stopped being an issue. So they found a new way. Walls were built up around key cities, and the people who had survived it all lived on as before.

But the story they told about the prison ships, after all was said and done, was a lie. The governments and scien-tists said that the original prisoners died up there: a brave, noble accident, volunteer convicts who had been willing to pioneer our escape from the tyranny of Earth, from the climate that wanted to swamp them, the ground which insisted on tearing itself apart, the water which constantly tried to rise up against them. When Ziegler saw me watching the lie being told, when he saw the tears running down my face, he introduced himself. I didn't hear him at first, so he tapped my arm. It made me flinch, pull myself into a defensive posture, ready to tear his eyes out. I was more scared of this new world back then. He said four words to me then – I distinctly remember: *Don't worry; you're safe.* Then he went straight into it, his spiel about the prison ships. He told me that he didn't know how they could get away with it; with lying to people the way that they did.

I listened to him as he spoke. He told me that something had crash-landed in the city recently, a pod. That almost nobody saw it land, and those who did were fobbed off: told that it was a helicopter, something secretive that they should just ignore. They were told, so of course they followed instructions. But not Ziegler. He saw it come down and he understood. At least, he suspected.

He asked me where I came from. I didn't look like I lived in the city, he said. Was I from New York?

I told him that I wasn't, and he nodded and smiled. I wonder if he knew, even then. When I came back, a week later, he was there again. The third time I came back was when I told him who I was. I told him about Mae.

He didn't really seem surprised.

When he left me, having written down his contact details on the skin of my hand because we couldn't find any real paper – and he seemed so bemused that I didn't have a contact chip, his face scrunching into a quizzical parcel when I told him – I spent the rest of the day there, trying again to catch up on a history that never meant anything to me. It wasn't my past. Even the stuff from before Australia had left wasn't *mine*, because everything I knew had become twisted and gnarled with time and storytelling. Some facts stayed, between the lies from Australia and the presented truths from the museum: that the Earth was in trouble; that ships were sent into space; that those ships were a failure. But beneath that was the great lie: Earth didn't tear itself apart. It stabilised, broken and hurting, but still here, still working.

On Australia, we told ourselves that it was gone, a blackened shell of a planet cindering in the void. I'll never know if that lie came from the people who sent my ancestors away, telling them falsehoods to placate them for what they were doing, where they were going, or from my ancestors themselves, ashamed of who they were, wanting some other narrative to tell, something that might have allowed them to sleep easier at night. I think, deep down, I know the truth. My ancestors were not good people. It's hardly a stretch to think that they'd lie about their pasts.

Maybe I'm being too harsh. Maybe they were ashamed of who they used to be, and of what they had done, so they lied, not only to themselves but to their children, and their children's children. They lied and their lies became my truths, until they were exposed.

And the world here is so different from what I knew. This city: the streets are clean. The buildings are new, bigger and better, space-efficient; and there are always shops, cafés, restaurants. Everybody's happy here. The happiest they've ever been; that's what the statistics say. Contentment levels are at an all-time historical high. The new infrastructure is perfect, unified. But then, as Ziegler told me, the poverty divide is so extreme. You're rich or you're homeless; you're inside the walls of one of the existing cities, or you're in the wilderness. There's very little in-between.

'So why don't the powerful help the people who need help?' I asked, because that seemed obvious to me; that they would give them money, help them get food, houses, whatever.

'Just because you've got power doesn't mean you know what to do with it,' he told me. 'They're scared of losing it, or of the people who want it. Everybody's scared.' He shrugged. Such an ineffectual little shrug. But you look at them now and you can see that. Everybody acts comfortable, but they're not inside. *What if this is all there is?*, they wonder. And it is. I know, because I've seen what's outside of here, and it's so much worse.

I watch the holo of the Australia's launch. I recognise that it's an old video – before the technology was as impressive as it is now, but still it's jaw-dropping to me, to see these people from this time hundreds of years ago, in their clothes that I don't recognise. People that are long dead, watching the Australia get assembled before being sent up to space. After that, the uniformed men and women being led up gantries towards the smaller loading ships, ones that look just the same as the one that I came down to Earth in. I can see their faces, turning to the cameras. Sad faces, worried faces, not sure if this is a punishment or an opportunity. Matching uniforms in this violent shade of orange; fragments of a fabric which I recognise from the ship as I knew it, somehow outlasting the people who wore it. These are the ship's ancestors – *my* ancestors – and they are both criminals and victims at the same time. There's no mention of the cruelty of their abandonment in the display. The holo woman who stands next to me tells me that all contact was one day lost with both ships, and the program was abandoned. She shrugs, as if that's the end of the story, a punctuation mark.

'What are you doing? I hear a voice ask, and I turn, ready to run, because that's my instinct. But it's Ziegler. He puts his hands up in the air as I turn towards him, and steps back. 'You think I don't have a tracker in the car?' He doesn't look disappointed, though. He expected this. 'I don't have to ask why you're here.'

'I wanted to see the museum again,' I say.

'You wanted the archives.' He shakes his head, like he's disappointed. 'You can't get in, I told you. It's too dangerous.'

'You shouldn't have followed me,' I say, and I go past him, down towards the section signposted *How We Used To Live*. He follows me, walking quickly to catch up.

'You took my car. I have a right to know where it was going. Besides which, somebody needs to stop you getting yourself into trouble.'

'I would have been fine.'

'No,' he says, 'you wouldn't.' He grabs my arm and stops me, right in front of a map of the world as it was once. I spent an hour here once; I pressed a button, and it showed me holo overlays for every conceivable variant between the world of the year 2000 and the world today. Population growth, urban sprawl, deforestation, animal extinctions, rising sea levels. The country at the bottom right of the map is where I focused before. Australia, just as the ship was called. That's where I once came from, where I was condemned. I press the button to bring up the census holo-gram, to show me the bright shining light that signifies how dense the population was. The country used to be bright, pinpricks of settlements, of light shining through. Then the holo updates, and one by one those lights go out. The coun-try collapses. Come the end of the holo, there's barely any lights left.

Ziegler pushes his hand out and through the hologram, scattering the image. It tries to reassemble around his wrist, the pixels not quite working, not quite lining up. 'If you tried anything, you would get caught, and you'd be thrown in prison. Where would I be then?'

'You don't need me,' I tell him.

'Of course I need you. You're my evidence. You know the truth. Do you know the hardest thing to find in the world? Actual proof of atrocities we've committed. You get taken and I lose the chance to make things right.' He starts to walk away from me, back towards the entrance, and I follow him. Then, quiet as anything, so quiet I barely hear him saying it: 'Besides which, I've grown fond of you.' I remind him of her, of his daughter. I'm a surrogate, that's what it is.

'You told me that you'd help me find Mae,' I reply. That's all I can manage. I don't say, *Also thanks for all the help you've given me, the food and clothes and bed when I needed it.* I don't thank him. I'm not sure I have ever; but then, I'm not sure that he'd ever expect me to.

And I don't say that I'm fond of him too.

'And I'm doing my best. But these things take time.' He sounds exasperated, which is fair enough, really. I've asked for nothing but Mae, over and over. I'm nothing if not bloody-minded.

'So help me now. We're here.' I grab his arm, stop him from walking. We're in the lobby. There are people everywhere. A security guard at the front stares at us, over the heads of the group of kids in front of him, each of them with a parent, for protection. 'We go outside, we walk to the archives, we walk around while I look at it. That's all. I'm not going to ask you to help me break in or anything.'

'Jesus, Chan,' he hisses. I don't want the security guard to scan us. He hasn't yet: his headset is round his neck, red sores on his temples from wearing it as much as he does, from the cheap tech that they give them. No way the company's paying for augments, because why would they? Soon enough, the guards'll be swapped for bots or terminals, that's what everybody says. This guard looks tired. Barely awake. But still, his eyes track us. We do anything interesting and he'll scan us, scan me, and that'll be it. Backup will swarm in here in seconds. I look down, away from him, try and move out of his line of sight.

'Chan, listen to me. You can't get in there,' Zeigler spits.

'I just want you to help me look.' I pull Ziegler towards the exit. I keep my voice soft. 'Or, I go by myself. Whatever happens, happens.'

53

He sighs. Resigned to it. 'Fine,' he says, 'let's go.' And he walks off, through the doors and down the steps, away from the museum, towards the manicured grass and white concrete of the sidewalk. I tread next to him, out of step. Anybody sees us, they'll just think I'm his daughter, that I'm following him somewhere. He looks like he fits in. Because of him, it doesn't matter what I look like.

The archive is a computer, but not one like all of the others. Everything else is networked, plugged into each other. Data moves around wirelessly and you can access pretty much anything from anywhere, providing you know the logins – providing you're the right person. Not the archive. There's a logic that anything on a network is hackable, and everything is fallible. When the chaos happened before, when the cities all collapsed, they lost a lot. Data was stored in the ether, and then suddenly that ether didn't exist anymore, and they had to start again. Now, you would never know to look at the cities, but there was a Dark Age that Ziegler has told me about – and I've seen it written about, in Ziegler's articles, capital D, capital A. A time without information, without computers and networking – and it lasted decades. They had to rebuild, had to put things in place to keep everybody safe, and stop another collapse from happening. People died, Ziegler said, billions of people. Lucky that my ancestors missed it, or I might not have been born. He said that like some joke, almost. I wanted to tell him that there was nothing lucky about being born on Australia. I'm not sure he gets, even now, just how bad it actually was. I could show him my scars, I suppose. But not yet.

So they built the new infrastructure, and now all information is protected, worried about. The archive is a computer that isn't on a network, isn't accessible unless you're next to it, unless you're actually there. It's underground. The whole place quake-proof, waterproof, fire-proof. And hack-proof, like it's the most precious thing in the world.

Maybe it is. Maybe, the knowledge of who people are, where people come from, what people do: maybe that stuff is what we should hold above everything else.

The Smithsonian used to be nothing but museums; a row of them, with hundreds of thousands of visitors a day, apparently. At one end, there's the building that once housed the government of the entire country. Ziegler had to explain that to me: that it was the most important building in the country, way back when; and that the people who passed laws, who kept the people under control, they worked here. This was where they did it from. It was the most secure building, Ziegler said, with underground space that was basically impenetrable. That's why, when they needed somewhere safe for the archive, they picked it. It isn't as fancy as some of the others – it's cleaner, more straight lines, less in the way of extravagant architecture. Pretty, though; but that's ruined a bit by the perimeter wall that's all around it.

Ziegler stands back when he reaches the perimeter, proud, somehow, that I can see as little as he said I would.

The darkened plexi walls all around it, unclimbable. Electric mesh at the top. One gate, with one panel next to it, for access, next to a raised vehicle ramp. It's a small gate. Through the dark transparency of the wall I can see the building itself. Stone, white concrete, insets. Windows. Clean.

'Used to be the home of democracy,' he says. I don't ask him what that is, because he's told me before. When I told him about Rex, that she was the Lows' ruler, he told me the meaning of her name. 'Rex means king,' he said, 'a word from some ancient language that refuses to die, clinging onto the remnants of the world like a louse. Your ship was an aristocracy, which is when royalty rule. Here, now, on Earth? It used to be a democracy, where we vote for everything we want to happen. Now it's a bureaucracy.' He seemed proud of that, like it was a joke. So I asked him who rules in a bureaucracy, and he said, 'Red Tape'. I didn't know what that meant either, so I didn't ask.

Now, Ziegler looks almost smug. 'They chose it because of how secure it was before there was anything *really* important kept in there.'

'Okay,' I say.

'They hollowed it out after the riots and fires. They lost pretty much everything inside. Amazing, to think of what was gone – so much of our history.' He turns and puts his hand on the glass, leaning forward, peering in. 'You used to be able to have tours, apparently. It won't look like this on the inside. It'll be servers, I'd imagine. Miles and miles of them.' He smiles at me, and a guard comes rushing towards us. One of the usual police: black outfit, white re-breather, red eyepiece. No striker, but he's got his hands held out. He runs, right up to the wall, and just as Ziegler's turning back to look at him, he slams his hand onto it, palm open. He's probably talking, but we can't hear him through the wall.

Then I do, like it's inside my head. I know what it is, and I hate it: targeted sound. 'Move away from the wall.'

'I told you,' Ziegler says. He shrugs, then raises his hands and steps back. 'This is what they do, Chan. They keep information from us. They say they're protecting it from disaster, but they're really just hiding it from the people.' He looks at the guard. 'We're going,' he says, and he makes a gesture with his hands that I know isn't exactly kind. He puts his arm around me and turns us away from the guard. 'You want to get in there, we're going to need help. I can't do that.'

A siren rings out, in the distance, in the yard in front of the Capital building. 'That means it's the end of their shift. Watch him,' Ziegler says, 'I'll get the car.' He turns me back around, so that I can see the guard. He's standing with other guards now, at the foot of the building's steps. He takes off his helmet, laughs with his friends. 'Car,' Ziegler says, and he waits at the curb for it to come from wherever he parked it up.

The guard pulls his gloves off and goes to the gate, and he scans his arm on a pad there to allow him to leave, a molecular read of his DNA; then leans forward and stares into a device for an eye scan; and then the gate itself fizzes and pops out of existence for a second, and he steps through. It re-forms behind him. He waves goodbye to his workmates, doesn't turn to look at them; eyes me, though. And I've seen that look before: where he's trying to act like he isn't staring, like he isn't looking at the bits of me that politeness might have taught him to pretend to ignore a little more. Here, on Earth, they're more subtle about it than they were on the ship, but the intent – the look – is the same. Then he glances away, as if he's ashamed of being caught. I imagine a partner, children, a life outside of his job.

I imagine him going home to them, having whatever counts as the rest of his day, relaxing or chores or seeing his friends. And then tomorrow he'll come back here and do this all over again: scanning himself to get inside, having all the access he likes to all the information in the world: information like where Mae's being kept.

I watch him wander into the distance until a voice behind me breaks my attention. 'Get what we need?' Ziegler asks. His car has pulled up, the door hanging open, waiting for me. It shuts automatically and the safety belt snakes across my waist.

'We?'

'You. I meant you.' He leans forward and points out of the window at the front of the car. 'Birds,' he says, and I follow his eyeline. A flock of them, soaring in the distance. 'Take us to Andrews Docks,' he says, and the car starts and pulls away from the curb. We drive through the city streets again, and this time, instead of getting cleaner, taller, more impressive, the buildings go the other way; and everything starts to fade, the city becoming worse as we travel towards the place where I live now.

When we stop, he turns to me before I get out of the car. 'Don't do this alone and don't do it now. Like I said, maybe talk to Alala. If you get taken, if something happens to you, there's nothing I can do to help you, you know.'

'I know,' I say. And then I'm out, onto the sidewalk, and the car is gone; and I can hear the docks, smell the docks, before I'm even at the fence that divides them from the rest of the city.

As I'm walking home, I think about Ziegler's promise to help me find Mae; and how it feels like it's slipping away from me, from him. We've been working on this for far too long. He's been looking, and I've been waiting. It's getting hard to be patient.

There was a time when I would just act: see, think, do. Done, and then it can't be undone. You just have to deal with the aftermath. That's how I ended up here.

I think about the guard. The security measures are meant to prevent anyone from breaking in, but the guard could probably circumvent them, if I forced him to. At night, that's probably safest – I'll bet their security is quieter when there aren't other people around, and the darkness could play to my advantage. I'd have to run. I'd have to have an exit route. I'll have to know what I'm looking for, because the guard would raise the alarm as soon as he had the chance. I'd have to knock him unconscious, and that would only buy me so much time. The alarms will go off sooner or later. I don't know how to shut them down.

Fine. There must be another way.

I persuade him. I find something that he wants, and I try and get him to help me. Getting what you want is the same here as it was on the ship: everybody's after something. Everybody wants more than they've got, doesn't matter how or what that is. He can't earn much. I'm not asking for the world, just access to the building. Or even just get me inside, through the gate, and I'll make it worth his while. But what will that be? No guard is going to risk their job for the cost of a good meal. They'll want education for their kids, or the cost of an extravagant augment. No way I can afford that. And then, even when I'm inside, there's the computer. It'll be hackable, but only from there, so I'll either need to have somebody with me, or know what I'm doing. And I don't. It takes me minutes to type anything, even though Zeigler's been teaching me. I don't even understand how computers work.

Every plan collapses as I run it around, as I try and pick holes. I'm good at that: weighing up the consequences, and seeing them as they are. I think I've developed a pretty good sense of what's realistic and what's not. Maybe Ziegler's right. I should ask Alala, see what she says, if she's got any suggestions.

And then, as I'm walking home, I see her. She's rushing along, carrying something – a small black case, shining in the blue lights that litter the wall. She smiles at me and calls to me to follow her. She knows that I was going to find her.

Of *course* she knows.

'Wait here, just a few minutes,' she says, when we reach her house. It's not fair to call hers a shanty, not really. It's a step up. She's got a repurposed cabin, fixed up on breezeblocks. The entrance to it has rotted away, but she's fixed up an old wooden door. Salvage, but if you had to live here her home is the one you would want. On an electricity junction, with a running water source, the security of the fence to her back and the cluster of other houses protecting the front. Because of the deals she does, she needs the protection, it seems. She makes people angry, and when people get angry you need security. When I've spoken to Ziegler about her, he's called her 'a big fish in a small pond,' which I suppose makes sense. Not that I've seen a fish outside the museum, of course. But still, I understand the concept, the idea.

The inside of her place is divided into two parts: one where she lives, and the other where she conducts business. There's another transaction already taking place: a worried man, barely older than I am, waits just outside the cabin. He's got an augment in his throat, a voicebox, and there's a soft mint-smelling vapour coming from his mouth, which lolls open, teeth missing, tongue limp and softened to the point of uselessness. No sense in not doing something with your mouth when you can't really speak any more. He has no shoes, toes poking through the holes at the toes of his socks. Scars and needle tracks run up his arms, but they're not fresh. Scars from another life, he'd probably say, if I asked him. From what I've heard, that life is always there, though; waiting, pulling at you until you crumble. The marks on his skin are going to be a constant itch; scars always are.

He doesn't make eye-contact with me, but I recognise him, from around. There are only so many people living here. I wonder why he's here, what he wants. There's clearly no money on him and he's nervous. But he's not here for drugs. It's something else.

Alala does a lot of trade. I've wondered why she doesn't move to the main part of the city. She's probably got enough money, given how good business seems to be, and it's got to be a better life than here. Though she lives here like she already lives somewhere fancier: there are fake furs all over the chairs, a small makeshift kitchen (the units salvaged, I'm sure), with a sink that miraculously has running water, and a direct line down into the city's electric supply. She's doing well for herself, compared to most in the docks.

The scarred man fumbles with the curtain that divides the two parts of Alala's place, pulling it aside to let her by, and she pushes through, fast, the little box held out in front of her. I see behind the curtain, and there's so much going on I can barely take it all in. There's a woman on a bed, her legs up, screaming, but with something between her teeth, what looks like one of the police's truncheons; and there's a man who I know from here, who used to be a doctor, who now will patch up wounds, or crudely fit black-market augments for the right fee (whatever alcohol or pills you've managed to get a hold of), and he's pulling a baby from between the woman's legs, his hands clamped around the head; and then Alala reaches out, face void of all emotion, to clamp her palm right down onto the baby's mouth. With the other hand she opens the box, and there's an injection in there. She takes it out and holds it up, and the man here now – the baby's father, it must be – holds the curtain open.

'Iona,' he says, his voice digitised, like the car's, and it takes me a second to work out that's the baby's new name.

The doctor cuts the cord. Alala keeps her hand clamped on the baby's face. The doctor slaps the infant, and the baby bucks, trying to scream through Alala's grip. They ignore the mother: she needs attending to, but she'll wait. The baby is more urgent, if they don't want any alarms to be raised.

The doctor takes the syringe from Alala, his hands still dripping with the mother's blood, and he places the needle right up next to the baby's neck.

'Firm,' he says, 'hold her firm.' The baby is a girl. Alala keeps her hand over her mouth, even as she struggles. She's just been born and doesn't know what's going on, nothing but panic. The doctor slides the needle into her soft flesh, his hands remarkably steady – I've seen him when he's not working, and he shakes, as though his body has a constant shiver running through it – and there's absolutely no resistance to the needle, and the injection is delivered straight into the throat. The baby struggles more. You wouldn't think something so small could be so much trouble, but she's wet, sopping with whatever she was born in, fluid and blood and mess. So easy to drop. The needle comes out, the point of it wet with new blood.

'Try,' the doctor says. Alala – who still hasn't said a word – pulls her hand away slowly, and the baby's mouth arcs open, suddenly free to breathe and scream in equal measure.

Only, no noise comes out. I can't even hear the desperate sounds of her inhaling air, trying to heave it into her new throat, trying to understand what's happening. But then, why would she know any different? If she's never made a sound, she won't know what she's missing, not until she's older, frustrated at her own inability; at the choice that somebody else made for her, and which yet likely kept her with her parents, stopped the services from taking her somewhere else, to another life.

'Good,' the doctor says. 'Good.' He wipes his hands on his tunic, then looks at the mother. She's lying back, eyes lolling, craning her neck in order to see her baby. 'That was good work,' he says, but it isn't clear who he's talking to; and he takes the baby and places it in its mother's hands. 'It's for the best,' he says, and he sounds weary as he says it, because he knows that maybe that's not true. She won't speak again. She was born here in the docks, after all, and this is the only way of making sure she's quiet, that the Services won't find her. They'd take her away if they found her. And nobody gets them back after they've been taken.

I wonder if Mae would have been quiet. I wonder if she would have known how to keep her head down, stay silent. I wonder if I would have had to force her to; to take measures to make sure that she did.

But I let her get caught, get taken away, to wherever they end up being taken.

I shut my eyes, for a second. I think about my punishment; how I failed her, and everybody else.

'Sensible, isn't it?' I hear the words, and it takes a second for me to realise they're aimed at me. It's Alala's voice, and she's right in front of me. I look at her, and through the curtain, as it closes, I see the family reunited: the nervous man, cradling his new and silent daughter; his wife, exhausted but almost happy that this has gone as well as it could possibly go, given the circumstances. Alala clicks her fingers in front of my face, to get my attention. 'You look worried. You in the same way as her?' She means the mother. She puts her hands in front of her belly, puffs out her cheeks and waddles, then collapses in laughter. 'Sit down, sit down. Stop looking so worried, silly girl. Tsk.' She kicks a stool out from underneath the table, another for herself, and she lowers herself down to it, this long moan coming as she breathes out, hand pressed against the small of her back.

'I need something. Or, if I can get something . . .'

'You can always get *something*,' she says, 'depends on how much you want it, that's all.' She's hard to give an age to. She's older than Agatha was, I think, but they obviously grew up in such different places, such different ways. Alala's skin is weathered in some places, smooth in others. She's lived here in the docks for a while – not her whole life, but that's a story I haven't yet managed to be told. But then, there are augments, treatments, that people buy to make themselves look younger. Possibly she spent some of her money on her face. Maybe she's even older than she lets on. Her body creaks in a way that isn't like how Agatha's did, or how mine has done: not because it's been pushed, but because it's just degrading. Everybody has a story, and hers is one that I'm desperate to know. Did she start here, or out there? Her accent is different from everybody else's, that's for certain. She didn't come from this city, not originally, just as I didn't. She's had longer to adapt, though. 'So,' she says, 'what is this thing?'

'I need to get into the Archives,' I say. The best thing about Alala? She knows secrets, and she keeps them. She and Ziegler are both good at that, but for totally different reasons. 'I need to get access to the Archives.'

There's a pause where it seems like she's mulling it over, and then she laughs, slapping her knees, tears leaking from her left eye. The other eye stays dry. I wonder, in that moment, if it's even real.

'I can't get in there, little girl,' she says. 'You know how hard it would be to get in there? It would cost you more than you have. More than I have.'

I stay calm. I explain about the guard I watched, the security there. 'I thought we could persuade him to get them, to get the files for us,' I say.

And for some reason that sets her off laughing again, and it's a good minute before she stops, composes herself, tries to speak and then goes right back to her laughing.

I explain the entry process: watching the guard leave the same way that he must have gone in, the DNA scan on the arm, then something with the eyes. As I talk, Alala pulls the fake, ratty furs from the back of the chair over her shoulders. She's got heat in here, small radiators that look like they're decades old, maybe even older, but she barely uses them. She reaches down, underneath her chair, and pulls up a metal bottle, a cork stuffed into the mouth. 'You ever drink poitín?'

'No,' I say.

'I make it myself. Bit like vodka.'

'I've never drunk that either,' I tell her, and she uncorks the bottle and lifts it to her mouth and swigs, holds and glugs. I can see the muscles in her throat as she swallows. She gasps when she's done.

'You aren't even old enough to drink here. Pah. Start small,' she tells me, her voice sounding breathier. She hands me the bottle. 'Don't want you being sick in my home.' I lift the bottle to my mouth. I can see something floating in the liquid, not alive and not dirt. More like fibres. I wonder what she uses to make this stuff. It doesn't seem to smell of much of anything. Actually, no, that's not true. If there's a smell, it's of something far cleaner than it looks; like the smell of the middle of the city, of the whitewashed buildings and the strip-cleaned streets.

I echo her, open my lips, pour it in. It burns; reminds me of some of the worst drinks on Australia. Back there, it was a thing with some people who worked in the arboretum, to brew alcohol. To use whatever we grew, to let it ferment, to turn it into something that could – for even a few minutes – dull the pain, take you away from where you were and what your life was. And the Pale Women used to make their own grape wine, claiming it to be the blood of the saviour, channelling their faith by getting drunk. I never tasted it, though. And I've never tasted anything as harsh as what Alala's waving in my face now.

'Good, eh? Good.' She stands up, walks over to me, holds the bottom of the bottle as I hold the rim against my lips, and she tilts it. 'You have to drink it faster. Doesn't work if you dawdle.' And while I sip, while I try to stop it just rushing down my throat, stripping it clean (or so it feels), she tells me what I wanted to hear. 'I will help you get into there. But no, no, you cannot persuade him.'

'I can,' I say.

She shakes her head and tuts. 'We pick a different guard, not the one you found. Who cares about him? I don't know. I get you a name, somebody who owes me, so they do you a favour, give you what you need. Use his ID, get in when it's dark, when the patrols aren't watching. Lots of access points. Won't raise an alarm. No, that's good. Better. Sneak around, wearing a uniform. But you are so *short*! And you are a little bit funny looking, you know? You don't look like you're from here. Only people from Washington get to work in the Archives, because they don't trust the rest of us.' She pronounces Washington with the *t* dropped, *Washingun*, like the people here do. Strange, how different their words sound to mine. 'Grow more inches. Taller, taller. Get a leg augment.' That's a joke, and I know that I'm not the tallest of people, but her words actually sting a little.

'No, you stand on the toes of your feet, like a dancer.' She does a little tippy-toes jig, tottering left to right, and then collapses into her laughter again. Her throat sounds like she lived in the Lows' part of Australia, that same ragged, wheezing laugh that constantly threatens to tear itself up into a cough. She swigs from the bottle again, to dampen the sound. 'Go at a strange time. You be clever about wearing a mask, cameras won't get a fix on you.' She offers me the bottle again, and I raise my hand. I've had barely any, and already there's a softness to the edge of my vision, a dampening in my head. 'But yes, I can get you in. You get what you want. You get out.' She smiles. 'You get what you want, maybe you get what I want as well, maybe?'

It's not a question. It's a deal.

'What do I have to do first?' I ask.

She smiles. 'That's the hardest part,' she says.

FOUR

Alala doesn't give me a name. She gives me an address, a guard that she says is perfect for this. Same colouring as me, in case there's anybody glancing at screens and faces, to see if they match. He lives out in the suburbs. Because the city is a wheel, I know how to find him: the outside edge of the city, where I live, being the poorest part, with the houses spooling inwards and upwards. There are very few places that aren't new, that aren't designed to house every-body – those who can afford it, at least – in the most comfortable way possible. The richest can afford to keep the beautiful, centuries-old mansions, save them from the rest of the upward sprawl, and sometimes you spot one, nestled between tower blocks: old stone instead of glisten-ing plasticrete. People won't move themselves somewhere different if they can stay where they are, where their history is. History is where people feel safest.

It's not that different to being on Australia. When I imagined leaving the ship, I imagined a total change, a life that I wouldn't recognise. That was when everything was still a promise, a hope, a dream – when knowing that the new life, the better life we were looking for might come to pass. And then we found it; the new world, same as the old world, and in so many ways. There are walls around me that I cannot climb; towers, hundreds of storeys high, that overwhelm me.

And yet, in some ways, this is worse. Australia was hellish, dirty and terrifying, threatening and broken. But I understood it. It's cleaner here, and there are police making the streets safe. Food is abundant, and I don't mind eating the replicated stuff, even as the people who grew up here moan about the lack of *real* beef, of *real* chicken. There are people who want to help me. There's a way forward, and I can see it.

It doesn't mean I'm not scared.

I find the address Alala gave me. I've never been to this part of the city before. I never had a reason to. It's an estate, an entire complex, a kind of neighbourhood: buildings grouped around each other, all forming one large area. The towers here are older, a little less impressive. No built-in security here aside from the cameras, and very little sign of any private guards. As you get deeper into it, you can see that it's not as comfortable as other parts of the city: the paint is chipping; the grass overgrown, or barely growing at all. These buildings are cheaper to live in because they're older, shabbier, because they're less desirable. The government needed to build these places when they started working on making the cities hospitable. They didn't care if they were nice; just that they did the job.

Ziegler has explained it as being an act of government: everybody had the right to a roof, was the rule. Only after enough people had died was it actually practical to offer everyone who was left a place to live. Not everybody made it into the cities, though. If you couldn't contribute, or didn't want to, you were left outside the wall. Outcasts. Ziegler says he spoke to some of them once, for a story. There's no hope, no getting into the city, because when you're that poor, that lost, there's simply no way to come back from it. Nobody's going to give you a job, because you're unskilled, out of touch with the world as it is; you're opened up to disease, because so many things thrive in the heat; it's likely you're not healthy, because the sun will have whittled you away. Being out there? It's a death sentence.

This man I'm coming to find – he must be grateful to live here, as shabby as it is.

I sit at the back of the bus, keeping my head down, my face hidden. The clothes Ziegler gave me have a hood that I can pull down over my face, so I can act as though I'm sleeping. It reminds me of my outfit from the last days of Australia, the one that I made myself. I wonder, as I stare at my hands, at the corner of the window that I can see without exposing my face, if I'll ever be in a situation in which I don't need to hide. Not yet, that's for sure. At any stage, any of the cameras – the ones in the bus itself, the ones on the streets, the ones in eye augments – could recognise me.

As far as the people here are concerned I'm a criminal, just like everybody else who landed from my ship. They'll want to pack me off, take me away, lock me up.

The towers we pass in this part of the city are so much more dilapidated than Ziegler's. His is far nicer, cleaner.

There's an attempt at making it feel as though it's a part of the city's heart: clean and white, with reflective windows and balconies with flowers and plants on them. In this part of the city, the people don't have those luxuries. There are work terminals on street corners, where the queues to get picked for construction jobs or landscaping or wall maintenance happen. There are people here that I vaguely recognise from the docks, queuing with the rest, dressed in their best clothes, so that the employers might not realise that they live where they live and give them some paid work. Save enough credit, you'll drag yourself out. Spend too much, you'll plunge back down. That, Ziegler says, is the real wheel of the city.

My target – that's the word that Alala used to describe him, refusing to use his name – isn't paid enough to be of any real importance. He's just a worker, just a guy who does whatever in the archives, which is good. His home won't have security measures. I asked her how she picked him, and she said that he was perfect: not even much taller than I am. She knew him because he did some work for her once. ('Terrible liar,' she told me, 'nothing but false words. I don't like this. He owes me money, so.' That's her reasoning: this is how his debt is going to be repaid.)

I followed him home yesterday and he didn't see me. He didn't notice as I crept behind him, as I walked past his bus stop, where he waited for a bus that was five minutes away; or as I ran so that I could get onto the same bus at the next stop down the road, and sat right behind him. When we got off, I stayed twenty steps behind, far enough away to avoid suspicion. I kept my head down. When we reached his apartment, I watched him climb up the stairs on the outside of his block – these buildings too old, the elevators seemingly broken, nobody caring to maintain or fix up this part of the city, tired and creaking concrete covered in so many coats of now-peeling paint. The climb left him exhausted. Too out of shape to hack it. I watched the lights flicker on as he passed them, until the light outside one front door went bright, and he went inside. I watched his windows to check that he lives alone, and I saw only one shadow moving around inside, making food, going between the two rooms that he calls his own. I watched him shut the blinds (the building is too old for dimmable glass, even) and turn the lights off when he went to sleep.

I waited a few more hours to check he didn't have a partner who worked night shifts, anything like that. I needed to make sure.

It gives me a strange feeling to be here, in this decrepit old building, like I've been here many, many times before.

The rows of balconies going upwards; the gangways between them, the paths that wind their way through; the soft noise in the background, a buzz of generators, of power lines, the connections that run through everything here; and in the middle of this particular block – four towers, arranged so that they're all just about facing each other – there's an area of green at the base, between the buildings; it might have once been parkland. I wonder if they ever grew anything here, if there were ever plants and flowers and crops, pear trees and a stream of some sort; if they ever worked that land.

I struggle not to think of the people who live here as living in berths. I imagine living here, and feel afraid of the pit. The image of it keeps coming back to me, like an echo; a shadow, the darkness at the bottom so powerful.

There are no guards here, no sentry points or cameras; it's not like in Ziegler's building. Here, you have a broken door up to an exposed stairwell, and then you climb. It goes up and up, right to the top. Everything is dark, the lights only coming on as you pass them. Makes it harder to be sneaky, but then nobody seems to notice, or care. They watch out for themselves.

Be selfish. I hear my mother's voice in my head, for just a moment, and I remind myself that I this is what I'm doing, that all of this is for my benefit. Fine, I'm trying to find Mae. I don't know what's happened to her, where she's been taken. I imagine trials, examinations, probing. I think of the stories about the surgery floor on Australia, the stuff that the doctors there once did to people.

In the museum here there are bodies, skeletons. Humans from back before they were even humans, before they were able to walk around and talk as we do and wear suits and work and *live*, and in my worst dreams, I worry that this is what's in store for Mae. *Survivor of the Australia. See how she's developed.* That she'll be killed and stripped to bone and put in a museum. We're shorter than the people here, I think. As an average, they seem bigger, taller than we were on the ship – apart from the Bells, that is. And people here are healthier, their breathing better. Mae will be an anomaly to them.

As I climb the stairs, the lights flicker. I can hear them as they come on; a soft ticking. Outside the target's door, I look for a way in. Just a finger-pad attached to an elaborate series of locks, four of them, covering a quarter of the door each. It's very secure.

I grab the door handle and try it gently, but it doesn't budge. The door is metal of some sort, dented in places, the paint chipped off where somebody (years ago, going by the rust in the cracks) once tried to break through. Force isn't going to work, I can tell that. I can't even hack the lock. I'd need his finger for that.

It's an hour before I see the bus pull up on the street outside the complex. He's the only person who gets off. I watch him walk up the path, through the bit of wasteland in the middle of the buildings. He pulls off his re-breather while he walks and coughs, just a small clearing of the throat, really, but the noise echoes around the towers, bounces off them, repeating and repeating.

I stay crouched on the gantry outside his apartment. I hold my breath. Stay still. Wait.

A woman leaves a tower in the adjacent block and I track her. She pays no attention to my target. She has a child with her, a little girl. She's quiet, head bowed, hand holding her mother's. Down in the wasteland is the remnants of what I've learned is probably a playground: some metal frames, a round wooden thing with a shattered top that turns a little when you touch it. I imagine that, once upon a time, there was more noise in this part of the city. Maybe it sounded happier. I stop looking at her and back at my target, as they pass each other: not even eye-contact, both of them with their heads down.

My target gets to the stairs in his building and I lose track of him behind the concrete walls. I lean over the edge of the gantry and watch the lights flick on as he passes them, climbing up floor by floor, getting closer. I can't have him being wary. I look for somewhere to hide only now – I've left it so late, I'm slacking – and there's nowhere, nothing. The flickering lights will give me away. I look over the edge, catch glimpses of him in the windows that line the edges of the stairwell. Like the little girl, his head is down, staring at his feet. Okay.

There's a way to do this.

I grab the edge of the handrail and climb over; and then let myself drop so I'm just holding on, hanging seventeen storeys above the rusted playground below. Everything pulls in my arms as I hang. He won't see me here; maybe only the tips of my fingers as I cling to the railing. I used to do this all the time on Australia. Maybe I'm not as strong as I once was. I look down as I feel my fingers twitch, as I feel sweat on them, as I feel my grip slipping.

Don't die.

'I won't,' I whisper, under my breath. I can hear his footsteps now, the echoes of them on the floor, bouncing off the walls, his breathing behind them, one breath for almost every footstep, and then the soft rip of him pulling his gloves off, to expose his fingers. Then there's the buzz of him pressing his thumb to the pad, and then the whirring of the locks. A small, quiet voice, the same voice as comes from Ziegler's car when you talk to it.

'*Welcome home, Dave.*'

'Okay, okay,' he says, 'okay.' He sounds young. His voice has that tone to it, that lilt, that says he isn't happy, not truly. He doesn't sound like he's accustomed to his life being what it is. I hear the door creak open.

Okay.

I pull myself up and over the railing in one smooth motion, and my arms sting, because I haven't done that move in a while, but I land on my feet and push forward, arms extended, shoulder primed, and I barge into him, slamming my weight into his back, pushing him into his apartment, driving him into the darkness. We hit something, a chair, which crumbles under our weight. The sound of snapping. The guard tumbles, kicks out with his boots. One smacks into my thigh, but that's nothing. I've had worse.

The lights in the apartment flick on, picking up on our movements, and he looks at me, terrified, staring right at me. He's on the floor, on his back, and I scramble to get control of him. He's got a foot and a half on me, and he's getting on for twice my weight, I reckon; but again, that's nothing I need to worry about. He's slow. I jam my forearm into his neck, his throat, and I push just hard enough that he gags. But he can breathe, he absolutely can. There's just a moment when he thinks that he can't. It's more the threat of what I *could* do than what I *am* doing. I could push down much, much harder than this. These bits of the body snap easily. I could crush his throat: that'll stop him, and he knows it.

'I need your help,' I say. 'That's all this is. You help me, and I can help you.' His eyes are wide and red with welling tears, because he thinks that this is *it*, that I'm going to kill him right here and right now. I feel sorry for him, and I don't know if I should. I don't know anything about him. He could be a good person, could be a bad one. I don't know. And he's the first person I've ever attacked where I didn't know that, where I couldn't somehow justify it. 'Do you understand me?' He nods, the flesh of his throat softening around my arm. 'Because I could kill you,' I say. And this is when I reach down and pull out the knife that I got from Alala when I first arrived here, because I needed one and she had one to trade.

I ran packages to earn this knife, going to parts of the docks with the drugs that she was giving to people, packages I hand-delivered because Alala gave me food and told me how this place worked; this knife that's been getting blunted from rubbing against the sheath that I made for it; that's been used to cut wires, to make food, to help me build the tents and shacks I've been calling home, however temporary they might be. But I flash it up, hold it right in front of his gaze. I've polished it as much as I can, so he'll be able to see himself in it, his eyes reflected along the length of the blade: their redness, the tears on his cheeks, the fear singing out from them. 'I'm going to stand up now,' I say, and I do, pulling my arm away slowly. My target breathes heavily, heaving in air as if I'd been stopping that – and I hadn't, because I *know* how to strangle someone – and he rolls over, onto his front. He pushes himself up to a crawl, like some sort of animal. I sit on a chair and I feel my own ribs ache a little, my shoulder sore from ploughing into him.

'What do you want?' he asks. His voice is staggered, the words with pauses between them, broken down. He doesn't look directly at me.

79

'You owe somebody.' His body tenses. Maybe he owes a lot of people. 'Alala. You know her. She told me where to find you.'

He nods, his head going up and down, lolling like he's a doll. I wait for him to push himself to standing. He uses the wall and the sideboard to pull himself up. He isn't looking at me, which is a bad sign. Not looking means he's thinking.

He's going to try something, I know that much. But what exactly I can't—

He runs. The front door is still open and he charges out, his mass seeming to carry him with a lurch of speed. I'm up only a second after he is and I watch him almost bounce off the edge of the gantry, hurl himself towards the stairwell. And he shouts, his voice – surprisingly reedy, given how big he is – coming back to me, on the wind.

'Please! Let me go, I'll do what she wants!' he yells, his words echoing, beating around the walls, the towers. I don't know what he did to Alala. I don't much care, right now. He's got something I need, and running just means it's going to be harder to get him on side. I'm faster than he is, though. 'Tell her I'll make it right!' he shouts.

'Wait,' I say, because I don't know how else to stop him without charging him down. He doesn't give me a choice. He gallops down the stairs, thudding, jumping three or four at a time, trying to take them as fast as possible. Slowing at the corners. So I chase him. The corners are where I really gain on him, because I swing around them, almost jumping to save time, not missing a step as I hit the ground and bear down on him. Every corner, there's a window looking out, a hole in the concrete that starts waist-high. I wonder what the people down in the city can see of me and him; a flash of us as we tear past.

Two flights down, at one of those corners, he turns his head, cranes his neck to see where I am. I'm right behind him. He spends too long looking for me.

'I didn't mean—' he starts to say, but he smacks into the wall at the edge of the stairwell, the same stumpy wall and handrail as you find at every other edge in the building, and he topples, barely even stopping. He doesn't even seem to reach for the rail, or for me. I'm there, hand out, trying to save him – I don't know what his weight will do to my arm, wrench it out of the socket, maybe pull it completely off, for all I know – but I'm too slow. Or, just as likely, he's too fast. I watch him fall.

There's nothing soft down there to cushion his fall. Not even the pit.

Grey stone, sprouting patches of grass.

His head tilted downwards.

The thud as he hits.

On Australia, you never heard what happened at the end of the fall. Now I know that the sound is wet, and I wonder if it's been raining or if that's just the ground. I look. His eyes are open and they're staring up at me. I shut my own eyes, just for a second, to the sound of people screaming, of the Lows attacking them, killing them, hurting them, and me there, trying to help but, really, what am I doing but pushing everything forward, driving them into danger; and then Mae there with her dolls, dropping them and watching them fall, one, two, way down into the darkness of the pit.

*   *   *

I get out. Away from there. I don't risk the bus, because maybe I'll be spotted. I've been assuming the police are looking for me, all this time. I don't want my face on some screen and somebody to look around, nosing, to recognise me. So I walk, not quite run, head down to the docks, through routes with no cameras, or on the other side of the roads from them. I walk against the traffic, so I can't be seen on the cameras embedded in cars, hood pulled tight, tied off. I've got a re-breather on that I took from the target, after I had dragged him back to his apartment – his body, his weight, his heft. Stair by stair I heaved him up, his body weighing more than I imagined it could. I smashed the lights in the stairs as I went, praying that nobody would notice me.

Nobody came. It took me so long, but eventually I got him there; to his floor, to his front door, to his sofa.

Dave, I remind myself. He had a name.

The docks feel so much colder than the rest of the city tonight. They always do – it's been explained to me that what's pumped out of the wall comes from some chemical reaction, and here is where it's at its coldest – but I really feel it tonight, as my lungs ache from running through the city and my skin prickles when the warmth of my blood pumping meets the chill of the air. I feel the cold in my knees, which ache, and my ribs jut out as I run my hands over them, as I check for bruises and breaks. I don't think I've been eating as well as I could. I'm thinner here than I ever was on Australia, even though there's more food here, more variety, but so much of it is worse for you and delicious with it. I've been sick a few times – more than my

82

share. Ziegler says that it is because of the germs I never got used to, the bacteria. He bought me medicine and, when that didn't always work, Alala got me inoculations. You need to be on government lists for them, but of course, she has her ways.

I call her name as I approach her home. Her door is closed, which means she's not open for business. It looks polished, with the number 39 fastened to the middle in solid bronze, and protected, a lock keeping a clasp shut to one side. That's her rule: the door is open, you come in, it's shut – don't even think about it. I'm surprised it's shut. Maybe she wasn't expecting me to work so fast. Maybe she wasn't expecting me to return to her at all.

'Alala!' I shout, and I bang my hands on her door, and on the corrugated metal walls around it. It's dark inside. 'Alala, wake up! I need you. Please, please, I need you.' In the distance, somebody else shouts at me to shut up, that they're sleeping. 'Please!' I shout, one last time.

I see light trickle out from the gaps at the sides of the door. I hear noise, shuffling inside. She swears, loud enough that I can hear it. I've disturbed her and she won't let me forget it. Whatever the price I'm going to pay for her help? It's probably just doubled.

'Tomorrow,' she replies. Her voice sounds different, her accent thicker. Usually, everything she says sounds rolled and curled around her tongue before it leaves her mouth; but now, tonight, it's harsher, somehow more brittle, the words spat out against a throaty, guttural noise. 'Come back tomorrow, junkie girl.' She thinks it's somebody here for more drugs, somebody unable to control themselves.

'It's Chan,' I say. I lower my voice, even though there are no cameras here, nothing that can hear us. 'He's dead. I killed him.' She doesn't reply.

And as if that was the password, I hear the locks moving, and she lets me in.

She makes tea. I'm grateful it's not her poitin again, but right now I would probably drink it. It would numb me and I wouldn't mind – that's how people used alcohol on Australia. But instead, she takes tea leaves and a beautiful glass teapot, and she doesn't say a word or ask anything of me while it brews. She's given me a fur to wrap around myself and I hold it close. I keep my satchel clutched in my lap, my knife in its sheath. She pours the tea into a cup, hands it to me and I sip. It burns my lip. That's okay.

'Tell me what happened,' she says, as she sits down opposite me. 'Are you sure he is dead?' She shakes her head. 'Start at beginning.'

'I went to his apartment. I wanted to persuade him to help, you know.'

'But you killed him.'

'I tried to talk to him—'

'Then he attacked you, so you fought back.'

'I attacked him. He ran away, said something. He was scared.'

'Of a little girl? Some guard he was, scared of such a little thing.' I don't say that it was her he was scared of.

'He fought, and he ran. And that's when—'

'How did you kill him?'

'He fell. A long way.'

'Well, now. That's maybe not your fault. And you weren't seen?' She stands up, pours herself another cup of tea. 'We can find new way to get you into the archive. Plenty of guards.'

'It's not that,' I say. I shut my eyes. I don't want to look at her. They're nothing alike, but she reminds me strongly of Agatha, all of a sudden. But there's one major difference: I'm sure that nothing I could say or do right now could shock Alala. She's seen it all. 'I couldn't just leave him there, not when I was so close.'

All that I wanted was to get him to do the job for us. I was going to tell him what we needed – something really easy, really simple. Take something to the archive computer, put it inside, and then one of Alala's people – a hacker – would get the data we needed. Then the guard – Dave – would bring the device back out to us. He had his ID card, linked to his blood, his eyes, his pulse – his genetic make-up.

I put his ID card on the table first. Alala shakes her head at me, because the card isn't enough. 'We need DNA, ocular patterns. This is no good,' she says.

So I put his hand on the table, the stump of it wrapped in cloth I took from his kitchen; and I hold his right eye out on my palm, and I say to her, 'I think we can still find me a way in.'

Judging by the look in her eyes right now, I was wrong. I can *definitely* shock her.

She swears at me, wild eyed and furious and, using a towel, stuffs the hand into my bag for me. She opens the door and stands there, a sentinel, waiting for me to leave.

85

'Get out of here,' she says.

'I don't—'

'No excuse. What if he has a tracker in the blood? They will know. Sometimes they have health trackers as well, and now? He has no pulse! Get away from here.'

'They won't find him,' I say. 'They don't know. I put him in his apartment, and I . . .' Did I shut the door? Did I close the windows? Will anybody stumble on his blood?

Did I leave a trail?

'You stupid little girl,' Alala says, and she shakes her head. But I can see something whirring inside her brain, something happening. She shuts the door and traps me in here with her, then reaches out and takes the hand back out of the bag. She walks to her kitchen – nothing more than a sink, really, and an age-old cooker that seems to rattle almost constantly – where she picks up a box from underneath the sink, thick and grey and lumpen, like she made it herself (no hinges, nothing delicate to it). When she opens it, I see a few vials in there, some full of blood, but one empty. She takes this, pulls the cap off with her teeth and holds the hand above it.

'Hope you're not squeamish,' she says, and she looks at me with something like disgust. Then she squeezes the hand, holds it in hers as if she's shaking it, meeting it for the first time; and blood runs from the wrist stump, then quickly slows to a thick drip. I hear the sound of it, pit-patting into the vial. 'All we'll need,' she says after a minute or so, as the flow slows to a stop. She reseals the vial – she doesn't seem to mind having her mouth that close to the guard's blood – and puts it into the box. 'They can't track it if it's in there,' she says. She wipes the ID card clean and puts that inside the box as well. 'Now, the eye,' she says, 'and to get rid of this' – she holds Dave's hand up – 'we need ice.'

I follow her out of her house. Somebody is waiting: a girl, a junkie. She's been nodding off, curled up outside Alala's house as if she's a cat. As soon as she hears us she's up and on her feet, her mouth open, her eyes slits. 'You're awake,' she says.

'Not now,' Alala tells her, and I feel special, for that second; that what I've got going on is more important. Alala and I start almost running, darting around the other homes, her holding the hand to her chest, while I carry the eye in my palm.

It's so soft that I think about squeezing it, just to see if it will pop.

And suddenly I feel sick.

I tell myself that it's not my fault that he – Dave, the target – died. He shouldn't have run. He was afraid; whatever he was into with Alala made him scared, and scared of her, not of me. He was unfit, out of shape. It would have happened sooner or later, I'm sure. If it wasn't me it would have been someone, something else. But I have needs. I had to do something. What I'm doing is bigger than him. It's more important.

It's crucial, for Mae's sake.

I tell myself that it's not my fault, but I know one thing that I simply can't shake: he wouldn't have been running down those stairs if it wasn't for me. I might not have killed him, but I certainly helped him die.

Alala walks through the shanty town and people try and speak to her – she's almost a celebrity around here, and she *never* comes this far into the docks, this close to the water and the wall – but she brushes them off. Head down, eyes forward, she keeps moving ahead. She's got one of her furs wrapped around her like a shawl and it keeps slipping. I rush to keep up with her stride and put my hand on the fur, to steady it, and she almost leaps away from me.

'Do not touch me,' she says, and then, still not looking at me, still powering forward: 'You have no idea what you are going to owe me, Chan.'

She's always known my name, since the first day we met; but I think that this might be the first time she's ever actually called me by it. I'm shaking, my arms wrapped around myself, but still, I'm shaking.

The wall juts from the iced-over water, the most impenetrable barrier: a hundred storeys high, littered with lights that mark out the hatches and vents for the climate generators. It's nothing like Australia, not really, because you can only climb the wall if you're working on it, if you've got the equipment. The noise of the generators is overwhelming today. I'm sure it's never been this loud before, and something inside me feels like it's itching, almost. Somewhere deep inside me I'm still stuck, still trapped. I swapped one prison for another.

No, I tell myself. This is action. This is moving forward, taking control. Saving Mae. Saving myself.

And yet here I am, letting somebody else talk me through

the things that have terrified me, that I have done wrong; fixing my screw-ups, holding my hand as I try to pick up the pieces.

Alala stands right at the edge of the concrete. The ice has holes in it. It doesn't always – it depends on how hard the air conditioners in the wall have been working – but today, we're lucky. 'The cold should freeze this,' she says. She looks down and I can tell that we're both thinking about the bodies that we know are down there, trapped in the ice, even though we can't see them through the darkness. People drown out here and their bodies sink to the bottom of the bay and the cold keeps them from rotting. And there they stay, forever.

The light from the red beacons that mark the wall out along its length is barely enough to see by as Alala hurls Dave's hand out toward the wall. I hear the splash as it hits the water, but I can't watch it sink. 'You used your own knife?' Alala asks. I can hear the shivers in her teeth, the slight chatter as she speaks. 'Throw that as well.'

I take the knife out of the sheath and I hold it up. The blood is gone, as best I can make out. I remember: I wiped it on my clothes, on my side, under my arm. I wanted the blade clean. I tell her this and she sighs.

'Then you have to throw those also. The cold will kill the isotope they use to track.' She softens, puts her hands onto my biceps and squeezes. 'Just get it done, and then we will get you warm.' She reaches out with her fur, jabbing it towards me. I take it and I stand there. 'I won't look,' she tells me, and she turns away.

I wrap the fur around me and take my clothes off. My

only good clothes. I kick them into the break in the icy water. They don't even make a sound as they sink.

'I will take care of the next part,' she says. We're back in her home and I'm wrapped in more layers of fake fur. She's given me stuff to wear, garish things that look like they were once hers, until they became a little too threadbare; they're Alala's style, her taste – or lack of it – in even more faded glory. 'I will talk to the hackers. Leave it with me. Come back tonight. It's morning, too early to do anything now.' She's right; there's the cold, red light of morning in the sky. Somehow the entire night has been and gone.

'What do I do next?' I ask, but I know the answer.

'You have to go into the archive, get the information you need.' She pats me on the knee. 'This is a window, an opportunity.'

'I can't,' I say to her. No question, I'll get caught.

'Cannot is not a word where I come from. You know that? My language, closest thing is *Will not*. A choice.' She tuts.

'There must be another way,' I say. It sounds like begging. Balking.

'You *will not* back out, little girl. No, no. You owe *me*, now. This is a deal. I save you and you help me.' I haven't seen this side of her. People talk, but of course they do, about how she's *a nasty piece of work*, about how she's been involved in things that no one would ever admit to. Rumours, which sound like lies until this moment; until I see this look in her eyes that says that she is not kidding around. That I have absolutely no choice.

'Okay,' I say. I'm shaking – my hands, my fingers, every bit of them. I try to stop it, putting one hand over the other. My skin feels even colder now than it did before, when I was naked at the water's edge.

'Will anybody find him? They cannot find him before you finish this.'

'I don't know,' I say. 'He's in his apartment.' I propped him up, on his sofa. He's sitting, facing the door, waiting for somebody to come in.

I wonder when he'll start to smell. I wonder when his work will ask why he isn't there.

I hadn't thought about all this before. I hadn't considered it properly.

'Chan,' Alala says. She clicks her fingers in the air, in front of my face. 'They could find him. We need to fix, okay? And when we have, I will let you find out where your daughter is.' I told her that Mae was a little girl that I needed to find. Not my daughter. That's her assumption and I don't correct her. And, more than that: she will let me find Mae. Her words. Like she's in control; which, I suppose, she is. 'I tell you, because I help you? You will do favour for *me*. Very big favour.'

'I owe you,' I say, and she nods; and I think about the target – Dave, he had a name – and how scared he was; and what he was actually running from. Me, yes, but something else – whatever it was that he owed to Alala; that made her pick him.

I haven't tested her yet, but I'm fairly certain that Alala doesn't forget a debt.

* * *

91

I've got some credit left over from what Ziegler has given me in the past. I hoard it, have been hoarding it for a time like this, when I actually finally really *need* something. It's on a chip registered to my fake name, and Ziegler puts money onto it when he thinks I might need it. I haven't had the chip implanted, because I can't bring myself to. I don't want to put it in my body. So I have that and some cash – actual money, which is a real rarity here. It's legal currency, but nobody ever uses it. It tends to get you glares if you try, that's what a hassle it is. But it's what I've got.

I'm cold, and that won't change unless I do something about it. The wind, the breeze from the wall, cuts right through this whole place, billowing out gusts that seem to find exactly where I'm coldest and make it colder. They say it's sweltering outside the city walls, so hot it'll cook food if you leave it in the sun for a while; cook *you*, if you stay in it even longer. I watch the usual lot waiting for Alala to wake up, to get their fixes – she went back to sleep, leaving me outside her cabin, telling me to wait, just as they do – and I pace, to try and get myself warm, but it doesn't work. Some days are colder than others. I had one set of clothes and I need more. Alala's cast-offs don't fit, and they jangle when I move, rattle almost. I could buy clothes from the people who live here, but there's no point. Those things will only fall apart. I have a blanket wrapped around my waist, tied off as a skirt; Alala's fur around my shoulders.

I feel ridiculous.

I leave Alala's as the junkies start getting anxious, arm-scratching and signing at each other. So many of them are muted, because that's what living here – being born here – can mean. They don't get the choice to speak. And the drugs: they're not from Alala, not originally. She's not the reason they're addicted. She just profits off their addictions. I've seen what happens when they go into withdrawal. My first week here: the pain in a man's face, as he scratched at himself, his skin rotting off his frame.

From where I'm standing, if you look straight up, all you can see is the wall. But in the distance, above it, there's the sky, the colour of it changing as night gives way to dawn, which gives way to the rest of the day. And the birds, the morning birds, starting to flock, casting shapes – arrowheads; wings; clusters of galaxies that seem to form, explode and re-form – against the pale blue that's starting to creep through the reddened black, advancing into its territory.

I stand up and walk away, just as the mist settles in. It comes every morning, a haze of vapour, plumes of white cloud that spurt out from the generators in the walls and settle in over the edges of the city. Eventually, as the sun creeps into view above us, the air warms up and the cloud dissipates. I pull the edge of the scarf that's covering my shoulders over my mouth, to protect me.

The buses are running, but they won't be full of commuters yet, which means there's more chance of my face being caught on camera. I don't have my hood. I don't even have a hat, so that means hair down, over my face. It needs a wash. It's a bit of a joke for me to even have hair. I've never had it this long, not my whole life. On Australia, we cut it back regularly, because there was such a high chance of lice. But it's been growing since the moment we landed. I haven't had to cut it. I can't tell if I like it this way, or if it's just easier not to bother. And when I see the local people, with their hair done so elaborately, touch-dyed and tip-lit and all of these other augments and processes that I don't understand, a part of me wants to feel like that *could* be me. That, maybe, doing it would help me fit in.

I take to the streets that don't have cameras: trade entrances, throughways, slip roads that never go anywhere, that just seem to join one avenue to another. As I walk, the pavements cracked and ignored, the roads pretty much empty, I watch the street lights twitch out, their brightness giving way to the darkness of the dawn, and the buildings cast more of a shadow than the night itself, for a few moments. Some are so large that you can walk in the shade of them for so long you forget what time of day it is.

I had imagined that when we landed there would be a horizon, a far-off that I could stare at and wonder what was there, what was so distant that I couldn't yet see it. That's what I wanted. And yet now I live in a city surrounded by a wall a hundred feet high. There's no horizon. There's no distance.

Cars pass me, and commuters. They rush. They don't worry about the fact that they're trapped here. We were told what life was like before Australia left Earth the first time: that people were free, that life was open. The world was swollen, sure, but everything was allowed to swell more. The swelling was our right, our destiny. Now I know how much we can be lied to; the capacity for those in control to tell us what they think we want to hear, to keep us from the truth. These people: they don't even know how free they are. There have been calamities and there have been traumas; technology halted for a while, because everything – everybody – was focused on saving the planet. We were their backup plan: people sent into space, to see if that was viable. If all else failed, would being trapped in a box in the stars be enough? If the climate couldn't be controlled, humanity would have abandoned Earth.

Instead, they abandoned us.

I get angry as I walk. I notice that my feet are hitting the pavement harder. The city gets cleaner, shinier as I walk towards the centre. There's better lighting, even if I don't factor in the sun. The streets are wider as I get to the shopping district, and this isn't even one of the bigger ones. It's mostly market traders, a few smaller shops, a couple of much bigger stores that sell clothes. I head to one of these. No need to wait for them to open. Nothing like the markets here, with set times. The automations mean that almost everything is available around the clock. Doesn't matter what I want, when I want it. All that matters is that I can afford it.

That's another thing I hate: there's no haggling here.

The clothes are all described in terms that I still barely understand, six months after I arrived here: they're all *active* or *enabled*, lights blinking as you walk past them, colours shifting, hues going from darker ends of the spectrum to lighter, the fabric twitching, almost, begging to be bought.

I enter the one with the least obnoxious sign, the least-loud music pumping out of the doorway. 'Good morning,' a girl says, smiling at me. She works here, you can tell. Her outfit's a mess of colours, like ink in a painting being pushed around, like a blurred tattoo. She's my age, taller, skinnier. Of course she's taller; everybody's taller here. There's not an ounce of muscle on her: all sinew, all bone. 'I love your shrug,' she says. She means the tatty fur, wrapped around me, pinned with a ludicrous safety pin. 'Custom?'

'Yes,' I say, the words stumbling out of my mouth. And I don't know why I don't tell her the truth: that it's all I have, a loan, that tomorrow I'll be dressed as I always am. Or, no. I do know. She likes it, so she doesn't see me for who I really am. Right now, I don't live in the docks. Right now, in this moment, I *belong*.

I walk past the dresses, past the shoes, towards the *Standards* section at the back. No bells or whistles: T-shirts, hooded jacket, jeans, sneakers. One of each, in black, or as close a shade of grey as they sell. A t-shirt in something called Midnight Ink, which looks like it's wet, a moody lake, the pattern swirling. In the fitting rooms, I try everything on, watching them adjust themselves to my body in the mirror: shrinking away from me in places, bulking up in others. The hood extends, fitting itself around my head, smoothly lowering, the technology in the fabric making sure it does what it should.

'Lower,' I say, as I rest my finger on the edge of the material. Then, silently, the tip comes down, covering more of my eyes. 'Lower.' You can't see my eyes at all; can't see what I'm going to do any more.

'Miss?' the girl from before asks, through the door. 'Miss, can I get you anything else?'

I want to barter. I want to trade. I think about running.

'I'll just take these,' I tell her. I try and make my voice sound like I'm smiling.

The checkout machine doesn't take cash, that's the first hurdle; and my credit isn't quite enough to cover all of my purchases. I press for help, and that sends the girl over, and then she goes and fetches a manager, who fumbles his words as he tries to unfold the notes I give him, presses the authenticator strip to check that they're not fakes, then scans them against stolen banknote records. He watches me the whole time. Cash apparently makes him suspicious.

'This takes a while,' he says, his tone suggesting an apology that never comes. 'It's inconvenient.' It's only inconvenient because he doesn't trust me, because he decides that he has to run five or six different checks to stop his store being even slightly out of pocket. 'We don't have change,' he tells me, when he's finally satisfied that the notes are legit. 'I can give you store credit.'

That's when I see the bracer, hanging from a rack at the side of the counter. Thick black leather, or something close to it. It has spikes, but these are softened down, the tips sanded off. No one could hurt herself on them. I pick it up and turn it around in my hand, feeling the tautness of it.

'How much?' I ask, and the manager puts it under the scanner. It's less than I have left over. I tell him to bag it up.

Outside, I find a stoop, sit down, and I don't care who watches. I pull my t-shirt on, then discard the fur from Alala into the bag my new clothes came in; and I pull the jacket on, yank the hood over my head, again feeling it moulding to me; then I pull on the trousers, then the shoes. I let everything adjust again. The clothes have forgotten who I am since I last wore them. They only have a memory of a few minutes.

And then I put the bracer on, and I think about Jonah. How he had one around his neck when I met him. The bracer tightens around my wrist, pulling itself closed until it's tight around my skin the whole way, until it's secure. This is when it catches me out. When something reminds me of him, it's so strong that it pushes me back, almost, it knocks the wind out of me and forces me to take stock. A flash of red hair in a crowd; something tied to a neck; a kiss in a holo between people I'll never even know. Or I'll hear somebody saying a prayer and I'll remember his voice, hear it saying that same prayer, explaining it to me. I haven't thought about him for days. The memories hit harder when that happens.

I learned that the people have his *Testaments* here, which surprised me. I thought they were a ship thing for the longest while. But Ziegler showed me a copy, and it was sort of the same, like a broken, not as exciting version. On Australia, they were much shorter. I appreciated that. Also, here, there's not the last bit, the bit about the nine levels of hell. I think that *must* have been Australia only. Too convenient.

But then the sharpness of the memory fades. With Jonah, it takes triggers to remember. The others? They're there the whole time. I can never escape thinking about my mother or Agatha or Mae, or even – for some reason, as if she's been burned into my brain, seared and scarred – Rex.

I remind myself that Jonah is dead. And that's awful and terrible and sad, but there are a lot of dead people out there, and I can't cry over them all.

I pull the sleeve of my jacket over the bracer. It's there, holding me; a pressure that's so tight it almost hurts, but I can get used to it. It fades into the background.

I need to speak to Ziegler. I need his help.

FIVE

'No,' Ziegler says. He doesn't even let me finish saying what I need him to do. He slams his hand down, he almost stamps his foot, and he shakes his head. 'It's absolute madness.'

'Please,' I say, as if that will work. *Manners will get you everywhere* was something that my mother told me. Not quite, I know. Not everywhere.

'I can't even have this conversation with you. You tell me what you're planning and I can't deny anything if they catch you. If they bring me in for questioning? I already know too much.' The café we're sitting in is heaving with people. A few tables over, a group of girls talk about going to pick up something from a contact in the docks – drugs, probably. That's usually why people go there, if they live in the middle of the city. Their money's always good. Behind me, there's a couple fighting about babies: she wants one, he doesn't. She says it's almost too late anyway – *I'm not getting any younger* – so why are they even bothering? Where is the relationship even going?

Even when Ziegler raises his voice, he and I don't stand out. An older businessman-type, his face bearded, his eyes (every part of his skin, really) tired and sagging, nurses his third refill of coffee as a teenage girl, likely his daughter, hiding her face, pleads with him for something.

'So I don't tell you anything. You give me a ride. You wait for me. When I get out, you take me to your apartment. They won't think to look for a car. You just need to be there when I finish what I need to do.'

'*If* you finish.'

'You think I can't do this?'

'I don't even know what you're planning,' he says, but he does. He just doesn't know the details. Maybe that's the best way of beating a lie-detector: if you don't know the exact facts, you can still make a convincing denial. But not if they dope him, get the information out that way. And not if he betrays me, gives me up. Doesn't matter how close you are to somebody: you can't ever trust them entirely. Not a hundred percent.

'I'm not telling you,' I say. 'All you know is that I will be somewhere at a certain time. I'll call you.'

'How? You don't have a chip.'

'So I'll get one.' I hate the idea, but if I have to, I have to.

'Which I'll pay for? Anyway, it won't be registered. You'll be better off without one. Otherwise, the systems will make you as soon as you're in the building.'

'Which building?' I ask, smirking. And he smiles as well, because this is almost actually funny. He's used to sitting back, to trying to fix the system – that's what he calls it – from the outside. His articles, his books, his beliefs: they're all intangible, theoretical. What I want to do is not. It is a crime. And it is, I think, intriguing him. 'I could get a burner chip. I know Alala's fitted them into people before.'

'So now you're getting black-market augments? Look, Chan. This isn't going to work. It can't work, you know that.'

And that makes me lose my temper. I'm furious with him. Now is the time to do, not think. 'Have you always been such a coward?' I ask, and that works. His face reddens as if he's been slapped.

'This isn't that.'

'Because you can't get in trouble here. Just say you had no idea what I was planning.'

'If you don't do this, you can't get caught. And then I won't have to say a goddamn thing.' He shakes his head. His fingers run through his beard, scratching at the skin, pulling the hairs apart. I can see tiny scars underneath, almost like paper-cuts on his lip, probably from teenage acne, or cuts from shaving. He still uses a blade to keep the beard in check, close to his face – I've seen the razor in his bathroom. Like the rest of his hair it's grey, white around the corners of his mouth. On Australia, that would have been a tell; because you couldn't trust somebody who didn't want you to see their mouth. Here, it's fashion. All the men have beards, or they have augmented follicles to force styles onto their faces. Ziegler's is his own, at least. He's not pretentious. I'm pretty good at reading people, and I know he'll do what's best for me. He'll help me. He just needs more of a push.

'You want your evidence about Australia, you'll have to help me,' I say.

'Chan.'

'You don't even know the best stuff yet. You don't know how I killed Rex, do you? I didn't tell you that part yet. And I've got stories about my mother, and Agatha; about the Nightman; about the Feeders, who were around before I was born, used to eat people. And not like the Lows, not all shady and *maybe, maybe*, they actually, you know, *ate* people.'

'Chan . . .'

'I mean it. I'll tell you everything, straight away, all in one go. I don't care. Put my name on the front of a newspaper. Put my picture up there. Tell my story. Sell it. Call your publisher. You can have it all.'

I stop talking when the waitress appears at Ziegler's shoulder. He likes this place because they have real people serving you, nothing automated. In the kitchens there's somebody actually making the food and putting it on the plate. He likes that. Me? I couldn't care less, beyond the fact that it makes this place much more expensive. The waitress smiles because she's working for tips. She has a pencil behind her ear that she never employs, using her finger to tap orders into her pad instead. Ziegler's told me that the pencil's an affectation, like it's part of the uniform. It's how things used to be done – people used to write orders down with pencils on pads of paper – so pretending to do it is what's fashionable now. It's a reminder of a time they never knew.

'Coffee?' asks the waitress, and Ziegler nods. She refills the cup in front of him from a big glass carafe she's carrying. 'And you?' she asks me, and I smile up at her, my best *there's nothing to pay attention to here* smile.

'Juice,' I say. 'Apple, please.'

'Right with you.' And then she's gone. I look at Ziegler's face, and I see that I've lost him, if I was ever even close to having his support for my plan in the first place.

'You can't do this,' he says, and then he corrects himself. He knows full well that I can. 'I can't do this. I can't help you. There's too much riding on it.'

'Nobody has any guts here. Why am I surprised you don't either.' And then, to kick him harder, as hard as I can: 'No wonder you're alone.'

He blinks that back, but holds firm. I can't even tell how much that hurt him. 'You're still a child,' he says, 'and you don't know what you're doing. I know that I can't stop you, that I can't persuade you.' Not going to stop him trying, I know, from the way that he says it. 'But you have to remember: you're building a life, here. I can help you get a job, a real place to live. I can help you start over. I've told you that.'

'I don't want that. All I want is to save Mae.'

'Sure. But maybe this isn't the way to go about it.'

'Tell me what is, then. Just tell me.' I'm nearly shouting, now. He's made me angry. But not with him, not exactly. It's just this place, this entire situation. I'm angry that I'm even having to try and persuade him. This isn't the way that it was meant to go; and as the waitress brings me my juice, and he blows to cool his coffee down, I think that maybe he knows that. He can see that I'm desperate, and yet still he won't help.

How it was meant to go is this: I was meant to step off the ship, having saved the lives of the people that I cared about, the good people who did nothing wrong, who didn't deserve the fate – the curse – that had been put upon them. I was meant to look back at everything I had lost – my mother; my childhood; even Agatha, so recently departed – and still see something resembling the future I had dreamt of. Mae would be there and we would be a family. Family is what you make it; that's something I learned. It's not blood. It runs deeper than that, and stronger.

That's how it was meant to go.

But it didn't.

So what I have to do next is not my choice.

We stand on the sidewalk. He calls for his car and we wait. He doesn't speak, doesn't even look at me. He knows he's let me down. We both watch as the car comes around the corner, as it slides towards us. You can't hear it until it recognises him and speaks to him.

'Mr Ziegler,' Gaia says, as the door opens for him. He stands next to it, one foot inside.

'Are you coming?'

'Are you going to help me?'

He shakes his head. 'Anything else, you know I'll help you. And you know that I want to publish the book. It's important, even if you don't think it is.'

I don't say anything more. I need his help. I'm alone here; that's what he's forgetting, or what he's ignoring.

I watch him get into his car and pull away from the curb, silent as anything; more silent than if he was walking.

The docks feel, for a second, like home; like a relief. I ran the whole way, not because I was being chased, or because I had to, but because it felt good. When I'm running I'm in control: of my breathing, of my feet on the streets, of where I go. The hood on my sweatshirt has reacted to the exercise, pulled itself off my head as I sweated, as I got warmer from the run; the clothes splitting vents in the fabric to let the heat out. There are no cameras in the docks. Here, I don't need to worry if somebody sees my face, and I can let the sweat run down my cheeks, down the back of my neck, and I can feel it chill in the coldness of the air. I stop and breathe, and feel the air cooling me down.

That's when I hear the voice, cracked and stammering, a local accent, somebody who's lived here their whole life.

'Alala's searching f'you.' The girl is sad-looking, her skin a mess as she staggers up to me. I've seen her before, in the junkie queue. A lot of them look the same, but she sticks out. Her hair is pulled right back, hiding where it's gone from her head. Fallen out or torn, I can't tell. Whatever she's on is responsible in one way or another. There are a lot of bad (or maybe just stupid) things that people do to themselves here: not exclusively in the docks or the other slum areas, but we get the cheapest, nastiest versions. In the rest of the city, people manage their habits and addictions. Here, they run rife, and they're ruinous. This one scratches and pulls at her own skin, and her eyes are gammy and weeping, and her nails have dried blood underneath them. 'Told me t' find you, fetch you t'her.' She waits for me to say something. I'm still catching my breath. 'And here y'are.'

'Tell her I'll be along.'

'She says t'give you a message. This is why you'll want t'see her. She says, she's got what you wan'ed. Tha' make sense?' What I wanted. The archives? Mae? I feel my heart race with something like excitement, even as I know I shouldn't let it. She touches my arm, a loose grab at me, for attention, and I flinch away from her. 'So you have t'go now.' It's not a request.

I head towards Alala's house and the girl follows me, just a few steps behind; I can hear her dragging one of her feet. She's slower than I am, but I don't like her being there. You can't watch your back if you're facing forward, and there's nobody here to watch my back for me. I think, for a moment, how it once was: Jonah and I, side by side, knives out and teeth bared. If he was here now, I wouldn't be doing this alone.

It's darker in the shadow of the wall. Even when it's daytime, the sun doesn't quite reach here. It's blocked on one side by the wall, and on the other by the buildings in the hub of the city itself. It's like we're in a perpetual dusk from which we can't escape. When we're still hours away from nightfall, it feels like the sun has already set. I turn and look at the girl, because I still don't trust her. She blinks at me and rubs at her eyes with her sleeves, her hands – her whole arms – shake as she tries to clear her vision. She's not a threat, I realise. She's just desperate.

Alala is waiting for me, foot on an upturned barrel, doing something with her boot. She clicks her fingers as I get closer. 'Come, come,' she says. 'You're slow today, little girl. Zoe's been looking for you, on her toes all morning.'

Zoe must be the junkie. Alala palms something to her, so small it'll last her an hour and then she'll be right back again, queuing for whatever Alala sees fit to dole out. 'Get inside,' Alala says. She's smiling at me, but there's no sound of it in her voice.

She shuts the door after me, then puts a chair across it, so it won't open. We won't be disturbed. She leads me to the back, where I saw the woman giving birth before. On the table where she once lay there's a thin grey tray, metallic, reflective. On top of it is the box from before, the one that had caught the blood. Alala reaches into it and pulls out three items, then lays them out on the table for me. 'You got these out of my home, you understand? You know the trouble that I had to go through for these?'

'And I'm grateful,' I say.

'You be more than that. You owe me, little girl. You said that, remember?'

'Of course,' I say.

'So I need favour from you. I have many things from archive that would be useful, you understand? More useful than where to find your daughter.' No sense in correcting her. She won't listen; or simply won't care. 'So I will get you in there, and you will . . .' She waggles her fingers in the air, some approximation of an action that I don't understand. 'You will make this happen. Get information for you, and for me, you understand?' This whole time, she hasn't lost that empty smile. I wonder what emotion it's hiding.

'Okay, so, now,' she says, and she bends down and picks up something. She's wearing thin blue gloves that show her flesh through them, the veins and bones of her swollen knuckles. The thing in her hands is a needle: a hypodermic. 'The ID chip is in here. I have changed the picture on it, so it is your picture now. If cameras see you, they will be fooled. It is also your genetic information. So they scan that, and you will get blood tested, and it will be you. So only you can swipe it. But not your fingerprint! That is his, still.'

She holds the hypodermic up. 'Give me your wrist,' she says, and I do. I have to. She presses the needle to it, and she squeezes the trigger. I feel a sharp pain, like being bitten by an insect. 'Done,' she tells me, and she rubs the place where the chip went in, before turning my arm over and squeezing my index finger. She picks up something else from the tray with her free hand, a thin film of pink flesh, it looks like; and she spits onto it, the saliva coming out from between her remaining teeth, her nearly blue gums. She rubs it, and sucks the remaining spit back up into her mouth with a slurp. 'Needs wetness,' she says, 'activates the glue.' Then she lays the film on my fingertip and presses it down. 'Good.'

I look at it. It looks like my finger, but subtly different. Something in the swirls, where before mine were like a shell. This one has harder, thicker lines. There's a scar on it that I don't have; a nick, down through the lines. 'It's perfect; it works perfectly. His finger, on yours. Don't get it wet. Then it might rot; it might ruin the pattern, because of the glue,' she offers, like that explains everything. 'And now the eye,' she says, and she picks up the final tray. At first I don't see anything in it but some liquid, a thin film. She takes another syringe from the siding, a sterilised packet. 'Open your eyes,' she says. 'Head back, hold them open with your fingers.'

'I can't,' I say. She presses the needle to the liquid and sucks it up into the chamber.

'Temporary augment,' she says, 'changes your eye patterns. Very temporary, only a few hours. Like when children have the colour changed.' That's a fashion thing, a gimmick; almost a tattoo into the eyeball, changing the shape and shade. I've seen it and been disgusted by it. We change enough without meaning to; why change things about ourselves if we don't need to? It's like the Lows, ruining themselves, damaging each other. Like Rex. And why would anybody want to be like her?

'I can't,' I say.

'You have no choice,' she tells me, the smile gone. 'This is what needs to happen.' Her words come out focused, almost spat out, one syllable at a time. 'Hold your eyes open, little girl. I do not want to blind you.' She comes at my right eye first, and my fingers, pressing my eyelids back, tremble and flinch, my reflexes forcing the lids shut. I'm terrified. It's not often I'm scared, but my eyes work, and they're mine. And if I lost them, for whatever reason, how would I find Mae? How would I even survive here?

'There is not time for this,' she says.

'I'm trying,' I tell her.

'Look away from me. Do not focus on me, on the needle.' I breathe, deep, and hold it. I keep my eyes open and I stare at the far side of the room. I stare at the wall and the corner of the floor, where it meets, just out of my vision; and I can see blood there, on the ground, dried and black, and I wonder where it came from. Who it came from.

I think about Mae, and Agatha, and Jonah; and how important what I need to do is; how necessary.

I feel the needle press against my eyeball, and then wetness, a rush of liquid, flowing down my cheek, and I can't see anything but dark red for a second. Alala touches my cheek with a cloth, wipes away something, and I don't know if it's blood or tears.

'One is done. Now for other.' So we repeat the process, me still looking at the same place, this time trembling slightly, trying not to cry. Now that the vision is gone from one eye I can't see the blood. Now I can only see the edge of my own nose. My skin, the freckles on the bridge of it. I flinch much less this time, and when it's done she tells me to blink. I do, over and over. 'Okay, better. Two minutes. Take two minutes. Keep them shut, and then open.'

I sit in the darkness I've made for myself and listen as she clatters around her home. The sound of her drinking from her bottle – which I'm grateful she's only doing now, not before she stuck the needle in my eye – and of her preparing something, tidying away what was on the table. Then, she pats me on the leg.

'Open now,' she says, and I do. I can't see the blood on the floor any more, and it takes a few seconds for my eyes to focus; and then my vision is back as it was, exactly the same. Not only that, but everything is clearer. I can make out details that I couldn't earlier. I look at the blood on the ground, and see that it's not blood. It's paint – old and faded, chipped away from whatever this place was used for before it was Alala's home. And Alala herself: she's older than I thought she was. I can see the details on her face as if I'm right up next to them, examining them, poring over them.

'I can see,' I say.

'Of course.'

'But better. I mean, I can see better.'

'I put other augment in the liquid. Adaptive, to fix problems. You don't know you have astigmatism?'

'No,' I say. She starts laughing.

'Little girl, where did you come from that you don't know that? My eyes, steady as anything. Perfect. My parents wanted me to have perfect eyes, so they had them fixed. You know that? Did your mother not try and fix you?'

'She did,' I say; but I don't give her any more than that, because I don't want to talk about her, not here; not with Alala.

Alala explains the plan again, once more, like I'm an idiot. I press my hand to the pad. It reads my genes, scans my fingerprint, all the while I lean forward to let it scan my eyes. The door will open, no alarms, no surprises.

'If you get caught, you can't get out. The security is tight for a reason.'

'Okay,' I say. I try to not play with the fake skin on my finger. There's a loose part at the very edge of it, a lip, and all I want to do is pick at it. Willpower, I tell myself, it's not that hard. 'How long will this last?' I ask.

'What do you mean?'

'I mean, the eyes. The –' I hold up my finger to her. 'How many days will they last?'

That sets her off laughing again. 'Days! Not days. Hours, little girl. Hours is all. You have to go tonight,' she tells me, and she cackles. I think about the stories we used to tell on Australia about witches. At moments, Alala is exactly how I imagined them to be. 'Last things,' she says. 'You need his uniform, because this?' She points to what I'm wearing. 'This will not do. You need to look like him. Will be adaptive, so just get it. Easy.'

Easy, she says, but it was on him. He must have a spare. He has to have a spare.

'Now when you get to the archive, this is what you need.' She has something in the palm of her hand, held out towards me. I didn't see her bring it out, or where it came from. It is a small metal disc, thin and black. She hands it to me. 'Safe, safe,' she says. I lay it on my palm and feel a soft tremor, as though it's vibrating slightly. It's cold as anything and doesn't feel like it'll warm up, either. 'You put this onto drives in archive, on computer. Just as long as it is very close, it will do the rest. It copies material we need, for you and for me.'

'Mae's location?'

'Every location. All the names, all the places. Everything we need. I have information in there; you have information in there. So you get and you bring back. My people will do the rest, read all the results for us; find out where you get your little girl back.' She closes my fingers around the device. 'Is very easy. Very short time to do. You do, you get out of there. Through door, come back here. All will be . . .' She smiles and she shrugs, as though this is nothing to worry about, as though there's nothing dangerous to it. I can hear the rain outside. The walls muffle the sound, but now that I'm listening, the storm – and the heavy thunder, when it happens – echoes everywhere. I stuff my hand into my pocket to keep it dry. The pocket closes tightly around it, a seal around my wrist.

'You're sure this will work?' I ask her.

'Little girl,' she says, leaning forward to kiss me on the cheek, 'would I lie to you?'

There are children outside the guard's apartment block, on the strange, bare patch of grass that might once have been a playground. A few of them are throwing a ball around and a couple of others are clambering on trees and wooden posts and the remains of something made of concrete blocks. It is strange to see so many children. Their parents are on one side watching, nobody caring about the rain. Rain is rare enough that it's quite nice, really.

I wonder if this is the sum total of the children who live in this apartment block. Once there would have been so many more. Before the wall went up, they would have pretty much swarmed all over it.

I make my way up the stairs. I get a few glances from the parents, but then they go back to watching their children; they don't want to let their kids out of their gaze. I can't imagine what that must be like: being afraid that your child will be hurt or killed, of being left childless, with no way of having another. There's no way of picking up your life after that. I remember a woman on Australia that my mother knew, who lived a few floors down. She lost her kid one day, when she fell off the edge. No one pushed her or threw her. It was just a tumble, like kids have, but with a finality to it. The mother had another. Straightaway she was pregnant, months later there was another little girl, same name as the first. It was like tempting fate, almost; but maybe she saw it as putting right what went wrong.

And Bess, Bess, who lived next door to me. Her son went missing and she went to Rex. She found solace there, somehow. Betrayed me. I never found out what happened to her son, where he went, if he was alive or dead.

I can't even remember his name, now. I try and find it, somewhere, deep inside, but it won't come. I grit my teeth. My jaw aches, I'm thinking so hard.

I pass the window, the gap where the guard went over. I search inside myself for what happened, for whose fault it was. I promised Bess that I would find her son. I promised.

I said that I wouldn't hurt Dave, and I did.

What was the boy's name?

I get to the top of the stairs and the memories keep coming, like a flood that I can't dam, even though I wish I could. It's the smell. I'm sure I can catch it on the air even here: the stench of the pit at the bottom of Australia; the rot of bodies, of blood. I remember wading through it, dragging the others, trying to give them something safe that they could own, that we could all own. That smell is here now, faint as anything, but here, right outside the guard's door. Whispering at me from the gaps between the door and the frame.

I didn't know bodies decomposed so quickly. My hand shakes. I tell myself it's okay, that it will all be okay. Or, at least, that this is necessary.

Even as I tell myself that, I think how easy it is to lie to ourselves.

I try the handle to the door, but it is locked. I totally forgot. When I left here before, I flicked the latch as I shut it. Okay.

I take a breath and jam my shoulder into it. It swings open, giving way almost too easily, the latch snapping off the door frame. My shoulder howls at me, a pang of an injury healed long ago, but my body loves to remind me of my past.

'Dave, there is a guest,' the voice of his home system says.

It knows that he's in the apartment already. It thinks that he's just sitting there, doing whatever. About to stand up, get on with his day.

The smell from him is a fog. It's a wave. I clamp my hand across my mouth and gulp back to stop myself from retching. How long has he been dead? A day? Nothing can smell like this in a day. And how can it bother me? On Australia, it was weeks, months, *years* worth of death and decay, spilled into liquid. The smell was everywhere and I didn't bat an eyelid.

Maybe I've forgotten, just as I've forgotten Bess's son's name. I spent hours – days – thinking about him, searching the ship for him, and the memory of his name is not even on the tip of my tongue. It's just not there. Like this smell, I don't know what's making me feel worse, feel more sick: the wanting to retch through the weird almost-taste in the air, or the fact that I never found him. The fact that he died and it's on me – just like Dave, now.

His body, propped up on the sofa, head lolled to one side. Bess's son, who knows where. Certainly dead.

Dave looks fine. He still looks alive, if not the colour that he should be. There's blood on his face, from where I struggled with his eye. I shut his eyelids, because I couldn't bear to look at the hole I'd left; the mess I'd made. His remaining hand rests in his lap, holding the wrist of the other arm. I don't know why that made sense to me, but I didn't want it hanging limp at his side. I put them onto his lap, folded. Neat.

I'm finding it hard to keep my own hands under control. They are trembling so much, they don't even feel like they're mine. There's a picture hanging on the wall, a printed photograph (not a holo, an actual, tangible thing) of the man before me. He's younger in the picture, thinner, with more hair on his head and a smile on his face that I just can't imagine being something that he ever had; it's a look so simultaneously calm and joyous that I have to distance it from him right now, distance it from me. He's holding onto the shoulders of what must be family

117

members: an older lady, a younger lady, an older man propped up in a chair. I can see Dave's face in theirs, some single through-line in their noses, their cheeks, the shapes of their heads: the things that made them family, that he inherited.

I turn back to his body, on the sofa.

'I'm sorry,' I say, and I crouch down next to him. I didn't kill him. I've killed before. Rex pushed me to do it. This was an accident; and while I've had those before as well, they were never like this.

He ran. He died. But somewhere in that, his death is my fault.

I never found Bess's son. She betrayed me. I lost her. I lost Jonah. I lost Mae.

But I can get Mae back.

There are no other uniforms in his apartment. I check his wardrobe, his drawers. I can only see the one that he's wearing. It's self-cleaning, self-adjusting, self-repairing. In theory, one was all he'd ever need. It's all I need as well.

The suit is a one-piece, a long seal down the front. I yank it undone. My hands are shaking still, but they work. I make them work. I start to worm the fabric off his body. It's a struggle to get the arms out. They're rigid, still. I don't know why. It's like he's fighting me. And his head lolls towards me, like he's trying to look at me. His eyes stay closed, though. I don't know that I could cope if they were to open. I position my head close to his, to help myself pull the suit off. It's a struggle.

I'm trying to get his left arm out of the hole at the wrist when there's a buzz, loud enough that it scares me, that I jump and let go. I look at the door, but it's not that. It's his cell, the buzzing coming from his ear. It stops, and I freeze. A voice, and I'm close enough to hear it: a cheap augment. Expensive ones don't make a sound; they just put the signal right into your head. This one is a speaker, at least a few gens old, older than they sell on the black market, even.

'Dave? It's Marek. Full day docked unless we hear from you. Can't keep you on if you keep doing this. You're in first thing in the morning or we find somebody else to fill your slot.' The voice is faint, like an insect trapped on the far side of the room.

I ignore it. They're expecting him tomorrow morning, and after that his access will likely be wiped. If I wait too long, everything will be lost; everything I've worked so hard for will be wasted. And the fingerprint, the eye augment: they'll fade or fall off and I'll be screwed.

I have to work faster.

I get the arms out and start on the legs. The suit is clean, small mercies. The body does *things* when it dies, evacuates itself, collapses. But his is fine. His legs feel so strange, like loose limbs that aren't connected to anything. Bodies go stiff when they die, and then those muscles relax. The smell, and his flesh under my fingers as I pull the trousers off, makes me think of the pit. How scared I was, at first. How I had to pretend I wasn't, come the end of Australia. I struggle getting the legs over the boots. I'm not taking those; there's no way that they'll fit. My shoes will have to pass. Then it's clear, and the suit is in my hands.

I go to the balcony and I hold the suit out over it, to get it wet. It will clean itself, but I don't know much blood it can handle. Besides, I like the rain. It's calming, for a second, just for a moment, hearing it fall, letting it soak my arms while it washes the suit. I like the idea of rain, of something so natural and clean and pure coming from so high in the sky, from the air itself, down here to us.

Then I remember the false skin on my finger, how I wasn't meant to get it wet. Stupid, stupid. I check that it's still there. It is. The lip at the edge is more prominent now, like it's actually beginning to peel. So stupid. I press it down, hoping that the water will give it a second stickiness. It holds, just about.

Stupid.

Back inside, I pull the suit on over my clothes. As soon as I press the seal together, it adjusts itself, shrinking to fit me, drawing itself tighter, drying itself, the fibres adapting to shed the water from it. I have the hood from my jacket up over the top of the collar, and I catch a glimpse of myself in the mirror in Dave's bathroom. It's so close to what I wore on Australia, the suit that I made for myself.

There's no time left. I apologise to him again, because I don't know what else to do. When this is over, I will tell people where to find him; maybe have Ziegler do something anonymously. I don't know. The people in the photograph will want to know where he is; they'll want to do something for him, something for his body.

It's only as I'm walking down the stairs – running, really, but trying not to lose my step, trying to hold on as I feel my legs shaking – that I remember the name of Bess's son. It was Peter. I never found him.

I hope that he died quickly.

The rain has stopped.

The children have all gone in now, the night swallowing Dave's apartment complex whole. It's too dark to play and there are no lights. I can hear voices, that's it. There are some people hanging around the playground, but not parents and children. I can see smoke billowing from one of their mouths, and I can smell something like stale sweat. I hear them squelch through the mud towards me and I pick up my pace, walking faster towards the road. I'm scared and holding it together, but my courage feels a frail thing; like I could lose it at any second. I need to hang on. There'll be time enough for fear after I've found Mae.

I stand at the edge of the road. Come on, I think. There must be a bus soon.

The people from outside Dave's complex start walking towards me. There's nobody else around, just me. It isn't an accident that they're coming towards me.

'Not now,' I say, loud enough that they should be able to hear me. I want them to wonder what I mean.

I hear the cocking of a pistol, maybe. Something sharp and metal coming out of a sheath. The fizz of a striker.

One of them laughs, then the others join in. I pick out their voices, count what I'm up against: two males, one female. I start walking away from them, fast enough that I'm nearly running. I don't need a fight, not now.

'Come back t'us,' one of them says. It's dark here, lit only by the ambient lighting from the buildings around us. I can just about see their shadows on the ground. They will be able to see my silhouette. 'You hear what I said? I said, come back, have some fun wi' us.'

So I stop walking. I put my hands into fists, which feels better. It stops them shaking, at least. I wonder how long it'll be before they wish they'd never told me to stop in the first place.

I wipe myself clean on the bus. I stayed away from blood, which is good. Can't have blood all over me, making me conspicuous, getting me spotted, turning me into a target. But I've got mud on my knees and my elbows, from where one of them managed to do this awful leg sweep thing to trip me up, something that they probably saw in a holo once and tried to emulate. It was so bad, so clumsy, that I almost laughed. I wanted to tell them, That's not how you fight. *This* is how you fight.

It was over nearly before it began. Afterwards, I had to roll them over out of the mud, to make sure they didn't drown in it. They didn't resist.

And now, on the bus, I'm thinking about how glad I am that the suit held up, that I could move in it exactly how I wanted to, as tightly fitted as it is; and how whatever's going to happen next, it's all a gamble; I can't predict it, not even close. I think about how this bus ride was the route that Dave used to take every day on his way to work at the archives; how he would sit here and stare out of the window, maybe, thinking about something else, anything else, about how much better or worse his life could be. But he'll never do that again.

The bus goes on into the night. Nobody looks at me. I keep my head down and don't look at anybody. My neck aches. I try to not flick the fake skin on my finger. It's tempting, like a scab that needs picking, that will peel away; only this one I can't afford to lose.

And then the view changes: the buildings turn into white palaces, columns and statues and grassy verges; the roads are wider. Everyone gets off the bus, and then it's just me, heading towards my final stop, as if I'm going to work. I have a few hours to go, so I find a bench and curl myself into a ball on the seat, and I wait.

SIX

There's a parade of people ready to start their shift, queuing on the street for their turn through the access gate. It's still so dark out. This is a time of day – night, really – that nobody wants to be at work for. But that's what happens here: you get a job and you have to be there when people tell you to be. These people, they don't want to risk losing what they've got. They're very big on punctuality in the city. I learned that right away. Everything runs to a perfect, exacting clock. That took some adjustment, after the vague nature of time in my life before all of this. Before, it was *In a while* or *Later* – an approximation of when things would be done. This place, though, is regimented to the second.

I look at the clock above the entrance: five minutes until the shift starts. People stop talking to their friends and get themselves ready. Everybody wants to hit the ground running. There's no warm-up.

There's a beep, a car horn. The whole queue turns and looks, to see if it's to get their attention, but nobody moves. I watch their faces, scanning them, trying to see who they are. There's a collective shrug as they don't recognise whoever it is, and the line to get through the gate tightens. You don't want to give up your place in the line for anything. Somebody wants you badly enough, they'll get out of the car.

The car beeps again, and this time I look. A hand, beckoning me over.

It's Ziegler.

'What are you doing here?' I ask, leaning in through the open door, as he eases himself back onto the seats. I'm holding my arm across my face, blocking as much of my eyes as I can.

'I wanted to give you an out,' he says. 'Get you away from here. You don't need to do this.' He looks me up and down, takes in the uniform. He gets it now, how serious I am about getting into the archive. 'You can't do this.'

'I've told you some of the things I did on Australia,' I reply.

'And they're impressive. They weren't anything like breaking into a government building. They were stories. You saved lives, and I'm sure that it was –' He can't find the words and I realise, right then, that he's not sure about the truth of what I've told him about my life, about who I was, who I am.

'I was on that ship,' I say. 'You believe me.'

He nods. 'Of course I do,' he says, but I can see something in his eyes that wasn't there before, a little doubt. He was sure about the prison ship, about us landing, but the government denied it, didn't tell a soul. Nobody owned up to it. The stories about it took place on message boards, in

125

clandestine meetings where true believers called the government liars. They were unifying, driven by faith. There was no evidence, but they believed in a ship full of prisoners trapped up there, desperate to come home, or dying up there, ships full of skeletons, drifting up there forever.

There was a reality about the prison system, about the government's desperation, about death. But I told him a different type of story: one of demons, of blood and bodies, of torture and pain; of a teenage girl taking revenge against bad people, and saving the good, who killed her own mother. Death, the only real unifying part of both.

He heard about my life, and he heard stories, not the truth he thought he knew. And there was a part of him that just didn't buy them.

'Go home.' I slam the door on him and walk away. I hear the door open and he follows, whisper-shouting so that the people queuing to get into work won't hear us. I keep going and he persists.

'I've got something for you, to help you.' He spits the words out so that I hear him. I turn around and he's holding some kind of device in front of him – a small bar, cream-grey in colour, with indents for fingers. 'For the electric systems. If you're stuck, it'll shut them down, but only for a few moments. A minute at most. Don't waste it.'

'I don't want your help. Not now.'

'You might not want it, but you need it. I've tried to talk you out of this and you're ignoring me. So this is the best that I can offer you. I used my contacts, the nastier ones. This thing can't be picked up by scanners.'

I take the button from his hand. It's odd, feels like the same material as Alala's device. I put it into my pocket and for a second I question whether it was cowardice that's stopped him helping me more than this. I think he's afraid of what might happen to me. In his face, I can see actual fear, the same as I saw in my mother's face before she died; and in Agatha's face, when I told her I was going to save the ship.

'Thank you,' I say. It feels hollow, like a goodbye that we'll never properly have, because we're both so worried that we already know how my breaking into the archive will end.

'You aren't Mae's mother,' Ziegler says. It's not spiteful; he just wants me to understand. But I already do.

'I know I'm not,' I reply. 'And I don't want to be. This isn't that.' I push myself up on my toes a little. I used to do this on the ship. I do it now and only realise when I feel the stretch in my foot. 'This is about a little girl who is scared, who I *promised* to help, to save from whatever. I told her she would have a better life with me, somewhere else, somewhere safe. And I failed her.'

'I'm sorry you feel that way,' Ziegler says. 'But we all fail sometimes. We accept it and we move on.'

'We don't have to,' I say, and I think I get the tone right: the sense of finality, that the conversation is over. That doesn't stop it feeling hollow.

I go back to the line. Ziegler watches me for a minute or so, and then gets into his car, and sits there, in the darkness. The line shuffles forward as the gate opens. I check my finger for the false skin. The peeling at the edges is worse than ever. I don't know how bad it has to be to stop it working. This could all be over before I'm even inside. I watch the people in the queue ahead of me going through the gate. They stand at the station and there's a beep; then they press their finger on the pad, and stare into the visor at the same time and there's another beep; then they walk through and collect their mask, and go to work. I'm going to do this the same as everybody else. But once I'm in, I'm on my own. Everybody in here knows their role except for me. I have been assuming that no one will care where I go, but I don't know. They might.

ID, first beep, finger and eyes, second beep and through.

I'm three away from the front and I realise that I have no evidence at all that the hacks Alala gave me to get in are genuine, that the tech is going to work. I feel an ache in my gut like a fist closing on my insides, squeezing.

Two people in front of me. The one at the front coughs as they're scanning themselves, and they apologise, taking their time to do the scan. The person between us shouts.

'We don't got time for this.' He stamps his foot a little, like an angry kid. The one at the gate apologises, scans, gets through.

I'm at the back of the line, the last one through. The guy in front rushes, gets scanned, swears, angry that his pay is getting docked for these precious missed seconds.

Then it's my turn.

I stand in front of the gate until I hear the beep, and I realise I've been holding my breath. Bend forward, chin onto the rest below the eye scanner, press my finger to the pad below, feeling the fake skin between my finger and the glass. I keep my eyes open wide and I watch as a blue light flits around in front of me.

I hear a buzz. It didn't work.

'Try again,' Gaia's voice says, from the system. If it's possible, it sounds even more dead-toned and passive here. I look around, to see if anybody's noticed, if anybody cares.

Okay, try again, slowly: finger on the pad, all of it. The fake skin is still there. The print is clear. It hasn't come off.

And then I feel a hand on my shoulder and my whole body tenses up, a reflex that I have no way at all of controlling. I never thought I'd be fighting before I even got inside.

'Sometimes happens. Flaky with the fingers, that's what it is.' I look at the woman who's speaking. She's probably ten years older than me with a nice face, soft features; thick hair pulled back tightly. She smiles. 'You new?'

'Yes,' I say.

'Okay, so this happens? You just get some spittle on your finger. Sometimes it needs a bit of *phhht*,' she says, spitting on her own, 'clean out the grooves. You'd think your eyes alone'd be enough, right? But no. Security's akin to this being a fortress or something.'

She watches as I mimic what she did; a tiny globule of my saliva on the fake fingerprint, and then she nods at me to try again. Eyes in, finger on. Blue light scans me and I blink, and I pray that it doesn't happen again. Again is when people might take notice. That's when this all falls apart.

There's a beep. A different noise. The gate opens.

'See? Things are so old, you can't tell what they're gonna do. Flaky as your worst ex, that's what I say.' She smiles. 'I'm Ruby, good t'meet you.'

'Chan,' I say.

'You got a placement today, Chan? You need help with where to go?' She looks around. 'People here, they get on with it. Nobody helped me when I started, and that was a real pain in the ass. So, you know, whatever I can do.'

'I'm in the archives,' I say.

She whistles. 'And you're new here? Must have quite the resumé. Or quick fingers.' She wriggles her fingers in front of her.

'I guess,' I say. I don't know how to act. I think about Agatha, telling me to have more confidence. Confidence makes it seem like you know what you're doing, even as you're inventing who you are. 'I've always been good with my hands.'

'Some of the pigs who work here, you're gonna want t' keep that t' y'self,' she says, and she laughs like it's the funniest thing she's ever heard. 'I'm topside, so I'll take you to the elevator and get y'set, okay?' She reaches behind me, picks my pass up off the gateway and puts it into the pocket of my – of Dave's – suit, then pats it safe.

As we walk, I wonder if she knew him. I start to invent the story of them: of their friendship, and how it maybe became something more, something stronger; a love, perhaps. How I stopped that. Even if I tell myself it wasn't actually my fault, there's still a sickly feeling of guilt about what happened. She won't know yet that he's dead; but when she finds out, she will be inconsolable. Broken.

I think about Jonah. My hand starts to shake.

I can taste my own blood in my mouth. I've been chewing the inside of my cheek. I don't know how long I've been doing that for – long enough that all I can taste is the bitter metal wetness on my tongue, running down my throat.

Ruby is talking and I'm not listening, just nodding, agreeing. I can't panic. I just can't. Act like you belong here and people will assume that you do. Confidence, shoulders back, head high. Don't slouch. *Carries herself like she knows this place.* Like I used to be, on Australia. Back then, as nightmarish as it was, at least I knew what I was doing. How to survive, how to thrive, even. Almost. I remember running through the ship, climbing the stairwells, working the arboretum, fighting the Lows—

No, I tell myself. Be *here.*

'How long's your shift?' I ask Ruby.

'Same as everybody else,' she says. 'Another eight hours and then I'm home and sleeping through the best hours of the day.' She laughs again, which I like. The sound of it, the casual way that some people use it, spilling out of their mouths, throats, their very being, as if it's something that they simply have to share with the world. Ruby's one of those people. 'I'm like, you know, vampires? From the stories?'

I don't. I'm not even sure I've ever heard that word before. 'Sure,' I say.

'Well, I'm like them. We only come out at night. That's what we are: vampires who get time and a half.'

She laughs again, and God I love that sound. It's relaxing.

I tell myself that I should laugh more, or try to.

She holds the door open for me. It's old and wooden, manually operated. Inside, the room is cavernous, every surface seemingly made from some sort of polished white stone.

'Through here,' she says. 'This is where you come first, okay? Straight in here. So, you're late at the front gate, pay gets docked. You're late to your station, pay gets docked.' She lowers her voice. 'Benefits of working topside: I'm logged in all the time. Means you can slack off a bit more. Get tired? Power nap somewhere, and you're still logged in. You get the chance, you move up here with me. It's not as glamorous, but I need my beauty sleep.'

She walks me through, beneath staircases which rise on either side of us, curling around the room. There are three doors along the back wall, metal shutters on the front. She yanks the middle one up. 'This is you. You get tired, don't feel like you can't have a break; come up here to rest or whatever. Hard down there: no windows, all that recycled air.'

I don't say that all the air is recycled in the city. People forget about the Wall. What it actually does. She presses a button inset to the wall and the doors open, and she stands back and watches as I step inside.

'Press to go down,' she says. 'And maybe you come find me when you're done? We can grab breakfast. You ever worked this time of shift before? That's what happens. You get used to having breakfast for dinner. And when you wake up, you get to have breakfast for breakfast as well. Best meal of the day, and you get it twice.' She waves as the doors close.

'It was nice to meet you,' I say. I blurt it out, desperate to get all the words through the rapidly closing space in the doors. I want her to know that, because she's so friendly, so kind. She's not getting anything out of this; she's just a good person.

'Hey, you too!' And then, 'Chan!' like a shout, but to remind herself of my name.

The door slams. At first it seems like nothing's happening. There's a gentle rumble to the floor, maybe, but I can't tell if I'm imagining it. Noiseless. I wonder if I've done something wrong, and then my ears pop, and I know that this box – with me in it – is going down. I can't even feel it.

I haven't thought my plan through. It was rushed; that was stupid of me. On Australia, you wanted to do something – to get something done – you just did it. Action first, then deal with the consequences. It's how everybody lived, and if you didn't, that was on your head.

The rules are different here.

The doors open onto an empty space, low ceilinged and barren. Every wall is concrete, unpainted and raw, with a bank of boxes, wires spooling off them, standing in the middle of the room. There's a metal cage surrounding the boxes – all that black metal, reminds me of bannisters, of stairwells, of grated floors – and in the middle of it, a terminal. This must be the archive. It's not like any of the terminals from the rest of the city. It's more like the stuff on

Australia. It's old, really old. I can see a keyboard attached to it: an actual physical keyboard. It makes me think of the stuff in Ziegler's apartment: a piece of archaic technology, like a relic, but preserved perfectly. The boxes around it hum, whirring lights and buzzing noises, thin grey devices in racks. The place is lit by strip lights so bright it hurts to look at them, and yet somehow that light is swallowed before it can do any good. The air tastes old, like it's too dry, somehow.

'You want something?' I didn't see him, I was so distracted by the room. A face is peering out from behind the cage. He's on his knees, wires in his hands. 'I don't know you.'

'I'm new,' I say, and he nods.

'Everybody's new. No one has any staying power. You know?' I shrug. *I guess.* 'What you here for?' He stands up and rubs his hands on his uniform. 'I'm Todd.' He holds out a hand to shake, looks down. I cross over. My hand trembles until it's in his and then he pumps it furiously. 'What are you here for?' he asks again, dropping contact.

'I'm looking for a name,' I say.

'Got the requisition?' *Think, think.* He shrugs. 'It's your first day. I'll cut you slack. Usually we need requisitions because they keep track of everything. But I know, it's a hassle. Hard to get a handle on all of this stuff. What's the name?'

'Mae,' I say. He rushes to the keyboard and stands in front of the computer. The screen flicks on, and he starts typing. I spell her name, because he had it wrong.

'Second name?'

'I don't know,' I say.

'Mae . . . Doe,' he types. I don't ask what that second word means, because he knows what he's doing, or he acts like he does. 'Nothing,' he says. 'No results.'

'Can you try Mae by itself?' I ask.

'You can. But there'll be a few, I'm guessing. This stuff goes way back. Like, before the *apocalypse* far.' He looks at his watch. 'I don't have time for it, so you do it? I can trust you?' He grins. 'First day, don't panic. Just, breathe.' He goes to the back of the cage again, bends down, starts on the wires. 'Go on,' he says.

I step forward, and I type her name. Press *Search*. The results rocket in, hundreds of them. Thousands, maybe. I open the first.

Abalette, Mae. A date of birth, a location. Names of parents. Abused, it says. Beaten. Sexually assaulted. It describes actions that I've known about, that I've seen happen before, but only up there. Things that people were killed for doing. This Mae's parents were put on trial, but there's no outcome listed against her name. She was taken away. Reassigned. It says where to: a nice family, a completely different part of the country. She's safe, now.

Not my Mae.

Aballo, Mae. No definite age, just *Baby*. Mother a drug addict, living in the docks. Or, *was* living in the docks, died giving birth, so they took the baby away. There's no sense of what that meant for Mae. Where she went. *Redacted*, it says, under the section discussing her whereabouts now. No names of who took her, no jobs, no idea who they could be.

135

As I scan the thousands of Maes I wonder how many people in this database are called Chan; how many were, in the past.

I never found out where my own name came from. It was just a name.

Abbot, Mae. The entries are from all over the place, the dates too; so many of them are decades old, the people they're discussing dead, or long forgotten, lost in the city, another city, the rest of the world. None are them are relevant to me. They are just names.

Abbott, Mae. Able, Mae. Ablett, Mae.

I whisper the names under my breath as I open the files, one by one, trying to find her. It's like an invocation, a spell. Like one of the Pale Women's prayers, repetitive and rigid, the words clipping into each other as I say them faster. *Mae, Mae, Mae.*

I read about so many of them, and none of them are right. This is going to take hours and hours. And then I remember: I can search in my own time. I've got Alala's device, the flesh-feeling disc that's in my pocket that will take the results back to her. She can help me. I pull the disc out and set it on the counter. There's no indication that it's working until I touch it, to move it closer to the computer; then I feel it warming up. I can almost sense the vibrations.

'You given up?' Todd asks, from behind the cage.

'No,' I say, 'just thinking.'

'We aren't paid for that,' he says, and then he laughs at his own joke. 'Where are you from? You're not from *Washing'on*, accent like that.' He exaggerates the local accent when he talks; I can hear him smirking as he says it.

136

'No,' I say. 'Are you?' Answer a question with a question. That's one of Ziegler's tricks: to defer, change attention, move the enquiry along.

'All my life.'

'And you've worked here long?'

'Kinda. They need somebody here for uploads. System's kept offline. It's old military hardware, totally unhackable. Doesn't even have a modem in there.' He laughs. 'You won't even know what a modem is, will you? You look pretty young. Anyway, I'm in here a third of the day every single day of my life. Sundays off if I'm good.' I touch the disc: still warm. Is that it? My only indication? 'What's your story?'

'No story,' I say.

'Nobody has *no* story. Even I've got a story and I'm really very boring.' He waits for me to ask him if I can hear more. I tap keys. I want to keep him down there, out of sight of what I'm doing.

Behind the computer, the buzzing gets louder, slightly more frantic.

It can't be a coincidence.

'What's your story, then?' I ask. I wonder if he can hear the nervousness in my voice. He stands up, stretches. His back cricks.

'You won't believe this but I was born outside the city. So, I'm Washington, right, but my mom, she was out in the colonies, outside the Wall. We got in when I was three months old, something like that, when she met my dad – not my real dad, but you know, he was there for me, so he *is*, you know? But then we got a pass. He's a pretty big deal

137

in the services. Good guy.' He stops talking. His mouth moves, like he's chewing something, and he squints a little. 'You hear that?' Puts one hand onto the cage. 'You still looking for that name?'

He comes round, walking quickly. I snatch the disc from the table, so hot that it's almost too painful to hold, and I slip it into my pocket, feeling the heat from it through my clothes, burning my skin. He pushes me aside and starts typing, brings up a totally different window, fingers so fast on the keyboard, typing strings of numbers and letters I don't understand.

'Is everything alright?' I ask. I start backing away, very slowly. I don't want him to notice, in case this is nothing. He stops typing, and pulls his hands away from the keyboard.

'It's fine,' he says, but he's lying. I can tell. He knows what I did. 'I'm just, you know.' He reaches to his belt, slowly slowly, and presses something.

I don't hear the noise, but I know that he's sounded an alarm.

When the elevator doors open, and the guards pour out, I'm holding Todd from behind, one hand across his chest, the other across his throat. I'm not going to hurt him, but they won't know that – it's easier to assume. Six of them. They almost sneak out, as if I can't see them right in front of me, and get into something like a formation, ready to take me on. No weapons down here, no metal, even for them, so they have their hands out, fists like boxers.

'Drop him,' one of them says. The voice is targeted, so I hear it like it's inside my head. Underneath it I can hear the sound of their feet on the floor, the slight squeak of their shoes, and mine.

'Let me go,' I say.

I probably don't look like much. Small, and weak, they'll think. They don't hesitate. One rushes towards me, swings at me. I push Todd at him; Todd howls as he stumbles forward and collides with the guard. Another rushes me and I meet his fists with mine, grabbing them, snapping one hand back until I hear the crunch. I drive my elbow into his face, and he crumples. Another two are already running at me; I dive between them, grab their ankles, yank. Their faces thud into the ground. They're not quite out, but it's enough. The next guard who piles towards me, I kick in the balls and he crumples. I try the same on the other, but he grabs my leg, so I use that, spinning up off the floor, slamming my other foot into his chest.

I am about to finish what I started – the disc in my pocket has cooled, and I have no idea if I've got what I needed or not – when one of the other elevators pings. The doors open, and there are more of them.

But these are different – not guards, police – ten, eleven, twelve of them. They rush out. These ones are armed. They point their guns at me. The guns fizz with the pulse of the electrics in them, blue tips like the strikers. This is real hardware. They never use this stuff when they're just chasing junkies through the docks. This is actual weaponry for an actual threat. They don't tell me to give myself up; they don't even give me the chance. Fast as I can, I run behind the terminal, to put it between me and them, hoping they won't want to risk hitting it. They fire and I feel the pulses

139

loose in the air, the tingle of them as they miss me. The pulses veer in mid-air, designed to track their targets. I'm lucky.

Ziegler's device, the one he gave me, I can use it. That'll mean no more hacking the computer, but it's going to have to be enough. I can't get taken, not now. I reach down into my pocket, wrap my fingers around the EMP, and I squeeze.

The sound is strange: like every other bit of noise is sucked out of the room. The lights pop to black. The blue of the police guns disappears. The computer shuts off with a grinding noise, and everything goes dark and silent.

It only lasts a moment, and then the police rush towards where I was, howling at each other, trying to get lights working, to get communicators and their augments up and running. Relying on their voices in the absolute darkness to guide them towards each other, towards me; to hunt me.

I stay quiet, and they don't. They give themselves up too easily.

I know how to fight in the dark.

The power comes back to show them lying on the ground, clutching themselves and each other, trying to muster the energy to fight back. I'm breathless. This was a big fight, bigger than I've had in a while. That won't be the last of them, I know, especially not now. I get into the elevator, and I hammer the button to go up, to get me back to ground level. There's only one escape route, which means there's probably more of them waiting for me when I make it to the ground floor. I picture the waiting guards, their bodies making a wall of riot shields and weapons, armoured up, faces blanked by their helmets; more guns, most likely.

I roll my shoulders, crick my back. Something changes when you know there's a fight coming. There's a change in the air, like before it rains.

Maybe that's why I like the rain so much.

Clank.

The elevator jars, shudders, stops. A voice comes through the intercom in here, buzzy and faint. 'Remain where you are. You will be attended.' I can't tell if it's Gaia's voice, or an actual person; just that it's cold and efficient. Then there's a thud. Something on the roof of the elevator rolling around, and then a hissing, and smoke, pouring in from the cracks in the roof. I recognise this tactic. I have been on the other side of it. But this smoke stings, burns my eyes as soon as it touches them, and I can't see. I cover my face with my arm. The smoke sinks into the elevator. I have to get higher, I know, above the smoke. I cough, a retching from deep inside me that feels like my lungs are being tugged out. I look up: cracks, where the smoke is coming in. A hatch in the elevator ceiling.

So many things in this city feel like reminders of what I've done before. Nothing but callbacks to a life I tried to leave far, far behind; and yet apparently I can't ever escape.

I leap up, spring off the wall, hurl myself at the ceiling, slam my forearm into the hatch. It clatters open. The smoke comes in faster, pluming down, followed by the thing that's making it all. It drops to where I was standing, and I leap again, coughing and spluttering, trying to keep my eyes shut. I grab the sides of the hatch. I pull myself through. The air is clear on the roof of the elevator, all the smoke having sunk down. But my eyes aren't working right; everything's in duplicate, triplicate. I can't actually lock on to anything: something's in my vision and then it's suddenly gone, spiralling off and out of my view, and I can't pin it down. It's dizzying. I'm dizzy. I try not to collapse.

I stumble. There's a gap between the elevator and the wall, a hole I could drop down and fall. That would solve their problems.

Nobody gets killed in this city; that's a rule. They made it after they lost so many people when the planet was wrecked. They decided to not kill any more, in any situation. Nature is senseless so humans have to be sensible. All their weapons incapacitate. You're never totally broken: you can be changed, fixed. At least Australia's rule was punishment or death. There wasn't any waiting. Here, they want you productive, part of the infrastructure. It's more than a city and a people; it's everything about life here.

From the corner of my eye I see it, fastened to the wall. A ladder. They won't think I've made it out of the elevator, I have to count on that. I stagger towards it, feel about until my hands hit the rungs, trying to get a good enough grip that I can climb. I wrap my hands around the metal bars, put my feet on the lower rungs, but I can't coordinate my movements; my feet keep slipping, like my legs are loose, somehow, not quite able to lock as they should – but I start to heave myself upwards anyway. My muscles aren't working properly; they're not as strong as they were. Not as able.

But still, I go up, rung by rung, crawling. Like I'm a baby, desperate to stand, trying to reach its mother.

I squeeze my eyes shut as tight as I can manage and I shake my head. It feels like there's something inside it, something rattling, dislodged; a part of my mind that's broken off and trying to abandon me. I can hear it in there. My ears echo. Everything is collapsing.

Still I climb.

Another rung, and another. Everything echoes.

I think: what happened to being still? When was I last still? When was I last not moving, not pushing forward, trying to get something done?

There are two days that I remember, when we first found the down-below on Australia. Below the pit, below everything else, and I thought, for a moment, that I could be happy there.

Happy, and still.

I hear them above, waiting for me. Shouting.

'Bring it up!' somebody yells, and I clutch the rung, because I think I could fall if I don't. There's a grinding, the mechanism starting again. 'Masks!' The same voice. They're going to get in, to take me. I'll have failed Mae again.

That's what they think. But the smoke is cleared, and I'm getting myself back – discovering who I can be – things are less swimmy. I can hear the elevator moving below me, coming upwards. It's moving faster than I am, so I push off the ladder to stop it mowing me down, thumping and rolling as I land on the elevator's roof. The smoke is all gone now, the bomb just a metal capsule in the middle of the floor in the elevator cage below. I grab the door to the hatch and put it back as best I can. It's dented, and they'll see it, but it might buy me time to get myself together more.

Have I ever been at a hundred percent? The best that I can be? Have I ever not been wounded, disoriented, sick, afraid? Not that I can remember. Certainly not here, and not on Australia – or not recently, anyway; maybe when my mother was alive.

Okay. Get yourself together. Breathe. Eyes still shut, then open, and still everything is loose, like the world's pivoting, unbalanced. I shut them again.

The elevator stops moving. I hear the doors open.

'Go!' the voice shouts.

I hear the clicks of their equipment, the confusion. No sound. I know that they're looking around, spying the hatch. I try my eyes again and they're better: wet, foggy, everything is still rocking, but only gently.

There's no time to wait for my vision to properly sort itself out. The hatch nudges open, a hand gently lifting it. A head comes up, and then a body, and a light shines from the visor the guard is wearing. I grab it, hands around his helmet, reaching for his neck. He's heavy, but he was already pushing up, and his momentum makes it easy for me to slam his face into the roof of the elevator, once, twice, another time for luck. He falls, tumbling back down into his associates. No time to let them panic, so I follow him.

*   *   *

I had a hard time fighting in the vast empty room of the archives. It's easier in a small space like this. I'm smaller and faster than they are. There's no room in here for the guards to get out whips and use them on me because they'll take everybody out, so there's nothing they can use but strikers. The one I hurt first lies on the floor, a lump they have to trample over to get to the biggest threat. I launch myself at what looks like their leader, slamming him into the back wall. The elevator trembles, buffeting between the walls, the cable above strong enough to take the assault, but I wonder for how much longer – and then my fist finds another guard, catches her square in the face-plate, shattering it. Some part of her helmet cuts my knuckles, I think. There's blood, anyway. Could be her nose – hard, sometimes, to tell where blood comes from. I kick another. Something whacks me on the leg, the quick burn of a striker, and I feel the electrics running through my body, making my limbs weaker. I grit my teeth, kick out at where the pain's coming from. Kick high, foot into the side of her head. She falls. I grab her hand, spin the weapon, ram it into the groin of another one. There's a hell of a scream.

After that, the last one runs. I don't think they were expecting me to fight back. There's a clear path out into the courtyard. Incredibly it's still dark out. I see the workers standing around and staring at me, mouths wide. Blood on my hands, I wipe it on my suit.

On Dave's suit.

So I walk, purposeful, fast. The gate is too high to climb, and there's no way it'll open for me. I'm frantic. The alarm will be linked to the rest of the city, I'm sure. Other people must be coming: police and services and God knows who else. I've got to get out now, before they get here.

I see Ruby. She's closer to me than the rest, sizing me up, trying to work me out. The same person she spoke to before, the person that she helped out, and look at me now. I know I must look wild, covered in blood, my suit torn, my eyes running with tears. She shakes her head at me.

'They're keeping somebody prisoner,' I say, desperate. 'I have to rescue her.' I want to justify myself. I want her to understand.

But she doesn't. 'What's wrong with you?' she asks, and she looks disgusted, like I'm a disappointment.

There's a beep as the gates open. A vehicle rolls through them, armoured and colossal. Ten wheels. They've come to take me down. But not before I can move. There's enough of a gap in the gate for me to get through, to squeeze and run and vault, to springboard off the front of the vehicle before the troops inside even know what's happened, before they can react, before they can train their weapons on me. I'm on the top of it, and running.

I see a car. Ziegler's car. It beeps as I get closer.

'Hello,' it says. 'Mr Ziegler instructed me to wait for you.' He wanted me safe. He wanted to do something more. 'Do you need assistance?'

'No,' I shout, running past. I'm not dragging Ziegler into my mess, not any more, not if I can help it. I bolt down the streets, lit from the lamps that dot the sidewalks; and from the moonlight that comes from above, like a single spotlight that seems to know exactly where I am and exactly where I want to go.

I stop and catch my breath.

And immediately I know that I can't stop, that I don't have that luxury. I look into the skies, and I can see the birds.

They're coming for me.

SEVEN

Birds were always part of our dreams of Earth. It's because we didn't have any animals on Australia, and the idea of them was so strange, so alien and free, especially animals that didn't fall but flew where they liked. We were told about them: their beaks, their wings, sweeping and swooping across the world. When I came here I went to the museum and learned about them. They were real. But they were mostly all lost, it said. Not entirely, but mostly.

I saw them, though. When I first arrived, I would lie on the grass and stare at the sky, and sometimes I'd see them way above, soaring past in formation. It was only when I saw one up close, being tended to by a technician, that I realised the mistake I made.

Things can have the same name and not be the same thing, I know. Because the birds we have now, most of them are not alive. Most of them are machines, and they hunt.

I can hear the buzz behind me. They are coming. They could be silent, but the noise is to warn you, to scare you — like sirens or alarms. High above, they follow as I rush down the streets. I dive into dumpsters and hide in cubby holes and eventually I slip down into sewers that flow with the run-off from the houses and the wall; they are full of this freezing cold, weirdly thick liquid that laps at the sides of the tunnel; a river of sluiced, chipped ice that flows underneath the whole city. The drones scan the streets and they can't find me. I watch through a grate as they swoop in, their formation a complicated knot that covers every angle; they won't miss much. They move in a dance, forming shapes: now a circle, an endless loop of the birds chasing each other in a spiral; now a star, different points jutting, sending light out, pulsing to find me.

When they decide that the street is clear, they move on. This is my chance to escape. But I'm as cold as I've ever been. My feet are numb, my toes so tense they feel almost brittle through my shoes. I can't move them, I don't think. I'll worry about that later. They're still good to run on.

So I do: I run and I watch the sky, and I keep away from the birds. They're not remote-controlled. Apparently they used to be, but now they're automated, operated by some part of the Gaia intelligence that puts them in a flock and keeps them working together. Individually, each bird is a fraction of a whole, a fragment of a picture that needs to be assembled into something complete. But all it takes is for one of them to spot you. That's why they change formation so much: it's easier to cover more ground that way, to put more eyes in more places at any one time.

A few streets over comes the noise of fighting; a couple are having an argument, their voices raised to screaming. The birds swoop away to investigate, and that's when I run.

I go as fast as I can the other way, quiet as I can manage, hugging close to the buildings, hiding behind cars, behind railings, underneath awnings. I'm not far from Ziegler's apartment building. I can see it, one of the many towers, looming high. He wants me to be safe. He didn't approve of my plan, but he didn't betray me. He cares about me. I could hide out in his apartment. I'm sure that he would let me in, give me shelter. I can stay there until the birds are gone and things calm down, and then I'll leave, I'll fetch Mae, and—

No, I won't. I didn't get her file. I didn't find her. I don't know where she is. She might not even be in the city. She could be anywhere. Maybe she's not even here. Maybe she's in another city entirely.

Maybe another country.

I slump against the wall of the building I've stopped next to. I'm tired. I can't face Ziegler now. He cares, but I know he'll judge me. He'll disapprove. I've got the disc for Agatha. Maybe it's got enough on it, enough information that I'll find out where Mae is, and she'll find out—

Alala. Not Agatha. The disc is for Alala.

I push off from the wall and turn away from Ziegler's apartment, and head home; or, what passes for my home. I have only lived here for a few months, but it suddenly feels like all I've ever known.

By the time I get back to the docks, it's morning. The sun's heat is burning away the morning mist. I wonder what it would be like to sit up on top of the wall, closer to the sky, and let the light and heat burn your skin.

Something like freedom.

This part of the city is mostly quiet at this time of day. If you're awake, it's to get into the job queues or get a fix. There's nothing really in between. None of those people looks at me. Nobody even notices me; I must look like just another junkie. I'm stumbling from the tiredness, my feet dragging behind me. I have to sleep. I've been awake too long, been moving too long, too much. I just want to sleep.

But I have to see Alala first. Mae's waiting.

Zoe is standing outside Alala's home, scratching as she always does. She's not alone. Waiting with her, in various states of waking, are the other addicts. Some of them are in a worse state than Zoe: missing limbs replaced with cheap black-market last-gen augs, vacant looks in glazed-over eyes; many of them with augs in their throats, lifetime survivors of living as outcasts here.

'There's a queue,' Zoe says. She stands up, neck tilted, head almost lolling, dragging her nails along her skin in tracks of pulled-pale scars. 'Just because you think you're special,' she starts, and I cut her off.

'I'm going to see her now,' I say. I'm too tired to argue.

'I was here first,' Zoe snaps. She grabs my arm, her grip weak, but digs the tips of her fingers in as hard as she can. The feeling of her nail breaking my skin; the trickle of warm blood running down my arm. 'You hear me?'

'I heard you,' I say. I put my own hand on hers. 'But I'm not listening.' I slam my forearm into her shoulder, and she spins, almost ridiculously, tumbling to the ground. The other junkies stare. They're trying to work out what to do here: get involved, defend Zoe, or step aside and let me through.

They're sensible. They can see what I'm feeling on my face: hurt, anxious, angry. They part, letting me through to Alala's door.

'Come back!' Zoe howls.

'No,' I say.

Alala paces inside her small house. There's barely room, but she makes it work for her, using every little bit of space she can find. Up and down, left and right, and I sit on the table in the middle of it all, where the woman gave birth, where less than a day ago I got the mods that let me break into the archive. It's best to stay out of her way and let her talk when she's like this – let her get it all out.

'I told you we needed all of the information. Every bit! Nothing left over.' She punctuates these words with jabs of her finger in the air between us. 'Because I need the data as well, little girl. We made a deal. That is what happens. A deal. You said, Alala, you get me access to the archive. Help me.' She does an impression of me, simpering and pleading. 'So I helped you. I got you access. You understand the cost of what I did? The favours I used up for you? This is all a trade, all of it. Everything is give and take. I need the information that you went for, you understand?'

'So do I,' I say.

'You think what you need is important to me?' She whispers, almost hisses. 'You do not even know what I need information for, and you think you are just as important?'

'I might not have Mae's information—'

'And this is not my problem. No, not even close to my problem. Because you asked me: get me in there. I did that. Did I not do that for you?' I don't say anything. It's not that sort of question. 'But now, you might have let me down.' She looks through to the other room. 'Is it ready yet?'

'It's coming,' her hacker says, moving his hands in the space in front of the holo: numbers and letters again, lines of code. 'It's encrypted, obviously.' He has augmented eyes, to keep up with the speed at which he's working, along with thin metal slivers that run the length of his fingers to make them even faster: so fast they're almost a blur. It's expensive tech. 'Where did you get this?' he asks me. His accent suggests someone well-off; he speaks with clipped neatness, more like Ziegler than the people who grew up in this part of the city.

'Does not matter,' Alala says. She looks at me: don't say a word.

'There's some messed up stuff here: names and addresses. What are you planning?' He turns and looks at her. 'This sort of thing could get me sent to Baltimore.'

'Just get this done,' Alala replies.

'You're not paying me nearly enough,' he says, but then stops moving his fingers, locks them together and bends them back. I'm expecting them to crick, but there's a sound like a hiss instead, and he blows on them. 'Done. I've got the files out, at least the ones that were here. No idea if there's anything missing.'

Alala rushes to his side, to see what he's looking at. 'The name I wanted to find?' He types it, gets a result. Leans back. 'There. It's here. You got a system I can air this all onto?'

153

'Leave me yours,' Alala says. She's thinking, plotting something, not looking at us.

'Mine? It's custom.' He smirks. 'This isn't for sale.'

'Everything's for sale,' Alala replies, her attention snapping back. She pulls a tablet from the side and types something. 'Take a look at your bank balance.' He opens a tab on the holo and types in his login. His eyes widen.

'It's all yours,' he says, gesturing at his computer. He stands up, nods at me, and then he's gone and it's just Alala and me, alone with the computer. Alala grabs my arm.

'No,' she says.

'I need to find—'

'Enough of what you say you need. You need to help me, is what you need.'

'I helped you. This is your information, on here.'

'You think this was all? What I have here? This is only the first part.' She isn't smiling at me. She isn't being nice, isn't joking. Somehow, it even sounds like she's got less of an accent than she had before. 'I have another job for you. You do it, maybe I think about if we are even, if you get the information you say you need.'

I think about how I could attack her, now. Take the information. The computer is right here. Mae's name, address, everything might be somewhere on it. I find out where she is, and I go and sleep for a few hours – maybe at Ziegler's, maybe – and then when I wake up, I go and get her. I keep my promise to her. Then I take her away, out of the city, maybe; find one of the settlements that are out there; live quietly, without running. We can be a family. I'll save her, because that's what I promised I would do, and it's a promise that there is not a chance in hell I am going to break.

Alala reads it in my face. She steps back, looks shocked. 'Or maybe you think you can leave?' she asks. 'But you are wrong.' She brings a holo up, and it immediately starts playing. I recognise myself. I see myself in Dave's suit. It fits better than I thought it did. It's easier to concentrate on that than the look on my face as I fight the guards in the archives. The video has been slowed right down, and I can see that my teeth are gritted, my eyes wild. Somebody is speaking. 'I will turn it up for you,' Alala says, and the voice of a reporter fills the room.

The reporter describes how I broke into the archives, how I attacked workers and then detonated a device – her words – that caused the erasure of the locally stored files. It's not clear how such a device was smuggled inside the archives, they say, but . . . Alala turns the volume down.

'I didn't ask you to fight them,' she says. 'One of them is in hospital, critical. Wait until they find the guard that you took the outfit from. Maybe they already have.' She smiles again. It's a different smile. I don't trust this one. 'So you need my help, little girl. When this is over, I can help get you out of the city, get you a new identity, maybe. You know that I can do these things.'

I can feel my mouth trembling. I think it's my lip, but it's not; it's my jaw, my entire lower row of teeth, juddering against the top, as if I'm cold. But Alala's got her heaters on, and it's not even chilly in here.

'So maybe you need me, after all? Maybe' – she pulls out her poutin from the cupboard and takes a swig (doesn't offer it to me) – 'maybe you should not be so quick to dismiss what I can offer you; the deal that I want to make with you now.'

'No more deals,' I say; or maybe I only *think* I say, because Alala acts as though those words were never even spoken, as if I don't have a choice.

'You are going to visit somebody for me. Nothing too complicated. Then you come back, and we are even.' Hands into fists, stretching my fingers. Everything ticks in my mind. I look for my exits. I try and work out what could happen next, not what should.

'Look at you here,' she says, indicating the holo. In it, I have my foot on one guard's throat while I punch another in the gut. I look impressive; so much so, I'm barely sure it's actually me. 'You are quite the asset. And when you get back, then I give you your little girl's location. Here is the target.'

She shows me the file she was looking for on the hacker's computer. There's an image of a man, older than I am, but not by much; head shaved, with a scar running down the middle of it, to between his eyes. He has kind eyes, in as much as that is a thing, but dark – not sure if they're augments or not. He has more scars than just that one, and there's something wrong with his mouth on one side, because it curls up, a scar next to it running across his cheek. There's a name, across the top: *Hoyle Grant*. And under that: *The Runner*. Alala reaches over and spins the image of his head around, so that I can see it from every angle. 'Now I have details for him, and you can go to him.'

'Who is he?'

'You don't recognise him? You really have not been here for very long, have you?' She says it like she should be smiling, but she's not. She's deadly serious. 'You will go to him, okay?' She clears the footage of me at the archives, types something in, then picks up a small device, a wristband tracker. 'Use this to find him, okay? I have put his details in here. He is chipped; you should find him with that.'

'Is he a criminal?'

'Does it matter? You go to him, and you do me my favour.' She says it in such a way that I don't need to ask the next question. I haven't needed to ask it this entire time. That won't stop me, though. My teeth chatter. Everything seems darker than it was; like the sun isn't coming up outside, like it isn't morning.

It feels as if everything is going backwards.

'What do I do when I find him?' I ask, my voice sounding like it's not actually mine, my words controlled. She smiles, and I know the answer. Of course I do.

'You kill him for me,' she says. Her face drops back to stone, back to nothing at all. 'Maybe then I help you find the little girl you look for, okay?'

I try and leave, try and push through the curtains, but the addicts, still waiting outside her home, stand up and face me. Zoe is at the front, scratching again. She rubs her chest as she sees me, a reminder of what I did to her before.

'Let me past,' I say.

'Alala?' Zoe asks.

I glance at the older woman. She nods, face serious, like stone. The junkies – clients, mutes, heavies, whoever they are to Alala – step towards me.

Maybe they haven't heard that much about me, because they don't look prepared for me to fight back. As Zoe steps forward, slipping metal bracers onto her knuckles, I think, I should show them the news footage of me at the archive before they make their move, let them see what they're getting themselves into.

Zoe rushes first and crumbles easiest, because she's not a fighter. She's not the get-your-hands-dirty sort, and I only have to hit her gently before she runs, squealing like she's trapped somewhere. The bigger ones are harder to hit. The tight leather skin of their muscles hurts my fists. They're drugged, augmented. One of them is holding something: a lump of stone, it looks like, only when he swings it I see the metal on the end, the rusted iron jutting from it.

Just before it slams into me, I think how heavy it looks, how impossible it is that he's swinging it as quickly and easily as this.

I hear a crack from deep inside me. It feels like I'm wet inside, all of a sudden; it's like there's something actually running down the insides of my body. But there's no pain, not yet. I know it will come, because it always does. Adrenaline, Ziegler explained to me: it's like a drug that your own brain makes, that gets you moving and dampens the rest. Adrenaline blocks the pain, along with pretty much everything else you should be feeling when you're in a fight, or in danger, or dying. Suddenly I'm not as scared as I was before this fight started.

But adrenaline can only do so much. The big guy swings his weapon again and I move. I'm fast, but not quite fast enough, and I'm hurt badly. I can tell that. So when it hits, it's not where he intended – the middle of my spine. Instead, it's in the back of my ribs. No crack this time, but the pain is like falling and landing on your back.

There's nobody there to pick me up, though; to carry me off, to make me better.

Instead, I'm on the dirt floor, staring up at the sky, at the edge of the wall looming over us, and the faces of them all, and of Zoe, pushing herself to her feet and stumbling in front of me, leaning in and acting like she's the one who brought me to the dirt. She drives her hand into my face, the blunt of her palm right between my eyes.

There's another crack, and everything fades to black.

My eyes are open and I wish that they weren't. I am on my front, and they are standing around me. The feeling of something pulling in my back: like a tooth, loose in its socket, but deeper. It's actually inside me. The doctor is here, the one that Alala uses for mutings. I see medical tools in his hands, thin white gloves pulled up to his trembling elbow; Alala next to him, assisting him; thread between her fingers, the other end of it in her mouth, trapped between her teeth. I'm on her table, her operating table. There's blood.

'Don't wake up,' she says. 'Do not want to be awake for this, not while he fixes you. You can wake up at the other end, little girl.'

I shut my eyes again. She's right. I don't want to be awake for this.

159

There's no pain. I'll die, or I won't. But at least now I can sleep.

Click, click.

Her fingers in front of my face. I can smell the teas that she makes, the sweet perfume of things that don't naturally grow here in the city, but that she can still get her hands on, through back channels. She has her ways.

'Don't worry,' she says. Nothing like that phrase to have the opposite effect. I try to move, expecting rigidity, paralysis; expecting bandages. 'You're fine,' she says. 'No problems at all, everything very smooth. As smooth as anybody could want.'

'What did you do to me?' I keep anticipating that I'll be broken in some way, that there is something missing, like my voice (taken away, as she has done so many times in the past to so many infants) or changed, like the augments that she gets fitted into people, illegal and unapproved additions to their bodies.

'Incentive. I fixed you, to begin with. You had a broken rib. You want to avoid fighting, eh? It's sealed now, made okay. No stitches: special glue. Can't rip, no tearing of your skin, okay? Are you grateful?'

'It's your fault,' I say.

'Wasn't my fault that you fought back,' she says. That smile, a slit that could have been made with a knife, cheek to cheek, wider than it should be; I fixate on it, and I can see what looks like too-smooth skin at the edges of her lips. Her make-up spreads out beyond where the brighter pink of her flesh ends. I think of The Runner, of his own scarring. There's something there: a connection. 'But I gave you another . . . incentive. While I was in there.'

'What did you do?' I push myself to standing, which aches, but only like I slept badly, joints tugged into strange positions that aren't wholly natural; and I look down at myself. I'm whole, intact. I reach around, trying to feel my back, where they were operating. I think I can feel it: soft skin, smoother than it should be. A new scar.

'Won't find it like that,' she says. 'It is attached to you. It is a part of you.'

'What did you do?' I ask, my voice small, thin.

'I have helped you to help me.'

'What did you do?' This time I scream it and my hand shoots out, almost of its own accord. My fingers wrap around her throat. She is taller than me, but I'm in control.

'I show you,' she coughs. 'I show you. Come, come.' I let go of her and she rubs her neck. I can see bruising already. But she hasn't stopped smiling. The ache in my back grows. I stretch, and there's no click from my spine, not like there usually is; no pain, either. Instead, it feels numb.

Outside, it's still morning. In the sky, through the membrane across the city, I can see the dulled glow of the midday sun.

'Zoe?' Alala says, and the girl stirs. She's asleep on the ground a little way away, propped against a wall, half-buried under a blanket. She's spacey, blanked out, mouth hanging open, dried saliva all down her chin, dripped onto her chest. 'Lovely Zoe, get up and come here. Come here, now. You want another shot? On me?' Alala talks the girl to her feet, watches her push herself to standing. I don't

161

know if she has an actual home, somewhere else that she goes to. Maybe this is all she has; she sleeps close to Alala, close to where she always needs to be. This is where she gets her fix; and Alala might protect her, maybe. Maybe their relationship is closer than I imagined. 'You wake up now, the next one is free,' Alala says to her.

Zoe tries to slap herself, half-jokingly, gets it wrong, misses her own face. It's too hard. 'You're still here?' she slurs, looking at me. Or, looking below me, her gaze askew, as if she can't quite home in on exactly where I'm standing.

'She won't be here for long,' Alala says. 'She is going to do a job for me.' I don't know why Alala thinks I'll just kill somebody for her. I haven't killed anybody since I thought I killed Rex, since she—

No. The worker, from the archives. Dave. He died, and maybe I killed him. Maybe I'm to blame for that. That's what she knows: that I broke him and brought her his pieces, to break in somewhere else, to steal something that I wanted, that I needed. She doesn't care what I feel about how I got them; whether I'm responsible for his death or not. She doesn't know how much I care. She's seen me fight, seen me move. That's all that matters to her.

Zoe stands in front of us, her face still. Her body wavers, though, from side to side; a doll, threatening to topple over.

'Brace yourself, lovely Zoe,' Alala says. 'I am sorry.' She points at Zoe, with the finger that's usually half-missing. Now, it's not. There's a tip to it, a metal end, an approximation of what a finger might look like, clunky and gnarled. She switches the finger, only slightly.

162

Like flicking a switch.

Zoe drops to the ground, and she screams. It's a delayed noise, her mouth open long before the noise comes; she wasn't prepared and it was a shock, a total shock, and now the noise is struggling to come up. It finally brings with it bile, spit and sick, and she's totally powerless. She moves the best she can, tries – that's the worst part of watching her in pain, the knowing that she's really battling to get to her feet, to push herself up, to fight against whatever's going on inside her body – but she fails, and she slumps down, her face slamming into the hard concrete of the ground. Her teeth break at the impact, blood spilling from her mouth. Her head rocks back, and she gasps in air. Then, thud! Face back down into the dirt.

Alala twitches her finger again, and Zoe falls still, not even a tremble to her.

'This technology . . .' Alala says. 'It is so old. Outlawed. Radio bands. You know what a radio band is?'

'No,' I say. I grit my teeth.

'They were how we used to send information, before they found it was dangerous – like radiation. Once, way way back, people would listen to music through these bands on the air. Then we learned we could control things with them. The birds. Then we could control people. Now? I can make her dance for me.' She walks over to Zoe, nudges her with her foot. 'I can do so much more with her. You want a demonstration?'

'No,' I say.

'That is a good choice. She is a customer. A good customer.' She looks around. One of the lunks – the one

163

who hit me with the rock, I realise, muscled out of his skull – is standing a short way away, hands all over some poor girl, places that they shouldn't be. 'This one, though. He owes me more than he can ever pay back. And I can use his augments for somebody else. A repossession.' She nods to the other junkies, and they nod back.

They swarm him. They pile onto him from behind, drag him away from the girl and out of the house, drag him through the makeshift streets, holding him by his ankles, and Alala makes me follow. He struggles too much, fights back, so they drop him and kick his head until his tongue flops out of his mouth and his eyes glaze, and then they drag him by his ankles, face down in the dirt. Alala leads them – and me – through the docks, down past the houses. 'I put one in him when he had his muscles augmented. It's safer, this way. You need to make sure that if you want somebody to do something, they understand that I have insurance.' She points at his twitching body. 'See? A scar, like yours.' She's put one inside me. I look at the other junkies, the ones carrying him, and they've all got the same scars. This is how she controls people. 'You kill this Hoyle Grant, and we're even. I take it out. Then I help you get your little girl back.'

Then we reach the edge of the docks, the water between us and the wall not quite still; the ice shifting, melting a little in places, where it's warmer..

Alala's people pick up the lunk and haul him up over their shoulders and then heave him into the air, out over the water. He smacks into the water and starts to sink, still unconscious. I thought the body reacted to water, woke you up when you were submerged, some last-chance survival device. I keep waiting for it to kick in for him; to save him.

I turn my head. I don't want to watch him die. But she reaches over and she grabs my face with one hand, turns it towards the water, and with her other hand, the metal finger, she points to him. His body finally twitches back to life as he fights against the cold water, struggling, barely visible through the broken ice that floats on the water's surface. She flicks her finger, and there's suddenly an explosion, a geyser of water blowing up into the air, then raining down all around us. Carrying with it fragments of ice and his body.

'Please take it out of me,' I say. I don't want to beg. I will.

'When you have done the job. But you had better go, little girl. The Runner waits for you, and I wait for you. Let us say, six hours. Six hours, if you're not back here with his blood on your hands, I find you.' She comes close to me, and she kisses me on one cheek, then on the other. She holds me close, presses something into my hand: an EMP, just like the one that Ziegler had, same black-market tech. At least I know how it works, this time.

'You will need this. Don't be afraid to use it. And hurry back, Chan. Bring me evidence. Because if you do not come back here, if you run, I will save your little girl myself. I will find out where she is, and I will go to her, bring her up as my own. You understand what that means?' I nod. I don't, not really, but I've got an idea. 'Zoe, she came to me for help when she was a little child, and I helped her. Save me, she asked.' She mimics her voice, but it's nothing like the truth. It's some pastiche of a begging addict, like some punchline to a joke. 'So I did. If you want that for your precious Mae, then disappear, then never see me again.'

Then she's gone. She walks off, back to her home. Her people go with her, or disappear into whatever parts of the docks they live in. And I'm alone, the water around me freezing on the ground, some of it dyed red from the dead man's blood.

I don't know what to do now.

No. I do. I do.

The tracker on my wrist twitches as I half-run through the streets, letting me know when to turn, when to carry on. I repeat the information Alala gave me, over and over. Willis Tower. Financial district. Hoyle Grant. The Runner.

I know nothing about him, nothing at all. His face. I don't need to know any more, not now, not yet. Out of the docks, through the housing – the towers, the quieter, older suburbs. I think about what happens if I don't stop running, if I go further than I have before. I could get out of the city. I've never left. They always say, Don't leave. It's hellish out there. It's so hot, and it's ruined.

I've wondered, of course, if that's another lie. Maybe now is the time to find out. Only, that will leave Mae here, and Alala isn't lying. I could see it in her eyes; she will find her, and she will punish her somehow.

I promised that I would save her.

I walk along the edge of the freeway that heads into the centre, that cuts right through the city. There's no sidewalk but few cameras either, and nobody who'll recognise me.

That's my worry; that somebody will recognise me and then the police will come, or the birds (that would be worse).

I step onto the bridge, in the part of the road reserved for cars having problems. As the traffic passes, drivers and passengers crane their necks and stare at me. I need to get off this track, but it is the shortest way to where I need to be. Getting a bus wouldn't be safe, too many cameras. I have to walk this. I keep my head down, like always. I wonder if I'll ever be head up. They slow down sometimes, to see what I'm doing. My hand is in my pocket, clutching the EMP. It's soft, squishy. So strange, but weirdly comforting knowing that I could squeeze it harder and everything around me – cars, buildings, birds in the sky, maybe even the wall, if I was close enough – would just stop, when I made it so.

Small comfort, even so.

The bridge crosses the river that intersects the city, which is so polluted it's barely even a river any more. Once it flowed, but you'd never believe that now. Now, it's a mess. It's a scar on the city; a divider that serves no purpose. The ground is too soft to build on – that's what the museum said – so it stays, but no water comes, only what bubbles up from beneath the sediment.

As soon as I can, I get off the freeway, down a side street. It's not far until the scrapers, and then I can lose myself a little more. A car follows me, like a coincidence, but it's not. It stops, and the door opens, and a man leans out.

'You lost?' He's young. Not much older than I am. He's wearing a suit, tie yanked up to his chin so far that it doesn't look comfortable any more. Augmented facial hair:

cheap job, that doesn't look like it's taken properly; a beard he's too young to actually have.

'I'm fine,' I say.

'You don't look fine.' He shuffles across the seat, gets closer to the door. One foot steps out. 'I'm a doctor. I can probably help you. Give you a lift, maybe. You need a lift?' I need a doctor. I don't trust him. No reason that I should.

So, 'Leave me alone,' I say, and he starts to get out of the car.

'You look tired.'

'Go away,' I say. I don't let him say anything else. He'll scan me, I know, if he hasn't already done so. He'll ID me. He won't even have a chance to call the police; the central servers will do it for him, and they'll descend in seconds.

The girl who raided the archives.

The girl who fought the guards.

Maybe, if they put two and two together, the girl who came from the Australia.

I run away from him. He doesn't shout or try to follow me. I don't look back.

The towers in the heart of the city are enormous. A cluster of them, like fingers reaching up – stretching, to pluck something from the sky. Ziegler once said that they're like the *citadel in the heart of the bastion*. He told me about how castles used to be, thousands of years ago. You build a wall around the city, and you put what you *really* want to protect in the absolute middle. Everything around it? It's expendable, the most expendable parts being those furthest from the centre – like the docks.

As you walk between the towers, you can stand still and look straight up and the buildings make these lines on the edge of your vision, as if they're guiding you towards the sky. You're always in their shadow when you're in the centre of the city; they stand hundreds of storeys high, taller and more impressive than anything I could ever have imagined. The first time I saw them, I thought that climbing one would be like climbing in Australia, over and over and over, endlessly. Ziegler told me that they're wonders of construction, the best that humankind has ever made. Apparently they're perfectly balanced. But, as I said to him, perfect balance doesn't mean you'll never fall.

I've taken too much time getting here. I no longer know how long I've got left. I didn't set myself an alarm, didn't even look at the clock when I set out. Going by the sun, I'm a few hours in. What happens after six hours? What can Alala do? She can't see me, can't pull the trigger on me. She can't find Mae that fast, I'm sure. But I don't know, I don't know. I follow the pulses on my tracker, moving further and further into the city. I'm surrounded by people in suits. It's much busier here and they don't care about me. I look wrong to them, out of place, so they ignore me and they push me aside. All I want is to not let them see my face: to not let them get a clear image, in case they've got augments in their eyes; in case those augs are networked. There are police everywhere, and cameras. Anyone, anywhere could potentially spot me. I'm almost as conspicuous with my hood over my face, because I look like I'm trying to hide something. But it doesn't matter if they're suspicious. I keep moving; they won't follow me.

169

I'm scared, and worried that I'm lost, that the tracker is wrong; and I try not to focus on what might happen. Agatha says she'll help me when my task is done: get me out of here, a new identity, a new place to be. Another city. But what about Mae? Will she come? Will I get her first? Or maybe Agatha will— Alala. Alala.

Fingertips, nails, digging into my palms. A reminder. They are not the same. They're nothing like each other.

Willis Tower is tucked away between other towers, like it's ashamed. Compared to the other buildings I've walked past, it's almost faded, filled with offices that aren't attended to, or that look vacant. The building is from the city before everything happened, before the renovation projects and the rejuvenation. It's been painted, but that's not enough to disguise its age and its decrepitude. It's shorter than the others, stumpy. Floors have been added, struts jutting out at the base, but it's tired, and permanently in the shadow of the other buildings.

I have no idea what to do once I'm here. All I have is his pseudo name, his photograph, the address. The AI at the desk terminal inside the building asks me what I want. Gaia's voice, just like everywhere else, but this version of it – I'd swear – has a distinct tone: brusque, like it doesn't want to answer any questions. They've set the mood to sound hostile from the get-go.

'I'm looking for Hoyle Grant,' I say.

'Nobody by that name here.' *Get lost* is implied, a bit of programming that pushes you away. There's nothing to see here.

'H O Y L E, second word G R A N—'

'Nobody by that name here.'

You can't argue with a computer, so you circumvent. I walk past it, down towards the elevators. But I don't have a pass, and I can't get into one without it.

The fire doors, though.

'Exit the building now,' the computer tells me.

'No,' I tell it. The door only opens from the inside. *Alarmed*, reads the sign across it. I charge, slamming my shoulder into the wood, which buckles, almost crumbling under the weight, revealing a staircase beyond. I crouch, braced for an alarm.

Nothing comes.

So I start upwards. At the first floor, I prop the door open. It's vacant. Why is there a vacant floor in a building like this? This is the centre of the city. The important part. The protected part. I shout The Runner's name, because he might respond. Or, he might run. Either way, I'll know he's here.

I try not to think about what I'm doing.

But then, it's the only reason I'm here. I never had a choice. I always knew this moment would come.

There's no coming back from murder. That's something my mother told me once, she and I sitting together, watching the chaos that consumed the rest of the ship, watching the gangs tearing each other apart like starving animals. She sat there, feet dangling off the edge of the floor we lived on at the time – I don't remember which home this was, which berth, which floor. I remember clinging to the railing that

171

ran along the side, so this was when the railings were still there, before they were wrenched out and turned into whatever they became. That was destiny on Australia: everything having one purpose, but another use. I was young then. I didn't have my purpose, not yet.

'They don't know what it does to you,' she said. Her voice was so soft when she wanted it to be. Talking to me – unless she was trying to scare me, trying to make me realise that she wasn't kidding around, that something was so desperately serious that she needed to drive the point home – she was always soft. It was for the benefit of others that she used her different voice: stronger, bitter, sharper, a smack of every syllable as she spat words from her lips. 'They don't realise that it's not inside us to kill.'

I asked her what she meant. Inside us? Like guts? Like blood, bone?

'Something else. In here.' Tapped me on the skull. 'It's not part of who we are. It's part of what we can become, and those are different things. We're not born with it. It's not in the blood, that desire, that ability. The people here all started as babies. They were babies and then they were your age and then they were adults, and somewhere in-between all of that . . . somehow, they became these people.' Tap, tap to my head. 'Something changed up here, to make them think this way, to change who they are, to give them a different part of their personalities. Do you see me killing for fun?'

I told her that I did not. I had seen her kill, of course. But that was different. That was defence. It was protection, for me and her both.

'When you do it and you are the aggressor, something changes inside you. You kill somebody without a good enough reason – and the only good reason to act viciously is survival, Chan, that's the only thing that justifies blood on your hands – you will change. These people?' She pointed down to a group of Lows, holding a body between them, tearing it apart, starting a fire, licking their lips. 'They're not even human anymore. They have become something else. They're too far gone to be saved.'

We sat and we watched. There was nothing else that we could do.

I shout his name, but there is nobody here. I return to the stairs and I continue up. More abandoned floors, more and more. I can't do this all day. I don't have time, and even if I did it's likely that the desk called the police, or raised an alert with a security team. There will be somebody coming, looking for an intruder, and I don't want to be here when they arrive.

That's when I notice the elevator.

I'm on the fifth floor, and the elevator is stopped at the thirteenth. Somebody's been here, and they've gone up there. It's as good a place as any to start. So I run up the stairs, and I think about Australia, and about running, always running. That has to stop. I wonder if the body ever forces you to stop. Like, actually shuts down. Screams, *No more!*

I arrive out of breath, but this is his floor. I can tell. Everything in this building is abandoned apart from this floor. A policeman, asleep on a chair. Uniformed, street

173

police, but lazy. He doesn't wake up when I'm next to him, and he can't when I find the target. He's armed.

Okay, I tell myself. My mother's words, *Don't die.*

No, before that. Before that. *The only good reason to act viciously is survival.*

I put my hand on the cop's mouth. He doesn't see me as I stand behind him, hand clamping harder, my fingers pinching his nostrils. He wakes, struggles for breath, beats at me, but it's not enough. He's down faster than I thought he would be. But he's not dead.

I go quietly down the hallway. I don't want my target knowing I'm here. If he runs – and I'm guessing, from his nickname, that's what he'll do – I don't know if I've got the energy to catch him. Besides which, he might not be alone. One policeman might mean more. I slip through the strong door, into a hallway. I can see four doors from here. I open the first. A bedroom, beautifully made and laid out nicely. Clean. Nothing else, nobody here.

The second room is the same. This one has been lived in, because the bed isn't made, some clothes on the floor, the bathroom messy with stuff. But he's not here.

The third, and I hear movement behind the door before I open it. Something soft and quiet, whirring. The sound of a weapon, most likely.

Okay, okay. Think, Chan.

I'm a pawn. That's what Ziegler would say. He tried to teach me chess: a game of war, he told me. People think it's thoughtful, intelligent, all about strategy and planning. It's still war, though. It's killing, and it's brute force, and it's scaring your opponent so much that they make rash decisions that betray them. You win by making them lose.

Alala is making me lose. She's making this Hoyle guy lose. That's how she wins.

He's waiting in this room. He knows. But the room I tried before had a window. It was adjacent. Maybe there's a way to surprise him still. I go back, flick the latches, push it open.

I'm good with heights. But I have never looked down at anything like this before. I never saw people below me, walking. I'm only used to a dark, bottomless depth. This isn't that. This is alive, full of movement. But nobody spots me. I hope that there aren't any birds doing circuits around here.

I cling to the ledge that runs from this window to his apartment. His window is open. I don't know what I'd have done if it wasn't. Broken the glass? I don't know. I don't have to know. I creep towards it.

I can't see much through the window – too much glare – but I can make out his outline by the door, waiting for me. He's primed to make a move.

Don't look down. It's scarier than on Australia. Who knew it was easier not being able to see what was beneath you?

Breathe. Hands on the open bit of the window. Breathe, quietly. And I wrench it open as he turns. The Runner. It's him. I see the scars, recognise him. He's a blur, moving across the room faster than I thought possible – faster than I ever could. A flash of grey and silver, of augmented limbs; the window open as he reaches me, reaches his hand out, grabs me around my neck. Cold metal on my skin. He pulls me inside, holds me up in the air as I kick out.

'Who are you?' he asks. His voice is cracked and broken, the buzz of something mechanical helping him speak. 'Who sent you?'

There's no time to pause. I kick at him, and he scowls.

'Don't,' he says, and he throws me – hurls me – at the wall. I collapse into it and it cracks, and I crack. My pain, all of it, smashes right back into me. I'm on the floor; push up, try to get to my feet, but he's already in front of me.

And then he's picking me up; I'm on my feet, his hand on the back of my neck. He doesn't know what to do with me, and I can see him now, while he's hesitating. He's broken and repaired. His skin is peeled back from bits of his face, and where there should be bone there's metal, or this smooth pink replacement that looks like skin, but with the wrong texture: like it's cheap, a lie. I take his whole body in, as much as I can. He has one arm, and a space where the other should be. The legs are there, but they're not wholly original. He's in shorts and I can see the lines on his flesh where the replacements swoop and slide through the skin that's left there.

I've never seen anybody as not-quite-still-human as he is.

'I know you,' he says. His eyes flicker. Augs in them, scanning me. They're like Ziegler's camera, his antique one: the shutter on the lens like a slow eye, closing and opening, whirring while it works out who I am. He's stronger than I am, I know now. He can stop me killing him, and now he'll know that's what I'm here to do. 'Who sent you?' he asks.

'Alala,' I say. I try to reach for my pocket, for the EMP. Now I understand why I needed it. He notices my hand creeping, and nods. 'She—'

I don't get a chance to finish what I'm saying. He throws me again, to the other side of the room. My head hits something – the bed, the wall, the floor, I don't know – and everything goes black.

He's propped me up in the corner. There's some sort of wire wrapped around my arms and legs. There's no give, and when I struggle – try to find a loosening, a fraction of something that I can use to escape – they tighten. He smiles as he sits down opposite me.

'It's an Unabler. They're synced to you. Touch your skin, they can tell what you're trying to do. They work with you or against you. You struggle, they go tight. You don't struggle, they stay loose and don't hurt you.' I stop wriggling because the wire is digging into my skin so hard I can feel it about to cut me. 'You should calm down.'

He pours a drink. Steam rises from it, and a smell of sweetness, of fruit, stewing. He tells me that it's Asian tea. Imported. He makes a joke about how expensive it is, how my shakes had better not make me spill any of it. 'That's a month's wages for every drop that doesn't make your lips,' he says. He smiles. His jaw is wired; the raised tracks of the electrics run underneath the skin, all the way down past his neck, up around his ears. That's what the scars are for. They're totally symmetrical, a perfect pattern etched into his flesh. He passes me the cup, which I have to lift both my hands at the same time to hold.

'Don't kill me,' I say, as he presses my fingers around it. It's metal, like cups we used to have on the ship, but painted nicely. We had no paint on ours. Maybe we did once. 'Please.'

'You think I'd kill you?' he asks. 'Police don't kill people. Drink that, all of it. You need fluids.' He seems calmer now. 'We're trained to keep you alive. Kind of the point.'

He's police. Alala didn't tell me that.

Oh god.

He sits and waits for me to finish my drink. He's quiet and still. When I'm finished, he takes the cup, puts it onto a table in the corner of the room next to the EMP from my pocket. He sits down again and taps his fingers on his knee: false on false, the hollow sound of whatever artificial material they're both made of. You glance at him and you'd never tell. It takes closer inspection: the stillness of his face, the smoothness of the skin.

'She made me do this,' I say, and he nods, waves the words away.

'How long have you known her?' He doesn't need to look at my face to see my reaction. 'What has she got on you?' I don't say anything. 'I'm not angry. I understand, okay? We're the same, you and I. I mean, not exactly' – a flex of his arm; the plates, sheets of metal, almost, folding over each other. 'I haven't been the same for a while now. I'm not angry.' He has a strange accent. I haven't heard it before. It's softer than it should be, for how he looks. There's a lilt to it, an airiness, from a different place altogether, I'd guess. He flexes his fingers. There's nothing threatening to the act though, I get that. 'She told you to come here, kill me. In return, what? You an addict?

178

'No,' I say.

'I didn't think so. You don't look like an addict. How old are you?' He's older than me. It's hard to tell his age exactly from the original bits of him that I can see, the lines and tone of his skin. He knows what I'm doing, what I'm trying to tell. 'You're still a kid. Seventeen?'

'Eighteen,' I say. I think. I think it was my birthday a few weeks ago. Maybe I got that wrong. It could be today, for all I know.

Maybe I should say that. Maybe, as a present, he'll let me go.

'I met her when I was your age.' He looks at my stomach. 'She put something on your spine? You know what it is?'

'Yes,' I say.

'You think she might have followed you?'

'Yes.' I'm close to tears, now.

'Blinds,' he says, and the windows darken, adaptive glass that makes the room almost pitch black. There are lights in his augments, I can see; pale trims of faded blue and green.

'Have you called for backup?' I ask. I don't want to be caught. I don't want to be.

'No,' he says. 'Not yet. Maybe we can sort this out. Chan, yeah?' He knows that's my name. He'll know everything about me. 'Let's see if I can get this right. You ended up in the docks, doing whatever you can to get by: odd jobs, probably some people telling you to join the queues, go and do some maintenance on the wall, right? The promise of those queues: get a job and an apartment. A proper life.' His face scowls, his mouth curling around the bit of his jaw that doesn't move. 'But she was a better option. Easier. She was for me, at one point in my life. What'd she offer you?'

'I've lost somebody,' I say, 'and I want to get them back.'

'So she said she'd help you find them. Guessing it was her sent you to the archives the other day? That's her handiwork all over it. And after that, she told you that you weren't quite done. One last favour, and then she'd give you answers, set you free.' He stands up. His legs move strangely, like the mechanics are a few steps ahead. He picks up the EMP, tosses it from hand to hand. The hands react seemingly of their own accord, like he doesn't have to think about it, and there's no chance of them dropping it – not even a slight chance. Silver flashes around his torso, where the skin is peeling. More and more of him is not quite right, not quite human. 'She builds these herself. She tell you that? Used to be in technology, then everything fell apart for her, so she rebuilt her life differently.' He puts it down, squats next to me, so that we're level. 'How did I do?'

It's more complicated than that, I want to say; because he doesn't know the full situation. There's a past to every tale, a complicated backstory that serves to be everything when you're making your choices. It's always there and it has to be important. It can't just be about now.

But I *don't* say that.

'You know why they call me The Runner?' He grabs something else from the desk to fiddle with. For the first time I look around and take in the room properly. It's temporary, sure, not somewhere that people actually live for any real amount of time. Everything is clean and must have come with the place, blended into the walls, fastened to the floor. There's no personality here, not really – not like Ziegler's place, or even Alala's. There's no stamp that says, this belongs to somebody: no clothes on the backs of chairs. The bed in the next room is bare, the sheets stripped, the curtains pulled tight.

He hands me the tablet he's holding. It's old – even I can tell that – solid, no holo tech. Instead it's running some software that I don't even recognise, and work has been done to it on a hardware level. The back of it is exposed so that wires jut and circuit boards are exposed.

'That's me,' he says. A video plays on the screen of a man running, sprinting: an athlete in a competition. It's him. His legs are pumping, no visible augments. Two arms, no scars that I can see. He's so fast that it's barely conceivable. He presses the screen and it slows down, showing me everything about him; how his body is behaving for him, the muscles all working with each other. 'She's rich,' he says. 'You know that? She doesn't need to live there. She's got resources, contacts; people all over. She could move anywhere she wanted, but she stays there still, in that shack on the edge of the outskirts, I'll bet.' I nod. 'Because it's not about money for her. It's about power. She got me the augments I needed to compete, to win. Simple as that – pulled strings. Don't ask me how. Told me I'd repay her afterwards.'

'You were fast,' I say. 'That's how you got the name.'

'Not quite. And I wasn't fast enough, not even close. Couldn't afford the augs for it by myself. She knew people from her life before: new models, prototypes. Anything's allowed on the circuit, provided you can mentally control it, so you do what you have to do. But, you know, it doesn't always work like that. If I'd have won, maybe I could have done something – paid her back, paid her off, whatever. But . . .' Then he plays another video. This one shows him fall, his limbs like spider's legs trapped underfoot, snapping and bending at strange angles; the ground beneath him churning as the mechanics in his broken legs keep going. His face is still. 'I've seen this hundreds of times,' he says, 'never get used to it. I was healing when she called in the favour. She said she'd make everything okay – outfit me with better augments, if I did everything she wanted. And I needed that, because I lost. I couldn't have refused, but I didn't even want to. She's like a genie or something; there when you want her, when you need her.'

'What's a genie?' I ask.

'From stories? They grant wishes. That's what she does. What makes her invaluable.'

'What did she ask you to do?'

'She didn't want anything, not at first. She waited. After I ran, I joined the police. With the augments, I was an asset. They wanted me, and I needed to work. Made sense.' He leans forward and looks away from me, props himself up on the table. 'Then, one day, she came to me. Turned up at my door. Told me she'd been watching. I'd almost forgotten her; or, I'd hoped she would have gone away. That's when she laid me out, and I woke up with something in my spine – I'm guessing the same as you've got. She told me she wanted me to do something for her, now. Get her information.'

'Did you go where she sent you?' I ask. I'm captured by the story. He seems like a good guy. He's just like me: scared, lost.

He nods. 'I went. She wanted something from the archives, and of course, I had the access to get in there. I stood there, by the computers, ready to get the information she needed, and I realised she couldn't see me. Couldn't reach me there, to do her . . .' He makes the same finger twitch Alala made. 'I called it in. Told my bosses what happened. I didn't tell them about Alala, though. Told them I didn't know who'd done it. I was just as guilty of rigging races earlier as she'd been; likely I'd have been kicked off the force. Lost everything. They got surgeons to diffuse the device, and told me to get back to work. That was about a year ago. Since then, I've been waiting. Doing my job, bringing down criminals, waiting for her to screw up; to make a move that I can use. I went to see her a couple of months ago, told her the device was gone. She told me that I would regret it, one day. Not helping her. And I thought, right there and then, that I could take her out. Solve my problem. Nobody would know why.' There's a glimmer in his eyes, and he's some-where else for a moment; and then he's back with me. 'But I couldn't do it. I have to do it right. She sent you here to kill me?'

'She said I had to,' I say, 'but I'm not going to. I can't. I'm not that person.' I say that, and I get a flash – a rush, almost like falling, like the ground is screaming towards me, but it's faces: of people who have died, who I didn't save; of Agatha and Jonah and Mae and even Rex and then Dave. And I feel sick, dizzy for a moment, my stomach knotting, churning.

'Did she give you a weapon?' He's quiet. He's ahead of me.

'Only the EMP,' I say.

'So what are you meant to do when you've used it? Slit my throat?' He draws his finger – one metal finger – across his neck, in the action. 'That's not the weapon, Chan. You are. She'll be waiting to explode you, take us both out. You're no use to her now.'

'I'm alone,' I say, and this suddenly feels like bargaining: for my life, for my freedom. I'm alone and nobody will miss me. Nobody will know I'm gone. Ziegler will publish his story as it is, and nobody will believe him without the evidence. Mae will be taken by Alala, or left where she is, and I'll never know how she is. Nobody will know. I want somebody to know, to miss me. 'Please.'

He moves away, sits on the bed behind me. I can't see what he's doing, but there's a hiss, the sound of something crunching. I bend my neck, to try and get him back in my sight. Then he walks back around, his other prosthetic arm fitted to his body. He tenses it, twitches the fingers.

'What are you going to do?' I ask.

'Nothing,' he says, 'and neither are you. And I'm not going to give Alala the chance, either.' He drags me, grabs my shoulders, props me up against the wall underneath the window. There's a mirror opposite, on the wardrobe, and I see myself, what I look like right now: a disaster, hurt and tired and wrecked.

He shuts the door, locks it, barricades it by dragging over the chest of drawers as if it's nothing; it's so light for him to move it barely registers.

'Now, we wait for my guys to arrive. Sorry, Chan. I wish we could help you more. But this is always how it was going to end for you, you have to know that.' His eyes flicker; he's sending a message though his augs, finally getting the backup he'll need to lock me away, to diffuse the bomb in me likely, before we get out of here. 'We can get you a deal, maybe. You help us to take down Alala, maybe we can help you find whoever it is you're looking for.'

It's a good deal. Safer. But there are no guarantees, and Alala's got the information now. That's faster. I don't want to kill him, but I don't know that I can trust him either.

I lunge for the EMP. I make it, both hands on it.

'No,' he says, but I squeeze it.

The lights pop off; the noise that I hadn't even noticed – all the noise from outside, from the street, from the building itself – comes to an end. Hoyle clatters to the ground, hissing coming from his limbs, which, when I look over, are limp, a stillness to them that they didn't have before this moment; his face has gone dead as well, though his eyes are moving; his jaw is tight, like he's gritting his teeth. The Unabler drops off my wrist, falls to the ground, suddenly useless. And inside me, something changes. I worry that what I squeezed wasn't an EMP, but a device; that I am on the cusp of exploding, of taking Hoyle out with me. But I don't. Instead, there's a gnawing pain from deep inside me that's like nothing I've ever felt before – like cramps, but a hundred times worse, creeping through my insides from my spine. From down below, noise rises again and then there's panic. Cars have crashed into each other. It sounds like chaos. People scream. Everybody's devices will have stopped working – augs as well. Some people will be crippled, blinded.

Then I hear the sound. It's a buzzing, a furious whirr. It's not right outside, but it will be soon enough.

The birds are coming.

I look over at Hoyle and he stares back, totally still. He can't move. Another surge of pain hits my insides – huge and horrible, scraping at me, like fingers clasping my organs. I struggle to my feet and Hoyle makes a noise, his half-useless mouth telling me to stop. But I can't. I push up, using the wall, the sill. There must be a weapon here, a knife or something. Something that I can use to defend myself.

'Don't,' he says. His voice is strained, the words forced out of a mouth that can't do what he wants it to, not just yet.

'I have to!' I scream, and I realise that I can't not scream, that the noise is pain and anger and terror, all coming out, one crash of everything I'm feeling. The birds are getting closer. The door is locked and I can't see the key, or how to open it, even. It's electric coded, likely. All that's left is the window. I can maybe go back the way I came in. I open it, try to make out the birds as they soar down the streets towards us. They're harder to see in the daylight, grit against the backdrop of the buildings in every direction, floating motes of dust, the sun only glinting on their shells when they're at the right angle.

I've got thirty seconds, I reckon. Nothing more.

Foot up, on the sill. The pain inside me hurts more. I'm nearly out; don't care if Alala sees me, because—

Hoyle's hand on my ankle. He's turning back on.

He grabs me, throws me against the chest of drawers and I thud painfully against it. I try to move right away, but I can't. My arm kills; legs as well, and neck. I'm out. I can feel it. I'm in too much pain to dig any deeper, find a last reserve to send me running. Something's broken. I look down, and there's bone jutting through my shoulder where it hit the drawer unit. I can't really feel my spine any more.

I'm done.

Hoyle stands in front of me, gasping as his body becomes operational again. Everything is slower than it was, twitchier. I'm guessing it doesn't happen often, that his whole system shuts down. I think about how vulnerable he must feel when it does. I know what that's like.

The birds are so close.

'I'm sorry,' he says. Then he's quiet, waiting, and I wait with him. The buzzing is right outside the window. There's a mechanical voice, Gaia issuing some sort of alert, telling the crowds below not to panic. Hoyle crouches in front of me. 'Who were you trying to rescue?' he asks.

'Mae. Little girl,' I manage. It hurts too much to speak. My jaw is broken, I think.

'I'll find her. Do what I can.'

I don't have time to say anything. I want to thank him. The birds are outside the window, a swarm of them, a shape made in the air as they orbit each other.

They drive through the window, smashing the glass with their mass, flapping and beating against each other with their tiny silver wings.

PART
TWO

EIGHT

Today is a day like every other. I wonder, during my waking moments, if my life is merely a dream, because it feels so much like a dream. The vagueness of it and the way that it seems so fleeting, as if everything – who I am, where I live, the people that I know – might just evaporate away from me. Everything that came before is suddenly not quite so real as maybe it once was. Perhaps it's not this day that I am dreaming but the past that I now barely remember. I try and call back to mind who I was once, and it's gone.

It's a shape I can't quite form, no matter how hard I try.

I can't make out the angles, the lines.

Instead, I understand the nature of truth. That is what's presented now. The truth is not vague and it is not slight. The truth is what's directly in front of me when I wake up, and absolutely nothing more.

'Good morning,' everybody says (without fail, every single person here). That is good manners.

'Good morning,' I reply. We are all so polite. Sometimes people say my name. My name, sewn into the back of my clothes; written in the front of my books; printed on my door, my private space, my room. Everything with my name on it is mine.

Chan. This belongs to Chan.

What do you feel? asks Gaia when I wake up. I hear the alarm first, every day, and then her voice, which for some reason is inside my head. I thought it was a mistake, that I was broken, the first time; and then it was explained. It's just for me. Talk to her, because she won't be there forever. Gaia's voice is cold. She's female, and she must live here as well, but I have never met her. But she is always here, every morning and every evening, and she is kind, and I'm told to not be scared of her. I'm told to open up to her, that talking with her is a private opportunity, just for me, for the moment.

So I do. I tell her if I have had a dream, and I tell her if I am unsettled. I can imagine her nodding while I talk, listening carefully, and really attempting to understand every little thing that I am saying.

We are assigned different tables for mealtimes, because – we're told – we have to socialise. We talk about our days and we discuss issues that have arisen. Sometimes we tell each other secrets and sometimes we talk about our morning conversations with Gaia.

Everything is as open as it can be.

One night I am on a table with people that I don't know; and then, the next evening, with more people that I do not know; and then, the next, with somebody from the first night again, and two people from the second; and the next, new people. Over and over. In the morning, the voice in the rooms asks us who we like; who we enjoy spending time with. *Do you think you form attachments easily?* it asks. *Do you enjoy the time you spend with this person?*

They ask us to remember the names of our friends. Names are important, they say. They have power, and they have meaning. A name is an identity. It's so much more than just a word.

Every few days we have a meeting with Doctor Gibson. He's a doctor, but of the mind, he says.

'Any doctor can mend a broken bone. We've gotten to be so good with them, you understand. We can heal those in minutes – moments even, as fast as it takes to take a breath, if the bone isn't too badly broken. But this is about something else entirely, Chan. This is about what's wrong with society. Sometimes, we have something we can fix, and so we should. We would think nothing of operating on that broken arm. There's always something that we can smooth over, you know? So, think about your art sessions.' In art, we paint and we draw and we sculpt. 'The clay you use? It's rough, isn't it?'

I agree with him. A lot of being here and succeeding is about agreeing.

'So when it's done and you want it to be pleasing to look at, to touch, to be something that is useable? That's when you smooth it down. That's when you have to make it what it can be. You see that? Not what it *is*, but what it *can be*.'

I agree again.

193

'We are all like that clay, Chan. Or we're like a canvas, if you prefer. Do you like to paint? What happens if we make a spill, if we paint something that we don't want to have painted, something that we need to get rid of?'

I tell him that we paint over it, that we start again.

'Exactly. Exactly!' He points into the air, like a punctuation mark. He chuckles. It's a fun little chuckle, quite sweet, nice to listen to. 'We start again. I was trapped once, so I started again. Now, I've got a family. Do you want a family?'

I want to say that I've got one, but, no. That's not true.

I want one.

'I've got children,' Gibson tells me. 'Two of them, because they're twins, which makes us rare, you know? That's like nature's way of giving you special dispensation, to get around the rules. But if you want a child, if you want a family, you've got to succeed and get out of here. Become a part of the infrastructure. That's all any of us wants.' He sits in a leather chair, and I sit on one that's exactly the same, directly opposite him. There's a table between us with a bottle of fresh water and two metal mugs. He pours the water out, like a ritual, even if I've only drunk a few sips from my cup. 'So, you should tell me what you remember. Tell me about your childhood, if that helps.'

I tell him that I remember being a child. He nods, as if that's progress, and he asks me to tell him more; but all I know is that I was. I was myself, but smaller, and I was cared for.

I absolutely remember that I was cared for.

* * *

I remember that I perhaps used to sleep badly. It's less a specific memory of why, of what used to wake me up – or, maybe, of whatever it was that used to keep me from sleeping – but I did, once. That's over now. This – waking up when I do, when I want to, feeling fine, sleeping safely – is the only truth worth considering. Now, when I sleep I don't wake up until it's morning, until that alarm rings out, when I hear the sound of birds and insects, and then Gaia's voice. I pass the day and then it's evening again, and the same as the night before. I put my head down, and I shut my eyes and go to sleep. They tell us to go over what we've done that day, to think about what's happened, and who we are. I do this, and it never takes long before I'm asleep.

And then I am awake again.

Every morning the room is exactly the same as it was the morning before. I think of it as being home, my home. This place is all that I have.

I dream, but when I wake up I can't remember what exactly it was that I dreamt, just the feeling that I've been somewhere else, that I *was* somewhere else, doing something that wasn't this. That I was a different person.

At breakfast, I'm with three people I've sat with before. We all say hello, and we introduce ourselves, because we're bad with names. There are so many people to meet, and so much to remember. And memories seem slippery, like they're hard to cling onto. You have to really try. You have to say names under your breath, until they properly take hold.

'I'm Cassie,' one girl says. She's younger than me by a few years, pretty, but with a look of permanent confusion on her face. Almost everything she says is like a question, lifting up at the end of sentences. 'You're Chan?' I nod. 'I remember you,' she says, 'from before. You're new here, right?'

'I don't know how long you have to be here before you're not new anymore,' one of the other diners says. His name is Tom, and he's enormous, aggressive, bearded (and it's scraggly, even though they cut our hair for us, it grows quickly on him, I think). 'I'm still new to some people and I've been here for months now. Longer.' He scratches at his face through the hair while he thinks. 'I don't remember.' We are told to not worry about things that we don't remember; that they don't matter, not in the grand scheme of things. That's Doctor Gibson's philosophy. We're here now.

I think: But where were we before?

'Anyway. New details this week. That's good. That's what I've been thinking about. Where I'd like to be working. I'd like to get something inside. I've been learning programming, which is good. That's a job I would like, when I'm out of here.' Tom scratches, as if he's got lice. He needs to have his beard shaved, but they only do that every few days. Hair itches when it's growing back in, I know. I don't know why I know that. 'Gibson says we should have a job that is practical, you know, because we can get a placement if we have a skill.'

'That's what we should focus on?' Cassie asks, or says. One or the other. She doesn't let anybody take the reins afterwards. 'Because I've been thinking about the art, you know? That might be something that I could do?'

196

'That's hard,' Tom says. 'It's not practical. To paint, you know. Do you have a viewpoint? Do you have something to say?'

'I think I do?'

I push my food around in its bowl: cereal, brightly coloured and so sweet it hurts my teeth. They cleaned my teeth a few weeks ago: sat me in a chair, sedated, and blasted away the dirt on my teeth with this precision laser, held in the shaking hand of a dentist who didn't seem entirely sure about his job; like he were too young, or too old, or just not trained enough. My gums still hurt. Cold food, warm food, sweet food: it seems as if everything makes my mouth ache.

'You've got to be sure. It's hard. That's what Doctor Gibson says.'

'I should get a proper job when I leave here?'

'Yeah, for certain. Something serious.'

Every conversation here is the same, I think. They sound the same. They start the same, end the same, drift off, with no sense that anything's finished. Everything is in progress.

The other boy at the table doesn't say anything, or look at the rest of us. He has stubble on his head and the red fuzz of it on his face – a beard, or the beginnings of one. It's nothing like Tom's though, which is patchy. This one is even. He stares down at his bowl just as I do, lifting the spoon, letting the milk run off it, onto the grains. Circles of pink and green swim in the white. I catch him staring at me, trying not to let me see. But he looks and then he looks away. We both let Tom and Cassie talk, and they go on and on until the bell rings, and we walk to our classes.

My stomach rumbles, because I didn't eat.

I ask Gibson what I should do, as a job.

'You think about that?'

I tell him that everybody else does.

'You don't strike me as somebody who cares what others think,' he says. Then: 'Do you have any desire about what you want to do?' I don't say anything. That's the easiest way to get the conversation moving, if you want it to, if you want to know what Gibson's angling towards when he asks you a question that he doesn't really expect you to have an answer for. 'So, there's working with your hands or your head. Either of those seem like something you'd enjoy doing?'

Head, I tell him.

'I don't know. You're pretty athletic,' he replies, 'maybe that's in your favour. Strong, as well.' I don't ask him how he knows that, because I don't much care. 'You'll work it out. We'll work it out, and together. You believe that, don't you?'

I do, I say. He makes a note of that. I think he's watching how fast I reply; what my face does when I reply. I don't know why he would care.

'Tomorrow, I've got another test for you. You feel ready for one?'

I do, I say. Of course.

'Good. Because I think we should step things up a little, see some real progress.' He smiles. Smiles make you trust somebody. Smiles are easy to understand.

*　　*　　*

198

The test begins the same way the previous one did. A warden leads me to one of the shops in the town. This is where they sell food that comes from the cities. We earn money through working and then we spend it here. Commerce, they say, it's a lesson in itself. He stands me outside the shop and he says that I'm to go inside and buy myself something. It doesn't matter what. I can choose. He gives me a card loaded with money. I ask him how much money.

'Your choice,' he says. 'You buy whatever you think you can pay for.' He stands back and folds his arms across his chest and he watches as I walk forward. There's no direct sunlight in this part of the town because we're inside what used to be a mall, and there's a roof over us. There's a huge entrance at one end, and they keep all the doors and windows open at all times. The air outside might be nearly too hot to bear, but they need ventilation – that's what they say. The ventilation lets the wind from outside in, and it brings sand with it that whips around, into shoes and eyes and hair. The shops are different. They're air-conditioned, cool and welcoming: a respite. It makes you want to open their doors.

'Good morning,' the shopkeeper says. I smile at him. 'You have a look around,' he tells me, and he whistles something, a song I've heard before, in this shop. 'You mind if I put some music on?' He doesn't wait for me to answer. The sound system in the shop turns up, some old song. I don't know instruments. Some people here learn them, play them, write songs, play in the band that performs every Sunday evening in front of the centre. The song jangles. *And your*

199

bird can sing, the singer goes, and the shopkeeper sings along.

I look at the shelves: pastries, the scent of chocolate wafting from them. I love that smell. It reminds me of something that I don't remember. In the corner of the room, a whirring fan; a counter for the shopkeeper to stand behind; expensive items, on rails and racks: clothes, shoes. More expensive still: technology, tablets and drones. And then, a locked cabinet: a new-model striker, it looks like; and a knife. I recognise it. I feel like I know it.

'Any idea what you're after?' the shopkeeper asks. I think I recognise him. He's a warden, I'm sure. Working here on his off days, or maybe the other way around.

I tell him that I'm not sure.

'When you are,' he says, and the sentence ends like that, trailing off.

I find a top. It reminds me of something from before. Memories like this, they're like a knot in my gut; I don't know where they come from, or when, but there's something about them, an echo deep inside me. This one has got a hood. I am drawn to these things; something to pull over my head, to cover my eyes. It feels like something I've worn before. I look at the rest of the shelves, and the memories that feel like they're trying to surface. Everything here feels like I should remember it.

'That's nice,' he says. He's watching me touch this top with the hood, watching me take it from the hanger and pull it around me, and discover that it fits me. They said to buy anything.

I tell him that I want this. He smiles.

'You want to wear it now?' he asks.

I do. He reaches over and finds the tag, and he keys the price into his tablet.

'Got a card?' I hand it over, and he scans it. He frowns, scans it again. 'There's not enough funds here,' he says. 'I'm sorry, but I'm going to have to keep this.' He reaches over and pulls the hoodie from my back, yanking my arms out. He puts it on the counter. 'Maybe don't try to spend money you don't have in my shop, okay?'

I apologise. He puts the top on the counter, right in front of me, and he coughs.

'Excuse me,' he says. He coughs harder, and then he covers his mouth, and he walks to the doorway that leads to the back of the shop. He coughs, and I hear him cough louder and louder. He can't see me. I can't see him. There's nobody else in the shop. The hoodie is in front of me, teasing me, taunting me.

I don't pick it up. I leave the shop. Outside, the guard asks how it went.

I didn't want anything, I tell him. He nods, tightens his lips and squints his eyes.

'Let's go,' he says.

Gibson asks about the shop. He's interested, desperately interested in everything I have to say. He records the conversation, and a small camera drone buzzes around the office, zooming in, noting everything.

'Did you not want to take the clothes?'

I say that I didn't.

'But they were there. And he wouldn't have known.' I don't tell Gibson that *he* would have known, and that's just the same. And it's a test. It's not a real situation. And beyond that, I wouldn't take them. They aren't mine to take. The shopkeeper was nice to me, didn't do anything to vex me. Why should I hurt him, in any way? 'Did you change your mind about them?'

I say that they weren't mine to take. That's stealing.

He nods. 'Excellent work,' he tells me. 'From where you were, to here. You're really doing so very well.'

That's the end of the meeting. He smiles at me, to let me know that I'm free to leave. But I sit there, for just a little while longer, in case I think of something else to say.

I notice that somebody's watching me while I'm sitting in the library on my downtime, sorting the books people have checked out. I go through them and return them to the shelves where they belong. It's a job, one that I volunteered for. I like the stories; I glance at the backs, trying to feel if they are something that I will fall into, or something that will push me away. And then I file them, · alphabetical, back into the racks. The ones that capture me, I sit and I read the first few pages, and I try to imagine where the story is going to go, where it's going to end up. The best ones take you away from where they begin, and then back again. They understand that it's the journey, not the ending. The end can be the same as the beginning, and that's okay.

The watching boy is pale, his skin the colour of dust. We are not allowed to bring dust here; that's a rule.

Some people clean and they make sure it stays clean. Dust is skin itself, and hair, and tiny parts of us that we abandon. We shed our skin and grow new skin, like snakes (as I have read). I know him. I saw him at breakfast. It's been two days, and his hair has grown more. Now it's a thin red sheen, a glow upon his scalp. He comes up to me when I'm reading a book about myths, things that we used to believe on Earth, but now we know aren't real: vampires, werewolves, mermaids. Lies, all of them.

'Chan,' he says.

He knows my name. I'm surprised, I tell him.

'I've got a memory for names,' he tells me. 'My name is Jonah.' He holds out his hand to shake mine, and his skin is somehow colder than I thought it would be. It's nice. Everything here is so hot, all the time, and he's not.

I have a feeling that I've known him. Like the items in the shop. There's something in the past. But, as Gibson says, that doesn't matter. What matters is the truth of being here; of being now.

I tell Jonah that it's nice to meet him.

At dinner, I see Jonah in the corridor, heading to the same room as I am. Dinner takes place across three large rooms, each with multiple tables set out. Tonight, Jonah and I share a room, not a table. He stares at his food, pushes it around the plate. Eats some of it, but not all. He looks over at me but doesn't stare, just a few glances.

As we're leaving, he hands me a note. We're shuffling out of the door, a queue to get back to whatever activity we're filling our evenings with, and he slips it into my hand. I don't read it until I get back to my room.

I feel like I know you, it says. *Isn't that strange?*

He comes to the library and he hands over a book, and he opens the pages to show me a line from it. We appreciate the words. He sits on the floor opposite where I am, where I'm putting the books back and taking my time over it. I give him some books for him to take away. Ones that I have enjoyed.

I ask him about the note, where he thinks he knows me from.

'I can't say,' he tells me. It's not a refusal, just that he doesn't know. I don't know either. They've told us – they tell us, when we first get here – that it's to be expected, because we've been somewhere before, we all know that. Different places, different lives. They say, You are here because there was something terrible that happened to you, something that is beyond your control, something that's too bad to think about. Trust us, they say; you don't want to. Sometimes, you'll wonder what it was that happened to you before, they say; what your life was like. There'll be a gnawing in your gut and a tugging in your mind that you're forgetting something that should be remembered. Well, trust us: you should not remember it. The truth that is in front of you, it is all that matters.

When they first woke me up here, they asked me if I remembered my name. It's the first thing that they said to me. Do you know who you are. I was in a room with devices that I have never seen since and don't want to see again. The memory of them – dense black boxes, whirring away, something medical and evil about them – makes me feel sick. I told them my name and they were happy with that. They asked me my favourite colour. I remembered that. They asked me why I was there, and it was gone. I told them that I didn't remember, that I couldn't quite reach the memory. Explain that to us, they asked.

So I said, It's a like a fog, and there in the fog are the things that I'm trying to say to you. They are there some-where, and I can *see* them, I can nearly catch them, touch them; but they're running, and faster than I am. That's how it feels. I know I was somewhere before this, and I know it was a place other than this. But the details? They're gone. I can't remember.

I cried, and they comforted me. They told me that it would all get better. This is the worst part, they told me. Before this, things were bad for you. Everything after this will be good. You forget the bad things. Why would you want to remember them?

I wonder if Jonah is my bad thing that I've forgotten.

Or, maybe, if I am his.

Here is my room. I have a space all of my own. There are four walls and a door. The door has a lock that I can control, but so can the people who work here, and that's important. We're taught it's for our safety. We understand that, because those are the rules. One door opens and another one shuts. Not literally, but inside us. We protect ourselves, but sometimes we need protection.

I have pictures on the walls, of what this place was like before. It's sweltering hot outside, so hot that you can only cope for minutes at a time. Your skin will crackle and pulse, and your sweat will pool and your lips will dry out, and you'll suffer. A healthy fear of death, we're told, is something worth having. I've been out there, because we're taught that freedom is allowed and isn't to be feared. But inside is safe, or safer, certainly. So the room has a device, a small box that maintains the temperature for me. I can change it, but only a little, if I'm too cold or too warm. Depending on the day, I could be both. Sometimes I just can't seem to settle on one side. I have a few things: a table for my books; a lamp on the wall; a mirror on one wall, which is dark and hard for me to see myself clearly in, and I don't like to look into. But it's mine. And bed sheets, which we are encouraged to sew ourselves: to build up designs, to thread needles through them into patterns, words. Mine has flowers, stars, the faces of a family that I don't remember, but that I know.

Agatha. I told the doctors that one of them was called Agatha, and they asked me where that came from, but I didn't know. They asked me to try and remember, and I have tried. But not too hard, because she is not here.

We all contribute to dinner. Everybody here has a job and we all bring what we can to the table. Family style, we eat. Some of the farmers bring their vegetables. From the growing rooms, they bring us beef and chicken, and it's roasted by the people who work in the kitchen. I don't have a job yet, because I've not been here long enough. I volunteer with the books, but it's not a real job. I'm still learning, they tell me.

The wardens ask, 'Don't you want to be productive?' if you say that you're tired or that something's wrong. Because sometimes something does go wrong. Sometimes my head buzzes, and I'm not here. I'm standing somewhere else and looking at my scars and running my hands through my hair and remembering when it was shorn, when I was another person. Blood on my hands, stuck underneath the bitten-down fingernails. So then they tell me that it was all a dream. They say, 'The problem with dreams is how easily they slip out; how easily they become a part of who you are. How unlike the truth of our reality they are, when you really examine them. Dreams are what make us individual; they are what make us special. You are special; we are all special.'

I want to tell them that I'm not. I could be anybody.

Jonah comes to me in the morning. He knocks on my door.

'I've been told to take you to your assignment,' he says. Which means that they've finally decided on where I'll be doing my proper job, and that I'm ready to contribute. 'You're on the roads,' he says.

I don't want that. I tell him that I don't want to go, not today. Another day.

'That's not how it works,' he says. He hands me a suit to wear that will keep the heat off. It goes over me, over every part of my body. It even covers the shoes that they gave me. There are fasteners right up the neck, to my hair, and Jonah helps me with them. 'It's not so bad,' he says. 'There are worse work details.' So I help him with his suit, and my fingers touch the scars on his neck that run all the way along like puncture marks; like rows of teeth.

I ask him how they happened.

'I don't know,' he says. I can feel the grooves of them, the scarred-over flesh.

I have my own scars, I tell him. Strange, isn't it.

'What?'

I say that we should probably remember them, because they were enough to damage us completely. When you're that damaged, how can you forget it?

'Maybe you need to? To move on. To deal with whatever it was happened.'

We walk out of the barracks, down through the tarpaulin-covered streets. No sky here, but the heat is overwhelming already. The suits don't stop the heat, they stop the sun. They protect us from real damage, but they don't stop the discomfort. We sweat as soon as we're outside the safety of the enclave, a gulf of heat blasting towards us. We head down the streets around where we live – swept clean by the bots, kept as pristine as can be – through to the outskirts. We don't really talk when we're out of the buildings, because it's harder to breathe; at least, until we've got the masks on, and they're reserved for those working on the road. Besides, it's easier to be quiet, to conserve your energy. Those are the first rules I learned here, and I never forget them.

Welcome to Pine City, a sign at the edge of the road says. It's a message from another time, when this was a proper town, when people lived here. People who weren't part of this facility worked here and went to school here, but the number is lost, scratched away. The town was abandoned, like so many towns. It was too expensive to convert them, to make them habitable. All we have access to now is the main street, which is where our facility sits: its abandoned shops, a few houses, and the entrance to a mall on one side. There used to be much more, but it's all in disrepair. The streets are overgrown, or they're barricaded off. We don't care; we don't need them.

I look at the sky as the tarpaulin ends, as we walk out into the open. There's a box here that's full of helmets, with masks that hang from the front of them. Jonah hands me one. It's dark, mostly, with an entire front made of something like glass. But they're all caked with mud and dirt, and the only thing you can really see through them are the eyes.

'On your face, like this,' he says. When he speaks, it's muffled, distorted. 'Just put it on, and breathe normally. It's fine,' he tells me. Reaches out, and he touches my shoulder. To reassure me. He knows that he should be protecting me from any fears I have, because that's what we're told. Don't rely on yourself alone. Trust your friends, the people around you. Everybody wants you to succeed.

I tug the mask down, over my face. It's so close, so tight. Unsettling, because then all you can see is grime through the glass. But I can still see Jonah. He mimes breathing deeply, and I do. The air comes through. It's bitter and stale – filtered. We need the air so we can breathe if we get too hot. There's coolant and repellent in the lining of it, and it's a relief. It's not like being in the cool of air conditioning, but it's nice. Out here, when you're working, you need something to keep you going. I'll be out here half a day, nothing more, Jonah has explained. They make us start before the sun gets highest, before it properly begins to cook the landscape. Then we go back and they run cold baths for us, and we recover, relax.

But first, we fix the road. The hard surface has bubbled and broken up, and it means that supplies can't get here from the cities. There are only a few cities left now. They taught us that the world roasted and collapsed. Everything went back a hundred years, more even, and there was murder and violence, and then it started going forward again, but at a creep, a crawl. We can't just reset to where we were. So now we are here. Here is Pine City: not a city at all, but a town that was lost, and now we are remaking it as we ourselves are remade. We are only here until we've been revised, that's what Gibson keeps telling us; and then, one day, we'll be taken somewhere else – to one of the cities, or maybe even abroad. Some other countries need a lot of help. They're worse off than we are. They've got people who haven't started going forward again. No patches, yet. You're person two-point-oh, Gibson says. None of us really understand what that means.

'Through here,' Jonah says. There's a path in between two rocks, like a vein in the side of the road, leaving off down towards crates covered in reflective stuff that shines and spins the sun's heat off in every single direction. There are tools here. 'These are what we use to break down the road, and then later – tomorrow – we go over that part, and we fill it in. Okay? It's a two-day cycle. Today, tomorrow. Always today and tomorrow. Three times we do that, then a day off. Take this.' His muffled voice is hard to hear. He hands me something that looks like a shovel, but pointed and sharp at the end. I can tell he's smiling; I can see it in his eyes. Even though his face is mostly hidden behind the filthy glass, somehow I know exactly what he looks like.

We walk back up the path, and then follow the road, him in front, me lagging behind. There are already people working here: four of them, working in pairs. One of each pair is digging into the road, the other is picking up the shards and throwing them to the side. The road itself is hacked and ruined, huge holes along it, and cracks.

'It's all about infrastructure,' Jonah says, as if that's something he's thought of; but it's from our lessons. We're told that. A road is infrastructure. So that's what we're doing, what everybody is doing: trying to rebuild infrastructure. Right now, we are the ground force; we do the really crucial stuff, the work that allows the rest of it to happen. 'Watch them. Do what they do, it's pretty easy work. And then we get out of here.'

I lift the shovel, jam it down, right into the ground. I push it down harder than I thought I might, putting real force behind it. The ground shatters, it seems, bits of the old covering and stone and mud flying up.

Jonah nods at me, that I'm doing this properly. Again and again, over and over, and something about this work makes me feel better. It's cathartic, is what Agatha would say.

No. Who's Agatha?

Everything blanks, for a second. A moment. I stand. There's wind, which I can't feel through the suit, but I can see, because the bushes at the side of the road are moving in it, pushing themselves this way and that.

211

I feel a hand on my arm, and a voice. 'What's wrong with you?'

I say that I'm fine, which is only really a reaction, the words that you're meant to say, even when you're not. When people ask that, they don't want the truth. But it's not Jonah's voice, and not his hand. I look up, and there's another girl there. No, not a girl. She's older than I am, but not by much. I can't see her face, can't really see anything but the shape of her, silhouetted with the sun high behind her, her dark outline, the pose of how she stands; like she's broken, barely clinging together, and yet somehow still so powerful it's unsettling.

And I know her. I don't know how or where from, but I know her.

'Don't fall,' she tells me. Her voice is jagged, the sound of coarse glass in a throat; and her speech isn't quite right, stilted, her tongue and teeth stumbling over the words as they come out.

I nod.

'I'm Polly,' she says, her voice muffled; and I tell her my name. She nods. I see her eyes staring out from the darkness of her mask.

And I *know* her, I'm sure of it.

I watch Polly while we work. I'm okay, I tell myself, over and over. It's like a mantra, every time I lower the shovel. I'm okay. Jonah and I work faster than the other pairs, maybe because I'm new to the job. They all talk about how they've been out here weeks now. This road, the good, smooth bit that we walked down to get here, that's been done by them, or a stretch of it has been. Past where we are, the surface is torn up, hacked apart by the heat, by nature, trees and plants growing through. There's such a long way to go. In the distance, at the end of the road, I can see something of a city on the horizon: towers jutting up, a mass crowded around their base. I wonder what city that is. I wonder if I've ever been there.

I ask Jonah if he minds not being able to remember the before.

'No,' he says. He doesn't pause. 'Because it's for our benefit.' He picks up the lumps of tarmac that I've brought up and throws them to the side. We don't clear them from that part. That's a waste. They'll be there until they're not; until nature swallows them up. The infrastructure is all that matters, not the mess that we leave behind us. 'If it wasn't, then, maybe. Maybe. But I know that I can't have been happy.' He touches his neck, reaching up through the line between the suit and the helmet. His voice, wilting. 'Some things are markers, I think, of everything that we should be willing to leave behind.' Then he's quiet.

The others take up the conversation, shouting so that they can be heard. They talk about how they're happy here, how being in the facility is good for them. They feel well, and they feel healthy, and they're learning so much. All of these things that they didn't know before, gaps which are being filled in, and they think it'll make life in the city that much easier. All except Polly. She doesn't speak, but I desperately want her to. I know her, could recognise something in her eyes, and it's like there's a word on the tip of my tongue that I want to spit out, that won't quite form for me.

I ask the others if they can remember where they came from. They can't, not really.

'But I have a sense of what the city was like, sure. That I know,' one of them says.

'When we see the pictures, I remember that. I remember how high the buildings were.'

'And I remember that they were cooler than here. That's true, isn't it?'

'I don't know if this is right,' Polly says, interrupting the others. She stops working, and she takes off her helmet, and she stares at me. Like a bell ringing, the memory chimes. Her hair is short, cropped close to her head. There's a scar on her face, more scars running down her neck. 'How can I know, if I cannot remember what my life was like before?'

'Because they told us,' one of the others says. 'They told us that we were in trouble. The truth is that they are saving us.'

'And we just believe it?' Her words are clunky, like she's struggling to find them.

'It's the truth,' Jonah says. 'They have given us something to believe in. That's as good as reason as any.' He looks at my shovel. I've stopped working. 'It isn't time to have a break yet,' he says. He waits until I start again, and then he picks up the pieces that I break away from the road, and he throws them to the side.

Doctor Gibson tells me that he's been listening to my morning conversations with Gaia, and that he's a little concerned about what he's heard.

'You've been dreaming?' he asks.

I tell him that I have. He already knows, so I can't tell why he's bothering to ask, what the point of the question is.

'But you can't remember your dreams? So I want to say that's natural. Some of the things we're doing here, they're going to be confusing to you, because they're new. Do you know, before you came here, you didn't have the education you're getting here? You were practically somebody else.'

I ask him who I was, then. He laughs out loud, and he slaps his knee.

'You were *you*. I didn't mean that literally. I meant . . . You weren't as whole as you are now. But you were Chan. You've always been Chan. That's crucial, your individuality.' He puts his hands together, like an arrowhead. 'You're special, Chan. We all are.' And then he relaxes again, sits back. He consults his notes with a side-glance. 'Are you feeling prepared for the world now? You're making good friends?'

He's heard me talk about Jonah, about Polly. I don't know if they're friends, or what they are. They're people that I know. Something gnaws at me, about friendship, about trust.

'Look, there are some simple rules here,' he says, 'and the biggest one is that we're working for you. We're doing all of this for you. This is my programme; did you know that? I'm in charge here. We're all making contributions to society now, as we rebuild, and this is mine. You're working on the roads? That's yours, for now. Later, you'll go to a city, probably one of the newer ones, one of the growing cities, and you'll get a job, and you'll make a family. That will be your contribution. Do you understand?'

I do.

He seems pleased. 'You'll want to think about what you hope to get out of here, as well. This experience that you're having here, it's second to none. Without this, you would be somewhere else. In a gutter maybe, or dead. Certainly worse off than you are now.' He pauses, then looks at the buzzing camera drone. It flies around, settling in front of my face. 'Do you ever think about death?' Gibson asks.

Don't die.

I tell him that I do, but that I don't know why. I tell him that I don't want to.

'That you don't want to die, or don't want to think about it?' he asks, but I don't have an answer. 'I think both are perfectly normal, rational, even,' he says. He smiles. The session is over.

It's been explained repeatedly, because this is what we have to learn: the history of how we got here, as people, to this point. How we ruined our planet because we didn't care. We overpopulated it; we crowded it and we robbed it. There's a story about cities that ran out of water because they acted as if everything wasn't getting hotter; a story about bits of the world that fell into the sea, because the tide rose up and wore away coastlines, lapping chunks out until the land just gave in; a story about how the cities died when the electricity did, and everybody had to try again, to build new infrastructures.

Ninety percent of the world's population gone in less than half a century; and then those who were left crammed into the cities that they built, that they thought they could adapt. Everything about this planet was set back in time.

We're not where we should be. I ask about the stars, about space. Because I want to know why we're not up there. They say that we never tried, not really. It was too much work. We don't have the technology. We're stuck here, and we have to make the most of it.

That's what moving on is: it's adaptation.

I am out on the road again, this time without Jonah. This time, I've got Tom, the bearded boy from breakfast a few days back. He's younger than I am, but he's been here much longer. He's used to everything here at this point. He's preparing to leave, to go to a city, to make a new start. He talks about his potential life while we work, while he shovels and I pick up after him. He prefers the shovel, he tells me.

'Because it's moving forward, you know? Everything with it, it's progress. That's what this is all about. You get going, get moving. Do something. Feels good to do something, that's what I've learned.' He talks and talks, and we stop when the sun is just too hot, and we drink water from coolers that barely work in this heat, the water being bath-warm, barely refreshing at all. With my helmet off, I can take a couple of minutes of the heat, nothing more. Then my skin starts to burn, slowly but surely. An hour of the heat and I'll be crackling. You lose water from your body quickly. Dehydrate and pass out, then that's it for us.

Don't die. I hear that again, a voice that I know. Somewhere deep inside me.

'What about you?' Tom asks me. 'You just have to have an idea,' he says, 'because that's how you move forward.

217

Haven't you had sessions with Gibson? He's amazing. Really helped me work out what I was doing.'

'Gibson's a liar,' Polly says. I didn't even see her. She keeps her head down, focused on her work. But now she stops, pulling her helmet off to join us, and she yanks the mask from her face. The sun is behind us and makes her squint as she stands and talks to us, her eyes narrowed, her hand raised above her forehead. Those scars. I wonder how she got them. 'They say it's the truth, but the truth would be answers. Did I ask to be here? Do I want to be here?'

'I do,' Tom says.

'Because you've been told you do. You've been told that this is what you want. They talk to us like we're children. I do not want to be here. I do not want to sleep here. I do not want to stay here, but they will not let us leave. They say we want to be here, that we are better. They say that they are telling us the truth; but I think that they're lying to us.'

'You're just pissed because you aren't learning as fast as the rest of us,' Tom says. 'Not my fault you're slow.'

Polly hits him. She's so fast I barely see it. Her hand is suddenly in his gut, buried in the belly of his suit, and then he's winded, on his knees, sobbing. He's desperately trying to take in breath, but it's hard with the heat, with the air as thin as it is. I help him, putting the bit from his mask into his mouth, pushing his helmet back onto his head, and he rolls back onto the floor, clutching himself.

Polly doesn't say anything. She steps back. Her face is blank. Her partner runs up and bends down to help Tom to his feet. Tom's coughing now, and there's blood bubbling

218

between his lips, pooling in the mask, near his chin. Washing clean the mud that was in there first.

In Polly's hand, I see a shard of something sharp. She opens her fingers and drops it. Tom's suit is a mess of blood soaking through the fabric.

'Help me!' Polly's partner screams, and I do, and the others do, lifting Tom up, supporting him as best we can. He sobs, and in his helmet the sobs echo around, amplified and muffled at the same time. We carry him back, his weight immense.

Polly walks behind us. I step away from Tom as we get closer to town, as he starts to shake, trembling and twitching, and the others begin to run with him. They head to the compound, bursting through the doors, howling for help.

'I did that,' Polly says. She's quiet and speaks so slowly, every word carefully chosen. She doesn't get anything wrong, though; she's just measured. Her own breathing is hard, so I help her with her helmet, with her mask. We put them to one side, and we go indoors. There's a trail of blood on the floor, and the sounds of panic from further in. I take my outer suit off, and I wipe my sweat down with the towels left by the door. I'll shower, but not now. I feel like Polly needs me, and I don't want to leave her alone. 'I have hurt him,' she says, finally.

I say that he might be dead. From the look on her face, in her eyes, I can tell that she hadn't even considered that she might have gone that far, done that much damage. She takes off her own suit and I notice her arm. It's been cut off just below the elbow, and there's a replacement, an augment that pulses with wet-looking metal and skin grafts where it meets her flesh. My brain hurts. It swims, clouding my vision. She wipes her forehead, then the skin on that arm, and she flexes the metal fingers that held the shiv that cut Tom. She walks away from me, down the corridor, both hands raised, as if she's surrendering to something that she knows they'll want her to pay for.

I don't see Polly or Jonah for the next few days. I keep my head down, and I work outside, with new people, who either don't want to talk or insist on asking me about who I am, how long I've been here, if I remember anything from who I was before.

I tell them nothing, because that's all I feel I have to offer.

Polly is being held in solitary, go the whispers. She's been taken off for more drastic teaching. She's not quite right, not working with the system here. She's been here six months, and she should be – the phrase that people seem to use a lot, far too much – *revised* by now. I don't even know what that means. I feel healthy. I feel fine. Even as I look at my scars, I can see that I'm not ill. There's no redness to the flesh anymore, nothing that hasn't healed up. My eyesight isn't good, so they give me glasses, and I wear them when they ask me to, when they remind me to. They say that they'll fix my eyes so I don't have to wear glasses someday. I wonder what else they'll try to fix, or maybe they already have.

Gibson tries to start as we always do: a summary of what I've been doing, how I've been feeling. I give him what he wants, because that's surely the fastest way out of the meeting. I keep thinking about Polly. That spills over into my story. I tell him that I've been wondering about her, where she is. I was working with her, the day that she stabbed Tom.

'Regrettable,' Gibson says. 'Sometimes, people are uncontrollable. You saw what happened. How did that affect you?'

I tell him that I didn't notice it until it had happened. I don't say how it made me feel. Honestly, I'm not really sure. I felt dull, that's the best way to describe it.

'Did you think that she was right to attack him?'

He didn't do anything, I say.

'No, he didn't. Not that we could see or hear.' *We. We* could see or hear. 'But there are often so many other things going on underneath the surface of us, aren't there? What he was saying to Polly, maybe that affected her in a way that's different to how it affected you. And me, as well. Maybe I would have reacted differently.' He smiles, the corners of his mouth gently pleased with the thought that's come into his head. 'What was the more truthful moment, do you think: what Tom was saying, or how Polly reacted?'

Polly's reaction. I don't even have to think about it.

'Because it was from her gut,' he says, trying to be reassuring. 'So, which was more interesting to you? Which made you ask more questions?'

Polly, again.

'Because it was so violent, so senseless,' he says, pleased that he knew the answer. That I am as predictable as he would hope.

I tell him no. I tell him that it was because I didn't see where the blade came from. It felt familiar, I say; watching Polly stab him. He glances up at me, and at my hands. Then he sits back, and he folds his own hands into his lap.

'Chan, what do you remember about where you come from?'

I tell him that I don't remember anything. I'm not sure how true that is. Faces, names, those words in that voice that digs deep into me and makes me feel sad and hopeful at the same time. But I don't tell him that.

'Because, that's good. That's good. This is where you come from, now; it's the truth. And this is where Polly comes from, and Tom. You're like brothers and sisters, really. That's it, all in this together, in this new beginning. We won't lie to you about that. But you have to remember: what Polly did, that was wrong. It wasn't here; or, it wasn't the person that she is *now*, you get that?'

I nod.

'I would hate to see anything thrown away, from her or from you. This is progression for you. You've been here such a short amount of time, and you've made such great strides. I see excellence in you, Chan.'

And with that, the session is over. Waiting outside to go in is Jonah. He smiles at me as I pass, and digs into his pockets, hands me another note, then he rushes inside. I don't read the note until I'm back in my room, his hand-writing this beautiful, delicate style, joined up and looped around, like one long, unbroken trail of ink.

I want to see you, the note says. *Find me.*

*   *   *

'Time for another trial,' the guard says. He leads me down the corridor, letting me walk a little ways in front of him. I know where we're going.

I ask him how long he's worked here, and he seems surprised.

'Inmates usually don't take an interest in us,' he says. 'Not saying it's not welcomed, but you're pretty much the first to ever ask me.' He pronounces everything drawled, his words sloppy, losing letters, changing others. *Intres; priddy; axe.* 'Three years now. Gibson brought me personally. We worked together before.'

I ask where.

'Now that's a secret. I mean, it's not, but it is for you. Loose lips sink ships.' We head to the outside, to the shell of the mall. 'So this time, you're just going to look around, okay? You go in there, and you see if there's anything you like the look of. Come back and tell me, and we'll see what we can do.' He folds his arms and stands at a real distance, the stretch of the mall between me and the shop. He shoves his hand through the air, like he's wafting something. 'Go on, haven't got all day,' he says.

The shop door is propped open. Inside, the stock is different. It's not stuff that I would want, not immediately. There are more expensive things in here – cases with jewels and gold bands. Nothing but shining, glittering gemstones throughout. Bright lights, so bright they're almost blinding. I've never seen anything like it.

I had a stone, once. I remember that. I was given it. I don't know what happened to it, or where it is now.

223

'I help you?' the shopkeeper asks. A different one. She's younger, much younger. Shaky delivery of her lines, a tiny bit too unnatural. Everything rehearsed for show.

I smile, say that I'm okay. She's uneasy, and I don't want her to be. I wonder if she's afraid of me, or something else. Is this a test for her or for me, I wonder. But her nervousness makes me nervous, and I feel my hands balling into fists. My nails digging into my palms just enough to hurt.

There's a noise behind us. Somebody else in the shop. I turn, and there's the butt of a striker in my face. The man holding it is wearing a mask, fully covered, not even a tiny sliver of his skin showing. He's out of shape, I can see that, but strong. Big arms, big chest, thick neck. Paunch where there shouldn't be one.

'Get down,' he says. He waves the weapon at the shop-keeper. 'Get down, hands behind your head.' The shopkeeper screams, and I –

I react. I grab the end of the striker while it's pointed away from me, and I yank it down. He's taller than me by a lot, and his arm bends. I whack his hand with my other fist, and he lets the striker go. He swings for me, but I duck away.

I'm acting instinctively. He can't get close. He's slow. I know that it doesn't matter how strong you are when you're this slow.

I flip the striker and lash out with the end, squeezing it so that it fizzes into life, but it doesn't, it's neutered. He moves backwards, but I go again, bringing it up into the bottom of his jaw. I hear his teeth clatter together, the crunch of something shifting, giving way, and he howls with his mouth closed, this deep-in-the-throat guttural sound. I kick him in the knee, straight on, and there's another click, another sound of something giving way. I wrap my fist around the striker, using it like reinforcement, and I swing it as he stumbles, as he slumps towards the ground, his bad knee shaking until he's fallen onto it, which probably hurts even more. I slam my other hand into the side of his face. There's another sharp crack, and he passes out. He falls to the side.

'Jesus Christ!' the shopkeeper screams. The guard runs inside. He checks on the man on the floor, pulls his mask off, puts his hand across his mouth to feel for breath, stabs two fingers at the man's neck.

'Get help!' he shouts to the shopkeeper, who runs off into the back, and I hear garbled words calling for backup, for a doctor. The guard looks up at me. 'What the hell did you do?' he asks, but it's not a real question. He can see what I did. He snatches the striker from my hand, and throws it into the dark of the shop.

I leave the building. I feel sick. I watch to see what happens as the medics arrive, as Doctor Gibson runs past. When he leaves, preceding the stretcher that is shunting the man who tried to attack me and the shopkeeper to the medical centre, he stops and stares at me. He doesn't look disappointed, or pleased, or anything; not really.

I have trouble sleeping for the first time that I can remember. Usually, there's a very set pattern. I get into bed and I lie down, and the lights go off; and I shut my eyes, because there's no sense having them open when all there is to see is the thin green light of the exit signs coming through the cracks in my door. Tonight I do that, but sleep doesn't happen. I feel myself getting antsy, itching underneath my blanket. I turn from side to side. I open my eyes, because I'm not tired. I shut them, and they don't want to stay closed.

So I stand up. I walk around my room, as little space as there is. I press against the walls, and I stretch my muscles. This feels good, and natural. I work them, exercising them. It feels like something that I need to do, the same burn in them that I felt outside, working on the road. I pace when I'm done. I listen to the sounds of others, shouting in their rooms. They lock the doors at night, apparently. I never knew.

There's a grinding in the walls, from the ventilation ducts. Something is going on inside there. I can hear voices, if I stretch up and get close enough. I move my bed, and I stand on it and listen. They're far away, distorted by being carried through to me this way. Little more than whispers.

'. . . when they wake up?'

'Just get it done and they won't even know. It's nothing.'

'Losing a day isn't nothing!' That voice is Gibson. I recognise it, even as angry as it sounds now. 'We don't know what effect that will have on them. It's crucial we deliver every night, you know that.'

'So tomorrow we find out. Nothing we can do. We'll get it working.'

'See that you do. There's going to be . . .'

I hear noises in the corridor: guards opening the doors, checking on us. I drag my bed back to where it should be and lie down, and shut my eyes. I don't know why, but I don't want them to see that I'm awake.

I sleep eventually, but it comes differently to the other nights. It's like I have to force myself, until it almost hurts, my desire to not be awake any more. And then, eventually, my eyes slide shut; and I feel them becoming harder to open. It's exhaustion, rather than whatever it is every other night, that makes me fall asleep. And for the first time since I remember being here, sleep feels natural, as if it's mine.

In the morning, there is no alarm; and for the first time since I got here, Gaia doesn't talk to me. The guards beat on the doors, telling us to wake up. Shouting, up and down the corridors, for us to obey them.

Gibson interviews us all. He asks us to line up, one by one (which we've never done before), and he spends the day talking to us: about whether we dreamt last night, about what we remember from before. I'm in the queue, and there's word going around about the sort of questions that he's posing: giving us situations and asking us how we would react in them; showing pictures and asking us what we can see in them. What we notice.

Jonah rushes up and pushes into the line behind me.

'Last night,' he says. He looks tired. 'You had trouble sleeping as well?'

I tell him that we all did. I explain what Gibson's asking, what's going on.

'You seem like you're excited about this,' he says. And I am, I think. I am. I reach for him, for a second. His hand, into mine. I don't know exactly why, but it's almost unbearably comforting. He squeezes; I squeeze back, and find myself wishing I could squeeze even harder.

We sit in the chairs, opposite each other, just like always. Gibson is rattled about something. He's not his usual self. He looks tired and he's sweating. The air conditioning isn't working, and every room with windows is stiflingly hot. He's got a fan in here, turned on his face, but it's barely doing anything. I'm being allowed to sweat, and the chair that I sit in is wet from the backs of those who were here before me.

'Did you sleep well last night?' he asks me, harried voice, twitchy hands.

I did, I tell him. He nods.

'You were moving around, exercising. You moved your bed.'

I ask him how he knows that. I already know the answer. They're watching me, all the time. But I ask him, because I want to know if he's going to lie to me.

'Just answer the question, Chan. You were awake?'

Yes.

'Good. Just, answer me. Makes both our lives easier. No withholding here, remember? So, you were awake. Why?'

I was too hot.

'So you exercised.'

Yes.

'Even though you were hot.'

Yes.

'You also looked at the vents.'

To see if they were working yet.

'But they weren't. So then you went to sleep.'

Yes.

'And how do you feel today? Different, the same?'

Tired.

'Did you dream, when you finally slept?'

I don't know. I don't remember.

'But, you feel okay? What do you remember?'

I remember yesterday. I remember working on the road. I remember—

'But apart from that. Before this. Do you remember anything?'

No.

'Look at this picture.' He brings up an image on his tablet, black ink on a white background. There are shapes there, amongst the swirls and blotches of darkness: a bat; a spaceship; a face that, in profile, looks like my mother's.

My mother.

'What do you see?' he asks, and I shake my head.

I tell him that I see a bat. The biggest thing, the most obvious thing. He nods. We're done. But I can tell, looking at Gibson now, stressed and panicked, that something has changed. I can *feel* it.

I have to be quick, I know. I have a few minutes between getting into my room at night and lights out, and I have to find some way to stay awake. I have to force myself.

I keep my eyes open for as long as possible. I don't lie down. I stand against the wall, and then I slump, and I know that I'm slumping, but I can't help it.

Then my eyes are shut, and I think – before I sleep – how I have failed.

I see Polly while I'm eating breakfast. No sign of Jonah, and I don't know how to get hold of him. I want to talk to him. His note, scrunched up in my pocket; I can feel it, like it's hot, burning a hole to my skin. I'm on a table with people who I know, but who I don't need to remember. One of them is enormous, bigger than Tom, bigger than pretty much anybody else I've ever seen. He's so large that the spoon for his cereal looks almost comically small in his hand, and he has three bowls of the stuff to sustain him. I haven't seen him before. But then, I feel like I have. I draw away from him. Scared, a little: not just his size, what it represents.

So I look away from him, trying to not make eye-contact. That's when I see her, in the corridor, being escorted by guards. They're leading her somewhere, down towards Gibson's office. She's shackled, her hands tied. Her metal hand doesn't stop twitching the whole time. She's been tearing at herself, I can tell: scratch marks down her face, across her scalp. She looks sickly, eyes red, mouth drooping. She looks at me. And she knows me, I can tell. Something in our eyes reflects.

On the road, I'm working with a different partner, but Jonah is there as well. I see him on the tarmac, working; the shape of him, and it's so familiar to me. I feel calm – only for a second but I carry that feeling, try to clutch it to my gut. We're laying pavement today, putting down the new tarmac. There are guns which blow out foam that we use to fill in the holes we made before, and it expands and hardens in seconds to fasten the road back together. After it's sprayed by one person, the other needs to flatten it straight away, dragging this long stick along the line of the road. And that's it. Repeat that, hundreds of times. I'm the one with the gun. I spray, and Jonah waves at me. When we take a break, he runs over and asks me how I am, even though we're not partnered. Nice questions. Nothing about the tests. Just concern, and I can tell he wants to say more, but doesn't.

I tell him that I'm fine. I want to say so much more, but I'm not sure what, so we keep talking, keep asking and answering. When the break is over, my partner asks him if he wants to swap. Jonah doesn't hesitate to say yes.

As soon as we're together, we move down the road a little, to work on our own section. On his knees, smoothing out sections of the road, he talks again, but more softly this time. At first it's hard to hear him, through the mask, so I move closer to him.

'I've missed you,' he says.

I tell him that I have missed him too. That I don't understand why. That I don't even actually know him.

He says, 'I've wondered if we knew each other before. Haven't you wondered?'

I tell him that I don't know what happened before. We've been told it's not important.

'But maybe this is the truth,' he says. 'They say the truth is in front of us. And you're in front of me.' He stops working and looks up at me, wiping the outside of his faceplate so that I can see his eyes. 'It's as if I remember you. I don't remember much, but sometimes I read something – a book, from the library – and it's familiar, like I've known it before. And that's how I feel when we talk. Familiar. Don't you remember anything like that?'

I tell him that I remember something from when I was a child. A voice, a woman.

'Your mother?'

I think so, I say.

'Well, maybe more will come,' he says. 'Or maybe it stays in the past, faded out. Maybe everything now is about moving forward.' And he doesn't say that he might see me in that moving, but it's implied. He looks away, and I keep staring, in case he looks back.

On our way back to the facility, I put the masks back into their box. It's our duty to make sure that they're charged and ready for the next day. If they're not, we won't have enough air, and it'll be our fault if something goes wrong. That's one of the things we're taught: personal responsibility.

I walk down the hall of the centre, past the room where they induct people, the showers, the dining halls; past Gibson's office. The door is shut, which means he's in conversation with somebody. The corridor continues on to the wing where our rooms are, past the maintenance rooms, the filters for the air conditioner, the electricity generator – we run our own, off the grid of the mainline, too far from the city to tap into theirs – and the laundry.

I want to see where they were taking Polly.

There's a room at the end of the corridor, sealed with a solid door, heavier than the ones on our rooms. There's no little window panel to see through. I try to push it. It's locked. I can hear noise from inside, though; murmurs. Polly, muttering something, I think. I wonder if she's in trouble; whether she needs my help.

Something feels right about how I'm standing; how I creep backward, until I'm flush with the wall opposite the door, and then turn my body, so that my shoulder is aimed at the wood, ready for impact. I've done this before. I can feel the pain in my shoulder already, like an echo from before; an echo of what I'll feel when I've done this again. I put my foot on the wall, ready to kick off, as much of a run at the door as possible, and—

'No,' she says. I can see her, then; the light of her body, her face, at the crack underneath the door. 'No.' I kneel down and look at her; at the tiniest corner of her eye that I can see. 'Why are you here?'

I ask her if she's okay.

'They are making me sleep.'

Making you?

'Something from the holes in the walls. Makes me sleep, I think. Why do they want me to forget? What did I do before?'

I don't know.

'Why can't they let me remember? I do not even care how bad it was. I want to know.'

Me too. She tells me that I should go, that I can't help her; that she'll be out soon and she'll find me when she is.

233

I agree to leave. I put my finger under the door, and she does the same. Our fingertips touch. And even that feels familiar; as though I've felt her skin before, somehow. Somewhere.

In the minute before I sleep, I look at the vent in my room. This is what Polly was talking about. I don't want Gibson or the guards to see me doing it, so I have to be careful. I don't know how they're watching us. Must be something in the walls, in the ceiling. The light, maybe. So I have to hide what I'm up to. I begin by exercising, pushing against the walls, bending my legs, cracking my arms behind my head. Moving as I do it.

Soon I'm close enough to the vent to see that the air coming from it is, for a brief moment, tainted; as pale a smoke as any I've ever seen. Like the steam that sometimes rose from the depths of somewhere I was before I was here; I have a a memory of it turning to wisps before it reached the higher floors. Or the mist that came off the top of a stream that I know I once saw, where the water that flowed down beat itself against its own surface, briefly, churning, spraying itself upwards.

And then I know I'm too close to it; because tiredness comes like a fist to the face; and I'm falling, falling down, wondering if I will die. I hit the ground in my room, and that shakes me a little. Awake just enough, I crawl to the bed, wanting to wake up there, knowing that will look more natural. On my way I take a pen from my table, and once in bed I hide myself under the cover. On my forearm I write *gas from the vents*, in case whatever happens while

234

I'm asleep means that I could forget what I've found. I don't want to forget it. I can't.

I see the note on my arm when I go to the showers, ready for the water from the faucet to clean every bit of dirt off me, ready to be put back all over again once I get out there onto the roads. I see it, and don't even have to read it. Something clicks inside me, the note nudging a brick through the wall in my memory that was blocking it off, allowing the events of the night before to rush back to me.

It must have been a pretty weak wall.

I scrub my arm first, getting the ink off, watching the water that comes off my skin blacken with it. Agatha used to say that water was purifying, that it had the effect of making you feel cleaner than you actually were; that that cleanliness was a lie worth telling yourself, if it helped you to sleep better at night.

I remember that, but I don't know where it came from. I can't even remember who Agatha was; only that she *was*, and we lived somewhere very, very different. I know that they are making us sleep, but not for our health; it's to change our memories, to enable them to rebuild us. Who we are here is not who we *are*. And they – Gibson, whoever else runs this place – are taking our selves away from us.

I wash my hair, my face. I remember something about my hair. It used to be so short, because of lice, because of stuff in their bites that could make you sick. That's why it was short. Why is it longer now? Was that my choice? When I'm clean, I stand underneath the dryer and let it completely buffet my body, pushing my skin, my flesh, forcing the droplets of water off it until I'm totally dry. Get dressed, go to the canteen. Take a seat, and sit with people who I know or don't know, and talk about the day. I stay quiet, and I eat my food, and I look around. No sign of Jonah. I want to ask him about what he remembers, tell him what happened last night. I want to understand why he's so familiar to me. We could have grown up together, and I understand now that we wouldn't know. We look different, so I know that we're not related: our skin colour, our hair, everything about us. But we *know* each other.

And maybe Jonah isn't his name. Chan, my name: maybe that doesn't come from who I was before here, either.

Tom comes in. He's stitched up, healed and cleaned. He's lost weight, it looks like; or maybe he's just sagging from the recovery. He raises his hand to wave to the table, like we're all waiting for him, all anticipating nothing more than his coming back to us. There's applause, and I don't see where it starts; and then I spy Gibson in the corridor, clapping, grinning. Tom takes a little bow, and he winces, something from his injury still stinging. I'm sure I've never met him before this time, but I don't know how I'm so positive of that. There's something, a niggling feeling, that his presence in my life is new. Doesn't matter. I feel bad that he was stabbed. I feel bad that Polly is in solitary. Both acts make me feel the same, but one should be worse, I'm sure.

'Tom has made excellent progress.' Gibson steps into the room, and he half-shouts this to us. 'But he won't be on rotation for a few weeks, okay? So go easy on him. Let him know how pleased you are that he's back with us. Somebody:

give him your seat, would you?' He watches and waits to see who steps away from the table first.

I do. I stand up and I push my chair back, and I smile, the biggest smile that I can manage. Gibson nods at me. I'm doing it because it's the right thing to do, because he was injured and he should have a seat; but also because I want Gibson to see that I'm on his side, that I'm making progress.

And he does. He comes to me, and he puts his hand on my shoulder, and he says, in a quiet voice, 'That was very kind of you, Chan.'

I don't say a word in reply.

Out on the road, and I'm working with strangers. Different partners on a different stretch of tarmac. We're back to digging up the path, and my partner – a smaller boy called Graham, who can't handle picking up the debris, and can barely hack up the road to the extent that it needs to be done to actually feel like we're making any progress – keeps moaning, whining that he's hot, that he feels sick in his suit. That he can't breathe properly. He's trying to take breaths that are too big. I tell him that, tell him that if he breathes softly, gently, he won't feel nearly as poorly. The masks purify the air, make it cooler for us. It's not like breathing normal air; it's concentrated. You need to relax into it. If he does that, it will help him to keep working. That's what we're here for. He's not been at this facility for long – less time than me, and this is only his first day on the roads; he's so not prepared for what it takes.

It's only when he starts to cry that I realise there's a solution here to a problem that I had barely begun trying to solve. I need to not fall asleep at night, because it seems like that's when we forget. The gas makes me fall asleep, makes me forget. But with one of the masks on, I won't be affected by it.

'I want to go back,' Graham sobs. 'I'm going to be sick.' And then he is, all over the suit he's wearing, all over the road. It fizzes as it hits the blistering tarmac, cooking, evaporating away. I tell him that I'll escort him back and he nods, pleased. He wears his re-breather until we get back to town, and then I tell him to take it off; that I'll clean it and put it back for him. And I do, but for the benefit of anybody watching, it looks as though I'm putting back mine. I'm not. That stays inside my suit all day, and after I change it's hidden away underneath my clothes, and then when I have a chance to go back to my room I drop onto the bed like I'm exhausted, and slide it out and under the covers, slipping it beneath my mattress, ready for when it's time for bed.

I go to bed the way I always do: on my side, bundled up under the cover. And then I slip my hand between the wall and the mattress, lift it just enough to pull out the re-breather then slide it back to myself, all under the covers. I put it on my mouth, head hidden from whoever might be watching, and breathe. I hear the sound of the vents, the hiss of incoming sleep, and I stay awake. I checked the volume of air on the mask earlier, so I know there's four hours' worth, but I take light breaths, shallow breaths. I stay awake for an hour or two, because I don't want to make any noise, or alarm anybody. I want them to think I'm asleep like the rest of them.

Eventually I feel tired. Not fake tired, forced on me; just tired.

And when I sleep, I dream. I don't remember the dream when I wake up, the mask empty, still on my face, the covers pulled up and over my head; and I don't remember my dream when I get dressed, when I shower, when I eat my breakfast, when I head back outside to the road, returning the re-breather to be charged, taking a new one. I don't remember it as I work all day, pulling up chunks of the road, work that feels as though it's designed to exhaust you. I try to breathe through the re-breather as little as possible, taking in real air instead, as warm and stale as that is, to make sure I've got enough air in the re-breather to get me through most of the night. I don't remember it at dinner, or when I'm reading or getting ready for bed, or looking for Jonah, but somehow failing to find him, feeling a hole, a desire to see him. Through all that I don't remember my dream.

But then I'm lying in bed, under the covers with the mask on my face, listening to the slow, soft hiss of air that's designed to send me to sleep and make me forget myself; and finally I remember my dream.

A woman, with hair knotted and long down her back; her face damaged from time and years of fighting, of surviving; her lip destroyed and rebuilt, a scar like a plait of muscle and healed tissue; and her strong arms holding me as she tells me that I will be alright, as I watch the dead remains of my mother burning at my feet.

I wake up, and it's dark. I don't remember waking up in the dark before. Here, we go to sleep when the sun's setting and wake when it's rising. I've never woken in the dark.

Except, I have. Just not in this place. I remember opening my eyes into a different sort of darkness, and hearing voices, the sounds of others in the distance, the noises of everything I knew shattering and breaking. There's a voice here now, as well, and for a moment I think that they've found me out, discovered my mask, that I'll be joining Polly in solitary. I'll be forced back into sleeping, into forgetting.

But it's not that. It's Gaia's voice, in my head. Like when she asks us questions, in the morning, but less gentle, more driven, more forceful. There's something different in her tone. *Everything begins anew*, she says. *There is no war; only peace. There is no imprisonment; only freedom. There is no cruelty; only kindness.* Words, over and over, repeated in cycles, and then new phrases dropped in. *There is no conflict; only resolution.* Ways to behave; things that I've heard Gibson repeat, tell us himself. *There are no lies; only truth.* There's a tranquillity to Gaia's words. Then it stops, a pause, as if she's taking a breath.

Her voice is replaced by a screeching, a noise that's utterly inhuman. It whines its way into my skull, as though it's a part of me, somehow inside me, coming from me and everything around me. And I cover my ears, but that does no good. I try to not make a sound, to not scream, because I don't want them to know I can hear it. I wonder if this happens every night, and if we just sleep through it. I don't know what it's doing to us, what it's supposed to be doing. My eyes water and my skin itches, and I scratch at my head.

I can feel my nails digging into the skin, making trenches; pain the only thing to block out the noise.

And then it's gone, and Gaia's voice comes back, a soothing balm, a relief. *There is no pain; only resignation*, it says. I breathe deeply into the mask. I don't sleep for the rest of the night. I keep my eyes pinned open until she stops telling me what I should feel and think, who I should be, until I see light and hear birdsong, and Gaia casually asks me, as if the night never happened, how I slept.

As I'm walking to eat breakfast, I see Jonah. He straightens his back when he sees me, opens his eyes wide.

'Chan,' he says. He takes my hands. His palms are warm against mine. I didn't know how cold my skin was until now. 'I tried to find you. They've taken me off roads duty – said it's for the best.' He pulls me closer, so that our heads – our faces – are nearly touching. 'I think they're keeping us apart, and I don't know why.'

I say that it's his imagination. I want him to calm down, to feel better. I'm not sure he's wrong, but I can't tell him that. I don't know how he'll react.

'They put me on comms, said it'll be good to get me out on the antennas; it might get me a job working the walls, when we get put in a city.'

The walls. I can suddenly picture them. I've seen them. I know how tall they are, and how imposing, how they curve over as they climb to the sky, as though they're cradling the city they enclose, like fingers, cupping people into a palm. He keeps talking, telling me about what his new work involves: the wires, and the panels. His job is to pull them back, to understand where they run, what makes the radio signals work. He talks about how, when it's all fixed, Pine City have an easier time sending messages to and from the larger cities.

'I'm not even sure what they know about us up here,' he says. 'There are satellites in the sky above us, above the planet, but they're not connected to us here at the moment. We're isolated.'

I think about the satellites, drifting somewhere above the clouds. Something clicks. It's like a light coming on, through the fog in my mind. 'I asked if they ever send us to the city with people from here, and Gibson said that they try not to, that individuality is easier if you've got no baggage. But I want to be sent with you. Is that strange? But I feel like I know—'

'Chan?' A voice from the doorway. It's Gibson. He's leaning in, clinging to the frame, casually. 'May I speak with you?'

Jonah lets go of my hands. My own hands are warm now, heated by his. He doesn't look at Gibson. We knew each other before this. I know that now. I can tell, I can feel it. It's so close a memory that it's almost tangible. But for Jonah, it's in his gut, nothing more. He's scrambling for a connection he only barely understands.

I tell Jonah that I'll be fine, that I'll find him later, and that we can continue talking then; and he smiles, reassured. I follow Gibson to his office, and he waits for me to go inside first, pulls the door shut tight after me with the closest thing to a slam I've ever heard him produce.

* * *

242

There's a holo in the middle of the room: a glitch-green view of what I know immediately is my bedroom; and the shape of me in the bed, facing the wall. The camera cannot see my face, which is good. There's no sound. Gibson indicates that I should sit down.

I ask him what the video is. I'm playing along. Is that me?

'This is something that we do for your safety,' he tells me. 'This is to make sure you're safe at night.'

I want to know why we wouldn't be safe. It's all about saying it in the right way, sounding surprised, but not too surprised. I trust him, that's the key. I'm surprised how easily lying comes to me.

'Because you've all come from places that you don't want to remember. We don't trick you, here. We want you to be better. Because if you're better, the world can be better. You see that, don't you?'

I nod.

'So now you have to be straight with me. How have you been sleeping?'

I tell him that I sleep well. Every night the same, really. I don't remember it.

He sighs. 'You never wake up? You never dream?' He doesn't look at me when he waits for my answer, as if he knows how this goes. I know what happens next; he's got video from last night, of me reacting to the noise that I heard. And, sure as anything, he says, 'Play,' and the video begins. I move around in the bed; I bring my hands up to my ears, visible through the covers, the shape of them moving; my fingers creeping over the edge of the blanket,

243

mingling with my hair. 'You look as though you can hear something,' he says.

I ask him what there would be to hear. I say that I must have been dreaming.

'You've already told me that you don't dream, Chan.'

I reply that I told him I don't remember if I do. Different thing. He nods. He seems tired. I don't really have any sympathy for him, if he is tired. I ask about where I was before this. Who I was. I say that maybe that will help me remember what my dreams are about. Or don't they want us to remember our dreams?

'You were you. I've already told you that. You were you, but worse. That's all we do, all I am doing here, trying to make you better. There's a version of you that you could be, and you haven't realised it yet. I have. Why wouldn't you want to be the best you that you can be?'

I ask why we don't remember the bad things from before; they might be important, to help make us who we are.

'Because the brain works hard to forget things that hurt it. It doesn't want bad things to be remembered. It wants the good. We try and give you the good here. That's what revision is.' He sighs again, and waves his hand. That's my cue to leave, and I do; and I work all day, on the roads, reserving the air in the re-breather again, staying awake for as long as I can that night, not breathing in the gas, waiting for the voice of Gaia in the night that I now understand I really have to ignore.

They teach us history as a way of making sure we're prepared to re-enter civilisation when we reach the cities.

There's a lot to cover. Some people remember the history, but some don't. They want us to know it before we get back to the cities, wherever we're sent, because then we can hit the ground running. We can start being productive members of society.

Today, we're talking about the weather, about what's changed over the centuries here on Earth. There used to be snow, they say. Sometimes it snowed as late as April. The spring began in March, sunlight breaking through the cold ground; it would warm the planet, but not like now. Now, the heat is brutal everywhere. Now, huge parts of the planet have been lost to it, are nearly uninhabitable. There's a poem, an old poem that she tells us. April showers brought May flowers. We have to remember these things we've lost, because if we strive, maybe we can get them back, see those May flowers again.

May. Mae.

I can feel something, in my head. The fog in there being lifted.

'Chan?'

The teacher has stopped, is trying to get my attention.

I say that I'm listening, I am. I'm trying. But she goes back to talking about the heat, the parts of the world that were hottest even before the worst happened. There was ice in the coldest parts of the world, she says, but the heat melted it, and the sea levels rose. Some of the hottest coun-tries – Australia, she says, which was a country far away from here, nearly the other side of the world – were completely lost to the sea, one of the greatest tragedies in

245

human history. This is what we don't want to repeat; what we're trying to avoid.

'Australia,' I say, hearing my own voice out loud, for what feels like the first time – mine, *mine* – and everything is suddenly there, in my grasp.

NINE

Keeping it from them – the guards, the wardens, Gibson – is the hardest part.

No, that's not true. Remembering. That's the hardest part. There's a lot to be said for having holes in your memory; or, maybe, one large hole, where everything has fallen out, and all that's left is the clarity of the now. I sit on the toilet, the only place here where I'm mostly certain that they won't be watching me, and I shake; I hold myself and I try to keep it together while everything comes back to me, clawing its way out of that hole.

My mother, and everything she did for me, her whole life. What I did for her in the end. Agatha, and how she looked after us, how she tried to protect me. How she lied to me, and I felt betrayed when I learned of it; and how she died, pointlessly, lost at a moment that I wasn't watching out for her. Jonah, who I know here and who I knew then, and whatever it was that we had: something so fleeting and so precious. And Mae, who I tried to save, because I wanted her to have everything that I did – security, safety, even in that awful place – and then even more. As much as I could give her.

247

The Australia itself; a ship that we were never meant to be on, that we were stranded on, not by the sins of our ancestors, but by the horrifying decisions of those who judged them, then left them to rot, to die, to kill themselves and each other. And then the fall, and my escape. Alala, Ziegler, The Runner. I can remember everything.

It takes me so long to get myself together, to stop feeling dizzy from the memories falling back into place. I miss the rest of class; when I come out of the toilet I'm taken to my room, told to lie down. I'm running a fever, they say. They tell me to sleep, but I don't want to, because I don't have my mask, don't have the oxygen to keep me awake, to stop me breathing in their false air and hearing their messages. I've got my memories back, and I can't lose them now.

They tell me it will be okay. They sedate me.

I can see the history of who I am slipping away from me. I grab at it, but my memories are weak – wisps, like smoke.

When I wake up, my mouth is dry and my head pounds. I remember something from last night; something that I wasn't meant to forget. I reach, for names, for places.

On my skin, letters I scratched onto myself with my own nails.

MAE.

There it is. All of it, back again. The wall, whatever they do at night to build it up, won't hold. I know exactly how to tear it down.

I sit at breakfast, first to the table, waiting to see who my companions are. I'm praying for Jonah. I don't know who

I'm praying to; I just uttered words under my breath, desperate to see him, to show him what I know.

He's first in. Jonah comes through the door, and he meets my eyes. He smiles, relaxed and comforted. That warms me like his hands did. I try to look serious and calm, to let him know something's important, that we need to talk.

'I've been waiting for you,' I say, as he sits down opposite me.

'Are you okay?'

I don't answer. I don't know how to answer. 'Do you dream of anything, Jonah?'

'At night?'

'While you're asleep. Do you dream?'

'No,' he says. He scratches at his neck, at the scars. 'No, I don't.'

'Do you remember anything about before?'

'I remember that it was bad, and that I wasn't happy. I wasn't productive.'

'No,' I say, wanting to grab him and shake him, to knock some sense into him and bring back everything the way I've done for myself. But then our tablemates join us: Tom, and some new girl, who's so scared and twitchy that I know she can't have been here for long. Jonah and I stop talking. We don't stop glancing at each other, though; we're desperate to be out of this room so that we can talk. Jonah doesn't know that it's deeper, for me, that desperation: I want to be out of this room, this facility, this town.

'I'm feeling better,' Tom says, sitting down, reaching for the juice that's in the middle of the table. 'The doctors say I'll be back working next week.'

'Good,' I say. I look at the new girl. 'What's your name?' I ask her.

'Nadine,' she says.

'I'm Chan. Where do you come from?'

She stammers. Unsure of what to say. 'From here,' she finally manages.

'No, you don't,' I tell her. 'You don't, you can't. You came from somewhere else.'

'Chan,' Jonah says, and he reaches over and touches my arm. More memories: the two of us helping each other, clinging to each other, fighting people who wanted to hurt us. Me kissing him, or him kissing me. But he died, or he was lost. I lost him, but here he is.

'You're scaring her,' he says.

He's right. She's terrified of me, of this place, of how little she knows herself. I remember being her, how it felt. I stay quiet. I eat my breakfast and I watch Jonah through the corners of my eyes; and he stares at me, and his gaze feels like it's etching something permanent onto my skin.

We're on the road and I hate it. I'm sweating, and trying to use as little of the oxygen in my re-breather as possible, but breathing is hard. It feels like there's sand in my lungs. Today I'm working with people I don't know, and I try to ask them what they're doing working here, doing as they're told, not questioning anything. And they all say the same thing: it's what they've been told to do. There's no purpose beyond that, nothing personal to it. They don't want anything. They're just digging up a road and relaying it, over and over, hoping to reach the city, the promise of something much better, of making themselves better along with it. And I realise that I can't do it anymore.

'I quit,' I say, and I walk off, away from them. I go back to town and I stand in the middle of the main street. There are buildings here that used to be shops. I can see their dusty signs, indications that there was something here before this. *Drugstore* and *Market* and a building called *Tunes*; clothing stores and technology stores and more, on and on, down the street. There's a playground to one side, iron wrought into shapes that have twisted and rusted. Families came here once; children played on these things. There are houses everywhere, spiralling off from this space. *Summer Rentals!* one sign shouts, in peeling black letters. This place was good, once. It was what life is meant to be; or some part of it. This is what I dreamt of when I lived on the ship, when there was talk of somewhere else, a planet – a home – that we were meant to find.

In the distance I can see radio towers, on a hill not too far away. I start to walk there. I need to speak to Jonah. I need to know if he can remember what I can; and if he can't, if I can make him.

He's up a tower. I know it's him from his shape, his gangly limbs wrapped around the metal rungs of the ladder. I've seen him climb ladders before; I've watched him climb, and I've watched him fall. I remember. I shout up to him.

'What are you doing here?' I beckon him down, and he comes.

'Are you working here now as well?' he says.

251

'No,' I say. I grab his arm and pull him away, off to one side. I don't want anybody to see us. 'You don't remember anything from before?'

'I've told you.'

'We were together. On a ship, a spaceship.' He looks blank, as though he doesn't understand. 'We were up there, in the stars. The ship was called Australia. That's where we came from. A ship like a country.'

He looks angry at that. He doesn't believe me, or doesn't want to. He pulls away, tries to walk away from me. I don't let him.

'Your name is Jonah, and you're older than I am, I think. Not by much. You didn't have parents, because they died when you were young.' He blinks. It should have hurt him more to learn that. Maybe he had already assumed. 'You were brought up by the Pale Women, who taught you about their book. Remember their testaments? Remember how you wore that spiked collar, that made those holes in your neck, tore your skin?'

'I don't remember,' he says; but he touches the suit he's wearing at the neck, presses it in, feeling for them, like that'll prove if I'm telling the truth.

'I freed you. Or you freed yourself. However it happened. The ship fell apart. Remember the Lows? Remember Rex? How they tried to kill us, how they tried to take the ship? But we found a way to escape. We found a way to come here.'

'I don't . . .' He doesn't finish the sentence. I grab his helmet and pull it off, and I put my hand on the back of his head and draw him close to me and I kiss him. Our lips press together, feeling the heat of our breath on each other's mouths. We've done this once before, and then he died; or I thought that he did.

I remember it, and I wish that he did.

I hope that kissing him wakes him up.

He pushes me away. 'I don't remember,' he says. He's confused, his eyes wet, suddenly shocked. He doesn't remember. It didn't work. 'I have to fix the radio tower,' he tells me; and he sounds sad as he says it. There's a finality to it: he doesn't want to hear any more of what I've got to say to him.

As I walk back, leaving him to climb the tower, not even glancing down at me, I look at the boarded-up stores, the broken signs, the smashed glass of the roof. Along the way is the shop that they bring us to, to test us, to see how we'll react. It's empty now, a blank slate of empty shelves and vacant counter. I try the door and it opens. I assumed they'd keep it locked. I assumed wrong. I walk to the counter, then clamber over to the back. This is where the shopkeepers disappear after our tests are done. I hope I can find somewhere quiet where I can sit, where nobody will know where I am.

Instead, I find a door that leads to another door, and I go through and find not a quiet room but a warehouse containing everything that they use in the shop, shelves stretching endlessly away. Here's the food, the clothes, the weapons: a box with strikers – new models – and knives. And then there are boxes labelled Frank, Dolly, Andrew, Grant. I run along the shelves, looking for familiar names.

Tom. Polly. Jonah.

Chan.

I yank my box down from the shelves. It's light, but not empty. Inside it is my knife. I *know* it. I remember it. It's not much, but it's mine. They must have taken it from me when I came here. It's been waiting for me. I can't take it, I know. Not yet. They'll notice. They might even be watching, though I can't see any camera drones anywhere. I can't have them become any more suspicious, or they'll do to me what they've done to Polly, put me—

I hear voices from outside. I thrust my box back into its place and run along the shelves to the other end of the huge room. There's a door here, an exit, but it's locked, a thick bar driven across it.

Okay. So, stay still. Wait. They may not know I'm here.

I recognise Gibson's voice talking with the guards. They're discussing a patient, a trial they're setting up.

'I want everything in here to be his, from before. As much as we've got. Do we have pictures of his family?'

'We can get them.'

'So, put them in frames, like they're the stock photos. See what he's drawn to, if he recognises them.' I can hear Gibson walking around, inspecting the boxes, the many items on the shelves. *Don't come back here. Don't come back here.* I'm holding my breath, crouched low, trying to keep them from hearing me, or seeing me.

I hear Gibson's feet slapping on the ground, coming closer and closer. Then there's a noise: something in the distance. A high-pitched trill, over and over. An alarm. Gibson and everyone here with him drop everything and run out of the warehouse, slamming the door behind them.

I've not heard this alarm before; I don't know what it indicates. I follow them, but they're so focused on getting wherever they're going that they don't see me. I hang back, cautious and careful. I don't know that they'll trust me at the moment, if I'm caught.

Outside the main doors to the facility that lead to our rooms, to Gibson's office and the food halls, I see Polly. She's free, somehow. She's got her arm wrapped around another person, and at first I think it's affectionate, that that's how close they are; but then, as I get closer, as the wardens and Gibson slow down, putting their hands out in front of them, shouting to her as calmly as they can manage, their voices carrying on the wind – 'Please, think about this, Polly; think about what you're doing!' – I see that it's the new girl from breakfast she's holding. If she looked scared them, now she's almost completely still and lifeless; not dead, just not entirely there. In shock.

I've forgotten her name already.

Polly's flesh is torn from her prosthetic. I can see the cylinders working in it, the liquid metal sluicing up and down inside transparent tubes as she twitches her fingers. Her shirt is torn as well, ripped away at the chest. I see scars there, exposed, faded but still the tops of the letters that I once watched her carve into her own skin the day she killed her predecessor; the day that I killed my mother.

Her name isn't Polly. I don't know if it's ever been Polly. I don't know if that was her name before she became leader of the Lows – before she became Rex – but I know it doesn't suit her. She's Rex. Nothing more, nothing less. And she's alive.

Rex says something something that I don't hear. I get closer, because I want to know. I don't care if Gibson sees me now. Some of the other prisoners – that's what we are – have crept off their duties to watch this. I'm not scared of Gibson, and I'm not scared of Rex.

I've already killed her once, and I can do it again.

'Let me go,' she says. Her voice sounds calmer than it ever did on Australia. Her hair has been cut back in the crudest way, hanging at different lengths. I can see cuts on her head from where she's mangled her scalp. She looks different than when we were on Australia. Softer. They must have tried to treat the scars, to whittle them away with lasers. They were too deep, I think. Too much a part of her.

I think about rushing forward, taking her by surprise. Pulling a striker from the holsters at the backs of the wardens and slamming it into her face.

But I don't have a chance. She doesn't see the guard that's crept up behind her; she doesn't see the fizz of their striker as it slams into the back of her head. She convulses, vomits, collapses to the floor. The other wardens rush forward, Gibson stamping his foot excitedly, running his hands through what's left of his hair. She's dragged off, sick and spit trailing from her slack mouth. She knew that something was wrong here; that she wasn't the person she was being turned into. Something of Rex survived. She killed people I loved, tried to take everything away from me and came so close to succeeding. She was ruthless and cold; the worst person that I have ever known. Maybe that's why it didn't work, why she didn't become Polly: the rot was simply set too deep inside her for it to ever be cleaned out.

She looks at me as they pull her away. She looks right at me, and I know that she recognises me as well. And something else, something deeper. A shared understanding, that we are not meant to be here.

TEN

Gibson asks me to tell him about my day, but I ask him about Rex – about Polly.

'What happened?' I ask. He pours himself a glass of water.

'You want some?' he asks, gesturing at the bottle.

'Yes please,' I say. They've taught us good manners here. That's the first thing they try and get us to learn. I can't show any signs of slipping now. He hands it over: chilled glass, chilled water. It's immediately slippery in my warm hands.

'Polly is a difficult case. Do you understand what we're trying to do here, Chan? I mean, really do. How this works?' He sits down and he drinks from his glass, half of it gone in two gulps. He wipes his mouth.

'You want us to be productive members of society.'

'I'm a doctor,' he says. 'I've always been a doctor. That's what I wanted to be from the minute I knew that there was a way to help this world. So that's what I try to do. There were attempts at ways to deal with criminals before this, you understand.' That's the first time anybody here has used that word – criminals – to describe what we are. No, what they *think* we are; how they treat us. He must notice me react to this; something passes across his face, so quickly that I almost miss it. I want to say that I'm not a criminal. I haven't done anything wrong.

'Crime can't be tolerated now. There's not enough room in the cities, and I mean that quite literally. So, we need solutions. This is one.'

He brings up a screen. 'Show *Brain*,' he says, and a picture appears: a lump of something organic, swirled in patterns, like a maze. 'This is what's in your head – in everybody's heads. And it controls you: all your desires, your fears, your hopes. It develops over your life, and some- times that development is . . . stunted. There are crucial points – toddler, teenager – where external forces can alter the brain's growth, changing who you are becoming. That can make you more susceptible to other external forces. It can make you selfish. But we need to make sure everyone understands that it's not all about you, never is, never will be. Living life in our society is about the people around you; the people who brought you up; the people you'll bring up. It starts with your home. Do you know where you lived?'

'No,' I say. I wonder what happens to the brain when it's lying.

'It wasn't a good place. It wasn't. I can promise you that, and you can choose to believe me or not, but know that I wouldn't lie to you. We tell you the truth. No sense in us not. What happened to you . . .' He drinks the rest of his water, and he holds the empty glass in between his hands, cradling it, swirling the last few drops around the bottom of the glass in a spiral. 'There's a theory, in psychology. The idea of nature versus nurture, where one is what's inherently inside you (your genes, the things that make you who you are), and the other is the external influences I mentioned. So, we're here to see that the nature doesn't win. You're genetically predisposed to being a criminal, Chan. You can't help it. Your ancestors did terrible things, and there are triggers, signifiers inside you that say that you will follow their path. You're what the people who came before you made you. The environment that you grew up in only made that worse. So, here, we change that. We get rid of the only nurture that you've known, replacing it with something new, something that can – cross your fingers – balance out the nature part of you: the part that cannot help who you are on a base genetic level. Does that make sense?'

I nod. I don't know why he's telling me this. He's only ever been vague before. He's telling me all of his secrets, all of the things that go on behind the scenes. That's a phrase that Ziegler used, that he taught me. He took me to see a play on our third meeting, a performance in a park. He said it would help me understand the city a bit more, and what people in it are like and what they value: the art, the music, life itself. It was a comedy, hundreds and hundreds of years old. A man dressed as a donkey – 'An *ass*!' Ziegler said, explaining the joke, explaining the dual meaning – and fairies and magic, all set in this world; a world that I barely understood. But I didn't get it. Before it, I saw the actors in their costumes; when it finished, one of them spoke to the audience, to thank them for coming. That's not the real world. That's a story that's nothing more. There's nothing behind it. It's a lie. Zigler told me that everything in the city is a lie, really; and behind the scenes of everything we're told is make-believe, layers upon layers of pretence in the stories we tell, or that we are told.

Layers of lies.

And as he speaks I know that Gibson is wrong. I'm not a bad person, and my mother wasn't a bad person. Most people on the ship were not bad people. They were trying, and they were surviving. My father *was* a bad person, however, but he wasn't from Australia. I never knew him. He was nothing to me. I survived Australia, and it made me who I am. And that's what Gibson wants to take away from me.

He can't. I won't let him.

'This program,' he says, 'is hugely important. We don't have the space in this world for people who can't contribute. Do you understand that we cannot sustain the lifestyles we used to live? Can you believe that we used to pack our criminals into prisons, into fortresses, huge concrete castles where we isolated those people we saw as a threat? We didn't try to help them, to work with them; to make them better, to discover what went wrong with our own society, to keep it from happening again. Instead we locked them up. Some people even got locked up on spaceships. Can you believe that?' He examines my face closely as he says this. Does he know? I am careful, and give away nothing.

'We sent them into space to orbit the Earth, and then . . . Well, then the collapse of everything here happened, and we forgot about them. Can you imagine that? What it must have been like, growing up there?' I look around his office for a way to escape. There's the door, and the window. What happens if I run? What happens if I'm chased out of here, into the desert? How long could I survive? 'One of those ships landed. It came from a country far away, but it landed here, because we're the only place who still has the programme active that would guide it back to Earth. That country doesn't even exist now, so the people the ship brought to us . . . They became our problem. Some of them were beyond saving, but some of them? I knew we could make them better. Give them to me, I said, and I can revise them. I can *fix* them, turn them into constructive members of society.'

'But what if they didn't need fixing?' I hear myself saying, my voice small and quiet. I could hurl myself through the window. I'd probably have a minute before they were onto me. The guards, maybe I could outrun them. They've got vehicles but I could hide. Do they have birds? I've not seen any, doesn't mean they're not lying dormant somewhere for a worst-case scenario. Ziegler would tell me to be careful, to come up with a plan before I rush into anything. But I haven't got the time to make a plan. Back on Australia, I would have improvised. Taking the time to plan something was time that would get you killed.

'They did,' he says, 'oh, they did. Everybody needs fixing. Even I do. We all have baggage, Chan, but they had so much . . . Some of them weren't able to be saved, like I said. And that is where we come to Polly. She was up there, on that ship – came to us scarred and broken, barely even human, such as we understand it. And we have tried, but there's something about how ingrained it is with her; how deep-set her rot runs. She's been here six months longer than you, and we've barely cracked her. We've removed what she remembers, but how she wants to act – her drive? – that's exactly the same as it was before. When we brought her here she was nearly dead, and yet she still found the strength to fight us. Bit us – she had no weapons so she used herself. We clamped her jaw until she calmed down.' He puts the glass down on the table between us, right next to mine, so close that they're touching. 'Do you want more water?'

'No,' I say. I can feel my fists balling. I remember this feeling: the tension welling up, needing to come out. The desire to act.

'Did you recognise her?' He swipes away the holo of the brain. 'Show *Polly A*,' he says, and her image comes up between us. Or, images: her now, as she looked outside – frantic, her hair torn, her skin scratched and broken. And her when I last saw her, when we landed here: the marks on her face from our fight, her eyes lolling backwards, looking dead; or as close to it as a person can be while still breathing. And then a holo of her at some point between then and now: hair, clear skin, tight lips, wide eyes.

'How long have I been here?' I ask Gibson.

'Half a year, give or take. Some patients fight really hard against the help we offer. Your friend Polly, for example.' He rolls his sleeve back, to show me the scars of a bite on his forearm, thick indents that must have gone so deep they drew blood. 'And she's still fighting. Not you, though. You didn't fight at all. It was like you gave yourself up to us as soon as you arrived. Like you were relieved to have us take your memories away. But then, you were tired. You kept telling us that, how tired you were.'

'I still am.'

'And yet you haven't been sleeping.' He puts his hand to his mouth, covers it. Rubs his chin. 'You remember her? Polly, I mean.'

'Yes,' I say, and I realise that this was never the comfortable normal conversation it was presented as. This is a trick, an interrogation.

I won't need a plan. I'm going to have to act now: take my chance, stick with it.

'You knew each other,' Gibson says. His voice is calm and controlled. There's sweat on his brow. Most of the time here, sweat means you're hot. Not this time. Now, this is him being tense. 'You came from the same place. I gathered, from what you told us when you arrived here, that you even had some . . . conflict.'

'You could say that.'

'One of the worries that's come up about this little project is that people who knew each other before might break down each other's barriers. But that's the test. You can't run a project like this and run the risk of you bumping into somebody in a city, when you're healthy, revised, with kids, a family, a job. That would undo all the good you've gone through. You have to be *perfect*. So I had to make you work together.'

'You've taken away who we are,' I say. I'm furious now, but anger won't help me. I don't know what will, but I know that I have to control myself, until I know how to get out of here, how to survive this conversation. 'You've taken so much.'

'For the better. Have you tried to kill her here? You have not. We took that away from you, and you want that instinct back?' He's exasperated, raised voice, spit on his lips. 'You want to be an animal?'

'I want to be *me*,' I say.

'And you are! Or, you *were*. You were you, just different. Better. So was she, I thought. She's too broken, Chan, I know that now. We did six months of reconditioning. Six months! That's more than anybody else. Some of the Australia survivors, they took weeks before they were on board with the new programme. That's because the brain wants an easy life. It wants simplicity, normality. It rejects the things it wants to reject. It wants to be rid of death and torment and pain. It seeks a baseline of stillness and calm. Yours did. You had three months of the process. That's it. We had you.'

'You never had me,' I say. I wonder how long Jonah took. I imagine him, fighting to keep a hold of me, of us.

'You can think that, but I tell you, Chan, some things aren't definite. They aren't set. You were fluid, receptive. And now look at you.' He's disgusted. I'm nothing to him, now. Not a project, not a success.

To him, I'm a criminal.

'You know that I remember everything,' I say. I look at the window, trying to work out how damaged I'll be if I dive through it – if I'll even be able to break the glass. I look at the door, wondering if he's locked it. He'll have been sensible too.

'I worked it out. Too much contact. And then we heard about your conversation with Jonah earlier.' Heard about it. How? A camera? Or – worse, worst of all, the thought making me lose a breath, the air briefly choking in my throat – from Jonah?

But I can't show that I'm worried about that. I need to keep control.

'What happens now?' I ask. I'm ready. If he's going to do something drastic, I'm ready for it. I'll fight my way out of here if I have to. *Don't die*, my mother's voice says, and there's something so reassuring to hearing her now, here, in this place.

'Now? We start over again. We spend months helping you, making you better. If it takes twice as long, three times, four times, I don't care. I'll fix you.'

'But I'm not broken,' I reply.

'Not yet.' I hear the sound of something in the distance. The same sound as in the cities: birds. I'm almost honoured. Gibson knows how dangerous I am. I reach for my glass, my hand faster than his, clasped around it, ready to smash it, to use it as a weapon. 'You can't,' he says, but I absolutely can. I smash it into his head, and it explodes into something like dust, harmlessly clouding his head before falling to the ground. He looks instantly smug that they planned for this, that these things can't be used as weapons. The door opens, and the wardens are there, along with three birds, buzzing into the room, circling us, glowing and primed. 'Don't fight us too much,' Gibson says, 'or your story will have to end a different way.' I want to ask what he means, but the birds don't give me a chance. They pulse, and then the whips come from them, the strings of metal, which snap and curl around my arms, tightening to coils; and then one around my neck, while I'm being held tight. They drag me towards the door, and I kick and scream but I can't make a sound, so tight is the whip around my neck. They drag me down the hall and I try to fight back, but it's pointless. They're too strong. We go down past the dormitories, past the dining halls, all the way to the end; to where they're keeping her. Polly; Rex; whatever she calls herself here.

Gibson comes up behind me as a warden runs to open the door. He leans in and whispers to me, so quiet that the birds won't hear him and his words won't be logged. 'I can't do anything to you, legally or ethically,' he says. 'But she can. We've stopped her treatments entirely, to see how fast her regression is. So this will be a different sort of test. I wonder if she remembers you now?'

Through the door I see her, lying on the floor, facing us. Her new arm, shut down, limp and useless; her hair gone, scraps of it cluttering the floor around her; her clothes torn, and those letters on her chest, those scars, freshly opened, traced into the skin anew. She looks up at me, barely moving; I am pushed inside. I hear the coils of the whips untying themselves, and I can breathe properly again. I stand there as the door shuts behind me; as the lock fastens.

She slams me hard against the door, which groans, the metal in the frame creaking with an abnormally human sound. It hurts; really, really hurts. I slam my forearm into her head, over and over as she pushes me forwards, driving into me as if she's trying to force me through the metal itself. She pushes, and I beat her.

Slam, into the side of her head. She moves.

Slam, my arm into her neck. Again.

She pulls back. This isn't like when we fought on Australia. We're out of practice. We're tired, and we're so hot we can barely breathe. This room is sweltering, the air conditioning turned off. She charges again and I move, but not enough. Her shoulder pushes into my side and I gasp, but the air's too warm in here to give anything like relief. I push back and she stumbles. I swing down, grab her leg and yank it, and she falls backwards, her back thudding into the floor, her head colliding a second later with a clang.

Everything sounds louder than it is, more brutal.

I'm on her, now, and I'm smashing my fists into her head, over and over. My hands hurt. They're not used to this. They were calloused on Australia; now, they're clear and clean. She spits blood, then pushes upwards, heaving me with her. She raises her leg, kicks me off, and I fly back, into the wall. Another thump, another fall, and I'm face down on the ground. I feel her hands in my hair, and she pulls my head up, grips my hair between her fingers.

She slams my face into the ground. There's nothing to cushion it, but it doesn't hurt as much as I know it should. I wonder if I'm just not feeling the pain, if it will hurt in the morning instead. If I will even see the morning.

Don't die.

I push back, and she tries to fight me off, but I grab her hand, pull it out from under her, and she falls face down next to me, her nose smashing flat. I smack her straight on, right on her nose. Blood gushes. She scrabbles backwards and I crawl towards her, hold her ankle, yank her back towards me, slam my hand – open, using the flat of the palm, closest to my wrist – into her nose again, and the blood starts fountaining out, spraying the floor. She cradles her face, screams. She pushes away from me, to the corner of the room. The floor is wet – blood and sweat and urine.

'Please,' she says.

I stop. She is not herself. The Rex I knew would never have pleaded, not for anything. We both breathe and we fall into a pattern with it, inhaling and exhaling at the same time, somehow in perfect unison.

We don't say anything for hours. There's no sense in talking. I don't know what I would have to say to her anyway. She stares at me from under her hand, still cradling her nose. I pull off my shirt, leaving only the vest underneath. She needs to stop the bleeding. I can't have her die from her injuries, and I can't stand seeing her with blood all over her hands and face. I go to her, shuffling across the floor. She takes her hands away, lets me tend to her. I press the shirt against her face, holding her head back, tell her to stay still, and she does. I hold the bridge of her nose until the blood stops.

'This is going to hurt,' I tell her. I put my hand around the nose. I can see where it's broken, where it's bent now. She doesn't flinch when I touch it, but she howls as I click it back into place, gasps as I let go. Better, I think. I give her the shirt, soaked in dark red, to hold there for a while.

269

I tell her it'll be alright, as if that's what she needs to hear.

I think about how much hurt she has gone through in her life, how many battles she's fought. She lost a limb, and still she fought. And now, here, in this room, a broken nose – shattered, maybe, because it's swollen and sore, the skin blackened and bruised, but still just her nose – is enough to finish it for her.

She pulls the shirt away, the blood ceased, and hands it back to me with a nod. She's grateful for my help.

I crawl away from her, to the opposite wall. I try to listen to the noises of the rest of the complex, but there's nothing – no sound of voices, classes, footsteps, whatever; just the echo of something down the corridors, and the hiss of Rex's – Polly's – breathing.

'I don't know who I am,' she says, out of nowhere, into the darkness. Everybody is asleep, but we're not. We're trapped here, and they won't let us out. There's no food. They want us to starve, or worse. Maybe they want to see how feral we can become. They aren't pumping the gas in to make us sleep. Neither of us has moved, not since we fought, and this is the first thing she's said. Her voice is quieter than I've ever heard it. I shift, to try and see her; to catch any light that's in the room. I wait, to see if she says anything else. That's it, though. Silence, after that.

So I fill the silence. 'When I knew you, you were called Rex,' I say. I hear something; I suspect it's her fingers on her skin, running over the scabbed grooves on her chest, feeling

270

out those letters. 'And now you're called Polly. Why that name?'

Silence, again. Then: 'I don't know. I remembered it.' More silence. Breathing. 'I don't know who I am,' she says. Her voice is desperately sad and small.

'Do you want to?' I ask. She doesn't answer. I tell her anyway.

I tell her about the people that she killed, the fights that she started, the violence she caused, the nightmares she enacted; I tell her about the wars for territory. I tell her about the night that I helped her – or, the night that my mother's death helped her, really, in the most terrible way – to take over the Lows from their previous leader. I tell her about everything that she did to me, how somehow she's the reason that we are here, damaged and ruined and broken. I tell her all of this and she doesn't say a word in reply.

In the silence, I think about my mother and about how, as a child, I would be given something and I would break it, because I would push it too far. She would give me a toy that she had worked hard to get for me, and I would want it to do everything for me, to be everything. It never lasted. Nothing does. And she would tell me: that's why you take care of what matters. That's why you don't push things.

I let Rex take in all that I've told her. I want to say that I blame her for everything: for Agatha's death, for Mae being missing; for the deaths of friends, of people who made my life good; the breaking and bending of lives to fit her own. But I don't. I let the silence tell her for me. I listen to her breathing; and then, I'm sure, the sound of her sniffling, rubbing her eyes. Gibson thought he didn't get through to her, that she couldn't be changed. But I wonder if that's true. I wonder if all it took was removing her from that place.

Because this Rex is not the person she once was.

'I need to leave here,' she whispers at some point in the night. I've been asleep and her voice wakes me. For some reason, I've slept heavier than any night on the bed. My back feels better. This hardness is what I'm used to; it's what my body needs. 'I have to leave here.'

'So do I,' I say. 'They want us to kill each other, though. We won't get out until they carry us out.' I stretch my body until it aches again, contorting myself to feel the still, cold hardness of the floor doing my muscles good.

I listen to a new sound in the darkness, as Rex touches her hand and her now-useless false arm; she plays with it, like it's another scar that she simply cannot stop scratching.

When I wake up again, her hands – the one good hand, the real one; and the fake one, which she's pressing underneath the other – are around my throat, and she is pushing down at me with all the strength that she can muster. Her grip is too tight. I'm already blacking out, already feeling the room, her, the world swim away from me.

I choke, or try to. I beat the floor with my hands and feet. I try to hit her, but there's no strength left in me, not even a little bit.

And then I feel Rex's breath on the skin of my cheek. 'Stay still,' she whispers. She's letting air in, but only slightly.

Enough. She shouts, 'She's dead. Chan is dead.' I hear the sounds of feet on concrete, running towards us; shouts. 'Get ready,' she says to me. So I am. I want to tell her that it feels like I'm always ready for anything, because I have to be. Now is no different.

The door clanks open. Screaming, shouting. Then: she wrenches. She pulls back from the false arm, which stays at my neck. I see the stump of her elbow, plugs and sockets exposed in the flesh from where she detached it. She grabs the false arm, holds it like a club; darts forward and smashes it into the face of the warden closest to us. He screams, falls backwards. There's blood, again. She snarls, swings once more.

'Get up!' she screams at me, and I do, I have to, even though I can barely breathe, even though my vision is cloudy, swimming in green and purple flashes. I'm dizzy, so I steady myself on the wall. She kicks a warden. He stumbles forward, towards me; on his face, I can see deep scratches from the wounds she's made, but can't tell if they're from the false arm or her fingernails. He sways in front of me, then regains control and reaches for his striker. But he's slow. I kick at his shin, really hard, and he slams forward, face on the floor. I stamp on the inside of his knee, and he howls as it crunches. Don't want him getting up again.

By the time I look up, Rex is already gone. I peer cautiously into the corridor, and I see the trail she's left: three wardens, and now a bird, which she smashes before it can whip her, the enclosed space somehow giving her an advantage. She's going for freedom, and I am going with her.

*　　*　　*

273

It's amazing how fast peace can turn into a riot, how quickly a single violent act can upend the status quo. She makes it to the dining halls, where the rest of the prisoners are eating breakfast, and she throws a warden into one of the serving tables, spilling the food, making the wood shatter. All the prisoners rush into the room to watch, their eyes wide. I recognise so many of them now, from Australia. Out of context, out of place, they look almost normal: their hair grown back, their skin clean, free of blood and grime; their tattoos and scars hidden. The wardens pile onto Rex, ignoring me, trying to keep her down, but she's a fury, unstoppable. I remember that power, even if she doesn't. They try to restrain her and she whips them around. A bird lassos her, and she grabs the cable and uses it to swing the drone around. It slams into one of the other prisoners. He lashes back, smashing the bird under foot, piling in towards Rex. The wardens turn to him and he slams his head into their helmets as they try to restrain him; he kicks out, hurls things around. He's not the man he was just a moment ago, and he doesn't know why. Others join in the fight as if their bones are telling them to: nothing's triggered it, not specifically. It's just a feeling they've got, that they should. That this is what they do.

Alarms sound, but they're distant. More wardens run in, clearly having just come from their bunks, pulling on their uniforms. They're carrying riot shields and weapons. The fight is a mess of bodies, of rioting that I can't keep track of. This is an opportunity. I run for the outside; to the mall, to the shop that they use to test us. It's locked up this time, but that's never stopped me.

The door collapses, and I run in and through to the back. Everything I need is here. I wrap some of the clothes I find around my fist, and I lay into the glass cabinets, over and over, watching the reinforced glass crack and then shatter, right around the time I feel the skin on my knuckles split, feel the fabric on my hand wet with my own blood. I smash them, all of them. Even the ones that don't hold anything I need, I smash, because breaking the glass feels something like relief.

Later I take the knife that they took from me. I've had a lot of knives in my life, but this is my favourite, I remember, a gift from somebody who wanted me to look after myself. Never be without a knife, I tell myself. I take a striker as well, in case I need it, and I run back, out of the shop and through the mall, towards the main centre.

I see Jonah. He's staring, confused, lost, standing outside the doors, watching the distance. He looks at me, and I stop running.

In the distance, there's a sandstorm rising. Every few weeks they hit, swirls of wind picking up the soil and turning it over and over. The wind here carries the debris, flinging it at us into our eyes, our mouths. We shield our faces with our forearms against it.

'Please don't do this,' he says.

'I have to,' I reply. 'This is a lie, all of it. You're not who you think you are. You're Jonah. I know you.'

'Don't say that.' Anger on his face, eyes red, because that wall, in his memory, it doesn't want to be destroyed. But I have to get through, I have to.

275

'You are Jonah, and I remember everything about you. You were with the Pale Women. You saved my life. You came with me down into the depths of the ship, and you helped me save Mae. You and I were—'

'This is my truth!' he shouts, screams almost. 'This, here. This is where I am meant to be!' He sinks to his knees and I rush forwards, hand to his shoulder, to the skin at the side of his neck, feeling that rough texture under my thumb. And he cranes his head towards me, as if that comforts him a little, to feel it there.

'Jonah,' I start to say, but then I hear somebody behind me. The soft crunch of their feet on the sand that's been thrown here by the storm. They're close enough to grab my arm, and I spin, hand darting to their throat.

It's Gibson.

'Do you see what you've done?' he asks. His hand tightens as mine loosens. He's no threat. He's shaking with fear, with sadness. With anger. I can feel his hands tremble against my skin.

'I didn't do this,' I tell him. He doesn't let go of me, even when I try to shake him off, so I push him, gently. He falls onto his backside, and sits there like a child, arms in front of him. He's crying.

'You could have been amazing,' he says. 'You could have been so much better. Special, even. I want to make you all special, make you all valuable parts of an infrastructure that abandoned you, that would have left you for dead. But you're too weak to see that: set in your ways. You think humans don't change? You think that they can't? Of course they can! I wanted to make you perfect, a contributor. I wanted to make it so that you could have been *anybody*. But you chose to fight. Look at you: a broken, sad little girl, who thinks she can save everybody.' The words hurt, but only ever so slightly.

'I don't think I can save everybody,' I say. 'Just the person I promised I would.'

There's a crash from behind me. Rex, dripping with blood, weapons in her hands, ready for more.

She heads for Gibson, eyes fixed on him. Her remaining hand, closing and opening, closing and opening. I know what she used to do to those she found responsible for wronging her. I wonder how deeply set that is inside her.

I step in front of Gibson, put myself between them. 'Please,' I say. 'No more.' I don't know if she's killed anyone inside. I know that it's quiet in there. I wonder what ended the fighting; and yet, I really don't want to know.

'He ruined me,' she spits, 'who I was.' Everything about her scares me: the look in her eyes, the gravel in her throat. But I stand firm, feet planted, and even as the sand whips into us, into my eyes, I don't blink. I feel Gibson tremble behind me, and I stare at Rex's eyes, and I let her know that she will not kill him. Not today.

She drops her shoulders. She holds her arm, the stump of what Agatha took from her, that I was so complicit in her losing; and she turns, looks down the road out of town.

She starts to walk. I don't know how far she'll get without help, in this heat, this storm. We're not far from the re-breather cabinet, so I let go of Gibson, who slumps to the ground, and I run to the box and take as many re-breathers as I can carry and some bottles of water, as well. There are backpacks here, for when we're working further away from Pine City. I grab a couple of them, and I stuff them full of anything we might need on our journey. No sense in leaving anything behind.

When I get back, Gibson has already gone, back inside the facility. Jonah is waiting at the side of the road. He is scratching at his neck, his only tell; he remembers something, even if he claims that he doesn't. I can't tell if the redness in his eyes is from the sand or not.

'Gibson told me to leave,' Jonah says. 'He said that he doesn't want me here any more.'

'It's for the best,' I tell him, but it feels wrong. Jonah is coming with me, but it's not his choice. I think about reaching for his hand, for his skin – using the warmth of it to comfort me, even in this heat – but he holds his arms close to his side, his head down. He doesn't look at me.

We walk away from the facility, towards where Rex is fading into the distance, framed by the haze of the heat coming from the road. I want Jonah to remember. He will, once he's out of this place, once he's had a couple of nights' sleep without the conditioning. He'll remember everything about who he is. Who I am.

Of course he will.

You are now leaving Pine City, the sign says. Rex stoops by the side of the road and grabs a rock into her one good hand. She walks up to the sign and swings the rock hard, denting the sign. She beats it again, over and over, until the sign bends back on its supports; until the letters painted onto it are so badly scratched they can't be read any more; until the metal starts to tear, and her knuckles are bloody and torn.

PART

THREE

ELEVEN

Way back, when I was a child, I got sick. I caught a fever so bad that – to hear my mother and Agatha tell the story, when I was older – I was as close to death as you can be without having a knife in your chest. They took me to the coolest place in Australia that they could find, the mouth of the arboretum stream, and they sat with me for hours on end, soaking me in the water then lifting me out, letting me shiver myself dry, before starting again. My mother told how the water would evaporate from my skin, my temperature was so high. For a time, she said, I was the warmest thing on the whole of Australia – engines, forges, everything included. But I didn't die. I survived that heat.

My mother told me that she knew that if I could survive that sickness, I could survive pretty much anything.

The blood smeared across Rex's shoulder has dried. To glance at it, it looks like the plates of soil on the side of the road: smooth, then cracked, like there are rifts underneath it, pulling it apart. The ground changes as we walk. Lumps of clay turn to dust, kicking up clouds as we tread along, splitting beneath our weight. I feel heavier, that's for certain: it's the heat, and how tired I am, how difficult the walking is. Gibson hasn't followed us; he hasn't sent anybody after us. which is something. We're prisoners, though. According to those in charge, we're dangerous. We should be punished. Gibson must have surmised that we'll die out here.

There are moments when I think that's a safe assumption.

'We go this way,' Rex says, the first words she's uttered since we left. I watch her as we walk. Her handless arm lies flush across her body, as if there's a sling supporting it. She pulls her re-breather off, to give herself a break; to try and choke her way through the gritty hotness of the air, instead. Jonah is refusing protection entirely. I don't know why, and it infuriates me. Freckled and shiny, his skin has turned a deep red. Sweat beads on his forehead. It's as if he's punishing himself. I've seen that in him before. But that's his choice. I can't protect him from himself.

We stare at the ground as we walk because looking up means looking into the glare of the sun. The heat is bearable, but only just. It's getting hotter and hotter with every minute.

'Keep going,' Rex says, though I wasn't in any danger of stopping. Stopping means giving up; and if we give up here, we're dead. There's no question of that.

For the rest of that first day, we see nothing. We keep walking along broken roads, along the shattered sections of what Ziegler told me is called a freeway. Sometimes the road disappears, swallowed into the ground; and then you see it reappear a way off, so you get back onto it. We reason it must lead somewhere. That's what a road does.

So we walk.

We don't talk, not really.

We drink the water, trying to be sparing with it, but it's hard.

We prop each other up when we stumble; and we rest when we feel like we might fall.

And then, when night starts to come, we find trees, the wilted stumps of a group of them, so dry and skeletal they seem like they must be dead, but I can't be sure; because I don't know how they're still standing, if they're no longer alive. As we sleep next to them, propped up against the trunks, I move closer to Jonah, huddling close to him, to try and protect both of us against the cold wind that kicks in during the night time; but he moves away from me, a subtle shift of his body over to one side, an arching of his back. I wonder if I am actually cold, or just cold compared to how hot the daytime is, and how brutal.

We're drenched in sweat when we wake up, the sky just getting light, the heat of the day not yet set in. I have no idea how the body makes that much sweat when it's so water deprived, but it does, and it has; Jonah is so soaked through it's as though he's sick. His clothes are wet, and he pulls at them, yanking them off. He stands there, red where the sun has charred his skin, the rest of him pale. I remember the welts that run all the way down his back, like the rungs of some awful ladder. I prop myself up and watch

285

him as he drapes his clothes on the dead branches of nearby trees. The scars bend and twist with his muscles as he stretches to get to the higher branches. I look at Rex, sleeping through this. Face soft. Her hand seems to be holding the space where once the other was. She looks so still, and so tranquil.

I don't have scars like they do. I want to feel mine, because I think that could be calming; to run a finger down them, to understand where they start and where they end, and to know that they are finite. But, like Gibson told me, the worst scars run deeper than skin.

'Chan,' Jonah says. He's standing in front of me now, his clothes wafting in the breeze behind him. The sun frames him, shining in my eyes from the horizon, and I have to squint to see him, shield my eyes with my hand. 'You did the right thing,' he says. I've heard that before, from him, but I can't quite remember when.

'What?' I ask.

'Bringing me with you.' I don't know if he means here and now, out of Pine City and into this wasteland; or to Earth, from Australia. He's somebody that I'm not sure has come out of this better. Back there, he was safe. Here, I think he'll be on the run now. We're all on the run. I wouldn't blame him if—

Then Rex is up and on her feet. 'Talking,' she says, not looking at either of us, but explaining what we've done wrong, either because it woke her, or we're wasting precious energy. The metal plug from her missing hand – where they attached the augments to her bone, her nerves – looks sore. There's red around it, like it's infected. It's not the neatest

286

augment job anyway, but I suspect she doesn't care about that. She picks up the water bottle she was carrying last, and she drains it. 'We're leaving,' she says.

'Jonah's clothes are drying,' I say, but she doesn't care. She starts to walk, the sun on the left of us; and Jonah doesn't even ask if we're going with her. He scrambles to his trousers and top, barely minutes in the warmth, and he pulls them on, grimacing against the dampness of them, but starting to walk all the same.

We see something in front of us, in the far-off. The haze coming off the ground makes it seem as though it's not really there. We've been fooled already, by pools of water that didn't exist, that disappeared as soon as we were close enough to understand that our own eyes were lying to us. This time we see tents, fabric stretched across poles jutting from the ground. Rex, walking at the front of us, stops and raises her arm into the air to halt us. She's still and silent, and we follow suit.

We watch. There are people there as well. Their shapes, moving around. Rex crouches. They aren't looking for us, and there's nobody watching this direction.

'They might be dangerous,' I whisper. I think about the stories that Ziegler told me, about those who were outcast from the cities. Criminals, or people who simply didn't fit in. Not good people, he insinuated. 'We should go around.' Rex glares at me – a look I recognise, that still chills me – and throws me her empty water pack. Her re-breather is almost empty. Our skin, our lips, are cracking in the heat.

She's right, I know that. I know. But Ziegler told me that the people who live out here, outside of the cities, only do that because they don't have any other choice. They're not allowed in the cities.

'Wait,' Rex says to us. Jonah reaches over and wraps his fingers around my hand, clasping it. He pulls me towards him. I try and remember if I've ever seen him this unsettled before, this scared. But I can't. Not even when we knew we were leaving Australia.

Rex creeps forward. We watch her go, moving so slowly a trail in the dust behind her is the only indication of her movement. Minutes later she's behind the tent; the sun makes it hard to watch, and hard to stay still. Sweat runs off my forehead down my neck to the small of my back, making me itch.

Jonah's grip on my hand grows tighter as Rex stands, as she walks up to the camp. We lose sight of her behind their tents and temporary fabric structures, but the sound of voices carries in the air. She says something. They say something. I hear a man's voice, then another man's voice; another, and another. Louder, they get. Rex stays quiet and measured.

Jonah's fingers are almost too tight on mine.

Silence, for a moment. A moment that lasts altogether too long.

Something's wrong.

I let go of Jonah and I run, and it's only as I'm at full pelt that I hear Rex scream; but not in pain. It's fury, and this is a sound I've definitely heard before.

*   *   *

I get tangled up in the tent fabric as I try to get through, and something behind me – a pole – comes loose, clattering, bringing down more fabric. It takes me a second to see what's happening, but the blood is a giveaway. Rex is covered in it, her hand clutching a curved weapon with a wooden handle. She's swiping at someone, or several people. One of them – a man, naked, his skin leathered and awful – clutches at his throat, blood coursing out from between his fingers. Another man is holding his groin, weeping. Another looks fine, until I step forward and I see that he's not quite whole any more; his shoulder is divided by a sharp line from his neck, threatening to peel away from the rest of his body.

Rex kills the fourth and last while I watch: two smacks of the blade into the neck before the head comes off the body. Watching her fight, every memory comes back. The last of the wall around her comes tumbling down. She is a dervish; dangerous and, in her own way, quite incredible.

Jonah rushes to us, and he sees the blood; and he falls to his knees, starts to retch. He's not ready for this. It's too soon for him.

'They started it,' Rex says. 'I asked them to share, but they . . .' She nods to the one who's holding his groin.

But behind him, there's a barrel; and around it, the floor is wet. There are a few tins of food sitting against the barrel's side. Rex pulls the lid off the barrel, reaches in and raises her hand to her mouth. She drinks, and she smiles at me.

She beckons me over to drink with her.

*　　*　　*

289

We take some fabric to make our own tents. When it's time to stop walking for the day – a slower day, bellies full from eating the tinned food – we drape it amongst bushes and dry shrubs and lie underneath it, as if it will give us protection. Jonah wakes us with screaming, with moaning. Rex stands up and walks away from us, until she's out of range of the noise; and I watch her lie down, underneath the stars, flat on her back.

I want him to feel better. I feel calm with him, but worried. He's not himself, not yet. He will be, I tell myself, eventually. It'll take some time.

But I wonder if he'll thank me when he is. I stroke his head, to try and calm him, half hoping he'll wake and look up at me, and show that he remembers me; but he doesn't even stir under my touch.

Midway through the following day we come to an abandoned town. A row of houses on either side of the road, a few other streets coming off that.

Welcome to Staunton.

We pass what used to be shops, before they were abandoned. There's evidence of fire in the buildings, and on one side of the road stand the jagged remnants of a forest, the stumps of charred trees, of blazed-out brush on the ground. Far off in the distance I can just make out a large depression in the ground. Maybe it was once a lake or something like that: now it's dry, cracked, running off in the distance, the ground like dried-up old skin. Jonah lags behind Rex and myself. He slept all night – unlike me – but is so tired and weary it's as if he barely shut his eyes. He doesn't say much of anything. Instead, he shuffles, trips over his own feet. Leaving the prison, us freeing him, it's exhausted him. I don't say it aloud, but I want to find a house for him, a bed where he can sleep again. Even if it's just for a few hours.

I don't have to suggest this, though. Rex is the first to turn off the road as we pass a house: big windows, wooden slats across them to keep the light and heat out. Nothing like the houses in Washington; it's more like something you see in a holo, of what life used to be like on this planet. Rex walks to the front door and doesn't even try the handle. She kicks the wood away, and it shatters, brittle and dry. The inside of the house reeks like rot. It's worst in the kitchen, where Rex scavenges for food, opening cupboards. Insects scurry out across the floor, over and under our feet, completely unconcerned by our being here. There are lizards on the walls, staring at us then dashing away when we get closer until they're all clustered in the furthest reaches of the room.

Rex finds a tin of fruit with a faded label and smashes it on the counter, tearing the metal apart. She looks and dismisses it, throwing it to one side; as it lands, it spills out the green contents, a mulch of paste.

'Useless,' she says. Her voice sounds so much more like it did on the ship than even a week ago: gravelled and harsh, coming from somewhere deep in her throat. It could be the heat, the dryness of being out in the world; could be her remembering more of who she is.

'We should stay here a while,' I say, looking at Jonah, then Rex. She doesn't make eye-contact, but nods. So I lead Jonah upstairs, opening doors.

291

There's a body in the first room I enter. The remains of one, anyway. I shut the door as fast as I opened it.

In the next room, there's an empty bed. On the blanket, a picture of a man in a dark outfit, a mask. Poses like he's fighting somebody. I lead Jonah to the bed, pull back the cover, and I lay him down.

'Stay here,' I say. 'We'll just be downstairs.'

'I missed you,' he says. Out of nowhere. His hand finds mine again. 'When I couldn't find you.'

'I've been here,' I tell him.

'Not now. Before. When we landed.' He lies back, shuts his eyes. He's remembering. I sit by his legs, our fingers entwined. I swear, something feels different in his touch. 'What they put us through. Do you know? Did you have it happen to you?'

'I did,' I say.

'I kept thinking: Chan will save us. But you weren't there. And then . . . Then I forgot.'

'I was trying to find you.'

'I know. But that's what you do, isn't it? You save us. That's why you're so good.' His speech slurs. He's drifting. 'That's what makes you who you are.' I lie down next to him as his words fade away. 'You want to save everybody, but you can't. Have to let us save you once in a while. But that's why you're special.'

'I'm not special,' I whisper. 'I was lucky. My family made me lucky.' My mother. Agatha. You, I don't say.

We lie in the silence for a while; his even breathing is so soothing I feel like I could sleep as well. But I don't. There's work to be done.

*   *   *

292

In the kitchen, Rex breaks open another door. There are stairs behind, leading downwards. She goes down them, into the pitch-blackness. I follow her. I don't want her to be alone. It's immediately cool as we head down. I keep my hand on the rail, hear her feet on the steps below me.

'Wait,' I say. 'Our eyes will adjust.' We spent years of our lives – from birth – in a place that was badly lit. The light from upstairs is enough, and I start being able to make out shapes: racks, rows and rows of shelves with circular shapes on them. She reaches for one, and she passes it to me. It's heavy. I go back up the stairs, into the brightness coming through the huge glass windows along one wall of the house. *Cabernet Sauvignon*, it says. It's full of liquid. I break it open and pour it out. It's a thick red colour, like blood, almost. Wine. Ziegler drinks this. I've seen him, bottles of it like trophies in a rack on his kitchen surface. Dusty. Better with age, he told me. I'm betting these are older than anything he's got.

By the time I get back down, Rex has smashed the neck from another bottle, and I hear the sound of her lapping at the liquid as she pours it out. I wait, expecting her to say that it's bad; that it couldn't possibly survive this long, under these conditions. But she doesn't. Instead she hands me the bottle, and I run my fingers over the shattered glass, feeling for where it could cut me. I pour it into my hands, and I lift it to my mouth, and I drink. It's ridiculously sweet; it's not pleasant, but it's wet. And right now, that's enough.

I can see the outline of her glugging from yet another of the bottles, raising the shattered glass to her mouth and taking it straight down. I hear it spilling over her, spattering onto the floor. She laughs. I've never heard her laugh before.

We've been here a long time. Everything swims in my head. It feels like I've been punched, kicked, hit in the gut, hit in the head. She's in worse shape than I am. She's drunk more. She slurs her words, while I'm sure mine are fine, sure that I'm making sense. I talk slowly, when I talk. But we're mostly silent.

'You could have killed me,' she says, and her words are quiet and slow, and measured. 'I remember that.' They broke her for months, but it wasn't enough to destroy Rex. 'You were going to kill me.'

'I was,' I say.

'Did I wrong you?'

'You were a murderer,' I tell her. You would have killed me, and everybody I loved. You took Mae.' I realise I'm shouting at her, my voice angry.

'Mae,' she says. 'The little girl.'

'You took her from me. You scared her. You could have ruined everything for her.' She nods while I'm talking. It looks like she's falling asleep, her head lolling as she listens, her eyes shut. 'You were a bad person.'

'You weren't better. You hurt me.'

'It's not the same,' I tell her. 'You gave me no choice. I had to stop you.'

'Maybe.' Then she's quiet for the longest time. I can feel the room starting to spin. I can't see it spinning, though. Perhaps that's better. She doesn't say anything else until I'm on my back, trying to focus on staying perfectly still, feeling everything – today, the last few months, years, maybe – drifting away from me. 'But I was stopping you, as well,' she says.

I can hear birds, real birds, twittering in the trees, those that survived the catastrophes that changed the planet. I used to dream of animals, of seeing cats and dogs and cows and birds, all the things that some on the ship remembered through their own parents, their parents' parents. The noises that those animals would make when they saw you, or when you stroked them. Some kids' song about a farmer, and the noises that the animals made; and all we had to tell us what the animals looked like was drawings from books or that people had made themselves.

Now, most of the animals are gone. The birds that survived aren't much to look at. They have patches of feathers on their bodies, and they're tired-looking, and they don't go anywhere near the cities, because they wouldn't have a chance with the air conditioners being as they are. Birds stay wild, unseen, away from people. Their survival instinct must have kicked in: running and hiding was the only way for them to save themselves.

All through the night I wake – to use the bathroom, which is a proper bathroom, and maybe it was once beautiful, though now the floor tiles are cracked and the paint faded; to get a drink, to try and find water before giving up, having more of the wine, as sickeningly sweet and now wrong-tasting as it is; to the sounds of Rex making this noise that's halfway between a sob and a growl; to just revel in this house, in being somewhere that is safer than maybe anywhere else I've ever lived, that's a dream of some sort – and I hear the birds in the far-off, twittering at each other, chatting. I listen to them until I drift off to sleep again. It's almost tranquil: the sound of life.

In the morning, I wake to the song of those birds again; but now it feels different, more forceful. The chirrups have turned into beeps that sound generated and fake, and are growing louder and louder. I don't know how long we slept for, but it's light. I run to the windows at the back of the house, that line almost the entire wall. In the distance, I see specks of dust – motes – moving. That's them. They're coming. I don't know if it's for us or something else entirely, but we can't risk it. They're heading this way, and fast.

I shout Jonah's name, Rex's name. They don't reply.

Jonah's room is empty. He's gone.

Their names again, this time screamed, as I run down the stairs, into the basement. Rex is splayed on the floor. I reach for her, shake her. She rolls over and vomits, onto the floor, onto my feet. I pull her upright and grab her face, my hands on either side of her head, and I stare into her eyes.

'The birds are coming,' I say, 'and I can't find Jonah. We have to do something.' She shakes her head, and she makes that growling sound that she's so fond of. 'Okay?'

'I need water,' she says, but so do I, and we don't have any, not now.

'Get up,' I say. I order her, and she responds to that. She nods. I scramble back up the stairs into the kitchen and I scream Jonah's name once more, but there's no reply.

Rex follows me up the stairs without missing a step, all of a sudden acting like she's not feeling the effects of everything we drank last night; and she drags open the windows, stands outside in the blazing morning sun, stares up at the advancing cloud of birds. I grab her by the arm – I reach for her hand, but it's not there, because I forgot; but from the way that she flinches she didn't – and I pull her back into the house, away from the windows. I don't know how far they can see, but I don't want them to spot us. They'll be scouring the landscape, following the roads, looking for us that way. And there's no way we're fast enough to outrun them, not in the state we're in, not with so little cover out here in the wilderness. 'We need to find anything that can help us.' I start to turn out drawers and cupboards, throwing cutlery around to find things that we can use as weapons.

'We have to leave,' she says.

'Not until we find Jonah,' I say. But she's right, I know she's right. We can't stay here. I shout his name again, but she hushes me.

'They'll hear you,' she says, and she's right about that as well.

We go through the downstairs of the house, as quiet as we can be. We know they can hear a long distance, and out here there's barely any other noise. We open doors, cupboards, wardrobes, cabinets, looking for weapons. There's nothing. And then we prise open a door into another dark, windowless room on the ground floor. There's something in the middle of it, under a tarpaulin. I pull it off, trying to be quiet and failing, but praying that the noise isn't significant. Underneath I see fabric, metal, thick rubber wheels; everything a deep, heavy black, polished to a sheen.

'It's a bike,' I whisper. Rex doesn't know what that is, but I've seen them in the city: going round the streets, people perched on the back. The noise that they make, like a roar of some long-extinct animal. 'It moves. It's like . . .' I don't know how to explain it to her. 'Just, trust me. It moves, and it's fast. Much faster than we are. Maybe as fast as the birds.'

'Do you know how it works?'

'No.' I look at the handlebars. People hold those. But the ones I've seen are automated, just like the cars. This one is older. The computer system here looks like it's hacked in, an afterthought. It doesn't wake up when I touch it.

'Then it's useless.'

'No,' I say, 'it's not. I can try.' There's a key hanging from the handles at the front, and a hole. I slide it in and turn it. The bike coughs, as if it's choking on something. I turn it again. The battery meter whizzes up. It's held a supply of power, even after all this time. Smoke billows into the back of the room, and Rex grins.

'Can you drive it?' she says.

'No,' I say.

'Can we learn?'

'We can,' I tell her. I look around, trying to find a way out of this room. On the walls, illuminated in the glare of the bike's light, are animal heads, stuffed and mounted on wooden boards, their teeth bared, as if they're all vicious, all about to attack. And in the middle of them is a kind of rack, mounted midway up the wall. Inside it, something black, long, metal.

298

'What is that?' Rex asks.

'It's a gun,' I say.

They banned them when the cities began burning, when the planet got too hot, when the riots started. That's what always happens, the museum told me, Ziegler told me. People live in a state of stasis for long enough, and then it gets hot and they explode. But this time it was on a scale that nobody had seen before. So to help keep the peace, guns were banned. Lots of things were banned, in those early days. But of course people found a way to keep them. Alala's got one hidden away in her home, that she thinks nobody knows about (but we all know). It's power, in a strange way: something so dangerous, so deadly.

'I've never held one,' I say. 'I don't know how they work.' But I've seen statues of people in the museum. Men from some war that happened centuries ago, clutching them with one part to their shoulders, pressed up against them, staring along the thick metal barrels. And their fingers on the triggers, aimed and primed.

I reach up and pull it down from the rack. It's heavier than I thought it would be. I feel the weight of it, spy down its length like the people in the museum diorama. I put Rex in the sights.

'They needed bullets,' I say. 'Things that they shoot.'

'Like arrows.'

'Like arrows but smaller, metal, pointed. Have a look.' We both turn out the drawers in here, throwing things onto the ground. Suddenly we're less concerned about the noise.

We know that they'll find us, because we're the only things out here.

It's inevitable.

'These?' Rex asks, and she yanks a small grey box up into the air, props it on her stump, and brings it into the light. They look like the bullets from the museum, sort of. Must be right.

'That's them,' I say, 'Get as many as you can. Put them in the bag on the side of the bike.' I leave her, to go back into the main part of the house. The birds are nearly here. They know where we are. I shout Jonah's name one last time, desperate now, because we have to go, if we stay here we're done for, and—

I see him. I see him, then, through the windows, on the land, at the back of the house. He is walking towards the birds, his hands in the air, raising them slowly, giving himself up.

No. I don't know what they'll do to him, why he would want to go, why he doesn't want to stay here, to learn more about who he is. To stay with me.

I open the door to shout at him, to plead with him. I want to tell him to stop, because we can get away, the three of us, we can be safe. But then I see how close the birds are and as I open my mouth to say the words, I'm not sure that I quite believe it.

He turns and looks at me. He doesn't smile – doesn't do anything – just looks at me, right into my eyes. And even as far away as he is, I can see into them. I can see them, green and clear. Unblinking as he stares at me, and I stare at him. He knows me. In that moment, I can tell. He remembers me perfectly.

The birds surround him, scan him, circle him. He falls to his knees, and he holds his hands up, and I realise that he's not running from me, back to them, back to the lie; he's buying us time.

The birds descend, and I shut the curtains, because I don't want to watch them drag him away. We can't waste the gift he's given us.

I rush back to Rex. She doesn't ask if I found him.

'Ready?' I ask. I want to ask her to come with me, to fight them, to rescue him; but I know there's no point.

And for some reason, I'm not even sure it's what he would want.

Rex raises her amputated forearm to show me. She's strapped something to the stump: a hunting knife, serrated edge on the blade, huge and unwieldy, fastened with thick grey tape to her skin. The tape is wound around and around, bulky and clumsy, but it holds the knife fast. It's threatening and, somehow, it's perfectly right.

'Ready,' she says.

There's a moment, just a brief moment, where it feels like I'm going to fall off this thing; where the sheer rush of it moving forward feels as though it could push me backwards, send me tumbling to the ground that's already far behind us. But I hold on, my hands on the grips that sit at the front, feeling the vibrations of it running up my arms, through my chest, into every single part of my body.

Rex hangs onto me as we tear down the road. The bike does most of the work for me, accelerating, steering along

301

the road. I'm just a passenger, but that's fine. The screen at the front lights up, shows us the route ahead.

'Where would you like to go?' the tinny voice of the bike asks. This one is definitely older than the Gaia voice, much more robotic. The battery is mostly full, the voice tells me, and the roads ahead are clear of traffic. 'Where would you like to go?' it asks again.

'Washington,' I say.

'Should I avoid toll roads?'

'I don't care. Just drive.'

So it does. The bike swerves to avoid the holes and cracks in the road. All I do is hold the handlebars, and Rex holds me. The sun is to one side of us, the streets, the burned-down forest, the dried-up lake the other. Rex clings on. I can feel the gun, slung around her body, pressing against my back, and as we judder on the road, it digs into me. Her good hand clutches my waist. She doesn't say anything; I know she's looking for the birds, and I know that they'll find us. But we're fast, and Jonah has given us time.

I can't think about him now. Not yet.

I watch the road. It's so fast, and we pass so much land that once was used for farming or living, but now lies sweltering and wrecked under the heat of the sun. I think about how I'll probably have to head back into the wilderness, when I've got Mae. I wonder where we'll go, what sort of life we'll lead. I'll need to start something new, for both of our sakes, something safe. I wonder if Rex will want to come, if I will even want her to.

I don't notice Rex nudging me, and it isn't until she leans closer to my ear and shouts that she gets my attention. She points behind us, into the distance. I turn my head quickly, to glance at what she's seen.

The birds are coming. They scream over the fractured bones of the trees that occasionally jut out from the land. I can see them framed against the clear crisp blue-white of the sky, swooping and swirling. The formation they make in the air is almost like the flow of water, tumbling and whirling. Jonah's sacrifice has taken some of them out of the equation, and kept the rest of them far away, but not nearly far enough.

'Can we go faster?' Rex shouts, and I turn the handlebar, but the computer voice cuts in. It can't calculate the path if it goes any faster, it says. The ground on either side of the road is ripped up and torn everywhere, cracked and scarred like Rex's chest, Jonah's back. It is impractical to ride on it. But the birds can find us out here, no matter which way we go. Maybe we'll outpace them, I think; so we'll stick with the road until we're somewhere that we can hide. I've seen them when they want somebody. I think about them in that block in the city, breaking through the windows, smashing through the doors. They're relentless, and that was only a few of them. I wonder what they'll do to us now, given how fast we're running from them.

There must be something we can do.

'Give me the gun,' I shout back to Rex. I let go of the handlebars, trusting the computer to keep us straight and balanced. Rex pushes it into my hand, and drops the bullets over my shoulder and into my lap. I fiddle with the catches, and I find a hatch that flips open. I flick the bullets into the only hole I find, which seems like the right hole, and I point the gun into the sky.

I pull the trigger. I don't know what I'm expecting. Not this. The gun almost kicks against me, and I nearly lose my seat, have to grab the handlebar again, wrapping my arm almost around it. The noise is insane even over the sound of the bike, so loud and so angry. Rex grabs me, holds tighter, stops me from falling. She needs me. We can't escape without each other.

'Take it back,' I say. She ignores me. I turn around, craning my neck, and I look at her.

She's terrified. I've seen her scared, angry, desperate to save herself; but I've never seen her like this before. On Australia she acted as though she didn't care if she lived or died. Agatha called it a death wish: because death was inevitable, and Rex acted as though she didn't care when it came. But here, now, I can tell that she doesn't want to die.

And neither do I.

'Take the gun and shoot them,' I say, channelling my mother's voice, her commanding tone, as best I can. 'If you don't, they will catch us.' I want to explain to her what they'll do, but she hasn't seen it for herself. She doesn't know. 'They will kill you,' I say. Nothing. She's frozen. 'And if they don't? They'll try what they did to you at Pine City, only worse. They'll take away who you are, and this time they'll make it stick.'

She snatches the gun from me, letting go of me, resting the barrel on her knife-arm, and she turns on the seat, bending backwards as far as she can. She aims up towards the birds.

'Just like firing an arrow,' I shout, 'think about them moving, where they're going, what we're doing.'

'I know,' she says. She pulls the trigger. I grab the handles to steady us, squeezing down hard, instinct kicking in. I try to compensate for the kick of the gun, and the computer squeaks, slams a word up onto the screen, a voice that I can barely hear over the sound of the ringing in my ears.

'Override,' it says.

'No!' I scream. We lurch, left to right. 'Just faster!' But it's in my control all of a sudden, and we wobble on the road, veer slightly, and I wrestle with holding the handlebars steady, trying to steady the bike.

'Again,' I hear Rex say, and she pulls the trigger once more. In the sky behind us, something explodes. I swear that I hear Rex laugh.

'Take over!' I scream at the bike, but it doesn't listen. I don't know the right command. It's old, and it doesn't understand me; or maybe it just won't. Maybe it's broken, unable to listen, to take orders. I clutch the grips, tell myself to hold them tight, tell myself that we'll be fine. The road is pretty much a straight line. As long as I don't move, the bike won't move either.

Then Rex shifts her weight, swinging around so that she's facing the birds, riding backwards, and I almost lose it. 'Stop moving!' I shout. I hear her plant her knife into the seat, to hold herself tight. I turn, to look at it, to see how close the blade is to me, and I accidentally squeeze the handlebars tighter, or turn them, or something. We go faster still. Rex screams, a noise of absolute pleasure and I look back at her in the mirrors, just a glance.

She's aiming at the sky, and she squeezes the trigger and, behind us, one of the birds collapses on itself, tumbling, colliding with the others around it. They explode, smoke and flames. The other birds swoop and churn around the falling debris, making a new formation; spreading themselves out, making the group harder to hit.

And I could swear that they're getting faster.

'Again!' I shout. Rex aims and fires, but they're ready for it this time. They roll and dive, carving through the sky, leaving empty spaces where they were only moments before. They're changing their tactics and edging closer to us.

I squeeze the grips again. Faster, faster. I need to see what the bike can do. The road is speeding by so fast that it's just a grey blur in front of us, around us, behind us. On either side the landscape is endless desert, peeling off into whatever's in the distance – trees; the remains of towns; places that I've never been and I'll never go. Everything blurs into colour and noise.

'They're getting closer!' Rex takes more shots, single bullets that ring out. In the mirror at the side of the handlebar, I watch as she makes the birds spark and tumble to the earth, or (when she really nails a shot) burst in the sky, a cloud of bright orange flame for a second, before the debris falls onto the road in the distance behind us.

The bike shakes. I look at the road, trying to focus on it. I can tell it's in terrible condition, cracked and riddled with holes, worse than anywhere we've been yet. I don't know what to do. I slow us down, then move the bars a little, and the bike tilts according to my direction, swerving on the road around the cracks. They're getting bigger; I can make out one giant one, running right down the middle of the road. I've got to pick a side, stick to it. I have no choice.

In the distance, I see where the crack ends in a crevice, a split in the earth that drives sideways through the road itself, driving it upwards into what looks almost like a pursed lip. I think about turning off, going onto the dirt, but it's too late. The lip comes, closer and closer: an upwards curve.

'Hold on!' I scream, and I feel her reach back, fumbling, clutching onto my shirt.

The bike roars to the lip. We go up it, and I see the front wheel leave the ground, and I shut my eyes for what feels like an eternity; but when I open them we're still in the air. Below us the crack yawns, so dark that I can't see its bottom. There's just blackness down there. An abyss. For a second, we're flying; there's nothing below us, nothing holding us down.

We're weightless.

Only for a second.

And then we slam onto the road on the other side of the crevice and I struggle to keep the bike steady. We skid to the side, off the road and onto the soil and the dusty remains of what was maybe once fields. The bike seems to slip out from underneath us, and then Rex is gone, thrown off, rolling along behind us in a cloud of dust kicked up around her; and I tumble after, helpless. I watch the bike spiral away, flipping, ploughing into the dirt, smoke coming from its vents.

I shout Rex's name, but she doesn't reply. It hurts to move, to push myself to my knees, hurts still more to get to standing. My clothes are ripped, shredded around the knees. My hands are torn up and bleeding, so I press them to my belly, trying to get the blood off, to see how bad the damage is; and I run – hobble – towards where Rex is lying, curled up.

My ears are ringing. I forgot about the birds for a moment. It's only as the ringing fades that I hear them, their tiny engines whirring in the sky, a buzz that's closer than it's yet been. I look up, and they're in a new formation, pretty much right above us.

'Get up,' I say to Rex. I nudge her with my foot. She could be dead, I know. 'Get up.' She doesn't. She stays perfectly still, and I can't even see the rise and fall of her chest. Her eyes are open. Your eyes are only open like that when you're gone. I've seen it before. I've closed too many eyes myself.

And I wonder, in that moment, why we close the eyes of our dead. When did we decide that the dead shouldn't face whatever comes next with their eyes open? When did we decide that they should be put into the dark, shut away, blocked out from everything after them?

The birds swirl. They make a spiral in the sky, round and round, and they start to descend. I hear the sound of a whip lashing out, and I shut my eyes.

The sound of the gun going off is louder than it was when we were on the bike. Here, without the rush of the air as we speed along the road, it's the most colossal noise. A few of the birds are caught in the blast, and we're showered with sparks and chunks of metal as they fall to the ground.

The rest of the birds disperse. For a second, they look almost like the shape of a star: different points going off in every direction. Rex coughs, breathing hard and heavy.

She's bleeding, I see; some wound on her chest, a spot of it coming through the fabric of her top.

'Let's go,' she says. She keeps the gun trained on the birds. They don't fly away, but they don't come any closer, either. I help her to her feet, and we run to the bike, half-dragging each other as we go. The birds stay back. They didn't get close enough to take us, but we were lucky. If Rex hadn't woken up . . .

'Get it started,' she says. We climb on, just as we were before, and I tell the bike to start, to put us back on the road.

'Operating at fifty percent efficiency,' it tells me, but I don't know what that means.

'Just go,' I say. Rex keeps the gun aimed back at where we came from. It's the longest time before she stops, puts the gun down, turns back around towards me; and I hear her sigh, feel the weight of her head as it rests on the back of my neck.

We stop to stretch our legs. Halfway to the city, the bike's screen tells us; but the battery is more gone than that. It wore itself down when I was in control, or when it was putting itself right after the crash. Either way, it's running lower than it should, I think. We're both aching, and neither of us says very much. We stand in the desert, and we look at the horizon, and we stare; as the sun starts to set, off in the distance, I know what I'm looking for. The shaking line in my vision that could be – should be – the sea.

TWELVE

'What happens when we get there?' Rex asks me. We've stopped again, because it's getting dark. The light on the front of the bike flickers, something broken inside it. It's too hard to see, and we can't keep going down this broken road without seeing where we're going. So we'll sleep. That's the easiest thing to do.

In the last light of the sun we found the trickling remains of a river. When we arrived, we sat and drank until we felt bloated and poorly, our faces pressed down into it. It was salty, but not too bad; the water warm and bitter, not unlike the taste of blood. But we didn't care. And then we lay back and we pined for food, and listened as each other's bellies rumbled. Neither of us said a word, not about the water, not about each other. Rex didn't even complain about her wound, about the pain she must be in.

Only now, moments from sleep, does she finally want to talk.

'Once we get there we find Ziegler,' I tell her. 'He's somebody I know. He helped me when I first got here.'

'You trust him?'

'As much as I trust anybody,' I say. I don't tell her how we left things when I last saw him. I think about how pleased he'll be, me bringing more evidence of my story about Australia. The woman who tried to kill me, her name carved into her chest, her arm gone: everything that I told him, true. Rex is proof. We watch the moon rise in the sky, pinks and deep blues, giving way to blackness; the stars creeping in, poking through, forcing their way.

'I want to know who I was,' she says.

'I've told you. I knew you as Rex, and—'

'No. Those are things that I did. Not who I was. Who I am.' I turn and look at her. Staring up at the sky, just as I have been doing; looking at the same stars.

'On Australia, those things are the same,' I say.

'Where is Australia now?'

'I don't know,' I say. What would it look like from here? A speck? Or would we be able to see it, floating around, still as it was when we left it; somehow static up there, unmoving, unchanged. 'I don't know if you're the same person. I didn't know you, when we were up there.'

'You tried to kill me.'

'You keep saying that.'

'It is one of the things that I remember the strongest.'

I sigh. 'I don't know if I'm the same person. But I know that I still *feel* the same, inside me. That's what matters. If you feel different . . .' I shut my eyes and turn away from her. 'I can't forget who I was.'

She is quiet for the longest time. 'What if I want to?' I don't know what happened to Rex: when she born; as she got older, either born a Low or inducted at some early age;

fighting to survive harder than I had to fight, not having the protection of somebody who wanted nothing more than for her to survive; being constantly threatened, not only by her enemies, but by those that she ate with, slept with, fought with.

I don't have an answer. During our final days on Australia, everybody looked to me for answers, as if I was going to be able to solve every single problem we had. And I knew nothing; I was a few steps ahead of everybody else, but it was just luck, or because I knew Agatha, or because I was out there, doing what I could. It wasn't like I understood the great secrets of life. Everyone treated me like I was older, wiser than I am. But I wasn't. I'm seventeen years old. Eighteen, now, maybe. I don't know the date, not exactly. Time's gone too fast.

Rex doesn't say anything more. At some point, we sleep. It's cold, and I can hear her teeth grinding in the darkness, in the silence of this place. I shut my eyes, and I think about Jonah. I wonder where he is now. If I'll ever see him again.

Starving hungry, mouths dry, we wake at the same time, at the sound of beating wings; as the sun starts to come up in the distance, a thick orange glow that hangs in the sky like fire. Rex sits up, looking around her, frantic, desperate. Then she smiles.

'Look,' she whispers. There are real birds all around us, scrappy looking, patches in their feathers, strange colours, pecked scars from fighting and surviving. 'Food.' She reaches for the gun, and I realise that I didn't even think about leaving it with her last night, while we slept; I just trusted that she wouldn't use it on me. It didn't even cross my mind that she might.

She takes aim at the birds. There's a thin whine as she turns it on, as the targeting starts to work. 'Hold still,' she says, though I don't know if she means me or the birds.

She pulls the trigger. One of them pretty much explodes with the force of the bullet that's been shot into it, and the others scatter, leaping up from the ground to take flight, crowing as they go.

'Food,' Rex repeats. She scrambles to her feet and runs to the bird, picking up the remains and examining them. It's dripping with blood, split nearly in two; one part dangles from the other. It's big, though. Big enough for both of us. I don't know what it'll taste like. I can't even imagine. She lifts it to her mouth and sniffs it, and she's about to eat it, raw and bloody, when I stop her.

'Wait!' I shout. 'You have to cook it.' She tilts her head at me, questioning. 'It will make you sick. You're not used to it. You have to cook it. We need a fire.'

She growls, and throws it at me. It lands at my feet, skidding in the dirt. 'Fine then. You get it ready.'

In the city, birds are served without feathers. I figure that's where I should start, so I pluck them from its body, carefully at first, then rushing it as the hunger takes over. I watch as Rex picks up sticks from the scrub, and small rocks. She assembles them in a delicate pile, a tent of twigs and dried up grasses, and then she kneels next to it. She takes a rock and strikes it against another, but she can't get a spark. Nothing happens. Again and again she tries, and she gets angrier, more frustrated with herself.

The last of the feathers come out, but they take effort. Some are set tight, and the skin around them is hard and leathery. Blood flows over my hands as I squeeze the bird to get enough purchase.

'I'm sorry,' I say to it. It can't hear me. I wonder if it even knew what was happening to it, as it died.

Rex throws one of the rocks away, pitching it far into the distance. We don't hear the thud of it landing, but it scatters some of the birds who have settled down again, forgetting what she did, trusting us again. She picks up another stone and changes tack, this time striking it with her knife; hammering the sharp edge onto the stone at an angle. It isn't long before she gets a spark, and then she dives to the ground, blowing into the small pile of tinder that she's made. The fire takes. It burns so quickly it's like there was a fuel there.

I walk to the fire and sit down opposite her. I take a stick from the ground and drape the carcass over it, and then hold it out over the flames. The blood drips from the creature, sizzling on the fire, making it smoke. The skin of the bird starts to change colour almost immediately.

Rex's mouth hangs wide, a slight trail of drool on her lip; and I don't blame her.

We eat every single piece of the bird. Everything. Rex doesn't care: it's all meat. She plucks the head from the body, charred almost to black, and she uses her knife to scoop the brain out of its skull, eating it right off the blade, a lump of deep purple and red that slips into her mouth with an ooze of liquids. She sucks the eyeballs from the head after that. Every bit is food.

She gives me most of the meat from the body. The bits that I recognise. It all tastes the same to her, or she acts like it does, eating as a means of survival rather than anything else. It's amazing: the energy that I feel after eating it. It's like the last couple of days haven't happened. I feel so much stronger. We stand up, stomachs aching, crying for more food and hoping we don't feed them at the same time, and we walk to the bike, start it. We get on the road again, driving slower, letting the bike's computer take control.

'Economy mode,' it tells us, and we get to watch the scenery some more. The engine cuts every so often, letting us cruise. We enjoy this part: the wind in our faces, brushing through our hair, across our heads. Later I feel Rex slumped against me, sleeping as we go, and I hold on, eyes wide, trying to concentrate on the landscape we're passing through.

We pass nothing and we see nothing, except for the landscape, and the broken tarmac that looks the same as it does everywhere else along this road.

I think, for a moment, that I could get used to being here. I could live out in this place, if I had only a little more: shelter from the sun; food, and water. I could bear the heat. I could dig a hole, like the downstairs room of that house outside Pine City where it stays cool, and I could live there.

And Mae. She's there, in the fantasy: playing in the stream, eating the birds with me.

*   *   *

I see it when we crest a hill, nearly to the city: the sudden endless blue that somehow meets the sky, almost as if they're one and the same. I have the view to myself for a moment. I try to take it all in, try to understand what it is. I've never seen it before: two not-quite-different colours colliding, then the green along the shore, grass and trees like they have in the city, but sprawling, untamed. The sea glistens under the sun. I want to drink it, swim in it, lie in it and float, let myself drift.

'Rex,' I say. 'Wake up. Look at this.' I feel her move, her arms unwrapping from my body, and I hear her gasp, softly as anything, when she sees it.

'What is that?' she asks.

'That's the ocean,' I say. The bike keeps going, slower and slower, trying to get us there. It won't quite make it, but we can see it; we can see where we want to be.

The bike gives up just as we reach the first sproutings of grass from the dirt. The wind is stronger here and the air doesn't feel quite as hot. And it tastes different: there's salt on it, it's wet enough that, if it catches you right, it's refreshing. I can't quite tell how big it is, not really, because there's not much to give it scale: just the stretch of ground that goes off, changes, slips underneath the sea. The sea stretches on and on. I say goodbye to the bike as we walk off, because it feels right. I thank it. It did a lot for us.

The road is less damaged than further inland, cracked and then settled back into place. You can see plants growing through the cracks, small green plants coming up through the little potholes and crevices. As we continue, the sand on the sides turns completely to green scrub: plants and grasses and shrubs. There are no trees, just bushes. The ground alongside the road is softer, not as dry.

Rex steps off the road and onto the plants, and she takes her shoes from her feet.

'I never had the arboretum,' she says, 'not until the end. I used to watch you all in there, on the grass, in the stream. I would wonder what it felt like.'

'You could have gone in,' I say.

'They would not have had me. I would have had to fight my way in.'

'We might have to fight when we get to Washington.'

'Then why are we going?'

'For Mae,' I reply.

'She's in danger,' Rex says. Not a question, more an assumption.

'She's been taken. I want to find her and get her back.'

'You want to rescue her.'

'Yes.' I watch Rex's face. She doesn't look at me. She presses her hand to her side.

'I had a daughter,' she says, out of nowhere. 'When I was very young. I had a daughter.' She presses her side, fingers on a scar I assumed was from violence, from conflict, but now it's so clear to me. It's deeper than the rest. Older. The only scar that really seems as if it's always been a part of her.

'Where is she?' I ask, but I already know.

'Dead.' She doesn't pause. The word spat out, full of fury. The Lows were like that. They didn't try and save each other. Individuals survived as part of the unit. I wonder

317

what happened, if the child was taken from her; if she tried to save it. If she even had the chance. 'You want to be Mae's mother,' she says.

'I just want to make sure she's safe.' I think about Agatha, taking care of me, teaching me everything I needed to know when my own mother was gone. How lucky I was, even if I couldn't see it at first. She wasn't a replacement for my own mother. She was something else to me. A guardian, and a friend.

'What if you can't keep her safe?' Rex asks.

'I will,' I say. 'I promised her.'

Rex doesn't take her hand off her scar. I wonder what she's thinking of, if she can remember her own daughter's face, as a newborn; if she can remember the sound that she made as she cried.

The sea is astonishing. When we reach it we stare and we watch the waves as they roll in, crashing over each other, slamming into the rocks that litter the shoreline like jagged teeth. The water churns, and it's beautiful and terrifying in equal measure.

We almost run when the grass at the sides of the road gets thicker, growing in and over the ruined road itself; and as we can see sand, sharp clifftops, chunks where the earth has fallen down and into the sea, chunks of earth lying on their sides, exposed and waiting. We find a path down, a steep slope. I skid and run down it, Rex right behind me, jumping as much as we can, landing on our feet, staying steady. And then we get to the bottom where the sand meets the sea, the water lapping up against it.

Our feet sink into the sand, overwhelming them, soaking us, but we keep going. We wade out into the sea itself, feeling the cool of the water on our legs, our bodies. We drink the water, cupping it to our mouths. It's salty, disgusting, revolting, and it makes me gag, but it's water, and my body takes it until it refuses, and I sick it all back up. Rex laughs. She drinks it as well, but less than I do, and doesn't reject it. And then she submerges herself for a moment, ducking down before springing up, throwing water everywhere. Feeling the blood that caked her, the sand in every line of our skin, the film of sweat: everything comes off, comes clean.

In that moment, I remember what it feels like to be free, and happy, and hopeful.

We walk south, towards Washington, following the shoreline. This wasn't always the shore. Once, the land went on for miles and miles before it fell off into the water. Then the sea rose and the land eroded and chunks of it were swept away, and there are still signs of that: the ruins of buildings clinging to the cliff edges; the signs that say *Welcome* where roads once led into towns; the tree stumps that might have been forests, jutting from the cliffs. It's rocky in places, impenetrable in others, and we're forced out of the sea to walk along the land for stretches before heading back down, letting ourselves get wet again, trudging in our damp clothes as they dry in the blazing heat. We're hungry again, needing more food; feeling our skin getting hot and dry. Hoods pulled close, burns on our heads from where the sun has found its way through, where the skin is peeled and painful.

We talk about fish, which we can see bobbing around, swirling by our feet, coming to the surface. Can we shoot them? I can't remember having ever eaten a fish, but I know that they're edible. In the city, I've seen them eaten raw. That seems like something we could do.

I say this to Rex, and she grins, a manic look on her face. She holds the gun above her head, primed to shoot, and she wades out into the water, and stands very still, perfectly still, waiting for the fish to swarm her, to gather around her inquisitively before she betrays them.

Towards the end of the day, as the sun starts to set, the sky goes black. Night is coming, but then more than that: a darker kind of dusk formed by clouds, strong and grey, swarming in from across the sea. We stand and watch them as they cluster. They move fast, the wind that carries them blows against us. It's warm, strong enough to push us back a step or two, to make us struggle against it. My hair whips into my face, so I tie it back.

'I don't like it,' Rex says. Her voice is small.

'It's only rain,' I say. I know about rain; I know that every so often, rain comes and it floods the ground, which can't absorb the water fast enough. The storm goes within hours, and when it's gone it's almost like it was never there; the sun boils the water off before it can do any good. There are mechanisms in the city that catch the water to use another time; but out here it just evaporates away.

I open my mouth, let the rain come in, drink it up. It's good. It's nearly cold, and it's wet, and it tastes better than the sea, and I feel better than I did; despite what's happening to us, better than I have in days.

The clouds keep getting nearer. Rex asks if we should stop, find shelter, but I can see something in the distance: a grey dot, a speck on the horizon that must be the city. If it's not, I don't know what it is. Another city, maybe. Somewhere else that could be safe. I point it out.

She nods. She listens to me. And just like that, it's agreed: we keep going.

There's no sun, no moon, just a strange half-light formed by streaks of silver lightning as the boiling sky rips above us. It's terrifying, the first time that it happens: the noise a stretched growl as brutal as gunshots, and then that light, those bolts. They're like scars running from the sky to the earth, but they come and then fade, as violent as anything I've ever seen. I'm sure we both scream, that first time, but I can't hear her doing it, and she can't hear me. That's how loud the noise is. It echoes around the beach, bouncing off the rocks, making the ground feel as though it's rumbling, ready to tear apart, to swallow us whole.

Then more rain comes, warm and heavy. I think of the first time that I stood underneath that shower in the secret part of Australia; how it felt unnatural, almost unsettling, the sound of it beating around me, slapping onto my skin. And now, the same feeling, of something bigger than me that thrills and excites and scares all at the same time. This storm is heavier than even the shower, I think, water driving down from the sky. I wish I knew how it was made, where it came from. I try and look up, but it's too strong; water stings my face and fills my eyes. Rex panics, shouting my name, reaching for me. 'It's okay,' I tell her. As we trudge along the beach I take her hand, squeeze it tightly, slippery as it is from the water smashing down our arms, meeting at the middle between us.

It will be alright.

The bolts – lightning, I whisper the name, lightning and thunder, hand in hand, like Rex and myself – keep darting down in the distance, and the sky sounds like anger, like the grizzled rage of somebody screaming in attack. Every so often it heaves a noise up, guttural and pained, and the rain seems to pick up pace. The rain pours down in waves: so heavy that we can't see a thing in front of us, but we keep going, sometimes losing the coastline, wandering into the sea, only realising we're wading when the water sluices over our shoes, that's how wet we are; and then it relents, as though it's breathing, or giving us a chance to set ourselves right before it begins again.

Every time a bolt comes, Rex jumps; every time the thunder rolls, she squeezes my hand tighter. She's got the gun strapped to her, and I hear the sound of the wind whipping it around in the wind. We don't talk; we just move.

We walk for hours, on and on, and it feels like we're getting nowhere. There are inlets dug out from the cliffs, the remains of walls that have slumped, that offer nearly enough shelter; we huddle in them for a few minutes, until the chill of our wet clothes drying makes us shiver so hard that our jaws hurt. It's warmer in the water, we discover, and we walk through that for periods. It's not like we can get any more wet than we already are. We keep going, and it's so dark we can't see where we're headed; but as long as we keep the water on one side, it's the only way we can go. If we go long enough, we'll get to the city.

Everything hurts, but that's always the way. I'm coming to accept that I'm simply never going to be comfortable.

I wonder if I need this feeling, this burn.

The storm rages harder, faster, brighter. There are flashes of white in the distance, and shapes behind them, silhouetted. Details are hard to make out, because it's so dark everywhere else. It's like staring into a light, the shapes and colours that are left when you look away.

The lightning comes faster and it holds, digs its feet in. The sky isn't black like it should be at night, but a dusky half-light that doesn't fade when the lightning does. In the distance, as the rain lashes, as we struggle, I see a cliff on the horizon: a jutting monument, taller than anything I've ever seen and sticking out into the sea. It's in our way. We'll not be able to pass it. We'll have to go back or over, have to find another way around. We'll lose more time. The lightning flashes again, throwing parts of the cliff into being, almost, and—

It's not lightning, not natural.

It's the wall that runs around Washington. This is it from the outside; not clean and polished and protected, but beaten by the wind and the sea and the nearly ceaseless heat of the sun, covered in dirt and plants and vines and sand.

I feel, for a second, like I've come home, and the swell that comes with that – of comfort, of a strange, brief kind of peace.

323

But then I realise that's wrong. This is just a place that I once lived.

And, now, it's a place where I've got work to do.

We get closer, as close as we can. Rex is amazed by the wall because it's like nothing she's ever seen. She didn't see it when we first landed here. She was unconscious, taken away, healed, and then her mind was purged and rebuilt. She never saw the city. She hasn't seen the streets, the cars, the people. What's beyond that wall is going to be a lot for her to take. I know that all too well.

Mechanical birds circle above, even in the storm, their lights shining down on the rubble at the base. We can see marks where it's been attacked, or maybe where the landscape has worn the metal and stone away. It resembles the rocks and beaches we've walked past on our way here. Chunks have been taken out, and the bricks have collapsed in places: enough that you can see that the wall is old and weathering badly. It'll need work to stop it collapsing in on itself, because they haven't taken care of it on the outside. They've worried about what's inside, what's visible. Ziegler told me that they – we, people, humans – always leave worrying about things we can't see until it's too late, until the very last minute, and then we have to repair problems and calamities. We should have been trying to stop them from happening in the first place, but we don't. That's human nature, he said; that's the problem with us. We don't worry about the future; we're always too concerned with living in the now.

We watch the birds' lights as they circle, shining down at

the base of the wall. They shine on what looks like trash or rocks, until we get close enough to see that it's not; it's tents. Rocks are arranged into shelters, into caves. Fires burn inside them. There are people here. Some of them notice us, and they stop and they stare. They raise their hands into the air, and they signal through the rain, picking up torches to wave, to get our attention, to show us that they're there.

'Who are they?' Rex shouts through the pelt of the storm. She has her hand ready to pull the gun, and her knife primed, prepared for battle. She doesn't trust them. I'm not sure that she's not right. 'What do they want?'

I stare, trying to make out their faces, trying to figure out what the waving means.

I'm sure they are smiling.

'They don't look dangerous,' I tell her.

'So why are they here? Why not inside?'

'They're exiled,' I say. Ziegler told me about them. Some people didn't want the city, didn't want the control over their lives that living there demanded, so they left. And now they're calling to us.

It should be a death sentence: forcing people from the cities, making them live outside of what we know. No prisons, no camps to hold them; exiling them into a broiling wasteland where there's barely food, barely shelter. There's no hope out here; that's the punishment. Exile is a death penalty delivered slowly and surely. An inevitability. It's cruel, and it's what happened to our ancestors: sent onto the Australia, given a chance to survive; a chance that, it was assumed, would be squandered. Out of sight and out of mind.

But we survived. And these people have survived. They're thriving. The woman who was waving to us rushes up as we get closer. She takes my hand. Her hair is long, threaded together into chaotic knots, and she smiles with a warmth that I haven't seen in a very, very long time.

'You're wet,' she says. Her accent is so loose that the words are a long slip out of her mouth. She reaches for Rex's hand, and then sees the knife. 'And you been in the wars.' This little chortle come from her, halfway between a cough and a laugh. 'You want some food?'

'Yes,' Rex says, before I even have a chance to consider her offer. She follows the woman back towards their camp, towards the fires in their makeshift caves, the smell of cooking food drifting towards us on the warm damp breeze.

They have chairs made from driftwood. Tents of stretched fabric, sewn together in patchwork. They welcome us in, ask us where we've come from. There are four of them, and more outside.

'We don't see many strangers here,' says the woman who greeted us. 'I'm Fiona. This is Mark. Mark!' A man rushes in, holding a spear of some sort, and a net. Rex flinches, and then relaxes. He's got soft eyes, soft features. Rex and I are very good at spotting the ones who'll hurt us. 'Get the girls some food,' Fiona says. 'They're needing it.' She picks up a kettle that's been warming on the fire and she pours whatever's inside into cups, passes them to us, tells Rex to watch herself, because it's hot, and harder to manage with only the one hand.

The smell of the food hits me. I don't wait for it to cool; I gulp it, because I know the scent, know what it's going to taste like, what it will remind me of. It's a stew of some sort, and it tastes just like we used to make on the ship. My mother used to make it, and then Agatha, Bess, so many other people. It scalds the roof of my mouth, my tongue, my throat. I don't care.

'Like I asked, where you from?' Fiona says. Another woman, much younger, sits down across from us, her back against a rock. She doesn't take her eyes off me. She's suspicious, and who can blame her? 'We don't judge. Some of us, we're exiled, sure. Some of us, we're here of our own choice. Whichever is your story, we won't question you. But we need to know. That's the deal. We're accepting of anything, as long as we're all on the same level.'

'We're from Australia,' Rex says. Fiona takes a second, sizing that up, unsure of what to make of it. Then she laughs, and she rocks backwards.

'Darling, you're not. I know an Aussie when I see one, and you're not one. She sank a long time before you were born. I should know, shouldn't I?' Her accent. That's why I don't recognise it. She's not from here.

'You're talking about the country,' I say. Her head tilts to one side.

'I was there until the day we were forced off – stayed well past everybody else, past the evacs, all that. What other Australia would I be talking about?' she asks.

'Up there,' Rex says. She looks up at the sky, and Fiona's gaze follows. 'The spaceship.'

'I see,' Fiona says. 'I reckon that's a story I'd like to hear, one day.' She stands up and cranes her neck, to see down the beach. 'After you're fed up, eh?' I stand up and look as well. There's a group of people down at the beach, where the wall meets the sea, circling around, digging its own trench underneath the surface. The rain has mostly stopped now, the lightning abated. The sky's gone back to its own colour. The water crashes and slams into the wall, and to watch it from here, it's like seeing the action slowed down, stretched out; the drawing back of the wave, then its push forward; a slam, a collision, and the dark water exploding across the stone.

Mark, the man who Fiona sent out, wades into the water as deep as he can. He jabs his spear down under the waves, trying to find something. A few jabs, over and over, and then he cheers, and wades back. He holds his spear aloft, the trophy on the end: a giant wriggling fish. No, it has tentacles: it's a squid. I've seen one of them, a giant one, hanging in the ceiling of the museum. This is much smaller, but it looks strong enough. The others have to help Mark restrain it, as it tries to wrap its tentacles around his arm, to haul itself away from him, away from land, back into the sea. They all pull on it. But Mark grabs the tentacles, bunches them together and walks up the beach, holding it proudly as it dangles and writhes in his grip.

In the darkness I can see Mark in silhouette, the clothes he's wearing clinging to his ribs, showing every single bone. His shoulder blades jut out from his back like fins as he raises the squid above his head, and then he slams it down, hard, into the rocks at his feet. Up and down, over and over, slam, slam, until it's nearly motionless. He brings it close to his face, plunges one hand in and pulls something out of it. Guts. Then he washes it in the water, and comes up the beach, thinking it dead, but it convulses to life again. Despite everything he did to it, there's more in it. So he slams it against the rocks again. And then again, for good measure. Back to the sea, to wash it one more time; and then the weak cheers as he presents it, brings it up the beach towards us. Finally triumphant. 'You ever eaten squid?' Fiona asks.

They drape the creature on the hot rocks, and we listen as it sizzles and pops, and the air fills with the salty smell of this thing that's going to taste so much better than it looks.

'So where are you going then?' Fiona asks later, mouth full of squid. It's cut into chunks, and they're chewy, but they're so tasty, so savoury. Salt and herbs on them. The flavour comes out the more you chew; there's something very satisfying about that.

'We're going into the city,' Rex says. She's more confident now that we're eating. She's speaking for us, as if we're a unit. *We're going*.

'You think it's that easy?'

'She was in there before,' Rex says, gesturing at me. 'She came from there, and then we were in Pine City. Assholes there.' She spears a tentacle with her knife, and raises the end to her mouth. Drapes it onto her tongue, and bites.

'But now we're going back. There's a little girl who needs us.' Fiona looks over at me and smiles. I'm smiling as well, I realise. The old lady nods, and stands up. She bends backwards, and we hear the bones in her crick and crack as she stretches herself out.

'There's a way in. We don't use it, not much, only for supplies. Things we can't get hold of out here.' She warms her hands by the fire, wipes them on the furs on her legs. 'It's not easy, but it's all we've got.'

'What do we have to do?' I ask.

'For what?'

'To get passage.' They'll want something. Everybody wants something.

'You say *thank you*, and you come bring us some supplies if you're ever passing this way again. Otherwise? It's your way in as much as it's ours.'

Or it's a trap, I think. 'Why do you live out here? Why not in there?' Fiona shrugs. The girl sitting against the rock throws something into the fire, which fizzes and sparks.

'Why would we?' she asks. 'Why live somewhere they're not learning from mistakes? We live here because it's free. The drones leave us alone, and the police never come out here. We do what we want to do, and we have a good life. It's not living in fancy towers, sure, but it's ours. It's actually ours, you know?' She pushes herself to standing, plucks the final bit of squid and pops it into her mouth. 'How many people in there can say that?'

Fiona walks us down the beach, past all the people making their lives here. She indicates a couple as we go by: a man whittling something from wood and then passing it to a little kid, watching as she clutches the figurine close to her chest, grateful.

'It's better here than in there,' Fiona reiterates. And I agree with her. Something about this little encampment reminds me of the nicer parts of Australia; the parts where, sometimes, I felt safe. The arboretum. My berth, that I shared with my mother. The secret part of the ship that I discovered. I can even hear laughter, somewhere. And I think about what it's like inside the city. It might be safe and clean, but there are so many rules, about where you can live, what you can do, whether or not you can even have children. Here, everything's free. I can't remember hearing laughter in the city, not like this; the sound caught in the air, carried through it like smoke. Here, kids play. Not just one or two – with their parents standing around like outside Dave's apartment – but a gaggle of them. They run in circles. Fiona touches their heads as they go, and they laugh. They plough into the sea, and we follow them; even in the dark, in the final sputters of the storm as it passes, in the light from the fires and the birds and the strange grey-brown of the post-storm sky, they're happy.

We keep walking until the sea is lapping at our feet, and Fiona nudges us to the edge of the wall, where it meets the sand and the sea. There's a rope here, leading away into the darkness. She picks it up.

'You follow this, don't let go,' she tells us. 'This goes round. Bit rough out there after the storm, I won't lie, so just try and keep your head above the water, okay? Just keep going until it ends, you'll be right as rain.'

331

'There must be another way,' Rex says.

'Nope. Well, there's the guards at the gates,' Fiona says, 'you can try going through them, if you want. They won't take too kindly to you, I'm guessing. And more than likely they're already looking out for you.'

'It'll be fine,' I say to Rex; and I reach over, put my hand on her arm. I squeeze it, trying to reassure her. We weren't friends. We have history. But now we're together. We're *we*. She's scared. I think that she's likely never been underwater.

But, she has. Of course she has. After I stabbed her, when she fell. She would have landed in the pit then, flooding as it was. She would have nearly drowned there.

She doesn't tell me that she's terrified, but it's in her eyes, and her one hand shakes as she takes the rope.

'Follow me,' I say. 'You get stuck, shout, and I'll help you. I won't let you fall.' I wade out, holding onto the rope as I feel the water get deeper, the sand below harder to reach while keeping my head above water. Rex takes it after me, follows me out, her good arm hooked around the rope, the other – complete with knife – free at her side. 'Let me know if you need me, and I'll help,' I shout. The water crashes around us and I turn back to Fiona. 'Thank you,' I yell. 'I won't forget this.'

'I know,' she shouts back. 'I still want to hear that story of yours, someday. Way I see it, we've got some shared blood.' She walks backwards, and she waves. 'Be safe.'

The tide is the strangest temperature: almost warm as it pushes in from the sea, then colder as it drags back, the chill from inside escaping. I'm shorter than Rex and I'm treading water before she is, almost swimming. With one hand on the rope, she launches herself along, kicking with her feet to stay afloat. The rope sags a little too much, though, under the weight of both of us. The water splashes over our heads every so often, soaking us. She spits when her head's above the waves again, smacking her lips at the taste of the salt, breathing in, coughing when she inhales it; she shakes her head again to get the water off her face.

'Not much further,' I say, but the truth is, I have no idea. I'm counting on finding something; seeing something that gives us an indication, a way in. They do this, Fiona said. This is how they get into the city. They come this way for rations, or supplies.

This is safe; until it's suddenly not.

There's something on my leg, something coiled around it, snaking and tight. I panic because I can't move. I try to look behind me, shouting for Rex, clinging to the rope; and the thing seems to pull as the tide goes, as the waves crash, and my grip on the rope slips. Suddenly I'm under the water, eyes open, mouth closed, desperate, being pulled down. I don't know what to do. I try and reach for whatever's taken me under, but I can't. I can't see.

I wonder how long you have before you drown. I can't hold my breath and I open my mouth, my lungs screaming for air. Water rushes in, and I remember this feeling, of thinking I could drown. Everything happens again and again. Everything is an echo.

My vision goes black, so much quicker than I remember it happening.

And then it stops. Then I'm above the water, and Rex is clinging to the rope, her knife-arm wrapped around it, her hand dragging, heaving me to the surface. I can see the glint of the blade reflecting the moon. The clouds have cleared, and the sky is now so clear, and so clean. I gasp in air and water, clinging to the rope to steady myself.

Rex pushes up. 'There was a weed,' she says. And that's it; she freed me, saved me. Simple. She starts moving on, following the rope around the wall, and she just expects me to carry on. So I do.

Ahead of us the rope disappears. All we can see as we follow the wall, as we hit a corner, a sharp edge, is the end of the rope where it's fastened, tied off through a chipped-away section of the concrete. There's no entrance visible and it's only when we're there, right at the end, that I feel the cold current underneath us, tickling at my feet. Our way in is down, under the water.

'How far?' Rex asks.

'I don't know,' I tell her. 'Not far, I'm sure.' I don't give her a chance to balk, to back out. I gulp a breath and dive, and she follows, holding my hand; and there's a tunnel, a tube that's big enough for us both, but only just, so we swim through, kicking our legs in unison. There's light at the end of the tunnel. It's so dark, and my eyes sting, so it's hard to make out any details, but I know that there's a light.

Shut your eyes and go, I tell myself. Do it.

Rex struggles. She didn't breathe enough, I know, but we're nearly there. I pull her with me. Kick harder, I tell myself. She does as I do, like she heard me, or realised.

And then we're clear, through the tunnel and racing for the surface of the water, which is so much colder than the sea. But we can't get through to the air – there's ice on the surface of the water, between us and it. My lungs are screaming for air. I already almost drowned once. The ice is thick, so thick, and the water is so, so cold. I beat the ice with my fists. Rex turns in the water, pivots, kicks out, slamming her boots against it, using me as a joist. But she gets nowhere.

In a last, desperate bid she tries her hand, the knife: not enough force, but it chips away a little. I grab her arm, and we both put all our force into it. Just as I think I can't do it, as I have to take a breath in the water, the ice cracks.

We're going to be okay.

The first time I went into the water at the edge of the city, I was running from Alala. Ziegler had told me to find her, that she was a good contact, that she would sort me out. I didn't trust him, not entirely, but I needed to try. I was terrified, five or six days into being here on this planet. I had escaped and now I was free, in hiding and alone, and I went to find her, only to see that she wasn't home, that her door was open. And there it was. Food. Not much, just bread. Then, as now, she left her door open at all times. The only time a door was shut was when she was asleep. The bread? I had to take it because I was desperate. I would pay her back, that was never in question.

She returned just as I was leaving, hands clasping the loaf like it was going to run away from me, clutching it tight to my gut. I was ashamed, that was it, and scared. Her head tilted, like she was intrigued. Quizzical, more than anything else.

'Little girl? What are you doing in my home?'

I shook my head, terrified. I prayed that she didn't see the bread. I could make an excuse, but there wasn't anything she would have believed.

So I bolted. I pushed past her, and I ran, fast as I could. I wasn't yet healed, my body bruised and broken in so many places, but I had to do what I could; get through the docks, away from her, pray she didn't follow.

She didn't, but her people did. The junkies, the mutes. They chased me to the edge of the water, and those who could speak screamed and howled that I would pay, that they would drag me back to Alala. She would deal with me. The ones who couldn't speak beat their chests like war drums instead. But they wouldn't catch me, I knew. They didn't have a chance. I could take them.

But I didn't want more blood on my hands. I didn't want any more chaos.

I hit the water before I even knew it was there. It was dark out and I wasn't watching where I was going. Keeping my head down as I ran, looking at where I was treading, not where I was going, I plunged into it blindly, and it was so cold I screamed. But all that came out was the muffle of bubbles. Water coursed into my lungs. I kicked out, and I had a moment of sheer terror: that the past week hadn't happened, that I was still on Australia, trying to get below, to the secret place beneath the bodies – to Mae, to Jonah; to leave Australia forever, and get to our new home.

I came to my senses and swam to the surface, chilled and sobbing, and they hunted me. They looked around, calling out for me, so I stayed out of sight, under the wood of a decaying dock or pier at the edge of the water.

When they gave up – it didn't take them long to assume I was dead – I found the remains of the bread floating on the surface, bobbing around, sodden. I crawled out of the sea and sat, shivering, until I felt I could move; and then I rushed to the place where I'd spent the past few nights sleeping – a shanty that somebody had abandoned not long before, that I had stumbled across in a lucky moment of synchronicity that gave me some vague sense of hope – and I found Alala there, waiting for me. She had found me, as she would always find anything she looked for. I didn't know that about her, then; didn't know that she had eyes everywhere. She was sitting on the ground, cross-legged. As I approached, she stood, dusted herself off.

'Silly little girl,' she said. 'It was only bread. I would have given that to you.' She smiled, and in that moment I trusted her. Nobody smiled that warmly and meant you harm on Australia. 'When you have something you really need help with, a real problem, come to see Alala, eh?' She patted my cheek, slow pats, almost slaps, and walked off. 'You're a pretty girl,' she said, as she went.

Where she had been sitting, there was another loaf of bread, and meat, and cheese, and a bottle of drinking water, all wrapped in brown paper.

It was a day later that the infections I got on Australia set in; that my wounds started burning, my skin peeling and blackening. Alala didn't seem surprised when I turned up at her door and told her that I had a favour to ask.

She smiled, that same smile. She could help me, and I would gladly accept her help.

Rex and I are in a part of the city that isn't supposed to have water in it, but no one has fixed the problem. This part of the city was abandoned a long time ago. That's obvious as soon as we reach the edge of the water and haul ourselves out: the ground is broken and torn up, with shattered glass everywhere, piles of garbage, metal and plastics. There are buildings all around us, windows caved in or boarded up, paintwork faded. Everything is the same grey-white colour in the moonlight, but overgrown. Nature has started to take this part of the city back. There are young trees springing up through the concrete, their roots making the ground bulge. Plants have grown everywhere, up the buildings, through those smashed windows. The doors we can see have been braced, sealed off with clamps. There's no noise here. The wall is kicking out plumes of ice-white smoke, and it spills over the water, seeming to float above it before resting at the edge, the lip that we're standing on. It's freezing here.

'Come on,' I say. We pass a sign, a faded green sign. *Goddard* something, it says. The ground is littered with the remains of the people who lived here: bars of metal, sheets of what look like chipboard, electronics, all lying around underneath canopies of trees. It reminds me of the arboretum, almost.

There's a clatter, and I turn to look at Rex. The tape that held the knife onto her arm has slipped, unravelled, and the blade is lying on the ground. She stoops to pick it up. Her forearm looks sore; where the implants for the augment were fitted, the skin is red, inflamed, a deep black in places. 'Does that hurt?' I ask.

'I don't know,' she says. 'No more than usual.'

'What do you mean?'

'It always hurts. I can feel the hand, as if it is there, still attached to me. It hurts like a burn. Or as if it is trapped.' She cradles the stump with her other hand. 'It hurts, but it always hurts.'

'You need somebody to look at that,' I say. 'It looks infected. Maybe we can get some medicine after . . .' I don't finish the thought. I haven't planned what happens next. I would have got some from Alala. Maybe she'll have some. I can find her, confront her, take it.

'How do we find the girl?' Rex asks, as she ties the tape around her wrist again, pulling it into a knot with her teeth to hold the blade in place.

'We need to find Alala first. She's got the information I stole.'

'So where is she?'

'South, I think. The other side of the city. Further along the wall, at a place called the Andrews Docks.'

'And she'll know where Mae is?'

'She will,' I say. 'I think she will.' We go deeper into the complex. That's what this is: warehouses and buildings, part of a large industrial estate.

'When you've got what you need, you'll kill this Alala,' Rex says. It's not a question.

'No,' I answer, but I sound unconvincing, even to myself. So I hammer it home. 'That's not me. Not who I am. Not now.'

'You want to change who you are,' Rex says.

'I was never that person,' I tell her. 'I won't kill her. I can't.' I kick something, which clatters; so I bend down, pick it up. A small figure: white, plastic, in a spacesuit like I saw in the museum. There are more of them all around here. Toys, most likely. What a waste this bit of the city is. These buildings could be turned into homes, where people could live a life that's far easier than they do in the docks. Fixed up, some of these places might be better than some of the houses that people have actually paid to live in.

Then as we walk through the ruin we see a building that's different to the rest. White walls, blacked-out windows that are still intact, still protected. Around it, there's a fence. It looks secure. It will do for the rest of the night, to keep us safe and warm until the morning, when we can work out exactly where we are and what to do next. We try the door and it is unlocked. It's heavy, hard to open, made of metal. The metal continues inside: there are metal grates on the floor, grey-blue walls. A sign reads *Ticket Office*; I can just about see it in the moonlight that's creeping in through the blacked-out windows, but that part of the building is cordoned off.

'Where are we?' Rex asks, but I don't know.

At the end of the corridor there's another door. This one opens for us, swishing to one side as we approach. I step through first, into a giant chamber, enormous and round. In the middle, there's another structure, suspended in the air hanging from wires. There's just enough light for me to see it. I know this place. I recognise it. I've seen it before, or something like it.

Three words, printed on the side of it. *THE NEW WORLD*. It looks exactly like the ship that we arrived in, the smaller one that brought us down from Australia. It's one of those, and it's here, and it's pristine.

'You are intruding,' a voice says. Gaia, she's everywhere. 'I am raising an alarm, and backup has been called. Do not attempt to run.'

I don't even have to tell Rex to ignore Gaia. She's out of the door before I am, careening down the corridor to the exit, and I follow her out into the yard we were in before, tearing away from this building and the wall, towards the city. We can't see anyone coming for us yet, but we can hear them: the thrum of birds assembling themselves in the distance, rising into the sky, getting ready to hunt us.

There's a fence looming. Birds circle it, pointing and looking in our direction; more guards. This whole area is cordoned off, kept secure. I'm panicking, looking for a way out, when Rex starts shooting. I forgot that she had the gun. The sound echoes off the walls, bouncing around, and the birds collapse, spiralling to the ground. She only stops when they're nearly all down, a mess of flames and torn metal. The gun clicks uselessly as the final couple of birds rise, out of harm's way. She's out of bullets. She throws the gun to the ground, and we climb the fence. It's tall enough to stop most people, but not us; and the jagged edges at the top aren't going to hold us back now.

From the top of the fence we can see the rest of the city: the buildings, tall in the distance; the streets; the lights, making it not quite night, not as dark as we've had the past few days. I stop for a moment and I stare, but Rex is already pulling away, leaping off the fence and pelting down a street, away from the flaming chaos of the birds behind us.

She doesn't even stop to stare at what's in front of us. She just takes it in her stride.

We stop because our lungs hurt. There's only so far you can run after what we've been through. We'll sleep for a week, I think, once we're safe. In Ziegler's home, if I can persuade him; in the bed he lets me use, assuming there's nobody else using it. Rex can have it. I'll take the floor, as long as it's warm in there.

We're cold and wet and sweaty and hot all at once. My heartbeat is so heavy, so loud. I can feel it in every bit of me: my chest, my head. I can even hear it.

Ziegler. We just need to get to Ziegler.

Exhausted, Rex and I slump down against the concrete support of an underpass, away from any cameras or passing cars, and after we catch our breath I tell Rex to stay and I walk to find a terminal. There's one a block away; it's old and lags, but it just about works. I ping Ziegler, hoping he'll know that it's me. I hope he hasn't forgotten about me. Or given up on me.

'Where do we go?' Rex asks, when I get back to her.

'We wait here,' I say, 'see if he comes to find us.'

'And what if he doesn't?'

'Then I don't know,' I say. We sit in silence, and I think about how much easier my life might have been if I had just let my mother's death pass quietly, not tried to defend her or myself, that first day I met Rex.

*   *   *

It isn't the noise of the car that wakes me, because it's silent, or the sound of Ziegler's feet on the pavement. It's only when he touches my shoulder that I react, and it's like the past year of my life never happened. I grab his hand, twist it away from him, bending his fingers into a shape that I know will nearly cripple him with pain. It doesn't matter who he is; I'm hard-wired to protect myself when I'm sleeping. Can't shake that. Doubt I ever will.

'Chan!' he says, trying to back away, 'Chan, it's me.' I breathe hard, open my eyes, let him go.

'Okay.' Then, 'Sorry.'

'Don't worry about it.' He rubs his hand, looks me over. 'You look like death warmed up.'

'What?'

'Something that my mom used to say. Death warmed up. It means . . . Not good.' He reaches out to me, pulls me to my feet. 'Let's go.'

'You don't seem surprised to see me.'

'You're easier to track than most. You make a loud noise wherever you go, it seems. You were in the Pine City Revision Facility,' he helps me to my feet, 'until a few days ago, when you escaped. That was all over the news. Car's over here.' He looks around. 'I don't know this part of the city that well. Don't know where the cameras are, and there are drones out, so you might want to keep your head down. Just until we're inside.'

I look over to wake Rex, to introduce her to Ziegler, but I can't see her. I touch the spot where she was sleeping next to me, and it's dry. She's been gone a while.

'What?' Ziegler asks. 'Have you lost something?'

'I think we've got a problem,' I reply.

'You're sure she was with you last night?' he asks. I stare out of the windows, but can't see enough, so I put them down and lean out, peering down streets as we pass them, trying to get a better view. The sun is starting to come up, the sky reddening over the wall. 'They'll be looking for you,' he says, as if I don't already know that. 'If they see you, they'll come down hard – harder than you can run from.'

'You don't have to tell me that,' I say, 'I know. We were chased by birds.'

'What?' His voice trembles, shocked.

'When we escaped. They sent birds.'

'They chased you? They've already followed you?'

'Rex shot them,' I say. 'We found a gun.'

He slams his foot on the brake and pulls the car over to the side of the road. 'They followed you?'

'No,' I say, 'I don't know. No. We escaped.' I see his hands as he squeezes the wheel, his knuckles whitening under the tightness of his grip. 'Okay.' Squeezes harder. 'Get out,' he says.

'What?'

'I'm sorry, Chan,' he says. 'But no. Not if they know you're here already. Stupid. Okay.'

'Ziegler, please! This is Alala's fault. Alala's fault I was screwed over, her fault that I was caught.' It hits me, like a fist: that's where Rex is. 'Please, take me to her. Then I'll—'

But his door is already open, and he's already walking

around to mine; and he pulls up and hauls me out, throws me, practically, onto the sidewalk.

'Please!' I shout.

He stands by the car, the door open. 'You've ruined everything, jeopardised everything. Don't you think about anybody but yourself?'

'I do,' I say, and I think about Mae and Jonah and Rex, and I want to tell him that, but he doesn't give me a chance.

'I came here because I thought you might see sense, see that whatever you're doing, whatever you're hoping to achieve, it's over. It was over before it began, before you told me your story. And now you're going to be taken off, and they're already here, already chasing you. I can't be seen helping you. There's too much at stake.' I reach for him, because he's all I've got now. But he looks angry, disgusted even. 'Don't ever get in touch with me again,' he says.

He climbs inside, and the doors slam shut. The car makes no noise as it leaves.

The city looks the same as I run through it. It's morning, just barely, and it looks like it always has, the rising sun reflecting off the glass of the buildings; the gloss of their polished marble, of their metals, of the haphazard way that what was old city has been mutated and beaten into something entirely new; pieces stuck on, changes adopted, adaptations made. People are leaving their houses and apartments to walk to work, or take the transports; they talk on their cells, project games in front of them, ignore everything but their own little world. There's traffic, queues of cars that slow but never stop; they're always moving, the computers dictating how the traffic flows. People on basket-ball courts, leaping, augmented; joggers running on the tracks in public spaces, their legs bowing beneath them; tourists from smaller cities, cities far less advanced than this, milling about, excited to see what Washington has to offer. Every part of the infrastructure of the city – every person, every car, every building – is automated, perfect, secure and safe. Every part but me.

This is not my home. It's just where I am. The glow from the signs above me spills down. When you look at the signs for too long, the technology recognises you and targets you with sound.

I've really only ever known three places properly: Australia, Pine City, and Washington. And really, they're not so different.

They're all prisons, in their own way.

It's late morning by the time I reach the docks. I can't remember having ever felt so wrecked. I'm so tired, but my eyes don't feel as though they could close. They're dry and painful but pinned open by adrenalin. Nothing in the docks has changed since I was last here; they're still quiet, still divided by the fence from the rest of the city. The fires burning in trash cans; the makeshift homes built from tents, old fabric, debris, garbage; the ramshackle divisions for each person's shanty. There's no sign of Rex yet. I'm hoping that I beat her here, because I know where I'm going, at least. She's fast, but she likely got lost in the city, on her way here. That must have bought me some time.

But as soon as I hear the shouting, I know I'm late. Not too late, that's all I hope. I see people running as I get closer to Alala's house, hear the sounds of panic: the screaming of some, the muted murmuring of others. Rex is here, and I know exactly why.

She came here to do what I said I couldn't.

She came here to kill Alala.

I can't get close to them at first. There's a crowd, but they're holding back, staying away. Alala must still be alive, or there would be no crowd, no noise. Everybody would have run, because the birds would be coming. So the fight must still be going on. I push through. I can hear them talking, shouting at each other; Alala, almost screaming, begging for her life, begging for the lives of those with her. I push through the crowd, who don't even seem to notice me, and I see her, sprawled on the floor. Her clothes are torn, and her face is a mess. Rex has already had a go at her, already taken a lump from her.

'Where's the little girl?' I hear Rex ask. It sounds like it's not the first time she's asked it. She's tired of the question, reaching the end of her tether. When I finally see her, she's got something in her hand. A striker? No. It's smaller. A gun. Alala's gun, the one she keeps hidden. Snub-nosed, really old. A proper antique. It should be in a museum. I only know what it is because I saw it, or one like it, in the museum, before I spotted it in Alala's house. She aims it at Alala's head, her arm tight and tense.

Alala is on the floor, scrabbling in the mud. The rain last night has turned the dirt to mulch underfoot. She's cowering, but there's something behind her back: something hidden, that she's fiddling for, trying to get loose. Alala's people – a few mutes, some junkies – stand back, hands flat and out in front of them. It seems like Rex is in charge, that she's got the upper hand. But this won't end how she wants it to. This isn't Australia. Even if Rex shoots Alala, even if she kills her, Alala's people won't hold back. There's no power vacuum to be filled, no licking wounds until a new leader rises. They'll tear Rex apart. They'll take revenge.

Rex might be strong, but she'll never make it out of here alive.

So I don't hesitate. I don't even think about it.

I run, and I launch myself head-first into a tackle that slams into Rex's body, that drives her to the ground. The gun flies out of her hand, slides across the ground in the mud.

'No!' Rex shouts, but I had to. I press her down, my face close to hers.

'I can't let you do that for me,' I say. Maybe I shout it. Maybe everything is louder and faster than I realise.

'It's who I am,' she spits.

'But what if it's not?' I reply. She's still, for that moment. One single, quiet moment.

I look back at Alala. Her people are helping her to her feet. 'Deal with them,' I say to Rex, 'I've got her.' And I leap up and charge head-first into Alala, smashing into her with my shoulder (feeling the pain of having used it over and over again), driving her through her people like they're skittles, slamming her into the wall of her shanty. She's no fighter. She's not ready for me, and she's not able to fight back as I club her in the face, as my fist finds its way to her teeth, smashing the bone of her nose. Rex is dealing with her people, but there are too many for her to handle, and some of them break loose and come for me. They try to pull me off Alala, but I fight back. I snap arms, drive my fist into faces, crack the back of heads on the ground, stamp my foot into the bones of their ankles. I wreck them.

I think I even enjoy it.

When they're broken and Rex is dealing with the rest – chasing them away, taking them out of the fight, stupid as they are – I'm alone with Alala, finally.

She cowers. I'm glad. I want her to feel what I'm going to do next.

Her face is swollen and bleeding. She's lost an eye. I think about how she can get an augment, if I let her survive; and I don't know if she will. I won't kill her outright. That doesn't mean she'll survive her injuries.

'Little girl,' she says, her mouth black with blood and drool, teeth crooked and loose. She coughs, spits up thick red. 'You came back.'

'Of course I did,' I say.

'So what is this? Revenge? You want your revenge on me?' She reaches into her mouth and pulls free a tooth; and she stares at it, as if it's going to do something. As if it's not even hers. 'You won't kill me.'

'How do you know? You would have killed me. You said that you would help me get Mae, and then you tried to kill me.'

'The little girl.' She smiles. That's the name Alala calls me. 'The even-more-little girl.' That makes her laugh, a creak that makes it sound like her injuries are worse than they first seemed, like there's something wrong with her insides. 'Everybody is somebody's little girl. You work for me. I work for somebody. On it goes, up and up.' She tries to stand. I let her. She's broken; it's more than the damage that I've inflicted. She was broken long before Rex and I got here. 'Maybe you should ask your friend Ziegler about that, eh?'

They knew each other. He told me to find her, when I first got here. And the EMP: they had the same weapon. Exactly the same sort. How—

She looks behind me. It's a trick, one that I've used. Act like there's something worth being distracted by, and you can get the upper hand.

But there's no upper hand for her to get. She's done, lost. In her way, she's won.

The expression on her face: it's not that she's won, not quite. But she's got hope.

'Step away from her,' I hear Zoe say. Alala's prime junkie. I look over, and I see her cowering, terrified. She's thinner than when I left here. She's twitchy, as well. Hasn't had a fix recently, and that's the worst state for her to be in right now.

She's got Alala's gun, I realise. It's aimed at me, pointed right at my head, too close to miss. Even if she's not used one before, it would be hard for her to not kill me.

The end of the gun trembles in her hand as her finger twitches.

Don't die.

Then . . .

Rex's knife flies through the air, plants itself into Zoe's arm, just as—

Zoe pulls the trigger, and the bullet screams at me, and I feel the thud—

Alala's on her feet, rushing towards me, past me, past Zoe, screaming this blood-curdling scream that's the sound of a nightmare, the sound we used to make when we were doing impressions of the Nightman, or what lived inside the pit, or the noise you would make when the Lows got a hold of you. She running faster than I've ever seen her, back to a few of her people, who cradle her, pulling her close. They want to make sure she's alright: not because they care about her, but because she's still got what they want. They're locked to her now. She points towards us, and a group of them charge us.

Zoe flies at me as I'm feeling myself, trying to find where the bullet went in – though there's no pain, not really – and then she's on top of me, scratching and clawing, Rex's knife jutting from her arm, dug in deep. There's a curious look in her eyes, somewhere between the withdrawal and her haunted devotion to Alala. The others are here as well, coming for me or for Rex. I can't see Rex now, though. I need to see where she—

I notice Alala, staring at us, at Zoe.

She raises her finger and points.

No, no, no. I kick Zoe off, hurl her back towards Alala, as close as I can manage.

The girl explodes. There's no pause, no stages of pain and suffering. Instead, a crack, like a bone breaking, but amplified; and then there's a spark, a shower of blood. We're thrown aside, and there's smoke where Zoe was, a crater in the ground.

The others either don't realise what happened or think that I did it. They turn, and they come at me. Rex has a jagged edge of rock in her hand, a blade made out of the ground thrown up by the explosion, and she chases one.

'Defuse them!' I scream. 'Base of the spine!'

So she leaps, trusting me. She barrels into one of the mutes and slams the knife in. He crumbles, and Alala points. She twitches her finger.

Nothing happens.

I charge Alala but am intercepted by another mute, his mouth open, like he's screaming in pain, in anger, but there's no noise from him. Alala's finger twitches, as I reach for his back, but there's no time, so I kick him, pivot and push off, and the blast throws me to the ground, face down. Another one comes at me, hauls me to my feet. I flip him, using his weight to toss him right into his friends as they pile towards me. This fight isn't my fault. These deaths are not my fault. They are Alala's fault. This is on her.

I feel the fire before I see it. Where Zoe was, where I threw her, something's caught fire. The cracked pavements are burning. There's a smell in the air, of rot. It smells like the pit – the blood, and the gases of the bodies . . . But the air is hazy. It reeks.

Rex screams at me. 'That smell,' she says. 'On Australia. I remember it. It burned.'

And she's right. It's the smell of the gases that used to burn off from the pit when they hit fires.

I catch sight of Alala, further away. She's created a distance between us. Her hand is raised, her finger extended. She knows about the gas, what will happen if she causes another explosion. The smell is overwhelming, coming from the cracks in the ground. Something down there must have broken. A haze drifts up with the smell.

Rex looks up and sees me as I run towards her. I grab her hand and drag her with me, and we run towards Alala, desperate, frantic.

Alala's finger twitches, like it's resting on a trigger.

I thud into her, snapping something as I do, her back bending forwards in a way that I don't like, that I know doesn't come without a mass of broken bones in her. We don't stop, Rex and I. We keep running.

As Alala lies on the ground, I glance back at her body. Her finger twitches. I don't know if she's making it twitch, or if it's out of her control.

Doesn't matter.

The body nearest to her explodes, and there's a quiet moment before the flame swells, like a balloon; and then it bursts, ripping through the air in every direction.

'Faster!' I scream. I don't know if Rex hears me. I don't care. I pull her hand harder, and I feel like I'm nothing but my feet slamming into the ground, over and over. Head pulsing, vision blurry. Through the docks, faster, faster. The flames behind us.

This part of the city should be cold, and it's not now. The fire licks our heels as we run.

I see the wall. I see the edge of the dock.

I see the ice, as we're in the air, leaping off; as the fire swallows the space we were just in, as it swallows everything above us; as we plunge into the ice, smashing through it and down, deep into the water; and we look up to see the air a glow of reds and yellows, and behind all that, the blue beyond the top of the wall, the sky the colour it should be. And I can see the floes melt away, becoming one with the water beneath under the heat of that fire.

The police are swarming the docks by the time we get out. We hide on roofs, paths that I learned months ago, when I lived here, scurrying out of view as best we can. We wait until night, when the cops go home – there's nothing they can do now; this is a bombsite, everybody who survived evacuated god-knows-where. And then we look for Alala's body.

We have to hide from the police who are guarding the site, but they don't really care. Dead junkies aren't high on their list of worries. We stick to the rooftops of the shanties, just like I used to, and then eventually find her, piled up with the others. There are too many dead to be dealt with in one go, so they're laid out under tarpaulin. They likely won't even try to identify them. Too much work for no reward. Alala's body is badly burned, but not so I can't tell it's her.

I reach for her hand. Rex doesn't ask what I'm doing; she doesn't care. I snap her finger off and pray it will still work. Then we walk to her shanty. The police haven't gotten to it yet. They will. They'll find contraband, drugs, medical equipment. They'll find things that will support their theories about the sort of people who live in this part of the city. But I don't want them to.

I go for Alala's computer first. I open it, and try her finger on the scanner. It works. I don't know what I'm looking for, but I know somebody who might. I put her finger in my pocket, and I feel the metal jabbing from it. I remember the other use it had for her. We take medical supplies, food, water; clothes; a bandage; another knife, for Rex's arm.

Everything else we pile up in the middle of Alala's home. Furs, papers, books. Everything. I take a bottle of the poutin and pour it over the mound, then I take one of the devices that Alala put into people, one of the bombs, and I throw that on top.

Outside, far away from it, I twitch Alala's finger, and the bomb explodes. The flame erupts into the sky, a tower of it, that I imagine you can see for miles.

Rex takes my hand.

She doesn't need to say anything.

Not yet.

EPILOGUE

I put Alala's computer onto the front desk, and the surly version of Gaia asks me why we're here.

'We're here to see Hoyle Grant,' I say. 'The Runner.'

'There's nobody here by that name.'

'He was here before. I know you'll be able to find him. Tell him it's Chan. He knows who I am.'

We wait. Rex is antsy. She keeps leaning over the desk, peering at the terminal.

'That won't make him come any faster,' I say.

'I know,' she says. So she hits it, smacks the screen.

'That'll do it,' I say.

'I'm not waiting,' she tells me, and she walks to the stairwell. She opens the door, and there he is. Police officers with him, and they've got weapons – real hardcore weapons, not just strikers. Uniforms on them all, and their eyes flicker with the glints of expensive augments. Rex backs up.

'Scan her,' Hoyle says. She raises her hand and he notices her arm, where the other is missing. He raises an eyebrow, then looks past her and sees me.

'Hi,' I say. I wave.

'You're alive,' he says. His men swarm me as well, ready to take me down. They could, I'm sure. I'm not quite equipped to win this fight.

'They're prisoners,' one of his men says. 'Escaped from—'

'From Pine City,' I say. 'We broke out. Or did you mean Australia? We were prisoners there as well.' Hoyle smiles from the corner of his mouth, the scar making it seem more subtle than maybe it is. 'You thought I was working for Alala.'

'You were,' he tells me. He makes eyes at his soldiers. There's something going on that Rex and I can't see, something under the skin – probably ESP augs. He's probably telling them what to do, preparing them for what could happen.

He's probably telling them how dangerous we are.

'It wasn't my choice,' I say. 'You know what that's like.' I'm sure it's a smile. 'But you helped me. It was for the best. I wasn't on a good path.'

'I hear that,' he says. 'So now you're here to hand yourself in?'

'No,' I say. 'The opposite.' I nod towards Alala's computer. 'May I?'

'Be my guest,' he says. I move slowly. I don't want to spook his people, and they look like they'll be pretty easily spooked. They'll have read my file by now, and Rex's. I spent the first six months here desperate for nobody to know who I was or where I came from. Now? Those stories about me are all I've got.

That and this computer. I open it, and I reach for the keyboard. The soldiers react, panicked.

357

'I need to type the password,' I say. The soldiers relax. He's told them to stand down. Must be ESP augs. Must be.

'You've given it a password. Old school.'

'Harder to crack,' I say, 'can't just cut off a finger and use the DNA.' *AgathaJonahMae*, I type, and the first folder unlocks.

'So what's on this?' he asks.

'Information,' I say. 'I think it'll be useful. If it is, there's more where this came from.' I push the computer over towards him. Rex's eyes dart left and right, looking for the best way out; the soldiers prime themselves to take me down, almost desperate to catch somebody as wanted as I am; and I feel my fingers shaking as I let go of the computer, as Hoyle takes it from me. I'm terrified that this might not be as useful to them as I've been hoping it is; and scared at the thought that finally – *finally* – I'm maybe getting close to finding out where Mae is. Getting her back. Hoyle peers at the screen and I grit my teeth. Hand into fist, ready to fight if I have to, if this is nothing, and if this hasn't paid off.

But Hoyle's smile doesn't break. He scans the files, flicking through them.

This is something.

'Where did you get this?' he asks. He opens documents, reads them, his augmented right eye flickering as it takes in whole pages at a time. 'There are more of these files?'

'There are,' I say. 'And they're yours. But I've got conditions. I want a pardon, for me and Rex. No more prisons.'

He nods. 'That's it?' he asks.

'No,' I say. 'Remember before? How you promised that you'd find out where Mae was?'

'When we got past this, sure. When Alala was taken care of.'

'Well,' I tell him, 'she won't be a problem any more.'

And that *really* makes him smile.

ACKNOWLEDGMENTS

Thanks first and foremost to my editor, Anne Perry. She's superb, with a really great eye for what makes characters tick. I think that both Chan and Rex are a hell of a lot more complete because of her.

Thank you also to the rest of the Hodder crew – Fleur, Oliver, Jason, and everybody else who has helped to get the books shipshape, onto shelves and into people's hands.

Thanks to Sam Copeland and all at RCW for their hard work.

And lastly, massive gratitude to Cath, Will and Amy for listening to me witter about the plot of this thing almost endlessly for the past few months.

Enjoyed this book?
Want more?

Head over to

CHAPTeR 5

for extra author content,
exclusives, competitions – and lots
and lots of book talk!

Our motto is
Proud to be bookish,

because, well, we are ☺

See you there...